Praise for Robin W. Pearson

"The journey of these three sisters wr
and trauma is a fascinating and insig
so visual—I felt immersed in the sto
Pearson's writing has that rare mix o
maintaining an undertone of humo
book club book for an in-depth conversation. I think this
be helpful to those on a road to healing from a difficult past. Bravo!"

CINDY MORGAN, award-winning singer/songwriter and author of *The Year of Jubilee*, on *Dysfunction Junction*

"There is healing for the broken, and Robin W. Pearson delivers a strong testament to that fact in her latest poetically written novel, *Dysfunction Junction*. Readers will be stirred and healed after reading this one."

VANESSA MILLER, bestselling author of *The American Queen*

"You can't help choosing favorites among the Winters sisters. Then again, you'll change your mind again and again as author Robin W. Pearson brings together three finely drawn characters—Frankie, Annabelle, and Charlotte—who must reluctantly join forces to wrestle the ghosts of their troubled childhood, come to terms with memories of neglect, and envision a future that's free of resentment and filled with grace."

VALERIE FRASER LUESSE, bestselling author of *Under the Bayou Moon*, on *Dysfunction Junction*

"Southern charm flows like molasses through barbed conversations in *Dysfunction Junction* as three sisters strive to find healing from festering mother wounds. Secrets and guilt wrestle their way to redemption in this quirky family tapestry. Robin W. Pearson's unique voice is complex and captivating."

TESSA AFSHAR, award-winning author of *The Peasant King*

"With her distinctive voice and gorgeous insights, wordsmith Robin W. Pearson takes a brave and deep journey through the tall weeds of a family's old pain, nagging fears, and challenging choices—painting a portrait of the path any willing family can take to finally walk into the promise of courageous, new life. Her invitation is beautiful, offered to our broken world at just the right time."

PATRICIA RAYBON, award-winning author of *All That Is Secret* and *I Told the Mountain to Move: Learning to Pray So Things Change*, on *Walking in Tall Weeds*

"There's a special kind of musicality to Southern fiction that delights my mind, and Robin W. Pearson's novels never fail to sing directly to my heart. . . . She's given us another gift in her newest, *Walking in Tall Weeds*. . . . Pearson invites us—a large family from different backgrounds, skin tones, experiences—to tune our ears to the song of unity and forgiveness that is only possible through the power of Christ. Robin W. Pearson's voice is strong and powerful. Listen up! You don't want to miss a note!"

SUSIE FINKBEINER, author of *The Nature of Small Birds* and *Stories That Bind Us*

"In her latest novel, *Walking in Tall Weeds*, Pearson weaves together a rich tapestry of Southern charm while exposing issues often hidden behind polite dialect. Where families will finally see the importance of looking at their past through a lens of awareness in order to do better, instead of allowing the past to rob them of the joy of the here and now."

T. I. LOWE, bestselling author of *Under the Magnolias*

"When I read Robin W. Pearson's latest, I saw my own heart. She mixes life's pain with Duke's mayonnaise and smoked sausages and fluffy drop biscuits. And in the tapestry she weaves with words, I find what I hold on to, what I need to set free, and the striving in between."

CHRIS FABRY, bestselling author of *A Piece of the Moon*, on *Walking in Tall Weeds*

"Robin W. Pearson has a gift for capturing the complexity and nuances of family relationships. She brings a remarkable tenderness and compassion to the struggle we all face to know and be known in a family. Prepare yourself for a rich and satisfying read!"

SARAH LOUDIN THOMAS, award-winning author of *The Right Kind of Fool*, on *Walking in Tall Weeds*

"Pearson delivers a satisfying tale of one woman's secrets returning to haunt her. . . . Pearson's excellent characters and plotting capture the complexity and beauty of family, the difficulty of rectifying mistakes, and the healing that comes from honesty. Pearson rises to another level with this excellent story."

PUBLISHERS WEEKLY on *'Til I Want No More*

"With help from her community, Maxine learns that by confronting her tangled past, she can face her future and discover her true self. Uplifting faith-based messages are included throughout, and the story's easy pace allows time to take in each lesson."

BOOKPAGE on *'Til I Want No More*

"This novel's slow pace allows readers to gain valuable insight into Maxine as she braves a great deal of soul-searching. A heartfelt tale about faith and family, readers can walk toward the altar with Maxine Owens as she tends to her past wounds."

***DEEP SOUTH* MAGAZINE** on *'Til I Want No More*

"*'Til I Want No More* feels like an extended afternoon at a family reunion barbecue, complete with mouthwatering food, spilled family secrets, and voices of faith that never lose hope. This brilliantly written story reminds us that God is bigger than the struggles that all families face, yet as a woman of color, I love that Robin's courageous characters look and sound like me."

BARB ROOSE, speaker and author of *Surrendered: Letting Go and Living like Jesus* and *Joshua: Winning the Worry Battle*

"Robin W. Pearson has done it again—she truly knows how to captivate her readers and have them eagerly turning each page, anticipating what is going to happen next. *'Til I Want No More* is no exception. Maxine's journey of love, longing, and finding her identity and worth is relatable to so many women, all of whom will be able to resonate with the many emotions of this bride-to-be as she seeks to find the joy and sense of belonging she's been missing."

ANGELIA WHITE STONE, CEO and editor of *Hope for Women* magazine

"Pearson writes strong characters who wrap their arms around you and pull you into the family circle, a hubbub of loyalty, secrets, faith, and yes, forgiveness. Nobody's perfect—but maybe that's the best theme woven through this book."

BETH K. VOGT, award-winning author of the Thatcher Sisters series, on *'Til I Want No More*

"Pearson's excellent debut explores forgiveness and the burden of secrets. . . . Pearson's saga is enjoyable and uncomfortable, but also funny and persistent in the way that only family can be."

***PUBLISHERS WEEKLY*,** starred review of *A Long Time Comin'*

"Pearson delivers a poignant debut that explores the faith of one African American family. . . . The writing is strong, and the story is engaging, and readers will be pleased to discover a new voice in Southern inspirational fiction."

BOOKLIST on *A Long Time Comin'*

"Robin W. Pearson's debut novel is a contemporary fiction masterpiece. . . . Set in North Carolina, readers will feel the heat, smell the food, and hear the bees buzzing in the background. . . . Pearson has created a story that makes you feel like you're in the same room as the characters. Do not miss this one."

CHRISTIAN FICTION ADVISOR on *A Long Time Comin'*

"Readers will cry, laugh, sigh wistfully, and even rage a little at this moving story. *A Long Time Comin'* is a wonderful tale of love, family, secrets, relationships, and forgiveness that will teach us all how to live well in the midst of real life."

***THE BANNER* MAGAZINE**

"Robin W. Pearson delivers a fresh new voice for Southern fiction, treating readers to an inspiring journey through the complex matters of the heart."

JULIE CANTRELL, *New York Times* and *USA Today* bestselling author, on *A Long Time Comin'*

"Robin W. Pearson's authentic faith and abundant talent shine through in this wholehearted novel. Bee and Evelyn will stir your heart and stay with you long after the last page of *A Long Time Comin'* is turned."

MARYBETH MAYHEW WHALEN, author of *Only Ever Her*

"Robin W. Pearson's singular style and fully realized cast of characters ring proudly throughout this novel. Her masterful voice is a welcome addition to the genre of family sagas rooted in hope and faith."

LIZ JOHNSON, bestselling author of *The Red Door Inn*, on *A Long Time Comin'*

"*A Long Time Comin'* is a tender and sweet story of a cantankerous grandmother and her dear family members. . . . Her characters are charming, endearing, and flawed. I hope we have many years to come of reading Pearson's work."

KATARA PATTON, author

Dysfunction Junction

a novel

Robin W. Pearson

Tyndale House Publishers
Carol Stream, Illinois

Visit Tyndale online at tyndale.com.

Visit Robin W. Pearson's website at robinwpearson.com.

Dysfunction Junction

Cover designed by Eva M. Winters

Edited by Kathryn S. Olson

Published in association with the literary agency of Books & Such Literary Management, 52 Mission Circle, Suite 122, PMB 170, Santa Rosa, CA 95409.

For information about special discounts for bulk purchases, please contact Tyndale House Publishers at csresponse@tyndale.com or call 1-855-277-9400.

Library of Congress Cataloging-in-Publication Data

A catalog record for this book is available from the Library of Congress.

ISBN 978-1-4964-5376-1 (HC)
ISBN 978-1-4964-5377-8 (SC)

Printed in the United States of America

30 29 28 27 26 25 24
7 6 5 4 3 2 1

To my family

You have always been my helper.

Don't leave me now; don't abandon me,

O God of my salvation!

Even if my father and mother abandon me,

the Lord will hold me close . . .

Yet I am confident I will see the Lord's goodness

while I am here in the land of the living.

Psalm 27: 9–10, 13

There are three sides to every story:

your side, my side, and the truth.

Robert Evans

Chapter One

Then

"WHAT TIME IS IT?" Annabelle's voice quavered as she studied the shadows huddling under the sliding board in Lincoln Park. She expected the streetlight at the corner to come on at any minute, and she didn't think her four-year-old legs could outrun those misshapen silhouettes if they had a mind to chase her. They were in spitting distance of home, but her fear made it feel much farther.

Apparently unperturbed, Frances Mae peeled off the paper from her second block of Hubba Bubba and popped it onto her tongue. Her teeth worked at the gum until she could chew more easily. When she opened her mouth to speak, she wiped a bit of spit from the edge of her lip. "Mama's not expectin' us any time soon. She likes time to herself after she closes the store."

They both knew their mama wasn't going to be alone for long.

But at that moment, all Annabelle could think about was that *she* didn't like being outside at this time of day. On top of that, she was hungry, and the overpowering scent of strawberries wafting from Frankie's mouth wasn't helping a bit.

Their mama had shooed them out of the house two hours ago with strict instructions not to come back until not one, but all the lamps standing guard around the playground were brightly lit. Annabelle peered up at the sky that had started out a pale blue but had transitioned to streaks of purple and gray. Birds flapped across the horizon and disappeared, as if they, too, knew it was time to go somewhere cozy and settle down for the night. Her eyes welled. "It's gonna be dawk soon."

"No, it's not. Besides, Mama's friend said if we listen, he'll get her to give us some more candy next time he comes over." Frances Mae used her index finger and thumb to pinch the end of her gum. She extended her arm as far as it could go while her teeth clamped onto the other end of the sticky treat their new friend had given her.

Annabelle scratched the inside of her elbow and watched her sister twirl and stretch her gum this way and that with her dirt-smudged fingers, mindless of the mosquitoes and gnats flying about.

Annabelle didn't want another piece of Hubba Bubba or a Reese's Peanut Butter Cup, even though she loved licking at the chocolate until she worked her way to the middle. Besides, wrapped or not, those miniature bricks Frankie had stuffed into her cheeks looked like they'd been gathering dust by the register in Mama's store more days than Annabelle could count with both her small hands.

All the treats from McNair's were either leftovers or stale. Her sister should know that as well as Annabelle did. But no, Frances Mae scarfed down all those soft crackers and chewy potato chips like they tasted better than the hamburgers and fries from McDonald's. Mama smiled and carried on like her new man had done something, making them shake his hand and say thank you.

Shoot, Annabelle didn't want any part of that gum.

Dry leaves skittered in a crackly circle near the swings. Fall was definitely on the way, shortening the days and lengthening the nights. Sure enough, the tall lamps began flickering on, one after another, along the sidewalk that encircled the park. The changing light redirected the movements and shapes of the shadows Annabelle's eyes had been glued to for the last ten minutes. She jumped and clutched at her sister's arm. "What's that?"

"Dang it! You made me drop it." Frances Mae squatted and reached for the gum that had plopped into the sandy space between her jelly shoes. She must have thought better of it because she stopped an inch or two before picking it up. Hands balled on her small hips, she glared at her younger sister. "You're just like a monkey, all over the place. Just can't be still. The monkey in the middle, that's what you are!"

Too agitated to be insulted, Annabelle spun, and her sneaker came down on the gum. When she lifted it, elastic threads connected her foot to the ground. Frances Mae's glob of Hubba Bubba was squished between the ridges on the bottom and plastered to the side of her left sneaker.

"Ugh, look what you did! Why can't you stop for once? Nothin's gonna get you out here! Haven't we been in this park a thousand times? Now I've gotta get this gum off your shoe or Mama's gon' have my head when we get home. Come on now, be still, Anna. Stop all that fussin' and movin' around. You heard what I said. Don't move a muscle, and let me go find a stick or somethin' so I can clean your shoe."

Tears streaming down her dusty cheeks, shoulders heaving,

Annabelle ran in place, her feet pummeling the dirt. Too frightened without her sister to stand still, and too afraid of her sister to leave that spot, she peered through the growing darkness as Frances Mae's outline trudged toward the grassy area near the edge of the park where a few spindly trees grew. Those pines provided meager shade when the sun was at its peak, but their cluster of thin trunks shielded her from Annabelle's view.

Wait. There! Another light buzzed, then clicked on. Something rattled across the trees as the wind picked up in force. *What's that creaking? The swings? What's that shadow?* Unable to contain her fear any longer, she let it fly. "Fwanna Mae!"

The girl crunched across the leaves toward Annabelle, holding a sturdy stick that the Lord must have pointed out to her in the faint evening light. Frances Mae squatted and studied Annabelle's feet. "You're makin' a mess of yourself!"

Sure enough, both Annabelle's shoes were speckled with bits of gum and clumps of dirt.

"Hush, and sit down." Frances Mae none too gently pushed her sister, whose bottom kicked up dust upon landing on the sandy ground at the base of the sliding board. When her aggressive action elicited more screeching, Frances Mae reached into the pocket of her denim shorts and withdrew a smushed orange packet. "Here, pretend this is your banana. Eat it and be quiet. Go on, eat your banana. Oo-oo-aa-aa." She shoved the Reese's Peanut Butter Cup into Annabelle's hand. Then she knelt, lifted the girl's foot, and started digging gum from between the treads of the shoe.

Annabelle's cries ebbed and then petered out altogether once she accepted that crying out and speaking up weren't helping. She hiccuped and blinked, her chest hitching, as she clutched the candy. Snot drizzled from her nose and mingled with the tears on her lip.

Frances Mae looked across and ran her free hand along her little sister's shoulder. "See? There's only the two of us, and your Frankie wouldn't ever let anything happen to you. Okay? Now, eat your banana, little monkey." She nodded at Annabelle's hand. "Go ahead, Anna Banana."

Annabelle looked down. She could barely make out the words on the orange wrapper as the last of the streetlights buzzed to life behind them. "Oo-oo-aa-aa," she whispered.

Chapter Two

Now

ANNABELLE MCMILLAN SHOULD'VE been used to feeling odd woman out after all these years. Still, she had to fight the urge to plop down between Frankie and Charlotte, angled toward each other on their spots on the sofa in Frankie's living room. Their heads bobbed back and forth, pecking at the conversation they were sharing, leaving only bits and pieces for Annabelle to snatch up for herself from her place in the recliner, several feet away.

I don't know why in the world I bothered coming to Frankie's. Oh, that's right . . . Miss Hattie, who couldn't be bothered to come! Why did she call me anyway? She's been around long enough to know that calling either of those two would've made more sense.

Annabelle rocked side to side to the rhythm of her thoughts and absently patted the baby on her shoulder.

Frankie pointed at Charlotte and chided, "Girl, you are no kinda good." Laughing, she scooted around in her seat and snapped her fingers at her three-year-old, who was halfway into a wooden trunk, throwing out one toy after another on the floor behind the sofa. Finally, eyes twinkling, she swung in Annabelle's direction. "Did you hear what Charlotte said? Are you gonna take that?"

Annabelle sighed. Swallowing the questions she'd felt compelled to ask, she offered a noncommittal shrug. She couldn't muster any outrage, feigned or otherwise. Miss Hattie was a longtime family friend. As trustworthy as they come. *I'm not sure what she expects me to do, or to want to do, but at least she cares enough to try.*

Frankie hooked an index finger with her baby girl's and led her through the obstacle course of discarded gadgets, doodads, and board books. Settling the child on the floor in front of her, she wedged her daughter's head between her knees and parted her hair with a narrow brown comb. "Mmm-mmm-mmm." Frankie shot a glance that ricocheted off the woman near her and landed on Annabelle. "Charlotte said *your* mama changed her wedding band as often as she replaced her coffee filter."

Annabelle forced a chuckle. "Now, you know good and well mine drank instant." Her tone was as dry as the child's scalp Frankie was greasing.

Smiling crookedly, Frankie nodded slowly at the comment, like a connoisseur appreciating a work of art. "*My* mama didn't bother gettin' a new ring, did she, Charlotte? She kept her finger oiled up so she could slip hers off and on when she got good and ready."

Charlotte shifted her hips that nearly covered her square cushion. "Well, mine never got 'good and ready' to take her husband's name. Probably because he had a foot out the door before they ever left the church." She raised and lowered her shoulder, her eyes rebounding off Annabelle as if she didn't want to get caught looking in her direction. "Of course, I was too young to remember."

Annabelle knew she wasn't the object of the affectionate glance. It was the baby on her shoulder whose every inhale and exhale Charlotte was monitoring. She knew the woman tended to look at life through lenses tinted green, not rose.

Frankie sobered. "Your mama was a mess, wasn't she?"

"*Our* mama," Charlotte said.

"Yes, *our* mama. A hardworkin' mess." Sounding as drained as she felt, Annabelle wasn't sure who she was talking to—herself or her two sisters.

Each of them slowly waved a hand high in agreement.

Frankie angled her daughter's head from one side to the next to see if any of her lines were crooked, then leaned in close. "Go on to the kitchen and tell your brother and your sister to settle down. I shouldn't be hearin' everything they're doin'." She sent her on her way with a tap on her bottom. "Then bring yourself right back here so I can finish doin' your hair."

The three women sat silently for a minute, watching the child do her mama's bidding, before Annabelle, feeling a little green around the gills, muttered, "You two are bound and determined to have your way. The way you and Charlotte gang up on me, I don't stand a chance against your united front." She stroked the baby's back, her eyes moving like bumper cars between Charlotte and Frankie.

"Common bond? Who, me and Charlotte?" Frankie sighed and started collecting all the tools of her mama's trade.

"I disagree, Annabelle," Charlotte spoke up. "Frankie and I may have the same father, but that doesn't mean we think alike." Of all the Winters girls, Charlotte had been blessed with the most of Mayhelen's attention, not that any of them believed it was heartfelt. "What sticks out in my mind is that coat Mama loved more than any of the men in her life. You remember, the one with the gold stitching and fleece lining? It definitely kept her warm longer than her marriages." Charlotte's chuckle was gossamer light and seemed to melt under the heat lamp of their tempers.

Annabelle knew Charlotte was trying to distract them, but her laugh bubbled up from her belly. She covered her open mouth with one hand and pointed at Charlotte with the other. A tear ran from the corner of an eye, and three-year-old Nora giggled with her auntie as she returned to her spot in front of Frankie. Annabelle wiped her face. "It was too big for either one of us, but Frankie and I fought over that thing for years! Mayhelen snatched it back and put it away for good. I didn't think we'd ever see it again, but then it turned up."

"Yeah . . . just like Mama." Charlotte hugged herself.

If only the three of us could've shared a father, like that hand-me-down jacket. The thought dried Annabelle's tears. "Maybe Mama didn't want to part with her classic denim because she was wearing it when she married your daddy." That was how the story went anyway. They never knew what really happened when it came to Mayhelen. They believed only what they experienced themselves, even though Miss Hattie warned them that trusting an eyewitness was like trying to catch the seeds of a dandelion. Annabelle remembered her saying, "Only God knows all."

"Ain't *that* the truth." Frankie's words were so low, she hummed them.

But Annabelle recognized their familiar tune, and she nodded a little as it played over and over in her head. She was Mayhelen's middle child, though her red-tinged brown curls, caramel skin, and grayish eyes testified to what had to be her own daddy's mile-long roots—whoever he was. Her outspoken ways were all her mama's doing, despite the fact the woman never took the blame nor the credit. Annabelle's art teacher called her student "headstrong, yet creative," and told the entire class she'd go far.

Mayhelen, on the other hand, declared her daughter "too mouthy for her own good" and believed her stubbornness would be the ruin of her. At least that's what Miss Hattie heard her yell once, from all the way across the street. Annabelle figured those very qualities provided her best offense and defense, her outspokenness then and her obstinance now. Getting rejected early on had readied her for life—once she stopped running from it.

"I'm surprised Mama made time to have one wedding, let alone four!" Charlotte's gaze danced around the baby once more before finally settling on the hot-pink blossoms of the camellia bush in Frankie's backyard, visible through the picture window to the right of her. In another month or two, one of North Carolina's late-spring storms would have washed away the last of the delicate petals.

Frankie's lips pursed. "Maybe we should consider it three, since she married our daddy twice, Charlotte. How does the saying go? 'When you know, you know.' At least you're supposed to."

What Annabelle didn't know was what to do with the five-month-old she was holding, though she'd best figure it out soon. Burp him? He was sleeping soundly, so that seemed superfluous. Her off-key humming or singing might make him cry—but then she'd have a reason to pass him back to Frankie with an understandable, oh-well-I-tried-here's-your-baby shrug.

Knowing at least this much—that it was a sin to disturb a sleeping child—she opted for shifting him to the shoulder he hadn't soaked with his drool and resumed patting his diapered bottom. She jiggled her elbow slightly to stop the uncomfortable tingly feeling in her arm.

Frankie snapped the last plastic butterfly around the end of the ponytail. The pink bow flitted among the lavenders, yellows, and light greens crisscrossing the glistening parts in the girl's hair. After admiring her handiwork, Frankie pressed her lips to the youngster's round cheek and nudged her in the direction of the sunlit room adjoining the den. "Go on back to the kitchen and play Uno with the twins."

The child took pains to wave at each woman as she toddled around their outstretched legs, bags, and various odds and ends. Annabelle, her hands full, grinned and nodded a goodbye, and Charlotte waggled her fingers at her. Frankie stretched for the towel she'd laid across the back of her green plaid sofa, causing the buttons on her short-sleeved blouse to work overtime. One finally gave up the ghost and popped free of its buttonhole as Frankie playfully swatted her daughter's bottom with the thick cloth to speed her along.

Neither Frankie, Charlotte, nor Annabelle was so quick to lay claim to Mayhelen Winters, the woman who had raised them from the ground up, like the pair of cherry trees Annabelle had planted in her own backyard. God did most of the work. Not one of the three dared to outright deny their mama, however, not even behind her back. Her hold on them was as firm as it was painful.

Frankie's baby stirred, and Annabelle bobbed up and down, causing the springs in the leather armchair to squeak. Truly, she was grateful he was awakening on his own so she could hand him back quick and in a hurry, the beauty of being his auntie instead of his mama. Not that her big sister was paying him a bit of attention, which surprised Annabelle. His teeny-weeny fingers had been splayed against her upper arm, but now they curled into a fist and rubbed at the bridge of his nose.

Blowing out a bang-ruffling breath, Annabelle pretended not

to notice that her little sister's eyes had again pinned themselves to their nephew's back. She grimaced at the sour taste in her mouth, and her stomach contents did a jig. Dealing with her mama on top of everything else just wasn't sitting right with any parts of her. "I still say we'll never get anywhere if y'all won't listen to reason. You're teaming up against me only to have your way! As usual."

The plastic bag in Frankie's lap crinkled when her hands flopped into it and the jar of grease and unused hair bows went sailing across the sofa. "To have *our* way? Huh, this is all Mama's doin'! I've made it almost thirty years without seein' hide nor hair of the woman, and I figured I could go more than twice that with my eyes closed and my hands clasped. Lord knows I have plenty enough to do without addin' her wants and needs to my list."

Frankie dropped snarls of hair into a plastic grocery bag in her lap, then scooped up extra bows, rubber bands, and the small jar of hair pomade. Never one to waste a thing—opportunities, hair grease, or otherwise—she used her thumb to swipe the side of the Nature's Blessings container and rub the edges of her own scalp.

"But you've been fine with heaping her wants and needs onto Miss Hattie's plate all these years." Charlotte's voice rumbled from her spot at the other end of the sofa. "Is that any way to treat Miss Hattie, who was so good to us? I'm willing to do your part and mine, even though I'm overrun with kids and grown folks alike. At least you have a husband to depend on. I had to shift my entire afternoon around so I could meet y'all here."

Annabelle considered the "here" to which Charlotte referred: Frankie's ranch-style house outside Jasper, North Carolina, where she lived with Melvin, her husband of eighteen years, and their four children, aged nine and under. One October evening, Frankie had been driving through a neighborhood a few streets over from their childhood home and spotted a couple raking leaves in their yard. Frankie had pulled to the side of the road, complimented them on their begonias, and spent the next hour convincing them to accept her offer for their home.

Frankie, you certainly made their place your place, Annabelle thought as her eyes meandered from the artwork mounted on the sage green walls to the cherrywood curio cabinet in the far corner, treasures Frankie had found at the Goodwill. Annabelle couldn't help but think her sister preferred other people's memories, something Annabelle could understand to some degree.

But there was no way Annabelle could build *her* house, figuratively and literally, in the backyard of the Winters family's old stomping grounds. For her, living an hour away was a bit close as it was. She caressed the baby's head, the family's youngest little piece of history, to the tune of the background music her sisters provided as they continued to harangue each other. The past might be behind them, but some things never changed.

Chapter Three

TRY AS SHE MIGHT, Charlotte couldn't keep her eyes off MJ, who couldn't seem to get situated in Annabelle's arms. Charlotte sensed that all the little one needed was for her sister to sit still and stop constantly switching him from one shoulder to the other. Though she itched to show Annabelle how it was done, she shifted in her seat, away from the baby and toward her view of Frankie's camellias, which were blooming earlier in the season than usual.

At nearly thirty-three years old, a part of Charlotte still cried for her mama despite the havoc she'd wreaked. Life with Mayhelen was like coming home from a day at Sunset Beach and having to deal with the sunburn, the sand in everything, and unpacking the car. Maybe that was why another part of Charlotte led her to avoid the beach at all costs. But there was no getting out of this discussion with her sisters. It was time to get down to the nitty-gritty. She eyed Frankie. "I had to disappoint several clients today to be here when I canceled their appointments or shuffled them off to other practitioners."

Charlotte could almost feel her hair move when Annabelle huffed from across the room, and Charlotte assumed a fair amount of eye-rolling came with it. But enough was enough. "I know, that's what families do for each other. Y'all need me more than those folks do, and that's why I'm here. Believe it or not, I can teach you both a thing or two—or even three. Only y'all never seem to want to know what your youngest sibling thinks, unless it's to agree . . . or disagree, depending on who's asking."

Her sisters were used to making their beds in the middle of a storm—Frankie, with all her bric-a-brac scattered among the books and photographs on every shelf; children's hand-painted pictures plastered to the front and sides of the refrigerator; toys and puzzles spilling from the cedar chest and against the wall; small, sticky fingerprints on the windows and mirrors. No telling what it looked like in the other rooms.

And Annabelle wasn't much different, the way she'd moved into another woman's remodeling project with her husband, Oliver. Nearly every room in that fixer-upper of theirs had been dismantled in some way or another, and now she'd come up pregnant. Annabelle was patching together a family the way she was piecing together a house.

But not Charlotte. Her life was as clutter-free as her modern town house. No extras, no muss, and no fuss. Everything was new, pristine, and well sewn, including her relationships. Her boyfriend might have thought he was sticking around, the way he kept "forgetting" his book or a sweater and even his wallet, of all things, on the hall tree in her foyer, but Max had better think again.

"My *ya-ya* told me when you leave something behind you, it means you're meant to go back," he'd told her, his lanky frame filling her door.

Charlotte had chuckled, her heart beating faster despite her internal *Whoa there, Bessy.* "Well, my mama told me you can't drive away if you don't take your keys." Two months was about as long as she allowed any man to hang his hat in her life. Any longer than that and he started to act like he belonged there and wanted something more from her than she could give. Two months, nothing more. *But it's been nearly six,* Charlotte counted, adjusting the new watch Max had bought her. It was a little tight on her wrist, but her pride wouldn't let her tell him so. *Perhaps I'd better drop some hints about my ring size,* she considered before squashing the thought. She wouldn't allow herself to imagine him popping the question or whether she even wanted him to. If she allowed such qualms to bob to the surface during quiet moments, they'd inundate her, so she resorted to her usual escape: her clients' needs, her own life preservers.

Charlotte made a show of checking her sparkly timepiece again. "Oh, my goodness. If y'all don't mind, can we please move on? I still have people to see this afternoon at the office."

"We know how busy you are, Dr. Charlotte." Annabelle looked toward heaven. "You've made that more than clear. We'll be outta your hair soon enough. A workaholic, like your mama."

"Don't call me doctor, Annabelle. You know I'm a psychologist, not a psychiatrist. Some people actually want my help." Charlotte's tone was as short as the fingernails she gnawed on.

"Shh, shh." Frankie patted Charlotte's thigh. "What Bella means is we appreciate you taking the time to come over here in the middle of the day, and we won't hold you up a minute longer than necessary. For some reason, all this seems necessary."

Bella. Ouch! Charlotte and Annabelle didn't see eye to eye on most things, but she knew how nicknames pained her, that one in particular—Bella. It was Oliver's favorite endearment for his wife, but he had no idea that growing up, Mayhelen had made her middle daughter feel anything but beautiful, as gorgeous as Annabelle was. Her skin glowed without a hint of makeup, and the professional side of Charlotte wondered if their mother had suffered from jealousy. Before she could speak up for Annabelle, she noticed the expression on Annabelle's face and spoke to her instead. "I see you've found something to smile about."

"I can tell you what I'm *not* smiling about, and it's those 'yo mama' jokes." Her sister tugged at a thick clump of her hair that was wrapped around the baby's fist.

Frankie snorted and inched to the edge of her seat cushion to drop all her implements and the plastic bag into the used IKEA bag Charlotte had snagged for her at a yard sale. It had seen better days, probably with someone who'd actually shopped at the Swedish-founded store.

Charlotte retrieved an errant hair ribbon and dropped it in the bag. "You know what I find funny? The fact that you're the one who started the jokes this afternoon, and now you're suggesting we stop." She wished she could see inside Annabelle's head so she could better understand how her brain worked. She loved Annabelle, but she was quite the conundrum.

"Is that new?" Frankie pointed at the slim platinum band encircling Charlotte's wrist. "It's pretty."

"What isn't new is how I feel about being called Bella. You know what I think about those old nicknames." Annabelle had a firm grip on the matter and obviously wasn't going to drop it.

"Charlotte, out of respect for your time, we'll hurry it up. Really, it shouldn't take long to come to some sort of agreement and nail down our plans for Mama because we're all grown here. Then we can all be on our way. That's what you came here to do anyway. Right, Anna*belle*?" Frankie angled a quick look at her sister, probably hoping to garner a smile.

But Annabelle only clenched her teeth and shifted the baby to her other shoulder. Again. "Well, if we're going to keep this discussion moving along, we should stop with the jokes. They're not really appropriate, considering we're talking about Mama. They're hitting too close to home."

"Maybe what's worrying you is the idea of *Mama* coming too close to home." Frankie shrugged.

"On that note . . ." Peeling her bare thighs from the leather as if they were Velcroed to the seat, Annabelle rubbed her nephew's back and stood. "Since Charlotte seems to be sitting there with time on her hands, she can make room in them for MJ. This pregnancy has already shrunk my bladder to the size of a pea, and I have to use the bathroom."

Charlotte extended her arms and waggled her fingers in a "come hither" motion. "You know y'all treat me more like a prop in a stage production rather than one of its main role players. I guess that's my lot as the baby of the family. Give me MJ. He's probably used to me more than you anyway." Charlotte cradled him to her chest, saying nothing more as Annabelle clip-clopped from the room and closed the door to the powder bath with a firm click.

"Somebody forgot to add sugar to her Kool-Aid today," Frankie said. "When did she start gettin' all defensive about Mama?"

"You know how she is. Always driving contrary to the flow of traffic. Maybe she's starting to realize why Mama worked hard. She did what she could." Charlotte tucked her hands under the baby's armpits and awkwardly bounced him on his tiny feet. Briefly touching her forehead to MJ's, she thought, *What was I thinking, asking for this child, as cute as he is?*

"Well, I wouldn't go *that* far."

Despite all her braggadocious talking to the contrary, Charlotte actually had no idea what to do with the wee one. She made googly eyes and fish faces to make him smile, striving to keep him in a good mood—and at arm's length—because she couldn't afford to get any drool on her new shirt. She didn't have time to change clothes before her date with Max.

The seat sank when Frankie leaned toward the middle of the sofa. Though she'd edged closer to Charlotte, she didn't bother to lower her voice. "That sister of ours. You need to pray for her and this burden she carries on her shoulders about Mama, what we all carry in some form or fashion. I want to help her, but I can barely help myself. She's gonna have to trust God with it." Frankie squinted in the afternoon sunlight streaming onto the coffee table. "It would bless her heart to focus on the good when it comes to Mama."

"To hear her tell it, there isn't anything good." Charlotte clutched the baby to her chest and reared back. "Not everybody can pray away their troubles like you can."

Frankie flinched. "Well, I wouldn't say I can 'pray away' *anything*."

Charlotte peeked toward the powder bath to make sure Annabelle was still down the hall. Hearing the faint sound of running water, she responded quietly, "You know how it is. Annabelle always thought we should've had it better and that she took the brunt, but I can't say. It seems my memories are interspersed with *your* memories, so I don't recall our childhood the same way y'all do. I do know that sometimes when I look back on it . . ." She used her shoulders to communicate her complicated thoughts. "You can get all high and mighty and say 'pray about it,' but it's not that easy."

Frankie sat still. When she spoke, her voice had lost some of its usual assertiveness. "Nothin' about prayer is easy. What Mama did nearly killed the rest of us."

No longer smiling, the baby coughed several times, gagging on the fist he'd stuffed into his mouth, wresting Charlotte's attention away from Frankie. "Oh, wonderful. As much as I love my nieces and nephews, a baby person, I am not."

Just as Frankie started to reach for MJ, her son Paul yelled out in the kitchen and snagged her attention. Charlotte stopped her before she could rush out of the room. "If you don't sit down! How in the world do you ever get any rest, the way you run after those children? If it's not one, it's another. Do you know how many clients I see who are burned out by their family? Too many to tell you. You're going to worry yourself sick, between hovering over us and them too!"

Frankie craned an ear toward the room on the other side of the wall from the den. Apparently satisfied nobody was dying at the hands of another under the kitchen table, she resumed her seat, her mouth a resigned straight line. "What I'm doin' now for my own, I did for you when I was doin' what I could to raise you, because you're my own too."

"Technically, I wasn't, Frankie. You weren't our mama, and your name isn't Mayhelen Winters. No amount of name-changing can mitigate Mama's effect on all of us."

Frankie saw an opening. "Now that you've brought up mitigation, let's talk about why we're here and try to agree on something before Annabelle comes back. Miss Hattie's right about selling—"

"Oh! He threw up! I told you, I'm not a baby person!" The infant hiccuped again and let out another cry, along with more of his lunch—his first taste of peas, according to Frankie's earlier announcement.

Charlotte wanted to toss the child to the sofa, but even with her limited knowledge, she was aware that was the last thing she should do. "Get me something!" Under her breath, she muttered, "And of course I bought this specifically for my date . . ." That last sentence was out before she could keep it from trip-trapping across her tongue and out her mouth.

Frankie upended the diaper bag. Riffling through the disposable diapers and other baby-related accoutrements, she came up with a thin plastic pack. "Here. Use these." She ransomed the baby with the wipes and hissed, "Did you say something about a date?"

Charlotte focused on dabbing at the gunk on her blouse. "I'm not talking about it."

"Come on, share." Frankie finished cleaning the baby, then slid a new diaper over his bottom.

Charlotte invested but a second on her sibling before returning her attention to the stain. "I'm not messing with you. We were talking about Miss Hattie."

The bathroom door squeaked open and Annabelle finally stalked into the family room, her flip-flops clapping against the hardwood floor. She posed in the wide entryway, hands on her hips. "From what I heard, there's plenty to talk about. You don't have to shout, Frankie, for goodness sakes."

"I didn't. My voice carries naturally." Frankie pressed the tape closed on the diaper and righted the baby in her lap. "Look at you, standin' there, gatherin' steam. No, I take that back. Don't look at her, Charlotte. She might put a spell on you."

Out of wipes, Charlotte looked around for something to scrape the last bit of smushed peas off the hem of her blouse. "What, you're afraid she'll turn me into stone? Like Medusa? I thought you saved and sanctified folk didn't do the Greek gods." She contorted her body to keep her chin pressed to her shirt and still cock an eye at her sister's face. "What?"

Frankie shook her head. "Child, you need some serious time with Jesus. I'm thinkin' about that snake from the Disney movie. You know the one."

"Oh, you meant Kaa!" Charlotte laughed and lost her grip as she wiggled her hips and shoulders.

Annabelle braced a palm on the side of her face. "If y'all don't stop all your shenanigans! Charlotte, you're always cuttin' up, whether you're showing off or pouting. Isn't it about time you grew up?" Jaw slack, Annabelle regarded her. "First the jokes about Mama and now this. How are we supposed to have a serious conversation about our response to Miss Hattie? If she makes the decision without us, Mayhelen will be in your backyard, and that's no laughing matter."

Annabelle's comment was a puff of air on a candle, snuffing out Charlotte's good humor. "Pouting! Y'all won't let me grow up. I'm not a cranky child, so stop patting me on my back and treating me like one. And Mama won't be my problem. I live in a made-for-one town house, remember? No extra room or a yard of my own to speak of."

"Never mind. Forget I said anything. Didn't you say you had to leave soon?" Annabelle returned to her seat and picked up a magazine, apparently glad to be relieved of her babysitting duties.

"There you go again, dismissing me, as if my feelings don't matter. I'm tired of it, Anna. I'm not your stepson." Charlotte and her temper were speeding away from the issue.

"Why'd you call him my *step*son? He's my child, same as MJ is Frankie's." Annabelle waved toward the baby, gurgling and freshened up, on their oldest sister's lap. "And why wouldn't Henry's feelings matter . . . because he's my child, a nephew once removed? As the 'expert,'—" her two fingers wagged in front of her face—"you should know better."

"Speaking of children, sounds like you both need a time-out and learn to play nice. I wouldn't call this a wise use of these precious few minutes we have together." Frankie threw her head back on the sofa and growled. She steadied MJ as his head wobbled in his mother's direction. "Who knows when I'll get the two of you in the same room again?"

"Not anytime soon," Annabelle pronounced.

"Not if I can help it," Charlotte grumbled.

For a second, the two younger sisters shot silent daggers at each other before Charlotte snickered and Annabelle exhaled a smile. The twins, Paul and Leah, scuttled back into the den and ogled at their aunts from the doorway. A small arm wedged itself between them, and Nora poked her head through the fence their bodies had created.

Frankie glanced over her shoulder at the ruckus and sighed when she again faced her sisters. "For a minute there, I thought I'd have to get a switch and take it to both of y'all. What kind of example are y'all settin' for the rest of my children?"

Annabelle's mouth fell open, and her head twisted from one sibling to the other. "Do you hear her, Charlotte? The *rest of her children*?"

"I have to agree with you, Annabelle." Charlotte held up both hands and hoped her playfulness masked her frustration. Frankie's world spun at dizzying speeds. Adding the weight of her sisters caused it to wobble and go off-kilter as it rotated. She always attested that the job had been thrust upon her, much like Malvolio's claim to greatness in Shakespeare's *Twelfth Night.* Yet Charlotte thought it possible that something inside Frankie could've wrested the role away from Mama because she felt Mayhelen was unfit. That she'd sapped all the mothering juice as a parasite in sister's clothing until their rightful parent had simply ceded the title.

"I know, I said it, Annabelle. You'd better mark this day down, because you probably won't ever hear me say that again. Frankie keeps trying to walk in a pair of shoes that don't fit her. Not anymore. It's time for her to be our sister, not our mama." She turned to Frankie.

Even if that was the case, Frankie didn't make Mayhelen kill anybody. Mama did that all by her lonesome. That much I do know.

Chapter Four

FRANKIE PRESSED A HAND to her chest and held Charlotte's stare. "Annabelle, would you do your big," she simpered, "*sister* a favor and get that large container of wipes from the bathroom? Charlotte's havin' a fit about her shirt."

After a beat, Annabelle did as she was asked. When she returned, she plopped the plastic box on the sofa and edged back around the table.

Annabelle tucked a stray hair behind her ear. "No offense, little sis, but Frankie and I could tell you plenty of stories about how you cried until you got what you wanted."

"I had the croup!" Charlotte looked like she would stomp her foot.

"Eight-year-olds don't tend to have the croup. You were spoiled." Annabelle smiled, as if attempting to divert the criticism so it was only a glancing blow.

Judging by Charlotte's face, however, it was a direct hit. "How would you know? Your stepson is what, four, five?" Charlotte depressed the button and extracted a wipe.

"You know very well he's five years old, so stop playing. I guess that makes two of us. Neither one of us has had a baby or an eight-year-old."

Annabelle resettled herself in her chair with an old issue of *Southern Living* and flipped the pages. Frankie knew Annabelle had her own internal wounds to dress. As only a half sister to both Charlotte and Frankie, Annabelle was sensitive to any adjective or prefix attached to her son.

Frankie pulled a new onesie over MJ's head. "Ladies, y'all know the rules. It's all fun and games until somebody gets her feelings hurt. No need to go there."

"But she did go there, didn't she? Henry may be only five, but I've certainly heard him do more than his fair share of whining." Charlotte crossed her arms. "Learned behavior, no doubt."

"Charlotte . . ." Frankie snapped the baby's T-shirt closed and smoothed his silky hair. He gazed at her with wide eyes, *Daddy's Boy* emblazoned on his chest, as she lifted the hem of her blouse and fit him against her side.

"You can't tell me what to do anymore, Frankie," Charlotte said. "I've got you by three inches and thirty pounds."

"You're wearin' high heels, so that's cheatin'," Frankie chuckled as she attached the infant to her breast. "And besides, child, my authority never had anything to do with your size . . . or mine. I may have perfected the short, but I let somebody else handle the sweet."

At that, Charlotte whirled toward her. "See, that's the problem. Mama may not have owned up to all the responsibility—"

"*May* not have? How about *didn't*?" Annabelle sounded incredulous.

Charlotte treated Annabelle's interruption like it was a pesky fly she could squash with her words. ". . . all the responsibility that you took on, Frankie, but I was never your 'child.' He is." She pointed at the nursing baby. "And all . . . of, of, of *them*." She waved a hand toward the kitchen, where Frankie's older son and two daughters were now laughing at the table over their game of cards. "Who knows how many you're planning to have, even at your age."

Charlotte positioned herself right in front of Annabelle and speared the magazine to the table with a finger.

Annabelle was not one to back down from a confrontation, something that used to get her in plenty of trouble, especially with their mother. Holding *Southern Living* in one hand, she picked at a crack in the leather arm of the chair with the other. "What is it, Charlotte?"

"You know what." Charlotte's voice squeaked as she tried to mimic her middle sister's slightly higher tone. "I can tell you've disengaged. Withdrawn. You're acting like you're above the situation after you've darn well caused the situation. And don't think I missed what you said. 'Neither one of us has had a baby or an eight-year-old.' As if I needed you to remind me. You forgot to add 'yet' to that statement."

Frankie shook her head, soul weary from the bickering. Her heart's desire was to evict the dueling duo and reclaim her house, this snug home that had opened its arms to her family, unlike the much roomier house she'd grown up in. She was eager to retreat to the comfort that her sisters considered chaos: homeschooling her precocious other three and nursing the baby.

When Frankie had called Annabelle to share the news about buying the decades-old, three-bedroom brick house, she'd explained that the two septuagenarians who'd sold it to them had raised their two children there, and it was where they ate breakfast with their grandbabies two Saturdays a month. The older couple was saying grace with them at the same table after tucking them into the same beds where their adult children had slept when they were young.

That was why Frankie had to have the house. Despite its recent renovation, it had a history that lived and breathed within its walls, a history that was theirs for the passing on.

"A history is different from the past, Annabanana." Frankie's normally boisterous voice had been little more than a contented sigh. It sounded farther away than the few hundred miles that had separated her from Annabelle at the time. "I think of the past as whatever happened before now. The dinner we just ate, that's in the past. But your history? That's connected to you and it moves with you. It explains how and why you came to be. It's more than an event or the forty years of baggage I've been totin' around."

She had paused, but not long. "Aren't you tired of thinkin' about all that stuff that happened to us when we were growin' up? I'm ready to set that down. Me and Melvin are makin' history, and we're goin' to pass all that on to our children and our children's children."

It didn't matter to Frankie that they were practically busting at the seams after giving birth to baby MJ. Charlotte insisted the boys would be scarred from having to share a bedroom, but Frankie disregarded the studies her baby sister attested to, letting them drain from her mind like the twins' dirty bathwater. If Annabelle's remodeling project went well, Frankie would talk to Oliver about a home addition, but either way, Frankie never planned to change her address from 323 Little Street. Maybe they'd sell it to a young couple who happened to drive by thirty years from now.

That is, if I make it through today and live long enough. Frankie squared her shoulders and projected her voice. "Okay, Charlotte. You need to sit down."

As usual, Charlotte and Annabelle ignored her and continued to bicker, looking like they would come to blows, so acquainted they were with violence. Charlotte's toes touched the legs of Annabelle's chair, and she seemed ready for a face-off.

Seeing Charlotte standing there with her arms akimbo, Frankie got so tickled, her belly jostled MJ and he squirmed. "Girl, sit down."

Her comment acted as the stalled car on the tracks that derailed a speeding train. An out-of-control Charlotte wheeled around and directed an accusatory glare at Frankie. "How can I convince you I'm not one of your children? You're still taking responsibility when it's not your place. Maybe Mama—"

"Why does Mama always get a pass?" Annabelle's monotone voice and lack of eye contact gave the impression that the recipes and articles she was perusing were more interesting than their discussion. "Here we are, still saying 'maybe this or that,' when we all know she wasn't a mother to us. But you weren't either, Frankie. You're our sister. You've always carried a load God didn't intend."

Charlotte flicked her hand over her left shoulder. "Oh, here we go with more of this God business. I'm used to hearing about it from that one, and now it's coming from your side of the room."

Frankie felt her temperature rise. Charlotte always knew how, where, and when to poke her sisters. Where the sore spots were. Other people thought Charlotte was the quiet one—the even-keeled *doctor*—but Frankie knew her youngest sister used her tongue like a rapier, cutting and jabbing. Ever on the offense and the defense. What preserved their relationship was that typically, Charlotte aimed somewhere—or at someone—else. At Annabelle.

Frankie took a deep breath to get herself together. She couldn't keep her eyes from landing on a photograph mounted in an antique gold frame. A shapely woman, posing on the hood of an Oldsmobile Cutlass, peered back at her. *Thanks, Mayhelen.*

Charlotte snapped two fingers. "Earth to Annabelle. Come in, Annabelle." At her sister's smirk, she shrugged. "Typical. You drop a bomb and then run for cover."

"Do you see me runnin'? Nobody's afraid of you, Charlotte."

"I didn't say you were afraid of me. I'm just making sure you're still with us. You tend to withdraw when things get sticky—when you *make* things sticky. You may not have an eight-year-old yet, but you will one day. I hope you don't plan on checking out on him the way you do when you're with us." Charlotte's accusatory thumb waggled between her and Frankie.

Frankie wished she could duck when their eyes connected. She didn't want to be swept up in the lifelong fray between her sisters and get washed up on one side or the other. There shouldn't be a "side" in the first place.

As her tongue searched for more words—the right words—to neutralize the resentful air in the room, Frankie watched Annabelle's expression undergo a metamorphosis. Her sister's anger became resignation before a world weariness slackened her mouth and jawline. She was shocked when Annabelle swallowed and a hint of a smile played around her lips. *What is she up to?*

"If you can grow out of your whiny stage, then I know Henry can too." Annabelle landed her words expertly.

"Wh—? I know you didn't—! Are you—?" Charlotte spluttered for a moment until her voice came to a stop. At last, like a balloon incrementally deflating, her fingers uncurled and she laughed when she swatted Annabelle's hand. "You know how to get me riled up, you and that quick tongue of yours. Just like

Mama. If you hadn't had to live with her, y'all would've gotten along like white on rice."

Wistfulness supplanted the humor in Charlotte's eyes when they settled on the barely discernible bulge at Annabelle's waistline. "Who knows? Maybe she would've thrown you a baby shower . . . if we weren't planning her funeral."

Frankie exhaled a tremulous breath in the silence, grateful to relinquish her role of umpire. She inhaled deeply and cleared her throat. It was high time they addressed the real issue that had brought them together today.

"Speaking of Mama . . . I'm not makin' a decision or doin' any of it by myself because practically and emotionally, I can't afford to. So what will it be? It's either a yes or a no; we bring her home for burial or we don't. Then we figure out what to do with the house and the furniture—burn 'em or sell 'em."

Chapter Five

Then

ANNABELLE ROCKED SLOWLY BACK and forth on the back porch. Her tailbone was sore at the spot that kept hitting the wooden ledge jutting off the top step. A soon-to-be six-year-old, she was smart enough to know she and Frankie weren't supposed to be left at home, despite what Mama had told her before she whipped down the drive, her tires spitting gravel from both sides like the red car in that TV show. Smart enough—yet scared enough not to say a word about it.

She'd watched when Mama had leaned down and cupped Frankie's chin with her long fingers, the squared tips of her nails leaving little half-moons where they'd dug into the sides of her face. "Don't let nobody in, Frances Mae, and get back inside and stay there. And you better not answer that phone unless it's me callin'. Remember, I'll ring twice and hang up, then call right back. That's when you answer. Y'all be in bed as soon as you see the flag come on the television."

"Make sure you listen, Anna!" Mayhelen had put a hand over her eyes and peered into the shadows behind the screen door, where she must have thought her younger daughter was hiding. But she tended to get it wrong when it came to Annabelle. When she'd turned, she'd spotted her younger daughter on the porch and shaken her head. "Mm-mm-mmm. Lookin' just like your daddy, poor thing."

As usual, Annabelle wondered why she was a "poor thing" and resolved then and there to ask one day. But it wouldn't be today, because her mama quickly tip-tapped down the steps, with only the toes of her spiky high heels touching the wood and her arms extended as if she were balancing on a tightrope. At the bottom, she'd winked at her older daughter. "Take care of your sister like a big girl while Mama goes to find somebody who can keep good company and help us 'round here. Bye now."

"But I'm not a big girl. I'm little, like Annabelle," eight-year-old Frankie had whispered.

Fear wrapped itself around Annabelle as she squinted at the oak tree in the far end of the yard. Her sister was twirling on the tire hanging from it, barely discernible in the evening light. She knew they were supposed to be inside, but neither one of them liked being in that big old house by themselves. It was too creaky, the ceilings too high. Something about the outside was less frightening. Annabelle didn't know about Frankie, but at this moment she would rather be at the park than at home.

Deciding to let her sister swing a little longer, she clasped her arms around her legs and propped her chin on her scuffed knees. Gazing into the cloud-streaked sky, she studied the oranges, pinks, and purples and suddenly and inexplicably felt less lonely. Her eyes followed the birds, flying in twos and threes before finding shelter in the branches that swayed together in the breeze and whispered secrets to each other that only they knew. A few landed in the ground-hugging flowers poking up in the weeds and picked at delicacies Annabelle couldn't see. She wondered at their peace, how they felt so at home when they had none to speak of.

A streak of far-off lightning lit up the approaching dark gray of night and thunder chased it, breaking the spell. Annabelle's sneakers skipped across the hard-packed ground through the yard. "Fwankie!"

Hearing her, Frances Mae grabbed the rope and pulled herself upright. "Stop that runnin', Annabananna! You'll trip and fall! If Mama comes back and sees your knees all bloody, she'll know we've been outside. What would happen then?" The order was more about self-preservation than prevention. Neither one of them could tie a shoe properly. Frankie's laces were a tangled mess piled on top.

But Annabelle kept going full speed across the wide stretch of grass in that hippity-hoppity way she loved to run, and her older sister didn't seem to have the sense to meet her halfway. Frankie screwed up her face as if preparing to take the brunt of the fall she must have felt sure to come.

"Fwankie, somebody he-we!" Annabelle panted, her voice the same size she was. Several feet from the swaying tire, she stopped and pointed in the general direction beyond her sister, her chest heaving in the long patchwork dress she was wearing, the torn hem of which dragged the ground.

"Anna, why you wearin' that to play in?" Frankie was too irritated to translate the girl's gibberish and see what she was looking at. "You're makin' a mess of yourself and Mama is gon' have somethin' to say if and when she sees it." She stomped to Annabelle and squatted at her feet. "Maybe if I tear off the dingy lace altogether, Mama won't notice."

Annabelle pounded the top of her sister's head with her palms.

Frankie swatted away her sister's hands and looked up. "Wha-at, Anna?"

"Hello there, girls."

The words were spoken softly, but they collared the older girl's attention, what Annabelle hadn't been able to do. Frankie toppled onto her bottom. Her arms reared back and caught her before she fell over altogether.

An older woman who didn't appear too much taller than Frankie approached the children and eventually stopped next to the large circle of oil that had dripped through the hole in the pan under their mama's car. She had dark curly hair sprinkled with white strands that sprang from the edges of her scalp. Large gold metal glasses encircled her deep-set eyes, the same ebony as her skin. The stranger was wearing the kind of dress old ladies wore, round at the neck and loosely belted at the waist and ending just below the knees; she would've fit in fine sitting on the church pew or standing in front of her stove. When Annabelle's inspection led to the woman's feet, she noticed the line bisecting her toes that showed she was wearing pantyhose with her sandals. Somehow she knew Mayhelen would sneer at them.

Annabelle liked her on the spot. Frankie must have too, because she allowed her to bunny hop over to the woman and tilt up her face and wave, a grin on her small face.

"I'm Hattie Mason, and I live over there." She threw her arm toward a neat, one-story, pillbox of a house way across the empty lot behind the Winters. The field was polka-dotted with blossoms that grew at summer's end, those tall ones that looked like the sun when it rose high in the sky. Her home had a pitched black roof that covered pale green clapboard and white shutters. Yellow light shone from one of its two double-wide front windows. The woman smiled, revealing a gold tooth in the corner of her mouth that glinted in the fading light. "Don't you look pretty in your dress, like a belle in a ball."

"That's my name!" Annabelle giggled.

"It is?" Her grin stretched wide enough to scoop up both Annabelle and Frankie and take them home with her. The girls' mama never smiled like that unless she was telling them something they wouldn't like.

Annabelle knew she and her older sister weren't supposed to be in the yard at all, let alone at that time of evening with somebody they didn't know, but at that moment, Anabelle felt safer outside with the stranger than she did inside with her mama sleeping across the hall. Feeling like the birds nesting and flying across the way, she settled into the crook of the arm that Frankie threw around her before speaking.

"My name is Frances Mae . . . Frankie. She's Annabelle."

"And your mama is Mayhelen Winters, who owns McNair's. I shop in her store sometimes when I'm buyin' things for my students at the Methodist church school where I work. Nice to meet you." The woman extended a small hand. "Call me Miss Hattie. My husband died a long time ago and took my *Mrs.* with him."

"You know my mama? You buy stuff from her?" Annabelle squinted one eye up at Miss Hattie. It had been dark the two times she remembered going to the store situated in the middle of downtown Jasper. Her mama had rushed her past clothes on racks and shelves full of bulky shadows—"merchand-eyes," she'd called it—to pick up some things in the back.

Feeling Frankie stiffen, Annabelle cocked an eye her way. For some reason, Frankie shuffled back a couple steps without shaking the woman's hand and inched behind Annabelle, as if taking cover. Maybe she felt better when the older woman was a stranger, when they all were unexplored land to each other. Then they could pretend they were two kids playing outside while their mama was upstairs somewhere folding laundry or running their bathwater. That was what they told people who came looking for Mama when the girls were home alone and still in the yard. This woman probably had some idea of the truth. Frankie might not want to feel known, but Annabelle found she didn't mind it too much.

"Why yes, to both of those questions. I've been shopping there a long, *lon-n-n-g* time, since your daddy worked there, before your mama ever owned it. I believe you—" she leaned down and tapped Annabelle gently in the middle of her sternum—"are wearing one of the cutest dresses I've ever seen, little Miss Annabelle. By the way, did you know *belle* is French for beautiful? You are, you know. You both are." She straightened.

"We are what?" *French, like French fry?* Frankie reached for Annabelle's hand and yanked her closer, causing Annabelle to stumble into her sister's side. Frankie squeezed her tiny fingers, commanding her without a word to keep still. It took some doing because Annabelle felt like a bumblebee attracted to the sweetness that oozed from the older woman.

"Beautiful. And maybe a bit hungry too?" Miss Hattie winked. "I saw your mama tear outta here like a bat out of Hades, and I thought y'all might like some comp'ny. I have some leftover baked chicken and macaroni and cheese if you'd like some. My doctor told me I had to cut back on fried foods, or else I woulda brought y'all some wangs."

Mmm. Fried chicken wings. One of their wannabe uncles used to make those, but he took that with him when he left. Warmth suffused Annabelle. Not the fuzzy kind she'd felt at first, when Miss Hattie had smiled at them, but the heat of shame. She took one step back and then another and barricaded herself behind the arm that had once embraced her. *I am hungry, and she knows it. She knows my daddy too. I wonder what he looks like.*

Frankie gave Annabelle a shove. "Mama told us not to talk to strangers. If she finds us out here when she gets back from the store, she'll light into us." Frankie headed for the house, looking back over her shoulder. "It was nice to meet you. Bye."

"Fwankie, I'm hungwy! What we gon' eat?" Annabelle didn't bother lowering her voice as she tripped up the steps and across the porch behind her sister. She turned with Frankie when they reached the back door and opened the screen.

Miss Hattie hadn't moved. "Go on in, Frances Mae," she called. "I'll wait until you're locked up. If I see your mama hasn't come back, I'll be over with a couple paper plates, and I'll leave 'em by the back door. You can throw 'em out when you're done, and your mama will be none the wiser." She waved. "Go on, now. I'll be watchin'."

The screen creaked shut behind them, and Frankie latched it for good measure, something they rarely did, and something she'd have to undo before Mama came sliding in sometime in the wee hours when the owl was still hooting up a storm from the tree that leaned toward Annabelle's window. The two girls stood with their hands pressed against the wood trim, watching Miss Hattie troop through the tall grass separating her house from theirs.

Chapter Six

Now

"ANYBODY HOME?" Annabelle bumped the back door closed with her hip and navigated the land mines her husband had left behind in the kitchen. She plopped down her armload of groceries, careful to avoid the big hole where their decades-old electric range used to sit. By the time they'd dragged it out of the house, only two burners worked—the small one on the right and the large one behind it—and the oven couldn't heat above 275 degrees.

Still, it had taken weeks of convincing to get Oliver to let it go. He'd stroked the cracked enamel top, careful not to scratch his finger. "Mama cooked a ton of grits on this when I was comin' up. It's been good to us."

Annabelle had lifted his hand and cupped it with both of hers. "Well, let's hope it'll also be good to whoever melts it down. We're going to need a fully operational stove to make enough food to feed this family, Ollie."

Those words had done the trick. Oliver had watched the truck until it pulled out of their driveway and disappeared around the curve at the top of the hill. Annabelle couldn't identify with such sentimentality for a hunk of steel, a tangle of wires, plastic knobs with faded numbers, and two barely working heating elements. It was an appliance, and it performed a specific duty. And not very well at that. Once it had served its purpose, they needed to move on to something better, newer, more functional. In fact, her brand-new natural-gas range was already sitting in a box in their garage, waiting for the moment the McMillans had installed the finished cabinets and Piedmont Gas had run the line to the house. In her experience, people shouldn't make room in their lives for clinging to broken things.

That day, when the truck hauled away their junk to the scrapyard, all Annabelle could do was muster a sigh and give her husband's shoulder a sympathetic squeeze. She decided to wait until the next morning to mention that the ancient Chevy's engine had dribbled oil from the middle of their driveway to the road. Certainly those stains were something they'd never forget.

Annabelle emptied the last of the plastic bags, and four apples and a net of clementines tumbled onto the countertop. She cut a hole in the net and stacked all the fruit in the cobalt blue ceramic bowl, a gift from Oliver's mother, who'd recently discovered the miracle of two-day delivery. Mother Mac was always trying to spruce up her son's demolition site with something pretty, as if a pop of color would lure the eye from the holes in the walls, paint splotches, drop cloths, and missing appliances.

She and her husband had passed down the house to Oliver, their oldest child, when they'd moved to a retirement village in

Colfax, North Carolina, to live near Oliver's aunt and uncle. Redoing the house had become Oliver's pet project. Owning a small construction business, Good Bones Construction, certainly helped, as did the assistance of his site manager, Thom Samuels.

Annabelle had to admit that the Granny Smith apples did look picture worthy sitting in that dish with the mandarin orange wannabes and the one remaining banana Henry hadn't scarfed down. What she didn't like the looks of was the empty hook on the side of the cabinet.

"Jimmy-jimmy cocoa pop, where are you, Oliver?" Frowning, Annabelle stared at the spot where his keys should be at that moment. Immediately, she maneuvered around the three-foot-tall ladder propped against the sawhorse in the middle of the kitchen and strode through the utility room to fling open the door to the garage. Sure enough, no sign of Oliver's pollen-covered black F-150. She'd been so distracted by thoughts of her sister summit with Charlotte and Frankie, she hadn't realized that his half of the garage was empty when she'd parked her Mustang a few minutes ago, not until that moment. She frowned at the full bicycle racks mounted on the wall; the shelves of canned vegetables and fruit they'd transplanted from the kitchen; stacks of jars, bins, and baskets; and bags of yet-to-be-donated clothing and asked, "Why aren't you and Henry where you're supposed to be? Where I want you to be?"

Taking her dejection back to the kitchen, Annabelle dropped her keys into her pocket as she invariably did, a habit that drove Oliver crazy and dulled some of their newly wedded glow. She sighed, her hand closing around her key ring as she eyed the space her husband had set aside for it, right with his own. Annabelle mulled over the questions Oliver had asked her a week ago—*Ready to go at a moment's notice, huh? Should I check the closet for a suitcase?*—before she looped the keys on their intended hook, as if doing so would make her husband and son materialize.

When they didn't, she plodded from the kitchen to open doors and peek under chairs, leaving no stone unturned in her search for clues that explained why the house felt bereft; it was never quiet at this hour of the afternoon. A teensy part of her thought she might find two separate piles of clothes—one topped by a pair of Fruit of the Loom briefs and the other by some underpants decorated with sharks, clown fish, and seahorses—as if Oliver and Henry had been caught up in the Rapture and left her behind. *What happened to my people?*

She retracted the pocket doors leading to the den, and light from the front of the house streamed in. They typically kept the shutters closed this time of year to keep the west-facing room cool, and the wood paneling added to its cave-like feel. Practically the only spot in their 1930s craftsman-style home they hadn't covered with sawdust or attacked with a hammer and nails, the den served as Annabelle's retreat, a place where she could pretend the walls weren't coming down and being erected around her. Oliver had dragged his wife into their home renovation—not exactly kicking and screaming, but with murmuring, rolling of eyes, and a great deal of passive resistance. Annabelle sighed, unable to clear her head of the ghosts of remodeling present, a faint sound of knocking that pursued her despite the absence of Oliver and his construction crew.

Sometimes, she sounded more like Henry than his mother because she was constantly questioning, "Why are we doing thus and so?" She still couldn't understand why they couldn't have refused the elder McMillans' *gift* of Oliver's family home and instead bought a house that was finished—completely new preferably—around the corner if they had to from his old neighborhood. Or better yet, in the next state.

According to Oliver, it would've been foolish to not only look a gift horse in the mouth, but to slap its hindquarters and shout, "Giddyup!" They couldn't refuse such generosity being slathered upon their small family. Annabelle had argued that newlyweds were supposed to strike out on their own, struggle a little bit, and churn some butter through their own vigorous efforts.

"We're too old to be considered newlyweds, and we've both struggled enough on our own. Now that we're together, we can use this renovation to make our own butter. Salted, sweet cream," he'd responded as calmly as he always did, with no hint of condescension whatsoever. He'd only drawn her close to him and planted a soft kiss on her forehead.

Thinking she'd heard a noise, Annabelle tipped back the leather recliner to make sure her stepson—*No, my son, not my stepson*—wasn't curled up in his daddy's chair. By 4:30, the intro music for *Wild Kratts* should be filling the downstairs, one of the few shows they allowed the five-year-old to enjoy relatively unsupervised. Thanks to Henry's penchant for watching those brothers explore nature via the PBS channel, she and Oliver had had time to paint three 30-minute episodes' worth every day—that is, until Annabelle's recent "discovery" got her relegated to the oversize lounger next to their son, right after she'd applied the last coat of semigloss in his room. Her husband continued to tackle their heavier-duty and fume-filled remodeling projects alone while a newly pregnant Annabelle learned how to tell a crocodile from an alligator.

"Oliver? Henry? Is that you?" Annabelle walked toward the house's center, her flip-flops slapping against the soles of her feet, the only sound to her lonely ears. She must have imagined hearing the two men in her life. She gripped the carved newel post and gazed up the fifteen unfinished treads curving toward their second-floor addition. The overpowering smell of freshly sanded oak made her gag a little, something else to get used to these days. She swallowed and called, "Ollie?" but her voice carried only an echo when it returned from searching the rooms above.

Swallowing the hard pill of disappointment, Annabelle tried to will herself to walk around the stairwell to the three rooms on the opposite side of the house from the kitchen, an area that faced the lawn on the right side of their half-acre lot. She'd claimed for her own the smallest of those spaces, where Oliver had slept as a child; she'd dubbed it her studio, the home of her jewelry designs. They were the same four walls that had snuggled Henry until they'd moved him upstairs so he could sleep under the watchful eyes of brightly painted jungle animals and googly-eyed insects. The first night in his new room, their three-and-a-half-foot-tall zoologist had informed them, "The spider only has six legs," and literally wouldn't rest until Annabelle had added two more squiggly lines.

Yet Annabelle had to admit that designing in Oliver's former bedroom got her creative juices flowing. She'd told him it was because the space captured the best natural sunlight. Secretly she wondered if maybe Frankie was onto something, the idea of attaching her life to somebody else's memories. Wasn't that what happened when you married someone? Deep down, where Annabelle secreted those thoughts she only wanted God to see, she believed she'd brought all her nothing and become a part of *something*, an established filiation that once was and would continue to be. And two years into her marriage, she'd grown accustomed to her new family's routine, despite her best efforts to the contrary. She leaned into their traditions and history; Annabelle Winters, once a solitary point, had allowed the McMillans to absorb her into their continuous family line.

Which was why the empty house rankled her—or rather, her *feelings* about the empty house. Annabelle didn't want to get absorbed by anybody, to lose that intrinsic loner within her that resisted depending on anything and anybody. She didn't want to find herself weeping over broken microwaves and old newspaper articles. Neediness was dangerous. She'd learned that implicitly from her mama's behavior, though it was something her mama never explicitly told her. The Winters part of her chided her newly wedded McMillan side as she wandered from room to unoccupied room, retrieving Oliver's black socks that were half under the sofa and scooping up Henry's Playmobil figures before she stepped on them and broke their fragile, outstretched arms. Annabelle could picture her mama shaking her head as her daughter cradled the items to her chest and deposited them in the laundry basket and the toy bin where they belonged.

Girl, you talk about me, but it's in the blood, Mayhelen Winters would say. *You're just as hooked as I am. I might've kept my own name, but that don't prove nothin'. They own you same as me. You're not one little bit better.*

"Yes, I am," Annabelle protested. The words seemed to reverberate off the walls, following her, even as they drove her, finally, to her office. She rested against the scarred, six-foot-long, repurposed, solid oak kitchen table that held her trays of beads, charms, chains, and other tools and findings.

As a wedding gift, Oliver had used his considerable skills to outfit the counter-high table into a true workbench that rivaled one of those fancier, more expensive numbers. He'd cut a half circle into the left end of it where she could fit comfortably—even the future, nine-months-pregnant Annabelle—and built drawers and shelves underneath. He'd given it a raised edge along those three sides where her chair fit to help prevent beads from rolling off onto the never-never land of their wood floor; on the end with the flat edge, he'd attached a high-powered, adjustable light that she could bring in for close-up work and an anvil and a bench peg. When she walked into the room that day and beheld the table topped with a large silky white bow, she'd recognized it for the well-appointed bribe it was, incentivizing her to see his "project" as her home. It had worked.

Annabelle plucked a pair of needle-nose pliers from one of the buckets mounted on the wall in front of her. Out of something better to do, she dipped the tip in a small container sitting along the desk's raised edge, fiddling with the beads she stored there for current projects. The noise didn't drown out her mother's words rattling around in her head, so she raised her voice over them. "Yes, I am better, because I *choose* to be here and do what I do. Nothing and nobody controls me."

A child screamed, and Annabelle knocked over the metal bowls on her desk with her pliers. *So it wasn't my imagination! All those thumps and voices!* Multicolored and shiny beads and spacers of all shapes and sizes bounced across the table and off the flat edge and came to rest in a crack between the wide floor planks, still original on the first floor. His name was first a thought, then an exhalation as she sprinted from the room and up the hall, toward the sound. "Henry . . ."

Chapter Seven

SOUNDS FROM THE BACKYARD drew her to the back door. Annabelle threw it open and had to catch her breath and the cry that hovered on her lips. There was her boy, safe and sound, home with his dad, who was kneeling at the base of a tall wood post near the open tailgate of his Ford. Oliver looked back over his right shoulder and grinned, then threw up a hand to beckon her over before returning to his work. Whatever he was doing with all his hammering steadied, then stilled, the rocking motion of the swing—not that it was worrying Henry one bit, by the looks of it. The little boy was pumping his little legs with all his might, sending his body soaring through the cool spring air toward the blues, pinks, and oranges of the early evening sky.

The laughter and at-the-top-of-his-lungs yelling finally spurred Annabelle to move. She let the screen door close behind her as she skipped down the five brick steps and jogged to her husband, who rose and met her in the middle of the yard. Annabelle locked her fingers around Oliver's neck as he encircled her with his long arms and lifted her from the ground; her feet dangled around his ankles. At six-foot-four, he towered over her by seven inches.

"Mmm-mmm, you feel good."

"So do you." Annabelle tucked her face into his neck and inhaled a deep whiff of him. He wasn't perfumy, just delicious, and she couldn't keep herself from nipping his collarbone. "And you're mmm-mmm good too."

Eyes wide, Oliver reared back and stared at her.

Annabelle laughed, surprised herself by her overflow of emotion—and relief—at seeing her menfolk. "Hormones?" She shrugged off her display of affection and raised her chin to accept the kiss Oliver was preparing to plant on the lips she tilted toward him.

"Ew, y'all cut that out!" Henry threw his head back and lifted his face to the sky as he continued to swing.

Laughing, Oliver gave his wife's cheek a wet smack, set her down, and intertwined their fingers. "Okay, little man. Then how about you do the honors and come give your mama a kiss."

Annabelle's heart beat a little faster at the designation, just as it always did. She was the only mother Henry had ever known, but still she feared she had no rights to the honorific. Her son's biological mother had walked away from her marriage to Oliver more than four years ago and divorced him soon after, then packed up and moved to Oregon to pursue a career in meteorology. Annabelle wondered if the woman regretted measuring raindrops for a living and giving up all her rights not only to the man but also to the boy. What was it about herself that was more important than her family? What great need had to be satisfied? These same questions had haunted Annabelle most of her life, pursuing her in the dark of night.

Apparently, Henry didn't believe in ghosts. Carefree, confident that he was loved and cherished by both his parents, he released his grip on the ropes of the swing and leaped to the ground. His bare feet kicked up dust as he raced across the sparse grass to Annabelle.

"Hey, there, baby boy!" She squatted and extended her arms.

He launched himself at her and wrapped his legs around her waist. "Mommy, where you been? I missed you!"

"I missed you too . . . this much. *Mm-mwa.*" A moist splotch near his ear marked where she kissed him. Annabelle had left early that morning while he was eating his oatmeal, searching for the perfect sterling silver hooks to complete a jewelry order before driving forty-five minutes over to Jasper to meet with her sisters. It was taking some getting used to, living within kissing distance to her family, being able to argue face-to-face and still arrive at home in time for dinner. Annabelle had let the wind blow her from place to place for more than half her life, and she'd claim—guilt free—"I'm from New Jersey" or any one of a half dozen states with just enough of a Southern twang to raise the suspecting eyebrows of the listener. She'd effortlessly leapfrogged over her first twenty years of life, though she shortened some words and stretched out others every now and again.

When she'd met Oliver and Henry inside the botanical garden at the Roger Williams Park Zoo in Providence, Rhode Island, she'd taken to the way he was with his young son. Oliver had never behaved like he was out of his element, babysitting somebody else's child. He'd worn both parenting shoes quite comfortably, whether he was pointing out different varieties of roses to the eighteen-month-old or setting Henry on his shoulders so he could count the spots on the giraffe. Annabelle's heart became Oliver's before she realized the two McMillans hailed from eastern North Carolina, a hop, skip, and not-so-long jump away from her sisters.

Something about the two of them had radiated "home," and she'd gravitated to it instead of running from it. They had a lot in common with Miss Hattie.

Her husband had explained that it was the Lord who called, and she had to answer. But at the moment, she had to respond to her son, who wanted her full attention.

"Do you see what me and Daddy did?"

"Daddy and I, and yes, I see it." Spending so much of her childhood around Miss Hattie had made her appreciate good grammar. "Y'all have been mighty busy. I thought you were going to wait for me before you finished setting up the play yard."

"We didn't need your help hauling wood. Henry and I made short work of it."

"And Mr. Samuels helped too. 'I don't know what we would've done without him.' Isn't that what you said after he left, Daddy?"

Annabelle crowed at Oliver's sheepish face. "Oh, I just bet you didn't need my help, what with your foreman lending a hand! Thanks for sharing that tidbit of information, Henry, although I'm sure your father would've told me later."

Her husband smiled and shrugged. "Caught, tried, and convicted. We made quick work of things without you. But your mustache is much cuter than his." Ducking away from her playful jab, he rubbed her back and leaned in close to her ear. "Do you think that's a good idea, Bella? That boy's got rocks in his pockets. Heavy ones. Maybe you need to put him down."

She snuggled their son's sweaty neck that hinted of baby days gone by. It reminded her of summer afternoons at the park, when she helped Frankie babysit while their mama was indisposed . . . Annabelle shook her shoulders to shed the memory and inadvertently dislodged the weight of Oliver's hand from her back. She set Henry on his feet, bent low, and tickled him under his chin. "You smell like spoons. Somebody's gonna need to get a good bath tonight."

He tucked his head, burying his chortle in his chest, and skedaddled back to the swing.

Oliver tucked an auburn tress behind her ear. "How was the meeting today with your sisters? Y'all come to any decisions about your mother?"

She squinted up into the sun that formed an orange-red halo behind his head and considered the man who'd stomped all over her best-laid plans of independent living with his dusty, size-thirteen work boots. "Only that we need to make some. Frankie wants to plan a sister sleepover so we can hash it out. She'll probably take my keys so I can't make my escape, then tie me to the stake and light a fire."

"She must not know how hard that'll be, wrestling those keys away from you. I'll have to call and give her some pointers."

"Ha-ha. I'll have you know my keys are hanging where they're supposed to be." Annabelle pulled out the fabric in her pockets to show him they were empty. "Unlike yours. Why is your truck in the backyard?"

Oliver glanced back. "Remember? I had a load of wood to empty." He aimed a thumb at the swings. "Speaking of . . . Henry! Climb down from there! The truck bed isn't a place to play. You know better!"

Annabelle shook her head as their son landed with a grin and raised his arms in a V after using the truck's tailgate for a springboard. "I see you didn't disagree with the burning-at-the-stake part."

"Who're you gonna burn at the stake?" Henry huffed back to them.

"Oops," Oliver grimaced over his head at his wife. "Nobody,

son. Mommy and Daddy are talking about grown-up stuff. Seriously though, baby, I think you need to give Frankie a chance. Charlotte too. You ran so far, so fast, for so long. But looky here, little mama: all that runnin's only led you back home. How does the song go?" Oliver rested a finger over his lip and peered at something over his wife's shoulder, as if plucking the lyrics out of thin air. A second later he improvised in a powerful tenor, "It's time to sit down and rest a little while."

Annabelle resisted rolling her eyes and decided to focus on Henry. She could appreciate Oliver's strong vocal if not the thought behind the gospel tune. "Why don't you show me how high you can go on the swing?"

"So you can talk to Daddy without me around? Is he gonna sing some more?" He didn't move an inch. His eyes seemed to be numbering every canine, incisor, and molar in her mouth, including her wisdom teeth way in the back.

"I don't know what we're going to do with this next generation." Oliver gripped his son's head with one of his large hands and turned his small body in the direction of their newly constructed swing set, guiding him as he'd use a rudder to steer a ship. "If you're so smart, Henry, why didn't you put up your tools like I told you to? Weaker and wiser, that's what my mama would be saying right about now."

Annabelle spared her husband a glance before returning her attention to the child. "Yes, so I can talk to your dad. I'm surprised you didn't get a splinter in one of those little piggies when you climbed in the truck, so before you get back on the swing, put on your sneakers. I don't want you stepping on something. Once you do that, clean up your tools—and your daddy's, too, while you're at it. It'll be dark soon, and we'll need to get inside and prepare dinner."

Henry couldn't spin around, though he strained against his dad's long fingers that looked like the brown tentacles of an octopus plastered to his scalp. Apparently giving up, he planted his feet in the dirt and stood there with his legs spread wide and his hands on his hips, facing away from them. "You never let me play outside in the dark."

She grasped her knees and propped her chin on his shoulder so she could whisper in his ear. "Do you know what else I don't let you do? Talk back or disobey. Maybe we'll discuss that later, you and I, but you need to stop looking like you own the place." She straightened and moved the child toward the play set. "Yes, ma'am?"

"Yes, ma'am." Resignation elongated each word. Freed from Oliver's hold, Henry sprinted toward his newly constructed toy.

Oliver sighed as the two of them watched him go. "That son of yours . . ."

Annabelle winked at her husband. "Is the second-cutest piece of work I know. After his dad. You're both too smart for your own good. In fact, you're too-o-o-o . . . everything."

He nodded. "I'll give you that, and I'll do you one better: I'm also too determined to let you get away with compliments, though you speak words of truth." Oliver draped an arm around her shoulders. "Now, tell me. How was today? Did you tell them about the baby?"

Annabelle relaxed into him, wondering how he could feel so snuggly despite the wall of muscle that was his chest. Construction work agreed with him—and her. She watched Henry hop on one leg, then the other, and spin in circles, retrieving both his father's large hammer and the smaller mallet she'd given him for his birthday. He placed the tools in their appropriate kits and lugged one after the other around the truck toward the shed near the fence.

She envied Henry his vim and vigor this time of day because she lacked the energy, let alone the desire, to rehash with Oliver today's heavy discussion.

"Have you thought about planting more trees to give us a thicker screen back here? What about cedars or pines? The cherry trees will look lovely once they grow nice and tall, but I don't think they're useful as a privacy hedge. And we only have a couple." She pointed at the house behind them whose yard abutted theirs. Tall hardwoods and evergreens sprouted on the half-acre to acre-size lots in their mature neighborhood.

Oliver pulled her closer and rocked her a little. "Uh-uh, nope. Stop with the smoke and mirrors. Details, details."

"I can't believe I let you talk me into moving back to North Carolina. Outta the frying pan . . ." She sighed.

"Love will make you do all sorts of things. That fire you jumped into keeps you warm and cozy on these chilly, North Carolina winter nights." He pressed his lips to the skin right below her hairline as he beckoned with his hand. "Henry, bring me the key once you lock the shed!"

She inched her left arm around his waist, which had thickened up a tad in the short time they'd been married, something Annabelle quietly took credit for. This family was reaping the benefit from seeds sown long ago in her life's hard ground. "Yes, love will do that, and so will regret."

Oliver's lumbar muscles clinched. "Regret?"

"Don't take that the wrong way, Ollie."

"Is there a right way to take it?" He bent to brush off his knee.

She dropped her empty arm to her side and tried to read his tone. "Of course I don't regret you . . . us." Her voice drifted toward Henry, who thundered up to them, shoved a set of keys in his dad's pockets, and dashed back to the swing set. ". . . Or the family we're growing. Who knew what family even meant? Not I, says the fly—until I stopped to smell the roses in that botanical garden. Watching Henry with you shows me what it means to have a father in your life, something Mayhelen denied me. I'm almost jealous." Annabelle reached for his hand. She thrust her fingers between his and pressed them into his knuckles.

His fingers remained extended for a beat before curling around hers.

"It's just . . . the Lord knows I'd never planned to call this state home again."

Oliver huffed. "Is it really home, or do you only live here? You don't even like to hang your keys on the hook next to mine."

Annabelle tugged him closer. "Since I've already proven that's not the case—not anymore—you can put that criticism to bed. You should be happy, though obviously quite surprised, to hear that my keys are thrilled to be hanging where they belong, and I am too. Home is where my menfolk are."

He faced her and placed their clasped hands low on her belly. "And babyfolk?"

Pressed against him, she knew she couldn't hide her shudder, and she did her best to explain it away. "Talk about hot topics. My psychologist sister loved hearing all about our news. The way she said, 'Oh, I see, you're joining Frankie in that whole "be fruitful and multiply thing."' I tell you, Oliver, I would've loved to multiply the size of her lip by knocking off that smirk."

He gave her a side-eye but pressed his lips together. While they'd only been married a couple years, Oliver knew her well enough to sense she was hedging by talking much about nothing. He also knew when to back off and give her the space she'd grown accustomed to freely wiggling around in before their two became one.

They swayed side to side for a minute, until Annabelle took a deep breath, kissed him quickly, and extracted herself from his embrace. "How about we chat while we cook? I'm beyond drained, and I'm going to lie down for a sec." As she stepped toward the house, she called over her shoulder, "And you, little fix-it dude, make sure you're inside before the streetlights come on!"

Chapter Eight

"UMMM." ANNABELLE PURRED and wiggled her toes, her back arching in a satisfying stretch. She blinked once, twice, then tucked her hands under her head and rolled over on the leather sofa, listening to the clanking and low murmurings coming from the kitchen. She wasn't sure what she expected to hear, but the sounds made her smile. Life—what she *hadn't* heard when she'd arrived home earlier that afternoon. After pressing her bare feet against the notches on the armrest, she took a deep breath and swung them to the floor.

A curly head the height of the middle hinge peeked around the door and disappeared. Footsteps dashed toward the kitchen on creaking floors. "She's awake, Daddy! Daddy, we can laugh now!"

As if Henry had given her leave to do so, Annabelle's low chuckle chased away the vestiges of sleep that had clung to her like cat hair. Crashing for thirty minutes or so in the evening had become a habit of late; the more she resisted it, the more her body craved it. Finally, she'd waved the white flag at Oliver's urging—she refused to think he'd given her permission—and as it turned out, that nap was all she needed to feel restored. Motherhood had already changed her daily routines, and now it was doing quite a number on her soon-to-be-forty-year-old frame.

"So, are you ready now to tell me about the big meeting today?" Oliver's back was to the open kitchen door.

"How'd you hear me? I didn't even have to push open the door, so I didn't make a noise." Annabelle slid her hands in the back of the white denim shorts she'd donned after her nap, feeling refreshed from splashing water over her face and the change of clothes. She knew it was a risk wearing them in the construction zone their house had become, but she figured she'd better enjoy them while she could still button them closed.

He rotated ninety degrees and winked at her as he continued to slowly stir a concoction in the crockpot on the counter behind him.

She nodded in the direction of his wooden spoon. "Isn't the purpose of a slow cooker inherent in its name? It's supposed to cook in such a fashion you don't need to tend to it. Maintenance free and all that jazz."

"This pot here serves as our deep fryer, skillet, and oven until we finish our remodeling project, so that's why I'm 'tending to' this spaghetti. I don't want it to stick." The lid clanked as Oliver replaced it and picked up the maroon-and-white striped dish towel that was looped over the faucet. He swiveled completely around and met her eye to eye. "Henry will be running into the kitchen before you know it to show us some Lego contraption, which means we have about two seconds to carry on a sensible, adult conversation. So stop avoiding my question, Bella."

Annabelle felt herself bristle, but she sheathed the sharp words she was ready to wield. No need to pick a fight when her husband came in peace. *What woman in her right mind fought over being called beautiful?* "You're right, I'm sorry. I did say we'd talk after my nap. Well, my visit with Charlotte and Frankie went about as well as I expected . . . Hmm, maybe not even that well," she sighed, thinking about it. "Now, what can I do to help?"

Sous chef, presumably Annabelle's role in the kitchen. She told anybody who would listen that she didn't like cooking and only did so under duress, but in actuality, she did the work of a ghostwriter, uncredited but integral to the finished product. When her husband's back was turned, she sprinkled, tasted, and seasoned and turned the heat up or down. Annabelle also offered offhand tips and suggestions along the way that she applauded him for when he applied them.

Oliver looked around at the mess he'd made. "Want to attack these dishes?"

She considered the splatters of red sauce on the countertop and her pristine shorts. "Sure."

"Thanks, honey." He retrieved his spoon, jiggled it in the sauce, then set it down on the peeling, seventies-style laminate, one of the next projects they needed to tackle in their renovation.

When he buried his head in the refrigerator, Annabelle nibbled what was bubbling in the slow cooker and added salt and a teaspoonful of sugar. She was giving it a whirl when he closed the door. "It's not sticking. Give me a minute to give you a clean spot for those."

He nodded and held on to his armful. "So, y'all didn't make any progress today?"

As the sink filled with soapy water, Annabelle wrung out a wet cloth and wiped the spot directly in front of him. "I'd say today was kinda typical."

"If that's what you want to call it . . . okay." He bobbled the English cucumber on top of the head of butter lettuce and the tomato he was holding. "What were they saying?"

She dug out the cutting board from a low cabinet and set a sharp knife on top of it. "First of all, they reacted to our news. No surprises with Frankie: she wrapped me up in a hug and gushed about all that I had to look forward to. She has tons of baby clothes for us, boys' and girls' stuff. I guess you could say Charlotte acted the way I expected too, when you think about it. In her mind, she's wanted a husband and a family almost as long as I didn't want one, but I ended up with both. Not that she'd ever admit it."

Annabelle watched Oliver open his mouth and close it, obviously searching for words while he juggled the vegetables. "I know. But it's okay. Really. We've survived harder things than my baby announcement—which inspired a whole round of those yo' mama jokes I love so much. We have bigger battles ahead."

"Yes, indeed, Bella." Oliver had finally found his tongue.

Annabelle had tried like the dickens to keep her husband from adopting "Bella," but his loving persistence was determined to wear down her resistance. He hoped the name would grow on her like the effects of water droplets on cavern rock. *Beautiful.* It was hard for it to stick because she'd never considered herself that way.

She'd have to be seen to be called beautiful. And her family never saw her, not then and certainly not now. What her sisters knew about her present life could fit in a thimble—her marriage, her stepson, her career, which they considered a glorified hobby. They had no idea the hours she spent bent over trays of beads, gemstones, and wire, how her fingers ached from gripping flatnose pliers. Never mind all her years of training and her certification as a custom jewelry maker. All to create something . . . beautiful.

"She was wearing my earrings. There's that. I almost said something, but I didn't want to make a big deal out of it." Although it was a big deal to Annabelle. At his questioning look she explained, "Charlotte. The pair I made for her birthday. Remember?"

He nodded, though *no* was written all over his face.

"What about your mother? What were their thoughts about Mayhelen?"

"They feel it's a no-brainer, that we need to move forward and embrace this final request, which I think is wackier than those jokes. Here, let me take that." She slid the cucumber from under his chin, rinsed it off, and returned it to him. Then she set the tomato and the lettuce beside the knife.

"I'm tired of trying to put a positive spin on what we went through and shrugging off my childhood like it was only a thing you get over. Forgive and forget. Accept the past. Let God take care of it. How am I supposed to do any of that in the face of Mama's latest emotional onslaught—right when I was trying to get over her rejection? I've been telling myself, 'That part of my life has to be over. It's okay to move on. I *need* to move on.' Am I crazy, or wasn't that natural to assume?"

Oliver sliced the cucumber into thin slivers. His mouth formed an upside-down U as he mulled over her question. "Mmm, yeah, I can see why you'd think that, however . . . Miss Hattie has been seeing to your mother all this time, making sure money was going to the right places and checking in on her—"

"Doing what we should have, you're probably thinking." Annabelle squinted at her bare feet.

Oliver didn't speak until his wife met his eyes, but his soft voice blunted the edge of his pointed look. "You did know she'd have to retire one day."

"When we were comin' up, Miss Hattie always looked out for

us, even when we didn't want her to, when we didn't know she was. And yes, long after she should have." Annabelle shrugged, palms up. "I suppose it didn't occur to us that one day, she couldn't."

"Or wouldn't."

She sighed. "Or wouldn't."

"It could be she's still looking out for you by stepping aside. 'God sends people into our lives for a reason and for a season.' That's what my mother used to tell me." *Chop, chop, chop.*

Annabelle finished wiping the rest of the counters. The spot where the dishwasher used to be was a gaping hole, so she commenced to scrubbing the dirty utensils and plates.

Oliver braced his hands against the counter's edge and balanced his toe on the thigh-high metal sawhorse in the middle of the kitchen, used at the moment as a makeshift island. "No Miss Hattie. No Mayhelen. But you still have your sisters. Aren't y'all pretty much at peace in your relationship, especially now that you've moved back? You don't have to jockey for position, figuring out who's going to step into the parent role, or fight for your mother's attention. The battle is over."

Annabelle snorted. "Over? Who says it's over? Charlotte, Frankie, and I are more like gunslingers in the Old West, at a perpetual standoff. We kept our guns cocked, ready, and aimed for so long, just waiting for somebody to shoot . . . We're struggling to accept it's peacetime. Now, war? *That* we can understand. We can trust that."

"Maybe you'll unite while you decide what to do with your common enemy."

After she draped the wet towel over the faucet, she took the knife from him and edged him aside. The vegetables weren't going to cut themselves. "Mama is the reason why I stayed on the run, Oliver. Why I ran so far so fast and why I nearly didn't accept your proposal. Marrying you meant moving back, so I had to do some hard talking to convince myself those days are dead and gone, and so is my mama's hold on me. I'm tired of scooting over, Oliver. I put up with it and made accommodations for her during my most formative years, and it nearly crushed me—to say nothing of my relationship with my sisters. We're still trying to navigate who we are to each other—parent, sister, enemy, friend, a bad reminder. Even an emotional trigger . . ." Her hands stilled.

Oliver reached around her and gently laid the knife on the cutting board. He grasped her by both shoulders and faced her forward. "Take a breath, baby. Watch me." He inhaled and exhaled slowly. "Do that." He waited until she'd followed suit. "No need to get worked up. She's not here."

"I know, but that's the point, Oliver. She wasn't around then, either. In body, yes, but not in spirit. Not in the way it counts when you're a mother—not that I'm an expert."

"You most definitely *are* an expert. Believe me, I know the difference. Don't forget, Eleanor taught me how to recognize the characteristics of an absentee mother."

Annabelle knew it cost him to acknowledge his first marriage. He'd been abandoned just as she herself had been, but his divorce had imprinted a scarlet *D* on his chest in the eyes of many, including his former church community. At least her situation had garnered sympathy, not condemnation. "The funny thing is, the opposite is exactly what nearly ruined my life: Mama's presence, not her absence. How ironic that we're building this addition in time for you-know-what," she patted her stomach, "and I'm supposed to make room in my new life—and in my heart, according to Charlotte and Frankie—for you-know-who. Again. Still."

"Still . . . we are talking about your mother, Bella. She's not coming back to set up house in Jasper. You've only got to decide if you'll bring her home." He brushed the side of her face with the back of his knuckles.

Annabelle's jaw stiffened. "She doesn't deserve to come home, and my pain is alive and well, thank you very much."

"She gave you life."

"She gave birth to me, Oliver, which any wild animal can do: procreate, deliver. Give *life*. There's a heap of difference between what she gave my sisters and me and what she stole from us through her sorry, self-serving choices." Annabelle knew he wanted to comfort her, but she shouldered him aside, moving out of the circle his arms had created.

He stood straight and thrust his hands in the pockets of his carpenter pants. "Anna—"

"Seriously, Oliver!" She glanced behind her, to check for tiny listening ears or the approach of little feet. Detecting neither, Annabelle lowered her voice. "Pick one . . . let's say a cat, a wild one. Any cat can birth a litter. She's naturally equipped to feed her kittens and care for them until they mature and they can keep themselves alive. But let some . . . some outside aggression threaten her, or she's gone hungry for too long, and those same natural instincts will lead her to kill those kittens, to gobble them up to save herself."

This baby must think I'm drinking salt water! Poor thing. In need of a way to mask the bitter taste of her words, Annabelle retrieved the spoon, dipped it in the sauce, and touched it to the tip of her tongue. Trembling slightly, she replaced the lid on the slow cooker and turned on the faucet. She could feel Oliver's eyes on her, sense the deliberateness of his quiet that flooded the room like the effect of a heavy rain.

After watching her rinse the clean spoon for a minute or two, he reached around Annabelle and shut off the water; it was serving as much a purpose as her hurt and grief. When he finally spoke, his voice was soft. "That doesn't sound like a fact you picked up on one of those animal shows our boy Henry likes to watch. Are you really going to compare your mother to a lion or a tiger or some stray cat? That's quite a leap."

His words gently dabbed at her wounds, but they couldn't completely staunch the flow of blood pulsating in her ears. Annabelle's hands stilled their frantic scrubbing of the spotless spoon, but she continued to turn it over and over in her hand, as if searching for indelible stains. "I'll let you decide. But let me tell you one thing. If I could show you my heart, you'd see the bite marks."

Chapter Nine

"HEY THERE, LITTLE MAN," Frankie croaked, her whisper creaky from disuse, as she leaned on the rail of the Jenny Lind crib. The sun was still slumbering, though MJ was not. He gurgled and kicked a hello, his chubby legs enclosed in a lightweight pair of footed pajamas. His mother was too nervous about covering him with a blanket, so she always sent him to bed fully clothed and set the thermostat in the hallway outside his room at a moderate sixty-eight degrees.

"Now, what are you doin' up? Daddy's gonna have my head, comin' in here at this hour. He'll say you know better." She reached for him anyway and fit him into the crook of her neck, chuckling when his small round head bobbed back and forth like a baby bird's along her chin line. "Okay, okay, hubba bubba. I'm going to feed you," she murmured. She was sleepy as all get out, but she couldn't pass up a rare, delicious bite of alone time with MJ. It was too precious. "Don't worry, Mama is never too busy to spend time with her little man. You'll always be my best work."

She and Melvin had fashioned a nursery of sorts out of the oversize hall closet near their bedroom. There was just enough space for the crib and a small chair she'd outfitted with a cushiony cover that was soft enough to get comfortable in but not roomy enough to sleep in. As an experienced mama, she knew better. Yet, her prior experience didn't keep her from snuggling with her baby boy in the wee hours when other mothers might have let him cry it out. Frankie had had enough of crying it out when she was a child. No way would any baby of hers wonder where his help was coming from or if it ever would. She swiped a finger gently across the fine hairs on the side of MJ's face as he suckled and promised him quietly, "Yours is comin' from the Lord and your mama."

Ten minutes later, he was lying on his back, asleep in his bed, and she was staggering across the hall to hers. Light was oozing into the house through cracks in the blinds by the time she adjusted the baby monitor. Frankie slid between the covers, determined to catch another hour or so of sleep, but Melvin threw an arm around her and attempted to pull her to his side, obviously thinking otherwise.

"Uh-uh, nope." She put some space between herself and her husband and drew the blanket up over her shoulders. "I love you, but . . ." Frankie shook her head *no* against the pillow.

He got the vigorously delivered message, for he moved his hand. Still, he stayed close enough to kiss her behind her exposed ear. "Thanks for gettin' up with the baby."

"Of course. Now, back to sleep with you." Frankie closed her eyes, but after a few minutes of deep breathing, she knew the slowly awakening sun and early morning activity had peeled away the fingers of sleep that had held on to her as long as they could. She flopped onto her back and absentmindedly played with the hair on the back of his hand, replaying the meeting with Annabelle and Charlotte.

His fist closed around hers and he scooted close enough to rest his warm thigh against her cooler one. "I thought you were going back to sleep." His voice was raspy and hushed, as slow to wake as the children were on Sunday mornings.

Frankie sighed. "That was the plan."

"You'd better shush or you'll wake the rest of the house. Then you'll never get any rest." Melvin's chuckle, buried deep in his throat, softened the admonition. He knew she was sensitive about the volume of her voice.

She turned on her side and moved lower in the bed so the sheet partially covered her mouth. "My sisters drive me batty the way we talk to each other. What if our own kids treat each other like that when they grow up? I'll kill 'em." Frankie picked right up on all her ranting and raving she'd started the minute Charlotte and Annabelle had walked down the sidewalk to their cars. It was like the last several days hadn't happened.

Melvin pushed his arm under her and spooned her. "Woman, stop it. Paul, Leah, Nora, and even MJ know better than that."

Frankie rubbed her temple. "But Charlotte . . . she's the dedicated psychologist. You'd think she could communicate better than she does."

"Helping other people with their problems is much easier than seein' your way through your own. Dealin' with men takes a lot of heart work, not head work, and y'all's mama didn't even try to train y'all up the way you should go or how to love each other in spite of your differences. Back then, you were scrabblin' for your very life, like those carrots we had to cut back on my granddaddy's farm—"

"Melvin, what are you talkin' about?" Frankie fought the covers to face him, forgetting to lower her voice.

Melvin gently laid a finger across her open mouth. "No, baby. Hear me out. Remember when we took the kids to learn what hard work really looked like, and we visited my granddaddy and grandmama? Right after we left the barn, they took us out to the garden, and Grandmama was cuttin' back the seedlin's. Their roots were all tangled up, so they couldn't get enough nutrients. She showed the kids how to snip the stems."

Frankie relaxed a bit. She'd loved that day, and Melvin had actually spent some good quality time with her and the kids. "I suppose I get your meanin'. And I'm grateful you didn't compare us to those runts and the hog."

"You know what, Frankie? Sometimes . . ." His laugh was low in his throat. He gathered her close, creating a nest for her in his arms. "Y'all weren't ever gonna get the love you needed from your mom. She just wasn't capable. Tangled up roots, all y'all fighting for the food below and stretching for the sun above. That's how I picture you and Charlotte and Annabelle."

Snip the stems. Frankie restrained a shudder. Her mama made room all right.

"If it weren't for Miss Hattie . . ." His beard scratched her shoulder when he pressed his lips to her skin right below her satin headscarf, completing the sentence he'd left dangling.

Miss Hattie was as much a marriage counselor as she was a mother figure. Her wise teachings before and throughout their marriage had come to the rescue more than once in their seventeen years together. Melvin was well versed on all things Mayhelen; he'd heard time and again about Frankie's upside-down relationship with her mother and its resultant effect on her interactions with her sisters. But they'd both been unprepared to make room for Frankie's childhood. It had taken much prayer, Bible study, and wise counsel to get to the point where she could sift through her emotions and discard the unusable, bitter clumps that remained.

"She saved our lives." *The ones she could.* A tear squeaked out the corner of her eye onto the pillow.

"I know." Melvin edged closer.

"But she's asking too much, Melvin. I don't think I can do it. What good would it do? The ghost of Mama past is what chased Annabelle away in the first place. The Lord knows what the ghost of the present might do. Why would I want to bring Mama here to Jasper now that Annabelle is back? How would that help my relationship with my sister, if it looks like I'm once again putting that woman and her wants ahead of hers . . . ours? Mama did her best to get as far away from us as she could. I say, let her go. Let her stay gone. I don't need her now that she can't help us. And we've got everything we needed out of the store." Frankie didn't have to work to keep her voice low this time. The hurt was a thick wedge in the back of her throat, and she could barely speak past it.

"Well, the money didn't hurt." He murmured the words, but the truth came through loud and clear. "However, it's not your mama you need, baby girl. It's healing. None of y'all should give Mayhelen this power over you and your relationship with each other." Melvin kissed her again. "And by Mayhelen, I mean the enemy. Because we both know your mama can't do *nothing* to you, and Satan's authority is limited to what you allow."

Leave it to her husband to preach at this time of the morning. The Frankie part of Frankie wanted Melvin to agree with her. To tell her that there was no way in the world she should listen to Miss Hattie, as good as that woman had been to them her whole entire life—at least the part that counted. But the Jesus part of Frankie recognized the truth in what he said and silently thanked him for speaking it.

Though she still felt the onus of working through the matter with Charlotte and Annabelle, her family's warrior princesses, she felt more at peace having reached a decision, even if it was internal. Her eyelids grew heavier, and she wedged herself against his chest. She muttered, "Amen" right as Melvin's alarm sounded.

Frankie slathered peanut butter on a slice of bread, set it aside, and picked up another. "Leah, get out the grapes, and Paul, find the chips in the pantry." She spared a glance at the table, where Nora was coloring a page full of rabbits and other R-words, something Frankie had printed out earlier that day to ease her daughter's struggles with learning her alphabet. "Can you tell me what *R* says?"

Nora, the only southpaw in their family, was clutching her red crayon awkwardly in her left hand. She scrunched up her face and studied the ceiling. "Ssssss."

Frankie sighed. *This is going to take a minute.* She arranged the rows of prepared bread before reaching for the jar of homemade strawberry preserves sitting beside the Nutella. "Look at your crayon. What color are you usin'? Paul, grab a towel and mop up that water. Don't think I didn't see you spill it." Out of the corner of her eye she watched her son shuffle off to the laundry room but kept her attention on the other fires burning in her kitchen. "Leah, they're in the bottom drawer on the right, under the milk. Yep, test one and make sure they're still firm. Nobody wants to eat squishy grapes. Okay, Nora. You said *red*, yes! R-r-r-r-red. Just like the r-r-r-r-rabbit."

Tuesday was clomping along at its typical uneven pace. Leah and Paul had rinsed their cereal bowls and loaded them in the dishwasher and returned to their seats at the kitchen table by 9:00 a.m. MJ, her little vampire, slept more in the daytime than he did at night, and Frankie allowed Nora to sleep in bed as long as she wanted, freeing her to work uninterrupted with the twins. After breakfast, they'd started with Bible study and worked on their math, a four-letter word for Paul, who would bury his head in a Percy Jackson book all day if his mama was of a mind and in the mood to let him. That boy would rather read the nutrition labels on cans before learning his multiplication facts!

Frankie gathered her hair, twirled it, and secured a messy bun on the top of her head with the long bobby pins she kept on her shirt. Their full morning of lessons on fractions and diagramming and all the stops and starts involved in parenting-while-homeschooling had drained them all. Still, nothing would stop the train from moving toward their Tuesday afternoon at the library. Frankie knew she'd best gather herself during the hour or so of quiet time after lunch before they packed up all their overdue books and the baby and faced down that infernal self-checkout computer.

"Mommy? When will Daddy be home?" Nora's eyes never left her paper. The tip of her tongue poked out over her teeth as she concentrated on the squeak-squeak-squeak of her crayon. Any listener would've thought Frankie was standing in the next room rather than a few feet away in front of the kitchen sink.

"Mom-my?" the child singsonged again. "When?"

Before Frankie could hush her, the baby cried out from his crib down the hall. *Not soon enough.* Frankie closed her eyes and curled her hands around the curve of the countertop. *Not soon enough.* Feeling a small hand on her shoulder, she opened them to gaze into the light-brown eyes of her older son. Her exhalation was slow and tremulous as visions of her afternoon nap went up in smoke. "Yes, Paul? Did you get up that water like I told you to?"

"Yes, ma'am. I made you a snack too." He extended a small plate filled with tiny, evenly cut squares of white cheddar cheese and gluten-free almond crackers. "Leah is washing off some grapes for you. If you want some."

Trust Paul to act as caregiver, following in his mama's footsteps so closely, he often stepped on Frankie's heels. And here she was, fussing about some drops of water by the sink. He probably made

Leah rinse those grapes for her mama because that girl didn't have a thought in her head for nobody but herself. "Oh, thanks, baby. So thoughtful! Set it down right there, and as soon as I help y'all get squared away, I'll take my lunch out to the patio."

The baby squawked again, his voice growing more demanding.

"Do you want me to get MJ?" Paul blinked rapidly.

Frankie could tell he was getting more worked up than his little brother. He was such a sensitive child, that Paul. It amazed her—and slightly concerned her, she had to admit—how he picked up on her moods; he must have felt her tension and exhaustion after her broken night's rest. And she hadn't bothered to hide her frustration over the baby's interrupted nap—something she'd been working on, letting the children see her get riled up.

Though she was a seasoned mama, the early months after delivering a baby taxed her. Frankie did her best to get up with MJ during the night so Melvin wouldn't have to; his work as a TV cameraman got him out early most mornings. Frankie managed the household duties she categorized as "stay-at-home mom," developing her own hunter-gatherer, traditional system for her family. And she determined to do it with joy and pluck, the way Samantha Stephens carried on in those *Bewitched* reruns she'd watched as a child. Those blond children didn't ride their mother's emotional upheaval like some wild rollercoaster. Upside down one moment, plunging two stories the next. They didn't carry Samantha's problems and responsibilities, leaving them without a hand free to take care of their own.

But Frankie couldn't twitch her nose, utter a spell, put everybody's life in order, and make Nora magically learn to read at the same time. Not today, as tired as she was from taking care of her own family and wanting to fix everybody else. She needed help, but she couldn't see her way to leaning on her kids beyond delegating a few age-related chores to teach them responsibility. Frankie squeezed her nine-year-old's shoulder, which felt it might break, not bend, under his mama's weight. *But I won't break,* she resolved as she ruffled his hair. *And I won't break this child here.* Her eyes tearing, she turned her back to the children and wiped her sticky fingers on the damp dish towel. *Those cheese and crackers will have to do.*

Behind her, she listened to the children wrangle over whose turn it was to set the table, but she ignored them this time. MJ's cries had become coughs, dispelling Frankie's hopes that he would settle down. Hurriedly, she swiped under her eyes and moved to slather preserves on two slices of bread and some hazelnut spread on another. Then she smushed together opposite pieces and slapped the sandwiches on plates. She licked a schmear of peanut butter off her thumb and glanced wistfully at her own saucer before stepping around the bar. "Y'all, quit all that fussin' and have a seat. And hey, put some grapes on Nora's plate and take your baby sister her food. I mean it now; settle down."

Paul, always the first to snap to, retrieved his plate and mat. "What about your lunch, Mama?"

"I'll sit down in a minute. Don't worry, son. But I've gotta get the—"

The back door squeaked open, and Melvin stepped in from the carport. He beamed at them. "Hey, family! Surprise!"

The warmth of relief suffused Frankie from head to toe and stopped her in her tracks, just as she was rounding the corner into the den. Nora hopped up from the table. "Me first! Me first!" she cried as she squeezed through the barrier Paul and Leah created in front of their dad and jumped into his arms."Hey, hey, hey. There's enough love for everybody. Especially your mama." Melvin settled Nora on his right hip and held an arm wide for his wife. "Why are you standin' there with your mouth open? Come get some of this."

Frankie looked back over her shoulder as MJ screamed—*Didn't*

Melvin hear that?—and dashed over to her husband. Heaven forbid he felt like he played second fiddle to the kids. She kissed his cheek. "What are you doin' home at this time of day? It's nowhere near three o'clock."

Melvin shrugged. "We wrapped up our shoot early, and I was in the area, so I figured I'd do some work from home for a change." He cocked his head toward his large black knapsack he'd dropped by the back door. "Y'all can always use another pair of hands, right?" He bounced Nora, who leaned back nearly perpendicular to the kitchen floor and laughed.

Thank the Lord, Frankie wanted to exclaim, for this was surely God's doing. As fine a man as he was, it wasn't Melvin's way to help out with "her work," as he deemed it. They played their roles to a tee, doing jobs she herself had distributed, in a one-for-you, one-for-me fashion the minute they'd said, "I do." The father in him could play with and discipline the kids all day, and the husband in him worked faithfully, deposited his paycheck, and curled up next to her all night. But he rarely offered to cross the line delineating their husband-wife sides of the household unless she asked him.

And she rarely, if ever, asked.

"Yay!" Leah did a jig and pulled her father to the table.

"Daddy's home . . . Daddy's home . . . Daddy's home." Nora had transformed the words into a song in her high-pitched voice.

MJ's screech became a hoarse croak.

Paul smiled at his mama, who'd been left behind. "Dad can take us to the library and you can have your lunch!"

Laughing, puffed up like a hometown hero, Melvin set Nora down in front of her coloring pages and red crayon and perched in front of an empty placemat beside her. "Is that peanut butter and jelly? Hmm. Baby, we got any lunch meat? I'm hungry!"

With one ear pressed to her cell phone, Frankie eased her minivan into its spot beside Melvin's Camry. She hoped her tone didn't convey that she was half listening to Charlotte. "Mmm-hmm . . . Yeah, girl . . . I'm not sure what—" She angled the rearview mirror so she could peer with narrowed eyes at the twins, tussling over a pack of stickers the librarian had given them for their so-called good behavior. If anything, her children knew how to behave in public. But if that woman could see how they carried on within the privacy of their minivan? *Shameful.*

She snapped her fingers three times, quietly enough not to disturb MJ, who was snoozing in his car seat at this awful hour of the evening, but loudly enough to catch the attention of Paul and Leah. They dropped the plastic sheath in the empty middle seat between them. Nora must have had sense enough to know the finger-popping wasn't intended for her because she never bothered to look up from her picture book; the green snake on the cover of *Verdi* held her undivided attention.

"Go in the house," Frankie mouthed, jabbing a finger in the direction of the back door. "Take your sister with you. Read quietly until I get inside."

She pressed the button to open the back passenger door and watched them unsnap their seatbelts and lug the overloaded canvas bag of books from the back. Paul helped Nora out of her seat and they trooped up the steps. A quick peek into the car seat reassured her MJ dozed undisturbed. "So, have you spoken to Anna?"

"Huh! Now, when have you known us to talk on the phone?" Charlotte's voice sounded distant on the other line, nearly drowned out by rumbling and scraping.

Frankie pressed her ear to her device while simultaneously

trying to lower the volume of her own voice. "Well . . . I was hopin' y'all were talkin' more. We were all pretty close at one time."

"Sardines can say the same thing, but they don't talk to each other either." More thumps.

Frankie shook her head. "What *are* you doing? I can barely hear you over all that commotion." She listened to what sounded like the clip-clop of footsteps and shuffling.

Charlotte grunted. "Sorry, I was shifting the furniture around. Arranging some space between the seating, making us all feel more comfortable." Under her breath she murmured, "Making *me* feel more comfortable."

"More comfortable? I've seen your office. It's nice. I'd even call it cozy." Frankie twisted around in her seat to take a quick look at MJ. *Still sleeping. Thank you, Lord.*

"Exactly. That's the problem. Anyway, I didn't call you to talk about my redecorating efforts. Have you heard from Miss Hattie? When is she comin' here?"

By the familiar squeaking, Frankie could tell her sister was sitting in her chair behind her desk. Charlotte's favorite place. "What? Are you scared she's just goin' to show up with Mama and a tax bill from the sale of the store?"

Charlotte snorted. "If Miss Hattie knows what's good for her, she won't. According to the bank, I've got twenty-seven more years to pay these taxes on my new town house, thank you very much. That's the only bill I'm concerned about. Besides, we haven't decided what we're goin' to do with her. I wanna do right by Mama, and believe me, I've seen what happens when people don't take care of their business and have some closure. But—"

Frankie leaned her head back against the cloth seat and closed her eyes. She rubbed the bridge of her nose. "That's some of that psychological mumbo jumbo . . . *closure.* I'm talkin' about obeyin' the commandment that reads 'Honor thy mother and father, that thy days—'"

"Ooh, not the King James Version, with all those thees, thous, and thys! Go 'head, chile!" Charlotte's chair squeaked overtime as she clapped.

Frankie had to cover her amused snort with her hand, and she shook her head at her sister's irreverence. "Shhh! If you wake MJ, I'll give *you* some closure." *Why do I bother?* But then a voice answered. *Because you love her, even more than I love you.*

"Where are you anyway? It's awfully quiet where you are. I'm used to hearing kids breaking stuff and crying and Melvin yelling for you every two seconds. It's not like you to be able to talk this long without interruption."

Forgetting herself, Frankie let a laugh escape through her fingers and filled the confines of her Odyssey. Stirring in the middle row reminded Frankie that she needed to do a better job at keeping a lid on her voice. "You laid some truth on me right there, and I ain't mad at you. The kids and I are just gettin' home from the library, and I sent them inside while the baby and I rested in the car. We left Melvin in his studio, and he's probably still in there, tinkerin' with the film from his shoot." Her husband dreamed of being his own boss one day, so he had converted an unattached shed into a type of sound booth. Occasionally he worked from home—and he'd done exactly that after lunch, having concluded that Frankie didn't need another pair of hands after all.

"Oh, that's right, it is the second Tuesday of the month, isn't it?"

"Yes, it's Tuesday. The day I pay my mortgage at the library. It kills me to spend so much in fines when we could buy books for less at the thrift store."

Charlotte coughed as she shuffled papers on her end. "Well, here's a thought: turn your books in on time, and stop losing 'em."

Frankie propped her forehead against the heel of her hand and grumbled, "Ha-ha, very funny. We talk too much. I forget how well you know my schedule."

"Know it? I helped you create it! If it wasn't for me, you'd never have gotten organized after you had the twins and set out to fulfill your audacious dreams to homeschool." Sometimes, Charlotte met them on their field trips, errands, and jaunts about town. She even traveled with them each summer to the family's time-share in Myrtle Beach. The only place Charlotte wouldn't accompany them was to their church pew.

"I think you give yourself too much credit," Frankie joked, knowing full well Charlotte spoke the truth. "Maybe you'll also be able to help Anna when she has the baby. She'll have her hands full with her jewelry makin', the renovation, plus the children."

"Always managing folks and planning family reunions, aren't you? Didn't we talk about this the other day? I know Anna's back in the area now, but that doesn't mean we'll all be happy-happy, joy-joy."

Just the other day, Melvin had commented along the same lines. "I tell you, constantly playin' referee. Babe, what are you *doin*? Those women are grown. They don't need you sendin' them to time-out because they can't play nice. And don't let me get started on your mama."

With his words ringing in her ear, she asked Charlotte, "When have I not taken care of people? First Mayhelen, then Annabelle and you. Now my husband and our house full of children—even if he doesn't count himself as one of my responsibilities."

The problem was, nobody seemed to drop off the list. Frankie wouldn't dare abdicate the role she played in her own household, but her sisters? They were another story. She was quite weary of serving as the point of intersection for their two lines; Charlotte and Annabelle always seemed to be headed in opposite, equally dysfunctional, directions.

"But maybe it's time you stop, Frankie. Do it for your sake."

"That's why we're talkin' 'bout bringin' Mama home, Charlie—for our sake, not hers."

"So you can cart her to the library? I can just picture story time." Derision dripped from her every word. "According to y'all, living in close proximity to Mama never did a one of us any good. Not that y'all gave me a say-so to form my own memories. Whatever the case, it's too late, Frances Mae. Let the nursing home or the state of—" Charlotte broke off and seemed to be clearing her throat—"of wherever she was living take care of her. As much as it pains me to join sides with Annabelle, I can't see my way around it. Even with all my training in psychological mumbo jumbo." *Tap . . . tap . . . tap.* "That's obviously what she wanted."

"How would you know?" Frankie pictured Charlotte's long fingernails painted the color of hellfire clicking against the leather-topped desk in her office. It didn't take an advanced degree to know it was Charlotte's own need that had driven her interest in her field of work, and she put her all into helping her clients—more than likely, families like theirs. Her sister was good enough at her job that Frankie had toyed with the thought of asking Charlotte for her professional—and, she hoped, free—advice about Paul's nail-biting and eye tics.

I suppose there's no time like the present. Frankie opened her mouth.

"Hey, Frankie! Baby, whatchyou still doin' in the car?"

"Wahhh!" a startled MJ cried out.

"And on that note . . . Love you, girl. Bye!" Charlotte clicked off.

Frankie's chest rose and fell, and she stared at her husband, standing on the opposite side of the car. He was peering through the passenger window with his hand over his eyes, like he was staring into the sun, but he had to be able to see clearly that she and the baby were okay, if not happy.

Melvin moved his fist in a circular motion and with the other hand, pointed down.

Obstinately, Frankie deliberately ignored his request to let down the window. Instead, she dropped the keys into the diaper bag and grabbed her water cup by its handle, resisting the urge to hurry as the baby's cries intensified.

Footsteps rounded the car and a second later, Melvin's ten fingers gripped the top of the metal framing her window as she stepped out. "The kids came out to the studio to tell me they were hungry."

Frankie pulled the handle to slide open the back door. Without a word, she slung her heavy bag around her door in her husband's direction.

"Oof." Obviously taken unawares, he brought his arm down to clutch it to his side. Diapers tumbled from the unzipped bag onto the concrete.

Frankie climbed into the second row and sat in the empty seat. She unbuckled MJ, picked him up, and rubbed his moist back. Instantly, the baby started nuzzling her neck.

The Odyssey's front door slammed and Melvin stepped into the gap her open door had created. "You all right? I said the kids—"

"I heard you." She wasn't angry, only resolved to start putting out one fire at a time and to stop running if there was only smoke. Calmly, Frankie unbuttoned the bottom of her shirt and adjusted herself so she could nurse her husband's namesake. "It seems *all* the kids are hungry, so I'm startin' with the youngest. Y'all won't starve to death in the next fifteen minutes, but if folks start fallin' out, there are some leftover peanut butter and jelly sandwiches from lunch."

After a few seconds of silence, Melvin shuffled into the house, his words a low, indiscernible rumble.

Chapter Ten

Then

FRANKIE OPENED ONE EMPTY cabinet door after another. She could feel her sister watching from her vantage point at the kitchen table.

"My big gut's eatin' my little gut. What're we gonna have for dinner?" The heel of Annabelle's hand pushed up the side of her cheek, nearly closing her left eye. The fingers on her right hand picked at the thick lacquer on one of the table legs. Mama had popped Annabelle's backside the first time she'd caught her daughter doing it, calling the table an antique "worth more than all y'all put together."

"Your guess is as good as mine. Mama went shoppin' to get some new clothes 'cause hers weren't fittin' right." Frankie squatted and checked the pantry drawer under the sink. The pipe had sprung a leak under there, but their mama always seemed to have better things to do than to address problems she considered beneath her. The opened door only revealed the brown stain on the bottom of the cabinet, along with a line of tiny black pellets along the back wall, a can of Comet with a torn label, and a half-empty bottle of Dawn dish detergent.

"She thinks new clothes are gonna fix all our problems? We can't eat a dress."

Frankie had to shove the door to, since it tended to stick, and then opened another. "You know Mayhelen. She's your mama too. Lookin' like money is next best to havin' money, accordin' to her."

"What's next best to havin' food for dinner?" Annabelle peeled another strip, much longer than the last piece.

Mama is going to tear her up when she sees what she's done. "Why don't we go over to the old lady's house behind us? It's not dark yet. And we can go and come back before Daddy wakes up."

"*Your* daddy, not mine."

Frankie skipped over her sister's words. This wasn't the time to worry over *yours* or *mine*; their troubles belonged to both of them. "When we borrowed sugar that time, Miss Hattie said she loves to cook and that she always makes more'n she can eat by herself. She might even have biscuits—you know how you love those—and you can eat as many as you want. Remember those chicken wings?"

But she could tell from Annabelle's face that she wanted to eat in her own house with all of them sitting around their own kitchen table like the Huxtable family did on television. Her sister hated to mooch off other people, lapping up the milk of their kindness, when they had a mama of their own. Frankie looked at the refrigerator and back to Annabelle, staring at her from across the room.

They both knew there was no reason to open its door because it was empty; she'd just be letting the cold out.

Shoulders slumped, Frankie clomped over to her younger sister and pulled out the second of four chairs; its heavy feet scraped the large squares of terra-cotta-colored tile under the legs. She plopped into her seat and braced herself on her left arm as she leaned on the table. Like Annabelle, she trained her eyes on the clock connected to the oven as it ticked away the time.

Three minutes passed, and Annabelle's stomach complained loudly, as if it wanted to make sure Frankie knew how it felt about the situation.

"Annabanana, when Miss Hattie had your mama over for dinner, she was so lazy . . ."

Annabelle sat up, her eyes full of question marks, obviously not sure where that particular path was leading.

Frankie poked out her lips and bumped the younger girl with her shoulder. ". . . Um, she was so lazy that when Miss Hattie said, 'Help yourself,' she couldn't."

She cocked an eye at Frankie. "What are you goin' on about?" her eyebrows seemed to ask.

Frankie grinned. "Somebody told me your mama was so stubborn the mule came by to ask her for advice."

Snickering, Annabelle covered her mouth and shot a look over her shoulder.

"Come on, why don't you think of something?" Frankie tickled Annabelle under her chin. They weren't actually lying on Mama or even making jokes at her expense. Her words had a thick vein of truth running through the middle of them. And she knew that was what made Annabelle want to laugh. Which was better than crying and counting the seconds between the rumblings of her tummy.

Annabelle shook her head slowly from one side to the other.

Frankie shrugged and thought hard. She'd rather think of Mayhelen as somebody else's mother, not her own. To make a game of their hand-to-mouth life. But try as she might, she couldn't come up with anything at the moment; she was too hungry herself. "It's okay. I'll think of some while we're walkin' over to the neighbor's. Here . . ." She scooted back and jogged over to the drawer by the stove. Smiling, she reached in, then turned and waved a red packet in the air. "Look! I'll make some Kool-Aid. You love the way I make it. Miss Hattie's sure to have some sugar and we can add extra."

Annabelle nodded and hopped up from the table so abruptly, she knocked over her chair. It clattered to the floor.

Gasping, both girls' heads whirled toward the darkness beyond the kitchen, threatening to gobble up the light. A few desperate, yet quiet, seconds ticked off the clock. Then they dashed out the back door, the packet of powdered drink mix forgotten on the kitchen floor.

Chapter Eleven

Now

ANNABELLE WAS SURPRISED she still had teeth to brush. A chronic grinder since she was a child, she expected to find nothing but a mouth full of powdery enamel every morning when she woke. She replaced the cap on the Colgate tube and dropped it in the top drawer of the bathroom cabinet. Ugh, how she missed the taste of Crest, the paste she'd used until a month ago. These days, it tasted like poop. "Why am I using that as my basis for comparison?" she murmured around a mouth full of froth.

"Sounds like you've started talking to yourself." Steam poured into the bathroom from the opened shower door, and Oliver stepped over the tile threshold. Water droplets glistened in his curly 'fro.

She swished cold water, spit, then wiped her lips. "Talkin' to myself is nothin' new. Talkin' to somebody else on the daily is what I've had to get used to."

However amused he was, Oliver's expression seemed to concede the point, something they both knew to be true.

"I'm never getting married," Annabelle had warned Oliver two years ago, as the three of them shared grilled pizza at a restaurant in Providence. "And I certainly don't want any children. It usually doesn't last, as you know yourself, and children shouldn't suffer."

"You're doing everything you can to stick a sharp pin in my bubble, aren't you?" He'd grinned at her, his attraction obviously not deflated one bit.

Sure, the man was mighty fine, with his caramel-colored skin; sparkly, warm smile; and a crescent moon–shaped impression at the corner of his left nostril, a memory of childhood chicken pox. His baby boy, alternately crumbling his animal crackers and pulling strands of mozzarella cheese, was even more precious. "I'm sorry, but I've witnessed too many husbands and not enough daddies floating in and out of my life to willingly entangle myself with another one."

Yet, here she was, despite her protestations, married and a mother of two.

Okay, one and a half. She studied her head-to-toe profile in the full mirror mounted on the bathroom door. Her stomach was just starting to pooch. "Or is that the evidence of a lifetime without sit-ups? Or maybe the pecan turtle cheesecake we had last night?"

Oliver peeked out of the walk-in closet, his head poking through the neck hole of his T-shirt. "Are you *still* talking to yourself? I know you used to be your best listener, but my ears are more than willing to work overtime." He wiggled them and added his pectoral muscles to the dance for effect. "You have me and Henry to talk to now, and he's almost as much fun to talk to as I am."

Annabelle smiled at his reflection. "And for both of you, I'm grateful. I suppose my old habits die hard."

"Well, you need to put them out of their misery for good." He reentered the closet. "What else are you doing today besides engaging in such serious self-talk?"

She riffled through the earrings in her jewelry box with her fingertip. She plucked a pair she'd recently made, delicate birds crafted from thin gold wire that was wrapped around an emerald-colored stone called aventurine in each wing. The way they seemed to flutter around her earlobes would catch the attention of potential customers and give her some free advertising, the best kind. When she slid the curved post through the hole in her ear, however, she noted that the clasp needed some tightening.

"Bella?"

"Oh, sorry. I got distracted." Frowning, she removed the earring and laid the pair on top of her jewelry box and selected another style she liked, only not as much. "Looks like I'm going to spend most of the day in my studio. First, I'll fix these earrings, and then I'm planning to work on a sterling silver piece that's been kicking my—"

Oliver's head popped out from the other side of the closet door, and like a mole it disappeared just as quickly. "What were you about to say?"

Laughing, Annabelle froze before she could put in the first loop. "Bottom . . . kicking my bottom. You interrupted me before I could finish my sentence. What'd you think I was going to say?"

"I know exactly what you were going to say." His chuckle was muffled but hearty. "If I'd waited another two seconds, I could have earned another dollar."

"You wish. I refuse to buy you another large plate of Calabash shrimp."

"I don't know. It's been about two weeks since I had some seafood, and I'm starting to miss it. Hey, have you seen my blue sneakers?"

"Yes, in the box where they're supposed to be. Look on the right side of the last shelf. I got tired of tripping over your shoes, so I put them where they belong. A novel idea, I know. And the same goes for those socks you left in the den—which are now in the hamper, so you'll need to get a new pair if you're looking for them. Isn't messiness a sin too?"

"John Wesley thought so. But I'm starting to think organization is too." Hangers rattled and something heavy thumped to the floor.

She glanced toward the partially closed door and raised her voice to ensure Oliver could hear her over the commotion he was making in the closet. "Maybe I should get my own giant pickle jar and make you pay as much for leaving your stuff around the house as I pay for saying a bad word."

Oliver entered the bathroom, holding aloft his Nikes. "I'd say these are worth at least one dollar."

Annabelle closed the second earring and admired each lobe. "When did saying *stupid* get outlawed?" Mayhelen had left behind more than socks and shoes for Annabelle, Frankie, and Charlotte to pick up, and they'd carried those habits and hurtful words into their adult life, something she'd confessed to Oliver before the two had promised "I do."

"Doesn't Jesus keep you from saying bad words?" their son had asked one morning over his bowl of Cheerios, a little more than a year after the wedding. Annabelle had stubbed her toe and colored the air blue around her with an expletive.

She'd pressed her lips together as she bounced on one foot. "I'm probably keeping Him extremely busy with everything else

I've got going on, Henry. Maybe I'm gonna need you and Daddy to help me."

And so her son had enlisted his dad to do just that: help Annabelle. Oliver had converted an extra-large Mt. Olive pickle jar into a bank. Every time she resorted to words like "shut up" instead of "be quiet," she dropped a quarter into the container; four-letter words cost her four times as much. Oliver spent the money on the family's food and fun. One evening, after yet another coin had plinked through the slot he'd cut in the lid, he'd tapped the side of the glass and reassured, "This way you'll learn how to use your powers for good."

Oliver stepped from the closet dressed in slim-fitting black denims and a deep amethyst-colored golf shirt with "Good Bones" and a house stitched across his heart. He kissed her on the cheek. "Maybe I should make a reservation at Captain Larry's for the three of us, just in case."

"Only if *you're* paying because I'm not planning to give you another thin dime . . . or quarter." Annabelle gave up on trying to zip her green capris. Instead, she threaded a rubber band through the hole, looped it across the button to keep them closed, and draped her striped shirt to conceal her thickening—and exposed—waistline. She trailed her husband from their master bath into their bedroom.

Oliver opened the wood shutters, freeing the sunlight window by window as he moved about the room. "You look mighty fine to be spending the day hunched over your trays of beads and thread."

Annabelle retrieved her pillow from the floor and tossed it onto the unmade bed. "I use wire, not thread, and don't you worry, I'll change clothes as soon I get back from my doctor's appointment. When you get home from the construction site, you'll find me in my comfy paja . . . What? What's wrong?" Annabelle hugged a second pillow to her middle and frowned at her husband.

Oliver had been straightening sheets but was now standing stock-still on his side of the bed, silhouetted against the light from the window behind him.

Isn't he scrumptious? Thank you, Lord. Annabelle counted her blessings every day. She still couldn't reason through the list of whys Oliver had chosen her, some strange woman he'd met while he was vacationing with his son. Annabelle hadn't needed his mama to point out that he was the most eligible bachelor in all of eastern North Carolina, but the woman had gone and said it anyway. "And God-fearin'," the elder Mrs. McMillan had reminded her more than once, audible enough for a whole room to hear.

"You said you have a doctor's appointment. I'm assuming this is a baby-related visit." Frown lines formed parentheses around Oliver's full lips, a fearsome expression that had nothing to do with the Lord.

As far as she was concerned, Annabelle could've been standing in the principal's office, where she'd spent too much of her time as a high schooler. She swallowed all the emotions from that uncomfortable memory and reared back her shoulders. *I'm grown,* she reminded herself. *No one is ever going to reduce me to dust and make me feel like that again. Who does he think he is? He's not that cute.*

Oliver rubbed his forehead. "Wait a minute." He whipped out the miniature calendar the bank gave him every year that he kept in his back pocket, which he preferred over using the app on his phone. "You saw your sisters last Thursday. Today's Wednesday. I thought we were seeing Dr. Nagele next week, on Tuesday. How did I mix up that date?"

A frisson of fear snaked through her. Marriage and parenthood seemed fraught with unavoidable missteps and misgivings. It was hard enough to lock her knees and bear up under the weight of her own thoughts and feelings without carrying Oliver's on her shoulders too. And what about Henry and their new baby? She couldn't possibly explain she would've missed the rescheduled appointment altogether if she hadn't checked her planner, which she opened before reading the daily devotional Oliver had subscribed her to. Then he'd think her irresponsible, not caring enough for their family. Either way, she was in the wrong—she was a bad mother or a bad wife, and a bad Christian to boot.

The defiance she'd gulped down a moment before made her empty stomach roil, and the heaping serving of self-recrimination didn't help to sweeten it. Annabelle took a deep breath and dropped the pillow she'd been squeezing onto the pale gray comforter. "I'm sorry, Oliver. You didn't mix up the date. I didn't think to tell you I asked the office to move my appointment last week. I'm still getting—"

"Used to including someone else in your life, I know. You've told me a few times and then some over the past two years. I'm starting to get that it's not only about talking to yourself." He reached for the down-filled rectangle, fluffed it absently, and arranged it alongside the others. Without meeting her eyes, he ran a hand over the already-smoothed bed, then gripped the headboard. Oliver stared out the window, squinting in the morning light that was seemingly unaware of the clouds hovering between the couple.

Annabelle hesitated a moment before slowly walking around the bed to his side of the room. She considered reaching for the fingers that were picking at a loose thread, but her hands seemed to have their own mind. They found themselves clasped together behind her neck instead. She threw her head back and studied the popcorn ceiling that was crying out for attention. *Yet another project.* "No, Ollie. I'm the one who's starting to get it. You're so patient with me, and I love you for it."

Even to her ears her profession sounded half-hearted, more weary than fervent. It must not have sounded sincere enough to garner his attention, let alone reciprocation, for he kept his face averted. He was probably as tired of hearing her apologies as she was of offering them. Annabelle reached down deep inside herself, past the bubbles of resentment that resisted humbling and dependence, to the little girl who desperately needed someone more than that someone needed her. She whispered, "Really, I am sorry. I know you've heard it before, but this . . . this is still new to me."

"'This' meaning, thinking of someone besides yourself?" The muscles in Oliver's jaw flexed.

"Well, that hurt." The way his eyes were fixed on something on the other side of the windowpane, she considered the possibility that he was imagining what his life would look like without her. So many men had followed through on such "wondering" when she was a child, she figured it was a matter of time. *Not you, too, Oliver.*

"It pains me, too, Annabelle, hearing you use words like 'regret,' like you did the other day. We're making a family together—you, me, Henry. Do I need to tape memos on the bathroom mirror, or will you ever start naturally including 'us'—" he made one-handed air quotes around that troublesome two-letter word—"in your thinking and planning? It's not like this is still a long-distance love affair; we're up close and personal. Henry and I aren't going anywhere. And why'd you reschedule your appointment? Is there really something more important, more exciting than this happening?" Oliver waved a hand back and forth between them.

Henry had been a chubby-cheeked toddler when they started dating officially. Because Oliver wanted to shield his son, he'd kept him from seeing much of Annabelle for the first six months, until she was willing to admit she was in the relationship for the long haul, that it was time for their hands to do more than graze each other on the armrest between them. They itched to hold on to each other tightly. Permanently and intimately.

During one of her visits to North Carolina, they'd taken Henry to the zoo in Asheboro. There, Oliver had popped the question, and she'd tearfully accepted a proposal that was a tender commemoration of their first outing two years earlier. Less than a month after he slid the custom-designed engagement ring on her finger, they married at Oliver's church.

Now, firmly ensconced in their home, Annabelle saw she needed to put to death her residual fears of abandonment and the need for self-protection, what she constantly battled within herself. She slowly relaxed her arms and reached for his stiff, unyielding fingers and squeezed them. "You don't have to remind me there's an 'us,' Oliver. It's just that I've been going solo most of my life, even when I was living with Mama. I'm not used to somebody loving me the way you love me. Meeting somebody else's expectations."

Oliver's bushy eyebrows nearly met his hairline and his head reeled back as if he'd taken a punch. "Somebody else's—"

Wham! went their bedroom door against the wall, and Annabelle turned at the size-four feet pummeling the hardwood floor toward them. Oliver's fingers slid from hers though she scrambled to hold on, to him and the conversation.

"G'morning!" Henry hurled himself at his dad, one arm still looped around a stuffed grayish bunny that had been white once upon a time. Its remaining ear was crying out for a needle and thread. Something Annabelle never seemed to have handy.

"Oopf," Oliver grunted, catching him. If ever a child was his father's son, that was Henry. Like Oliver, when he opened his eyes, he was ready for the day. He didn't slowly greet the world each morning; he propelled himself into it with both feet.

Unlike his mother. Typically, Annabelle took twenty minutes to decide she was getting out of bed and another twenty to actually follow through with it—even longer since she started battling morning sickness. While Annabelle's heart had laid firm claim to Henry, it was obvious from his demeanor that not an ounce of her blood flowed through his veins. She pressed her lips together and swallowed a sigh. As her husband hugged their pint-size interruption dressed in T-rex-speckled pajamas with fangs that glowed in the dark, she mumbled to herself, "Why don't you look as irritated as I feel? Relieved, probably."

"Good morning, buddy. Have you brushed your teeth yet? Something tells me you haven't." Oliver waved his hand in front of his nose.

Henry covered his mouth and giggling, shook his head. He dug in the corner of his eye with the tip of an index finger.

Annabelle reached over and wrapped her hand around his. "A warm washcloth will take care of that, you know."

Henry's lips poked out. "I washed my face last night."

"But you can't go with me to the yard today to look at granite with those crusty eyes. How can you see which slab you like? I guess you'll stay home, and I'll go by myself." Oliver shrugged and set the boy on his feet.

"No, Daddy, I'll go wash my face right now!" The five-year-old sprinted toward the door.

"I'd better make sure he's picking out something that matches. That boy will come out with those red rainboots he can't get enough of and orange plaid shorts."

Annabelle caught Oliver's fingers as he took a step from the bed. "I thought we were all going to pick out our granite together."

He shrugged. "I could say the same for *our* prenatal appointments."

She could feel him pull away, but she held on more tightly. "Give me a second, Oliver." She plopped down on the bed, knowing his mother was somewhere rolling her eyes toward heaven, sensing her son was about to sit on his bed in his day clothes. *You'll have to thank that woman God gave him, Mother Mac.*

"What's so funny?"

"My sisters were asking me the same question the last time we were together." She shook her head and patted the mattress beside her. "You know who's funny? Your wife. And weird and strange and struggling. Feel free to pick an adjective from the list or add your own. Or better yet, feel free to stop me."

He eased down beside her; their thighs pressed against each other, and he smiled a little. "How about pregnant? And mine?"

"Okay, pregnant, thanks to you, and all yours." She leaned toward him, and his mouth met hers halfway. Their lips lingered for a moment, and she felt the tension ease from him. "I think about you and Henry and now this baby so much, I can barely get a lick of work done around here, Oliver. Which is part of the reason why I rescheduled the appointment, so I could meet with a client next week and invest in the me I'm losing touch with. Is that so bad?"

"No, it's not bad." Oliver inhaled deeply. "Now I feel selfish."

"Don't. I *want* to meet your expectations because I know you only expect the best from me and for me. I'm going to keep trying, but I'm also going to keep failing—"

"Baby, you're not failing. And I don't want you to feel like you have to work to please me. Just be my wife. Be a mother to our children. Love us. You'd have me think you lived like a feral cat, wandering the streets, living hand-to-mouth, but I know that's not quite the whole truth."

"Are you callin' me a liar?" She tried to infuse humorous, Southern grit into her tone, but she couldn't help but wince at those words ricocheting around her brain. Growing up, Annabelle had heard that phrase more times than she could count. She was always one to question her mother about one thing or the other; she never could simply accept at face value what the woman said. Mama didn't like back talk, especially not from her thin-as-a-stalk-of-wheat middle child who didn't have the sense not to stare down the person gripping the purse strings.

"Only when you talk to yourself, baby. When you talk to yourself. Remember that handsome dude who goes with you to your sister's? That's me. I've heard y'all talking about old times. Your mama might not have always done right by you, but y'all took care of each other. Sure as my name is Oliver McMillan." He scooted closer to her on the bed. "Now, what time is this doctor's appointment?"

Chapter Twelve

TRYING NOT TO FEEL SELF-CONSCIOUS in front of the posters of body parts and mammograms, Annabelle—*What am I, twelve?*—tried to study anything and everything but, and her eyes landed on the manila folder on the doctor's desk. "What's with this AMA?" Annabelle pointed to the white label affixed to her file. "What does that mean? Why did you put an American Medical Association label on my record?"

"Maybe it's 'against medical advice'?" Oliver shrugged.

Ignoring the only man in the room, Dr. Nagele followed the direction of Annabelle's finger. "Oh, no, sweetheart," she laughed lightly, "that AMA stands for advanced maternal age. You'll be over forty years old soon. Now, let's talk about these—"

"But I won't be over forty. I'm still thirty-nine. My fortieth birthday isn't for another few weeks. And even then, I won't be *over* forty."

Oliver was sitting to the right of Annabelle in a matching black leatherette-covered chair in front of the obstetrician's large desk. Photographs of expectant mothers and families holding their brand-spanking-new infants adorned walls painted the color of champagne, along with the doctor's framed diplomas from University of North Carolina at Chapel Hill and Duke University medical school. Artificial plants decorated the corners and popped up on shelves in between seashells and figurines and pottery. Oliver stretched out an arm, spanning the distance between them, and covered Annabelle's hands that were resting in her lap. "It's okay, babe. There's life on the other side."

Dr. Nagele had stopped smiling, but the twinkle in her dark eyes betrayed her delight at her patient's discomfiture.

"That's because nobody's plastering a label on your forehead that denotes advanced *paternal* age. You've had three years to get used to the view from the other side of the hill," Annabelle chuckled. When she rolled her eyes, they landed on a life-size model of a pregnant woman that showed the forty-week development of a baby. She swallowed, not quite ready to see how her skin would stretch and maneuver around this tiny creature slowly taking over her body, and focused on the old scars and new scratches on the back of her husband's hand.

"The only advancement you need to worry about are the changes that are going on in there, so let's not worry about labels and terms." The doctor tilted her head in the direction of her patient's middle. "Actually, we apply that term to any expectant mother thirty-five years and over, so *technically* you're already older than that. All this means is we need to ask some questions and take some steps to get prepared before baby arrives."

Annabelle glanced at Oliver and back to the doctor. "Like what?"

Dr. Nagele set the file atop a stack of manila folders and plopped a pink crystal paperweight on the pile, effectively covering the offensive label. She lightly tapped a rhythm on her glass-topped desk with her even, white-tipped fingernails. "Well, like genetic counseling and amniocentesis."

"So, we would be talking about these tests if my birthday was in, say . . . eight months from now?" Annabelle sat back in her chair and crossed her arms, taking Oliver's arm with her. When it became apparent Oliver wasn't letting go despite the uncomfortable position, she stopped pinching her elbow and held his hand instead.

"Bella is the same strong, beautiful, healthy mother-to-be today as she was last week, as she'll be when she turns forty soon. She hasn't gained but five pounds."

She tickled the palm of his hand with her index finger. "Four."

"I meant four pounds. And an amnio? That's pretty invasive, isn't it? What does genetic counseling entail? I've never heard of that."

What Oliver meant was that his first wife's OB hadn't mentioned genetic counseling. Annabelle fought the urge to explain that Eleanor was a dewy thirty-year-old when she carried and delivered Henry.

Dr. Nagele leaned forward on her desk, bridging the distance Annabelle had created when she sat back. "Annabelle, you've known me for almost two years now, right? When have you not known me to shoot you straight?" Her tone was matter-of-fact, more up close and personal than professional. Though the sound of her words proved she'd grown up in the Bronx, New York, their down-home feel attested to the four decades she'd spent in the South.

Annabelle nodded and slowly rested her hands on the sides

of her chair, appreciating that Oliver had never let go of her. She'd chosen Arlene Nagele because of her traditional, almost old-fashioned manner of practicing medicine, which seemed antithetical to her metropolitan background. The doctor kept her list of patients small so she could spend time getting to know each one; others she shuffled off to her partners whose exam rooms were more sterile.

"That's not going to change; I'll always be up front with you. Tell you what you need to hear, not merely what you want to hear. We generally recommend genetic counseling for our AMA patients. You're over thirty-five, and this is your first baby. You're older, which means your eggs are older, and that means a slightly higher chance of birth defects. Not a huge chance necessarily, but higher."

She pushed a hand in Oliver's direction as if she were a crossing guard directing traffic. "Slow your roll there. I'm not saying there are problems with your wife's pregnancy or with the newest little McMillan. Some patients opt for an amniocentesis—and I'm not pushing it, merely laying out your choices because it's my job—because they want to find out as much as possible about the baby and make some decisions based on what they find out. Now, I know what you believe and what I believe, but I have a responsibility as a doctor to tell you. And before you ask me, Oliver, yes, there are risks, but we'll talk about all of that later.

"As far as the genetic counseling goes, that involves meeting with someone at this stage of the game, and you're bordering on the edge of it at . . ." Dr. Nagele slid the file out from under the crystal weight and opened it, ". . . nearly thirteen weeks along. The counselor will ask you questions about your own medical history, about your cycle, general health, illnesses, conditions. Then she'll ask you about your family's medical history—"

Annabelle, whose head was already spinning, inhaled loudly and swung toward her husband.

The doctor, obviously sensing her patient's growing consternation, *tapped tapped tapped* again on her desk and shuffled the pages of the large calendar. "Y'all came here to have some fun, and we're not having any fun yet. Let's meet this baby. Oliver, why don't you step out? Annabelle can gather herself, step around the curtain, and get changed. Then we'll do the examination." Dr. Nagele waved toward the left side of her roomy office where a paper-covered table was set up against a wall, partially covered by a curtain hanging from a rail mounted in the ceiling.

Oliver's grip tightened on Annabelle's fingers. "But—"

Dr. Nagele stopped him with a brisk shake of her head. "Don't worry. You won't miss the good part. I'll do the ultrasound at the end. And if I remember correctly, you don't want to know the sex of the baby."

He stood and smoothed his slacks down over his thighs. "You're correct. So, no slipups." Oliver put his lips close to his wife's ear. "You're okay with me leaving? You know I don't give a whit about this doctor and whether she wants me to leave. You're already pregnant."

Annabelle cupped the side of his face with her free hand, enjoying the warmth of his breath on her cheek. "Give us a minute, baby."

When the door clicked closed behind him, Dr. Nagele faced her patient. She crossed her own arms and leaned forward on her elbows. "Okay, let's have it."

"What do you mean?" Empty without the press of Oliver's reassuring palm around hers, Annabelle's fingers curled around the wood armrests of her chair.

"Annabelle McMillan, cut it out. I'm your doctor, and for the next few months I'm your baby's doctor. I've seen parts of you you wouldn't understand, so out with it. When I talked about your medical history, specifically your *family's* medical history, you nearly jumped out of your seat. Now, out with it."

She took a deep breath. "Arlene, you know my family's background is . . . complicated."

"Yes."

It was obvious to her that the doctor wasn't satisfied with such an amorphous response. "Complicated" could assume any definition; it could mean everything or nothing at all. Annabelle narrowed her eyes, trying to see her way to a clearer answer. "I don't know half of it, to be honest. And what I do know wouldn't help you much—any history of heart attacks, high blood pressure, strokes. I've never met my father, and my mother never had much to say except that I remind her of him, a resemblance Miss Hattie supported. I didn't know to ask questions like that when I was little, not that Mama would've answered. My sisters can only tell me half my story." Annabelle made a face as if to say, *I've got nothin'.*

Dr. Nagele shrugged and relaxed her shoulders against the back of her gray leather seat. She swiveled back and forth. "That's okay. The counselor will work with what you've got. They'll ask you about any conditions related to your sisters and illnesses you experienced during your childhoods, with their children, any genetic disorders. Do blood work. That sort of thing. Maybe you could talk to your sisters and find out if anyone has died in infancy, about any sudden deaths—"

"You mean SIDS?"

"Well, these days, most medical professionals refer to it as SUDI: Sudden Unexpected Death in Infancy. That includes SIDS." Dr. Nagele used her fingertips to push back from the desk and rose. "And on that happy note, let's leave all that to the people who handle metrics and probabilities, and I'll do what I do best, which is focus on life. I know you don't want to find out about the baby's sex, and you may or may not decide on the amnio, but I have a noninvasive, yet highly reliable way of determining these things." She held onto the ends of her stethoscope looped around her neck as she wiggled her eyebrows.

Annabelle didn't move—her feet anyway. But her hands . . . Those seemed to have a mind of their own; they wouldn't stop wringing, a term she didn't fully understand until that moment. She stared at them because she couldn't meet the eyes of her obstetrician, who was standing behind her tall chair, her own hands clasped over the top of it.

"So, do you want me to get Oliver?"

Annabelle steadied her hands by grasping her denim-clad knees, then swallowed. The lump in her throat wouldn't budge so she had to force her words around it. "You said unexpected infant death, Arlene." She looked up. "Does murder count? Think that's a disease that could run through a family's bloodline?"

The peacock blue antique clock perched on the corner of the doctor's desk ticked loudly in the silence. The second hand counted off a full minute before Dr. Nagele rolled her chair back on the plastic mat and sat down.

Chapter Thirteen

FRANKIE SNAGGED LEAH'S ARM as she tried to race by her, sneakered feet clapping against the art museum's parquet floor. She leaned close to her daughter's ear and hissed, "Stop running! You know how to act in here. Let them act the fool, but you know better."

Leah nodded and slowed her pace until she was a few feet from her mama before sprinting over to five girls standing in front of an oil painting.

Frankie adjusted the thick cotton straps of the carrier so they rested in the right place on her shoulders. Four babies in, she still wasn't used to wearing one of these things. She'd much prefer to cradle MJ in her arms, but she needed both hands free to keep Nora and the twins from touching things they weren't supposed to. *These homeschoolers and their field trips!* Why they needed to spend a perfectly good Friday morning oohing and aahing over colorful splotches, sunsets, and old people from back in the day was beyond her. She loved exposing her children to new things and believed art was one of those lovely things God encouraged people to "think on" in Philippians. But her laundry room was piled sky-high, and now she'd have to spend precious weekend time finishing lesson plans and folding clothes.

She craned her head to look for Paul, who had volunteered to walk with Nora. "Why didn't I bring the stroller?" Frankie moaned to herself.

"Need me to take the baby?"

"Eyow!" She nearly jumped out of her skin. Clutching the front of her flowered blouse, she whirled toward the voice that had invaded her personal space.

Another homeschool mom stood there, palms out. "I'm so sorry, Frances Mae. I didn't mean to startle you." The woman lightly touched the back of Frankie's shoulder. "Everything okay?"

She swallowed and, like her daughter moments before, nodded silently, gathering her wits about her so she could speak. "Yes, I'm fine. Just counting piles of dirty towels in my head, and I forgot where I was." Rarely one to spare her words, she was so caught off guard, she didn't think to dress up the truth.

The woman seemed to appreciate her forthrightness. "I know what you mean!" she laughed, her blue eyes twinkling. "Remember me? I'm Carla Madsen. We met at park day last week. This is not my idea of a Fri-*yay*, if you know what I mean. We do three-day weekends at my house, so I'm typically playing board games with my peeps right about now. And that's after we sleep in." She fell into step beside Frankie, and the two women strolled up behind Leah and the other five children who were chatting in front of a large canvas.

Frankie's mouth fell open. "You too?" She'd only recently joined this homeschool group, and it was rife with overachieving mothers intent on producing the next Mozart, Serena Williams, or Condoleezza Rice. She herself was of the mind that God had charged her to shepherd her children's spiritual development first and foremost in her efforts to raise productive, critically thinking individuals. *Critically thinking individuals who know not to show out in public,* she stewed in a less holy fashion.

"Absolutely! Studying fine art is wonderful, but I'd prefer to do it on a Tuesday or a Wednesday." Carla's blonde eyebrows nearly disappeared when she raised them. "Driving home from Raleigh during Friday rush-hour traffic is not my idea of fun—especially when my children don't even know what they're looking at, and I'm too tired to explain it to them."

Laughing with the other beleaguered mother, Frankie extended the hand that wasn't stroking her baby's back. "Call me Frankie. I'm your long-lost twin, stolen at birth. Nice to meet you at last," she laughed.

Carla squeezed Frankie's hand between both of hers. "So, it's Frankie, not Frances Mae? Mae is your last name?" She let go and waved at a child across the room, presumably one of hers.

"No, Frances Mae is my given name, the one my mama blessed me with. Southerners tend to double up whenever we can. But my friends and family call me Frankie." She turned to look for Paul again and expelled a breath when she finally spotted him—and sucked in another when she saw him about to make contact with a statue in the corner. "Just a minute." She snapped her fingers and caught his attention. *Absolutely not,* she mouthed, shaking her head.

Carla snickered beside her. "I say we ditch these other people soon because somebody is going to collide with something expensive. And I don't know about you, but my budget can't handle retouching a Monet or Manet or Matisse . . . whoever." She flicked a hand at the canvases mounted on the walls.

"Are you kiddin'? Mine can't either." Frankie beckoned her three-year-old who was tugging Paul in a direction away from the two other boys he was talking to. She hadn't wanted her son assuming responsibility for his younger sibling, not when he was getting to know this new group, but she'd needed a moment to change MJ in the bathroom. Against her every instinct, she'd allowed one of the other chaperones to envelop Paul, Nora, and Leah into the larger cluster so they could keep moving through the exhibits.

"I'm relatively new to this group. What about you?" Frankie brought her baby girl close so that MJ's bottom in the carrier balanced on Nora's head. She widened her stance and waddled along at a slow pace to avoid tripping over the child.

"We joined two years ago after moving here from Ohio, but we took a few months off." She brushed at her strawberry blonde buzz cut, which complemented her heart-shaped face. "Cancer."

"Oh . . . I-I'm . . . I'm sor—"

"Surprised that a vibrant, relatively young mother like myself would get stuck in the North Carolina Museum of Art on such a lovely Friday afternoon?" Carla pressed her hands to her chest. "Why, that goes without saying, but thanks for nearly saying it anyway." Her eyes smiled though her lips didn't. "Really, thank you. I'm getting closer and closer to okay. When you think of Carla Madsen and her one, two, three—" she said, pointing to each as she counted—"kids, say a prayer."

"Happy to." Sensing the woman's desire to step out of the spotlight, Frankie aimed an index finger at her own children, chocolate chips in a sea of macadamia nuts. "You can probably tell which kids are mine, but I'll point 'em out anyway. That's my Paul, the little brown boy in the middle who really wants to manhandle that sculpture. And over there, the girl with the braids who shouldn't be runnin'—that's Leah."

"They're twins!" Nora piped up.

Frankie brushed her daughter's cheek. "They are indeed. And this is my soon-to-be-four-year-old baby, Nora."

"And that's my brotha!" Nora patted MJ's rump.

"Yep, Melvin Junior, my going-on-six-month-old, Melvin Jr. MJ. My whole crew is here, sans my husband, Melvin Sr., who works as a cameraman for WRAL. You might see him today if you're still here when he picks us up." By this time, they'd caught up to most of the homeschool group. Frankie watched one of the docents try to corral everyone so he could lead them to the next exhibit. "This is worse than trying to hold Crisco oil in your hand."

"Mmm-hmm. You said it. Maybe not the way I would-a said it, but that's exactly it." Carla nodded vigorously, tucking her fingers in her back pocket.

"So, what brought you to North Carolina?"

Her new acquaintance's facial expression was a kissing cousin to a smile. "Cancer. In a roundabout, God-only-knows type of way."

"Oh, uh . . ." Frankie tripped over Nora.

"It's okay. Here—" she reached for Nora's hand—"let me take her for you."

Frankie felt the tug and then let go so she could shift MJ in his carrier, relieving the pressure on her shoulders. She considered drawing her baby girl closer to her, but the other woman and Nora looked rather cozy together, surprising her. "Er, do you mind my asking—"

"What happened?" Carla shook her head and slowed her pace as Nora paused to study some artwork composed of bright colors and shapes. "My husband dragged me here after my in-laws moved to the area, and then I got diagnosed with breast cancer. The doctors at Duke saved my life. That's the long and short of it. Pretty simple and complicated at the same time.

"All of that taught me that God has a plan, not one I liked at the moment, but a plan nonetheless. If Rob's parents hadn't fallen in love with North Carolina winters, we wouldn't have sold our house and moved here, and I wouldn't have hurt my arm carrying moving boxes." She moved her free hand in a forward motion. "Then I wouldn't have visited the ortho who accidentally brushed my breast and thought it was weird when I went 'Ow!', which helped us discover the lump. And, and, and."

Frankie sucked in a breath.

"Most people would tell you, 'Oh, my husband or a job brought us here.' I tend to start at the end of things and work my way back to the beginning." Carla laughed. "I know. TMI. But we all focus on the 'A' side, the one that teaches you God is in control, no weapon shall prosper, Jesus loves you, 'ask and you shall receive.' There's also a 'B' side, the one most people don't want to play, that talks about thorns in the flesh and raining on the just and unjust. Crying out and brokenness and 'persecuted but not forsaken.' I've tried to dot every *I* and cross every *T*, but I've learned through faith that I can't prevent heartache. But He will heal it, one way or another."

Frankie squinted at her. "So no more fears and all that?"

"Not hardly. It's just hard to fear the unknown when the reality of a toilet bowl is staring you in the face." She tapped her hair. "Chemo joke."

A tiny part of Frankie coveted the freedom Carla had—hands free, strolling alone, no anxious thoughts for her three children who could have been destroying a priceless work of art at that very moment. It was nowhere in the realm of a Mayhelen Winters–type carelessness. Carla had learned to trust that all was well without having an eye or a hand on it; she had nothing to prove because God had proven Himself faithful. Frankie struggled to roll like that.

A tousle-headed boy about Nora's size hopped over to Carla. He looked so much like his mother, she could've spit him out. He tugged on her short-sleeved shirt that was hanging loosely around her shorts. "Mom. Mom. Mom."

"One time will do. What is it?" Carla squatted and looked him in the eye.

Isn't she worried someone is lost, scared, or hurt? Dead? Frankie marveled at the woman's calm.

"I've gotta pee, and that man . . ." He aimed a thumb over his shoulder at the museum volunteer who was sweating buckets. "That man said he can't help me."

Unable to restrain herself, Frankie, queen of the worst-case scenario, butted in. "You're darn skippy he can't!"

Carla straightened and raised a brow at Frankie. "Do you remember what my kids look like?"

Frankie nodded.

"Could you keep an eye on them until I get back? If that dude finally succeeds in leading these little horses to water, I'll have no problem finding the group, as wild as it is." She took about two steps before half turning toward Frankie. "Does Nora need to go? We can kill two birds with one stone."

You won't be killing this *little birdie.* Frankie shook her head. "No, we've been to the potty already."

Carla shrugged and led her son away by his shoulders, obviously assuming Frankie was fine with her spontaneous babysitting assignment.

And she was, if not incredulous that the other woman trusted her with her children, flesh of her flesh and all that. *Maybe she trusts Me more than you do. She knows who's really in charge. And it's not either one of you.*

Frankie looked down at Nora. No, she hadn't said anything,

and she hadn't heard anything either. The girl was dancing from one foot to the other.

"Mama, can we go with Paul and Leah? Please? Can we go?"

Frankie came to herself and realized that the docent had indeed reconnoitered the troop of homeschoolers and was leading them from the exhibition room. Reassuring herself that her twins were a few feet ahead, she picked out the auburn and dark-blond heads of Carla's children—"I don't even know their names," she realized, wondrously—and followed behind.

As she turned the corner at the arrow directing them toward African art, Frankie looked down the long hallway stretching to her left and saw a familiar figure at the far end. It was Charlotte, and she had an arm looped around the elbow of a tall, olive-skinned man with thick, luscious curls brushed back from his forehead. Pulling Nora close, Frankie flattened herself against the wall and studied the couple's profiles as the two peered closely at a placard posted next to the display of pottery. Charlotte flipped her braids—*Where's her curly wig?*—over her shoulder as she giggled over something the man whispered in her ear.

"What in the world? Or should I be asking, *who* in the world?" Frankie whispered, gaping as the couple moved a few steps toward shelves displaying vibrantly dyed fabrics. Charlotte looked happy and relaxed—and *short*—in a pair of leather flip-flops instead of the heels she normally wore rain, sleet, or shine. Her sister was laughing naturally, *with* someone rather than *at* someone.

Nora yanked her mama's fingers to get her attention. "What is it, Mama? Can we go now? They're leaving us." Her head was leaning so far back, her twists nearly touched the floor.

Frankie cast one more surreptitious look at her sister and her mystery man and then let Nora lead the way to the next roomful of exhibits.

Chapter Fourteen

"ARE YOU SURE THIS IS A GOOD IDEA?" Frankie moved in so she could get a better look.

"Oliver sure seems to think so." Annabelle stuck a finger through one of the metal squares of the large crate, despite her sister's warnings to the contrary. "And Henry will be over the moon on his birthday when he opens a wiggly box with one of these inside."

"What little boy wouldn't? Still, isn't this one of those major decisions pregnant women shouldn't make? New baby, new dog, new house? That's a lot of peein' and poopin' on your new wood floors." Frankie watched the four fluffy Moyen poodle puppies tumble over each other, trying to get to their new chew toy.

"You forget relatively new marriage. And technically, it's a relatively *old* house. Ow!" Annabelle snatched back her finger and wrung her hand.

"Told you." Smirking, Frankie crossed her arms and stood back, telling herself to focus on the sharp teeth instead of the cuteness.

The sun had emerged after a spring storm had blown in earlier that afternoon, and now its rays warmed the top of the sisters' heads. Annabelle's husband had built an addition for this dog breeder, and so thrilled were his clients about the project, they'd offered the McMillans a good deal on a puppy. One by one, the breeder had brought them out and set them in the crate, providing Annabelle the opportunity to study them individually and also to see how well they were socialized as they played together. The breeder looked on from the other side of her fenced backyard.

What Frankie saw was sleepless nights, work, and money—on four legs instead of two. *At least my kids grow up and look like me, and I have a chance* somebody *will take care of me. Troublemakers . . . just take, take, take.*

"Remember when we worked up our nerve to ask Mama for that dog?" Annabelle rose. She arched her back and stuffed her hands in her rear pockets, revealing the scar that snaked around her left arm. Her emerald green T-shirt clung to the barely visible curve below her belly button.

Frankie closed her eyes at the memory Annabelle alluded to and focused on the moment at hand. "I don't know what got into our heads, thinkin' we had a chance at gettin' it. Talk about pickin' our moment! Just askin' got us into more hot water."

Her sister fiddled with the hem of her shorts. "*Chasing* it is what got me into hot water—"

"And into a cast. She said all an animal would do was take what time we didn't have and cause trouble."

"But I didn't think so."

"And you told her so." Frankie stepped closer so she could get a better look. *Maybe it wasn't such a bad idea.* She leaned over the crate and listened to the puppies yip and whimper as they tumbled over each other.

"Why wouldn't I? It's not like she would've borne the brunt of the responsibility or one of her husbands. That would've been our job. So, somebody had to stand up to her. Especially when she compared the dogs to her children." Annabelle's low-top Converses flattened the moist grass as she circled the crate.

"I don't know if *somebody* had to, but you certainly believed *you* had to." Frankie squished through the long green blades in her purple Crocs, the soles of her feet getting wet through the holes.

"What do you think of that one?" Annabelle seemed to shake off Mayhelen's hurtful words as she pointed to the roundest and smallest of the four, an apricot-colored puppy crouching in a corner off to itself.

Frankie studied the one Annabelle had settled on. "Do you want to hold him . . . her . . . again to be sure?"

"I'm sure already, but yes, I'd like to hold her again. It'll be nice to have some extra girl power in that house full of menfolks. By the way, thanks for coming with me today. This is much more fun with company . . . with you." She glanced at Frankie and smiled a little, obviously a little uncomfortable making the admission.

Frankie's heart grew even toastier than the rest of her as the sun warmed her head and the back of her arms. "I'm glad you asked me. You called at just the right time. Melvin was home, dinner was in the Crockpot, and the baby was sleeping. A trifecta."

Annabelle ruffled her curls, making them stand out on her head like she'd been struck by that afternoon's lightning. "Between me and you, that's still taking some gettin' used to, the fact that my schedule isn't my own." She rubbed her abdomen. "My *life* isn't my own. I really couldn't wait to get pregnant. We were actively trying—"

"Actively?" Frankie cupped a hand over her mouth to smother her laugh.

Pink flushed Annabelle's high cheekbones. "You know what I mean. But a couple of weeks ago, Oliver and I had the strangest . . . I guess you'd call it an argument . . . because I forgot to include him in my plans."

"What plans?" A slight breeze lifted Frankie's bangs. She was cooking in her jeans and she was glad for the cool air.

"A prenatal visit." Annabelle held up a hand. "And before you say anything, I apologized profusely. I was totally wrong not to include him. We moved things around and went together." She waved the same hand back and forth. "Anyway, the point is, hearing you talk about that 'trifecta' makes it sound like you needed permission to come with me, and that takes some getting used to."

Frankie wanted to ask her younger sister more about her doctor's visit, but she refrained from taking that giant step into her business. Charlotte and Annabelle frequently accused her of trying to run their lives, but Frankie would do her best not to venture down the road unless she was invited to go. As the silence between them grew and started taking on an awkward shape, Frankie nodded toward the crate. "Talk about responsibility! You're volunteerin' to take on something else requirin' your time and attention. I should tell you now, I'm willin' to *baby*sit. Not dog-sit."

Annabelle's eyes lingered long on Frankie first, then the crate. "You sound like somebody else we know and—" She smushed her lips together and clipped off her sentence.

Frankie heard the four-letter word Annabelle wouldn't say. "Walkin' that thin line, are we? The distance between those two extreme emotions is actually pretty short."

The breeder ambled their way, squinting in the sun that had sunk a degree or two in the hour and a half they'd been there, and unlatched the metal door. She reached over the squirming puppies for the one that was the color of a Creamsicle and used both hands to plop her into the extended arms of Annabelle. "Here you go. She's all yours."

"How'd you know?" She nuzzled the furry head with her chin.

"I've been in this business a long time, ma'am. I've been watching you and the dogs, and dollars to donuts, I can usually tell you who's going home together. Every dog has her person, and vice versa," the woman drawled. "Let me know when you're ready to settle up, and we'll talk about pickup dates and shot records. It'll be a little while before she's ready to go."

Frankie watched the two bond for a minute or two before approaching them to scratch the back of the puppy's neck. She couldn't help herself. "Uh-hmm." She cleared her throat, hating to spoil the Norman Rockwell moment. "Speakin' of Mama . . ."

Annabelle rolled her eyes and sighed. "Frances Mae . . ."

"Don't 'Frances Mae' me. I don't mean to rain again on your already soggy parade, but you know we need to make a decision. I'm tired of huntin' you and Charlotte down. Y'all are grown, and she's not my mama only."

"But she was your mama first." Annabelle squatted to let the puppy romp freely in the grass. It immediately began sniffing and dropped its hind parts.

"Annabanana." Though she wondered how her forty-two-year-old knees would behave, Frankie lowered herself—a couple of feet from the golden puddle soaking the grass.

The puppy lumbered a few steps in the thick grass, then lolled onto its back. Annabelle accepted the invitation to rub its pink belly and smiled a little when one of its back legs moved.

"Nobody's asking you to do anything by yourself, Frankie. At least I'm not. I can't speak for Charlotte. But deciding to bring Mama home is way harder than choosing to bring a puppy home."

"Because she's our mother. We didn't choose her—"

"And she never chose us. We weren't her people." Annabelle scooped up the dog.

"Judge much?"

Using her fingers, Annabelle combed the puppy's hair from the top of its head all the way down its back. "I don't care what Miss Hattie says. An eyewitness doesn't have to judge what she experienced. Only report."

Frankie opened her mouth to refute her sister's quietly spoken words, but then she snapped it closed. The breeze picked up and ruffled the loose edges of her hair, and she cast a wary look at the sky. Purplish clouds off to the east toward the Raleigh-Durham area threatened the clear Tar Heel blue above them. They felt like a harbinger of the direction their once-pleasant conversation had taken.

"I tried to please y'all and almost lost who I was. I had to find me somewhere else. If I give in on this just to please you . . ." Annabelle flicked her hand.

Frankie wondered if she was shooing away a fly or her fears.

"I still can't believe I finally get to have a dog! I should snap a few pictures so I can share them with Oliver. He told me he was happy with whatever—*who*ever—I decided, but I still want to get his okay; we'll be living with this decision for a long time. Do I need to put down a deposit to hold Poppy?"

The woman had tromped over to them. "Poppy? Like the flower?"

Frankie's mouth flattened. "No, like the man who nearly ran her over. This girl just won't let sleepin' dogs lie."

Chapter Fifteen

Then

ANNABELLE AND FRANKIE HAD told her different versions and various parts of the story over the years. As best she could, Charlotte had fit it together as she would an old photograph that had been torn into smaller, irregular pieces; the tape covered bits of it and she had to reimagine what was missing. One thing was for sure: it always began and ended with the road.

From what Charlotte had heard, Annabelle nearly had to stand upright to pedal. The ten-speed had been handed down a few years too early for her nine-year-old legs. She'd been practicing the move for a week, how to navigate the right turn off Howler Drive without using the handlebars. The misshapen patch of white meat showing on her elbow attested to all the effort she was putting in to show how cool she was.

In case somebody was looking, Annabelle closed her eyes and bobbed her head to some imaginary beat as she craned to hear the crackling of her wheels on those tiny rocks at the edge of the road. But then a shout—*"You'd best get outta my way, Mayhelen!"*—caused her to zig when she should've zagged across the gravel bordering her driveway. When she did, the bicycle landed on her, and she lay spread-eagled at the end of their drive, one pedal digging into the uncovered skin low on the inside of her thigh.

Suspended in the air, the front wheel spun slowly and came to a stop. A dazed Annabelle peeled off the ten-speed, clambered to her feet, and peered up one side of the road and down the other. The only thing that seemed to notice her was the high, golden sun glaring down on the wide front yards and deep porches of the other houses that faced their own. Annabelle explained that most of the people living on their street that curved past empty lots, shady drives, and woods to a dead end, wouldn't get home from the clock factory or pharmaceutical plant until closer to six, and an after-school special on channel 13 was probably babysitting their latchkey children. Even the robins hopping from branch to branch on the dry, crackly dogwood tree stretching toward the road ignored her as she picked gravel out of her palms. Head down, Annabelle shuffled through the strip of grass in the middle of the packed dirt of her driveway toward the house.

"Don't worry, nobody saw you. Besides me, anyway."

The voice made Annabelle yelp, but whenever Charlotte heard this story, she thought to herself, *Annabelle should've known it was Frankie.*

Their oldest sister was perched on their stoop, her chin propped on the heel of one hand. The fingers on the other plucked at the grass poking through the cracked concrete of the bottom step, only stopping for a second or two when something crashed in the shadowy recesses beyond the screen door behind her. Green bits peppered the ground by Frankie's feet.

Annabelle ambled over on shaky legs. "Hey. Whatcha doin'?"

Frankie pointed. "Hey, Anna Fo Fanna. You're gonna need a Band-Aid before long."

Annabelle's eyes followed the direction of her sister's finger. A scratch snaked angrily from her knee to her shin. She shrugged. Like Frankie, she knew they'd only find Band-Aids in the nurse's office at school. Mama's heart couldn't seem to afford such expressions of care or kindness, so a square of wet tissue paper was about all their home had to offer her. That and a scolding. Annabelle was sure to hear a list of reasons why her fall and her scarred leg and elbow would turn off future prospects once Annabelle was of marrying age. "Yeah. Why're you outside?"

Slam!

"What's going on now?" Annabelle ducked for cover. There always seemed to be some commotion or upheaval bubbling within their walls, behind the windows flanked by forest green shutters and their many doors, whether they were open or not. Nobody would know it to look at the stately, two-story white clapboard house with a porch that wrapped from the left side all the way around to the rear.

"You can guess why I'm outside." Eleven-year-old Frances Mae sounded like she'd traveled around the world more than a dozen times, as if she'd seen all there was to see. She propped her elbows on the step behind her and leaned back, still yanking at the grass.

Annabelle squatted down on the walkway in front of her sister and dabbed at the trickle of blood with her fingertips. No way was she going inside to clean her leg. "What started it this time?"

Frankie shrugged. "The sunshine. Not enough mayonnaise on his hamburger. Charlotte cryin'."

Charlotte used to grin at this point of the story. She liked to hear her name.

"But we both know the real reason. Mama won't let him stay over, not until he puts a weddin' band with that ring he gave her." Frankie braced her weight on her left arm and rubbed together the fingertips on her other hand. They made a faint shushing sound.

Annabelle stared up at the house, her mouth a flat line. From all the commotion, their mama's man-friend didn't have the wherewithal to keep up the game they'd been playing for two months.

"Two months too long," Frankie whispered in Annabelle's ear one night, and they had to take cover under the blanket and scoot to the middle of the bed to muffle their giggles. Actually, Uncle Pete had stuck around about as long as most of Mama's friends, unless they counted Frankie and Charlotte's daddy, and that was putting the two marriages together. But Charlotte and Frankie didn't like talking about that relationship in front of Annabelle.

Annabelle shared that it had taken some time for her to realize he was as much their uncle as he was their daddy. She and Frankie didn't know what else to call the man, and saying "Mister" had earned them both a swat on their backside for being sassy. The engagement ring Uncle Pete had given Mayhelen had turned green before she'd worn it a week; she'd taken it off because she had to, not because she wanted to—a first for Mama—and started clamoring for a real one before she let him put a toe on the first step leading to the second floor.

They told Charlotte she was too young to do more than smile at Uncle Pete when he was around. And he was gone so soon, it didn't matter what they called him. If the man was anything like the others who'd come before him, Pete's side of the bed would be icy cold or warmed by somebody else before Charlotte even got the chance to call him anything but a memory. A pitiful one at that.

Ca-thunk.

Frankie had described for Charlotte the "cry from her gut" at the noise and the ensuing sounds of a scuffle. Several heavy somethings thunked to the floor above them. Eyes wide, Annabelle pushed herself upright as two sets of footsteps, one right on top of another, seemed to tumble down the four-foot-wide staircase to the entryway. The screen door around back rattled against the frame.

Annabelle took off around the porch, headed toward the sound, with Frankie inches behind her. They both knew Mayhelen wouldn't air any of their dirty laundry in the front of the house; their life had to look prettier than that. Sure enough, the girls arrived in time to see their mama, hair piled on top of her head in a messy bun, fling back the screen door with such force it slapped against the wood siding; the metal door handle gouged the paint and sent off-white chips flying. Then a tattered and patched duffel bag landed with a smack on the porch.

Mayhelen flattened herself against the doorframe, her frayed pink robe draping open to reveal a torn lacy neckline on a cotton nightgown sprinkled with faded moons and stars. She thrust a long cigarette between her thin lips and held a lighter to its end with fingers that shook slightly. When she took a long draw, the tip glowed bright red as it ate a half-inch of paper, then dripped ashes on the threshold straddled by her bare feet. Eyes narrowed and hand steadier, Mama used her tongue to flick the Marlboro to the corner of her mouth so she could warn, "You'd better not have none of my stuff in that bag."

"What *stuff* do you have I'd wont?" Uncle Pete's top lip curled. "All you've really got worth havin' is them girls, and you know I don't want no parts of raisin' nobody. I can barely take care of my darn self." Sidling around her, he toted nothing but a baseball cap with an orange tiger on the brim. He sneered at the children as he settled it so low on his head that Annabelle could barely see his dark-brown eyes.

Mayhelen cursed him under her breath but loudly enough that he took one step toward her, then another. She drew herself up to her full five feet eight inches, thrust out her chest, and didn't budge. More ashes fell, but a light wind swept them away before they could land and do any damage to anything more than her lungs. Mama laughed as he brushed off his shoulder and stared at her through nearly closed eyes. She didn't look down as Charlotte, clad only in a soggy diaper, toddled through the door and headed straight to her sisters, showing off her six baby teeth.

"You were a cute baby," Frankie used to tell her. "Even if you did cry a lot."

That day, Annabelle swooped up Charlotte and scooted down to the ground, what she reasoned was a safe distance. She sat on the bottom step and tried and failed to cross her arms around the baby to hold her still, all the while keeping her eyes on the standoff in the doorway. Frankie held her ground on the porch, though she looked like she might run if either Uncle Pete or Mayhelen said "Boo!"; she hugged the supportive post at the top right corner when he finally snorted and stomped down past them all without another word.

At the bottom, he spun and stopped, his heel crushing the grass that bordered the orangey-red clay they considered a walkway. "Little girl, you gon' miss your Uncle Pete, I can tell you that. You got your hands full. And I'm talkin' 'bout that piece o' work up there, not Charlotte."

"Charlotte!" Frankie never could identify the moment when everybody realized that Annabelle's hands were indeed empty and their baby sister had taken it upon herself to hotfoot it across the

field behind the house. Annabelle claimed she was the first to scream the baby's name.

At that point in the story, Charlotte once chided, "Serves you right. Always taking me for granted. Something else is more important. I still don't see how all y'all let a baby get that far." Regardless of how it happened, Charlotte had spotted a stray dog and chased it across the sunbaked yard and nearly through the ankle-high sunflowers in the acre behind their house. "And while y'all clutched your pearls, Annabelle of all people went to get me."

But her sister didn't get there until the car came, on the heels of the dog that Charlotte tried—and failed—to touch.

Mr. Poppy—what Miss Hattie called him because of the artificial bloom he stuck in his hat—was on his way home. According to the report he later gave the police, he'd just taken a draw from the bottle he kept under the seat of his car. "By the time I looked up, that baby was in the road and nearly under the wheels of my station wagon. If it hadn't been for that skinny little thing snatching her to the left, no telling what would have happened," he blubbered.

Their mama wept noisy buckets too, almost as much as when Frankie and Charlotte's daddy left them. But Annabelle said it wasn't over nearly losing their baby sister; Miss Hattie was consoling them both with a glass of lemonade. The girls knew that although Mayhelen stayed "in the streets," she couldn't stand knowing that some stray dog had put their family and their business there.

Chapter Sixteen

Now

CHARLOTTE PULLED INTO HER narrow space on the corner but let the engine purr quietly, hoping the air conditioning would cool her flushed cheeks. Nothing could get her worked up like the prospect of helping somebody, feeling needed. The thirty-minute drive to her office got her blood pumping as she envisioned her day. After taking a deep breath, she arranged the reflective shield on her dashboard that kept some of the day's heat out of the BMW, slid on her sunglasses, and gathered her bag. As she sidled between her car and the one next to it, Charlotte watched people stroll around the office park—six connected, two-story brick edifices that looked more like row houses than places of business. She forced herself to slow her pace and gather her thoughts to prepare herself emotionally and mentally to walk alongside her clients. "Girl, you need to get prayed up," she imagined Frankie advising.

Charlotte glanced at her watch. *3:45. Let's see. Who's on the docket this afternoon?* Tapping the top row of her teeth with a manicured nail, she thought a second or two before a tall, lanky man wearing a plaid suit popped into her mind. His image stopped her in her tracks in the middle of the parking lot.

LeRoy and Brenda saw her for family counseling, what his wife had deemed "pre-divorce care" when she'd called for their initial appointment. Charlotte pictured a skull and crossbones hovering over their sessions and had almost asked her assistant to write their dates in pencil. At the moment, the couple visited Charlotte separately, and she was working with LeRoy on his tendency to hyperventilate during job interviews, precipitating his need to go to one after another—and subsequently suffer one episode after another. The vicious cycle eased his anxiety nary a bit. Nor did it keep his marriage from dissolving at the edges. Together, Charlotte and LeRoy were examining the reasons behind his struggle and were working through different methods of mitigating it. So far, all efforts to help his withering marriage were for naught; they were fighting an uphill battle in an ice storm.

Clip-clopping across the lot to the sidewalk, Charlotte felt perspiration cooling the base of her neck. *Too much hair for this heat. Summer's going to be a hot one.* She couldn't do anything about that now. Her main focus at the moment was her client and his issues. For one, LeRoy tended to either show up late for appointments or cancel them altogether. The latest complication was that he had developed an obvious attraction to his counselor—Charlotte—and was starting to get a bit . . . "handsy," as Frankie would say. Miss Hattie would describe it as "fresh." Either way, Charlotte was going to have to put a stop to it, or she would be labeling him a "former client" and storing his file in the bottom drawer with all the others who'd either declared themselves healed or whole enough to live without her. Moving around her furniture wasn't going to cut it.

Hmm, she thought and whipped out her pen and her moleskin book and pressed it to a brick wall so she could write: *Is this self-sabotage, a subconscious way of destroying his marriage?* She put a pin in the thought and pictured running her finger down that day's page in her calendar. *That's my 4:15. Is there anyone else? Nope, don't think so.* Her teeth lightly clicked to the rhythm of *The Nutcracker* march as the tune played in her head, a habit she'd developed a month ago to replace gritting them. When her dentist had warned her she'd need surgery one day to remove the bony growths on her gumline if she didn't drop her longtime childhood habit, Charlotte determined to find a way to keep her mind occupied even when it wasn't, to focus her energies in a positive direction when stressed. Humming classical music and clicking her teeth did the trick.

"I'm no physician, but I healed myself," she quipped. Still chuckling at her own pun, she waved off a passerby squinting curiously at the would-be doctor talking to herself on the sidewalk. Charlotte dropped her book and pen into her leather satchel and headed for her office situated in the middle of the row of buildings.

Actually, she didn't think of herself as a doctor—though she held a PhD—or the people she helped as patients. She was no healer. And that proverb adapted from the book of Luke was the closest she would get to seeking Scripture for help. Charlotte didn't see why Frankie thought that Book was considered so good anyway. And now Frankie and Oliver were indoctrinating Annabelle. What had church ever done for Charlotte besides feed her a home-style meal every now and then that probably did more harm than good to her heart?

Buzz. Buzz. Charlotte set her things on the bottom step and dug through her bag for her cell. She read the text from her assistant. Sure enough, LeRoy had canceled. *Shoot!* Deflated, yet already reconnoitering, figuring out how to get him in the office, Charlotte returned to her midsize SUV and reversed out of her space.

Ten minutes later, Charlotte slammed and locked the door of her town house and tossed the key in the heavy crystal bowl sitting on the table in her small foyer. She leaned against the door and peeled off her jacket and kicked off her heels, losing three inches of height. The hem of her persimmon-colored slacks dragging across the tiled floor of her entryway, she sloughed through the den, passed the kitchen, and headed into the back of her home to the bathroom.

Charlotte stared in the mirror that spanned the double sinks at a woman whose face looked back at her despite all her efforts to the contrary—Mayhelen Winters. She sighed and reached under her hairline to whip off her curly wig, freeing narrow braids that started at her temples and flopped to her shoulders. She fitted the hairpiece over the foam head on the side of her sink. How her mama would've hated her natural style; that was something Charlotte did know about the woman. The only thing that came natural to Mayhelen was her ability to find a man, though keeping him was a skill she never acquired. She took painstaking care to maintain appearances even while her home life fell to pieces, and that included how she styled her long tresses that turned under at the ends. Nothing but the best chemicals or straightening comb would do for Mama.

Charlotte shook her head slowly and unlatched her new watch from Max. It had to have cost him an arm and a leg and maybe a finger or two, not that his bank account would notice. Next she removed the necklace with its simple diamond pendant that stood for understated success and the large silver hoops Annabelle had designed for her birthday the year before. Had her sister even noticed she'd worn them a couple weeks ago, Charlotte's preemptive peace offering? She scoffed at her mirrored self. "I bet not."

Finally, Charlotte turned on the faucet to the warmest temperature she could stand. While the water heated, she stripped off her blouse and stowed it in the dry cleaning bag and hung up her slacks. Standing in her bra and panties and pink toenails, she scrubbed at her face with her washcloth: off came the deep umber lipstick and lip liner, the purple and brown eyeshadows and the eyeliner, the cherry cheek color and dusting of foundation. Afterward, she rinsed with the hot water first, then the cold until her face felt free of its ornamentation, its mask. Before she dried her hands, she took out her contact lenses and disposed of them.

A fuzzy Mayhelen Winters look-alike returned her steady gaze after she finished her ministrations. Only Max Demos would recognize her now, certainly not her colleagues nor her clients. This was the Charlotte he'd met and the one he claimed he loved, though she rebuffed his declarations while quietly basking in the attention. Frankie and Annabelle would see the pie-faced girl they'd grown up with, with the mole in the middle of her chin, the slightly raised brown dot Mama had called her beauty mark. Charlotte had considered having it surgically removed but opted for the less-expensive option of a smear of Mary Kay makeup.

Readying herself for a different world than the one she'd greeted that morning, Charlotte took her time showering, toweling off, and selecting an outfit for her date with Max. *How do I love thee?* she thought, sliding aside one hanger after another to find a shirt that would flatter her curves. "You mean hide your waistline," she chided herself. She chose a short-sleeved white linen pullover and a pair of loose-fitting denims. After dabbing some grease in the parts between her braids, she sprayed perfume on her pulse points and slid her feet into sandals that were a mere slip of leather between her feet and the floor. Her new tortoiseshell frames and a touch of Downtown Brown lipstick were the only accents on the face Max said he adored.

Satisfied with her look, Charlotte went to grab a protein bar to take the edge off her hunger. *No man wants to see a woman clear her plate.* She wasn't sure if that was her voice or her mama's.

Chapter Seventeen

Then

CHARLOTTE'S PATENT LEATHER SHOES glowed with a soft sheen under the lace of her bobby socks. She loved the way her feet looked when she kicked them back and forth under the table, in and out of the wide band of light shining from the large window that looked down on the large foyer. That's where Frankie had set up a card table, in that square space in the middle of the wool rug that was starting to unravel all along its edges. While she'd been sitting there by her lonesome, she'd pulled at the yellow threads and tucked them under the folds of her frilly light-blue dress. Later she'd pretend to be the lady with the golden hair in the storybook.

"Hey there, baby girl."

Grinning so hard her eyes nearly closed, Charlotte looked up at her "bestest friend in the whole wide world," and her sun-kissed shoes lost all their appeal. "Anna!"

"Shush, sweet pea." But Annabelle attached a wink that softened the edges to her warning. She set two polystyrene plates on the card table, one in front of the two-and-a-half-year-old and the other at the empty spot to her left. "Here, let me scoot you up." She wedged her little sister under the table, where the youngster's feet swung happily several inches from the floor. Then the older girl handed Charlotte a plastic fork and laid a wide strip of cloth over her lap. Annabelle kissed her forehead and said, so low Charlotte barely heard her, "We'll pretend this is your napkin."

The words had tickled her ear, but she pressed her knuckles to her mouth to smother her excited giggles. Charlotte nodded several times without a sound; she'd already been shushed a few times, and she didn't want to do anything to make her sisters mad, not now. Today was special, and if Mama woke up too soon it would ruin their party, Annabelle's first. Charlotte peered up the shadowy stairs and murmured, "Rumpelstiltskin-Rumpelstiltskin-Rumpelstiltskin" under her breath for good measure.

She loved playing restaurant with Frankie, when her big sister would set up the table in the front hall and bring food for her and Anna. Usually, the game took place once or twice a week in the middle of the day, when Mama was out of the house, and Frankie would serve them boiled hot dogs, fried bologna sandwiches, or that cheesy macaroni in the skinny blue box. She "gave" her younger sisters a whole hour to eat while she found a show to watch on television, something that had lots of grown folks kissing and crying and carrying on.

But that afternoon was even more special—and even more secret—because the girls were celebrating Anna's tenth birthday, something they'd never done. As soon as Mama had shut herself in for her two glasses of grape juice followed by a nap—what her sisters had called her "con-si-*tu*-shin"—Frankie had held a finger against the middle of her lips and whispered that Miss Hattie was at the back door. The three little mice had scampered to meet her, and their neighbor had handed them a paper bag filled with a late-afternoon snack of Little Debbie Zebra Cakes, barbecue chips, grapes, and warm pigs in a blanket. *And ooh, a container of Country Time lemonade!* Frankie had even added an extra scoop of sugar with the water.

Anna pulled out her own chair and sat. Her mouth formed, *Yay!* as she made a clapping motion, carefully keeping her hands apart.

Charlotte's heart would have translated the word if her eyes hadn't easily read her sister's lips, and she, too, made sure her hands didn't touch. But she couldn't keep her bottom from wiggling so in her ladder-back chair, which caused it to rock from side to side on its left two legs and then the right two.

Her sister quickly caught one of the wooden slats before her seat tilted over and tossed her to the floor. When she'd righted Charlotte, Anna aimed a finger first at her before pointing upstairs, and finally, she made a slashing motion across her own throat.

Charlotte gasped and covered her mouth. Frankie had taught the child what that sign meant a long time ago.

For a second, Anna's eyebrows looked like they were having a conversation in the middle of her face, but they must have decided they were happy, because the two fuzzy lines moved back to their God-designed sides of her face, and the creases in her forehead smoothed out. She smiled and gave Charlotte a thumbs-up.

And just in time. Charlotte spied Frankie striding around the corner, bearing a large plate with enough goodies for three. She'd stuck a candle in one of the white-and-black-striped cakes! That time, the toddler couldn't keep herself from jumping to her patent-leather-clad feet and applauding, excited for the party and that Frankie was going to join them. Her laughter gurgled up her throat and encircled the room, bouncing off the plaster walls and stairwell. Frankie's and Anna's eyes widened.

A few seconds later, the floor creaked above and a door opened upstairs. "Are y'all gonna make me come downstairs?"

Charlotte trembled. Her mama sounded like she could've played the troll living under the bridge, the way Frankie read the story. But the girl didn't think his words were all jumbled together and slow like that. Tears flooded her eyes, which moments before had been full of visions of sugary cakes and cups of lemonade.

Before Charlotte could throw back her head and commence to wailing, Annabelle covered the girl's mouth with her hand and called, "No, ma'am! I tripped and fell . . . I'm sorry." Then she waited with her sisters in the silence, Frankie frozen with her hands gripping the plate. When Charlotte seemed to struggle for air, Anna removed her hand and pulled her into her lap.

"I already told you I didn't want to hear a rat pee on cotton! Seems like you need me to show you again what I mean." Mama's voice didn't float down to them. It fell as a heavy rain and drenched their party, washing away their joy.

The girls waited, Anna with her bruised arm enfolding a quiet Charlotte and Frankie, who set down the plate in the middle of the table. They all seemed to expel a collective breath as finally the bedroom door shut and two sets of footsteps creaked a retreat above them.

Chapter Eighteen

Now

TYPICALLY, Charlotte sat in a cushioned, deep red, barrel-shaped chair across from the two-person sofa that radiated—albeit in a muted caramel-colored cotton sailcloth—peace and reassurance. It sat as an island in a sea of navy, olive, and umber, in contrast to Charlotte's now empty, blood-colored chair, the focal point in her traditionally appointed office.

She missed it, the chair with its gently curving back that provided a comfortable place for her arms to rest while she attended to the various mothers, fathers, sisters, and brothers that plunked their needs into her capable, educated lap. Sitting there, she gave the impression to clients that she was close enough to touch, though she kept her hands to herself. And they'd best do the same. Appearances were important in her line of work. Whether or not

Charlotte felt confident, concerned, or invested, she wanted whoever was seated across from her to believe she was.

Today, she meant for LeRoy to consider her approachable but most definitely unavailable, so when he entered her office, she smiled and promptly marched herself around her desk and sat in her high-back rolling chair. "Hello there. I'm glad you were able to reschedule your appointment."

His eyes skittered around the creamy walls of the room, pausing at the empty seat, before landing on her face. A moth to a flame.

Charlotte propped her elbows on her large desktop calendar and chewed on the end of one arm of her glasses, the pair with the bold rectangular frames that were only for show. *I'm listening, but you'd better not cross the line. And you know your mama named you Lee-roy,* she chided internally, hoping it wasn't bad counselor juju when she drew out the first syllable of his name.

He touched each of the three gold buttons on his vest with shaky fingers. "Yes . . . uh, should I sit down?"

This was his fourth weekly visit. By now, that man knew to sit down. Her new position in the room must have thrown him, but no matter. There was no way she was moving from behind the shield of her desk. Charlotte extended a palm toward the sofa and intentionally avoided saying *of course*, her natural inclination, since she didn't want to imply he should've known something. That made him even more anxious, that thought of getting something wrong. "Yes, please."

With a last glance at her empty seat, he backed his long thin legs against the fabric of the sofa and flopped into the middle of it, then peered at her from under half-closed lids.

Charlotte tugged down the sleeve of her navy sport coat, covering every inch of bare skin that her high-necked white blouse had skipped. She'd do everything she could to help a client. "So . . . you missed your last appointment?" Statement of fact posed as a question that allowed him to supply information he knew, as much as he felt comfortable sharing.

LeRoy unlooped and looped his top vest button as his eyes toyed with the unoccupied chair across from him. "Yes, I thought it was best," he volunteered in a near whisper.

She nodded slowly a few times and squinted at a spot above his head, as if she was considering his statement. Actually, she hoped to give him space to expound upon what he'd offered.

"I didn't want to disappoint you . . . since my last interview didn't go well. I wanted to wait until I had some good news to share." In and out went the button. LeRoy's voice sounded a mite stronger.

"You can't disappoint me, LeRoy." Charlotte coughed a little. "You're not here to impress me. I'm here to walk alongside you. We're working together."

His nostrils flared as he inhaled her words along with a deep breath that steadied him. LeRoy exhaled a slight smile, and he leaned forward a bit. They sat in silence for a beat, and his eyes continued playing tag with Charlotte's chair. "Did you miss me?" His voice sounded slightly louder.

Okay, here we go. Charlotte adjusted her watch.

"Do you have somewhere to go?"

The uncharacteristic edge in his voice threw her off, and she spoke candidly. "No, but my sister will be here in less than an hour." Sitting straighter, she braced her hands flat on the desk to keep her chair from spinning. She slid on her glasses so her nibbling on the arms wouldn't become all-out chewing.

Both of these professional and personal visits were upsetting Charlotte's emotional applecart. "But that's neither here nor there. To answer your question, I'm always glad to see my clients. You and Brenda came to me for help, and I'm grateful I have the training to work with you as a family counselor."

He and Brenda had married twelve years before, and they had two children. LeRoy wanted a third, but Charlotte suspected his wife didn't want another child to bind her even more tightly to the quiet man in front of her. Was it his silence that so unsettled her? Perhaps it was his steady gaze that followed her every twinge. Or the shaking. *Not even fall leaves quivered that much before they fell.*

Feeling guilty and unprofessional, she ground the thoughts under her heel. "Now, how about those breathing techniques we talked about, LeRoy? Did you use any of those yesterday? We could try them now, if you'd likc." Charlotte modulated her voice and spoke deliberately. When she was uncomfortable or upset, her thoughts chugged faster than an Amtrak train, and there was no stopping them, another pesky family trait. Frankie had complained once, "You're as bad as Annabanana. Slow down! My ears can't keep up!"

LeRoy followed her directions and, after a few minutes, his trembling fingers stilled and rested in his lap.

Charlotte edged back from her desk, the casters on her chair smoothly rumbling on the thick plastic runner protecting the carpeted floor. She hesitated a second, then she stood and walked around to her red chair positioned across from her client. When she perched on the edge of the cushion, ready to take flight if necessary, she took LeRoy's sigh as appreciation for her move. Releasing a deep breath herself, she scooted back a little in her seat. "So, did you talk to Brenda about the interviews?"

His eyes widened, and he nodded. His wife was half his height and twice his width and presented a formidable force that he usually chose not to reckon with.

I can just imagine how that conversation went. "Is there anything you'd like to share about your discussion?" Charlotte tipped lightly down the middle of the road since she was seeing both him and his wife. It was important that neither of them feel she was siding with or against one or the other—especially the man sitting in front of her. Any hint of favoritism would either attract or repel him, and both were better avoided.

"Well . . ." He gave her a once-over.

She followed his gaze. Nothing to see here but her pair of loose-fitting navy slacks, worn to dissuade even the most determined letch. Charlotte rested her clasped fingers in her lap and sat quietly, waiting, an acquired skill she should've used with her sisters. It just wasn't in her to sit without moving her feet or saying or doing something to fill the space between words. Reacting to her environment in some way. The baby sister inside Charlotte always felt discounted, her cries attributed to her immaturity and inexperience; the all-grown-up part of Charlotte made sure she was not only heard and seen, but appreciated and valued. She was the scarlet armchair in the middle of the room.

Hoping to draw LeRoy's attention, she shifted in her chair and tried to communicate encouragement with her eyes. At this moment, it was her job to listen and look.

"*Ahem* . . . well." He unlooped and looped his button. "Brenda wasn't too happy with me for missing that interview."

"So, you missed it altogether, which isn't what you said earlier. I bet that didn't go well since you didn't bother to show up!" She dug around her seat for her pen and leather-covered binder and finally spotted them on her desk where she'd left them.

LeRoy's entire body vibrated, and he fussed with his clothing. "I-I meant she . . . I was . . ." His hands worked with his vest until it draped open. "Please don't be angry. I'm sorry, Dr. Winters."

A chagrined Charlotte came to herself, realizing that she'd forgotten she was in therapist mode; she'd allowed her true self to jump into their session. *But girl, you better keep all four eyes on him,* she warned herself as she switched to the chocolaty leather ottoman between his seat and hers. She'd specifically positioned the three-square-foot piece of furniture right there for another client who seemed more comfortable propping his shoes on its rounded edge instead of letting them hover slightly above the floor. At that moment, it situated her close enough to LeRoy that she could almost pat his knee reassuringly. Almost.

"Oh, no, no, Lee-roy. I mean, Le*Roy*. Don't apologize. You merely surprised me by what you said. It was completely your decision not to go to the interview, and there's no need to explain yourself. Not to me, not to Charlotte." She didn't consider herself an authority but a help, so she always did away with titles in her client interactions.

He swallowed and his fingers continued to dance along the blue threads in the seams of his vest.

Charlotte inhaled deeply and rotated her hands counterclockwise toward him. Nodding slightly as she held her breath, she then exhaled on a count of ten before inhaling again on the same slow count. After a minute, he followed suit. Instead of focusing inward or on some happy place he envisioned, he pinned his eyes to her chest as it expanded and contracted. The urge to halt the exercise warred with the whisper of *retreat! retreat!*

Finally, LeRoy breathed normally and regained control of his fingers, though his eyes continued roaming. Beads of sweat sprinkled his forehead as he settled against the back of the sofa.

Charlotte spared a glance toward the door. To the left, a miniature grandfather clock ticked away the time as it perched on a small wood and wrought iron side table, one of Frankie's few good thrift store finds. All this hullabaloo had gulped down a huge chunk of their allotted forty-five minutes. "Better?"

He nodded.

"We still have a few minutes. In our remaining time, would you like to share with me about your talk with Brenda? The interview?"

LeRoy swallowed.

"I'll get you some tissues." Tapping her own warm forehead, she murmured, "I could use one too." She rose, presumably to reach the box on the corner of her desk, but really to put some space between them; the walls were starting to smush together. Charlotte tried not to flinch when her leg brushed his. *I didn't know we were that close. I should've known better than to sit on that ottoman.* When she took a second step, she bumped her ankle against the hard braid lining the ottoman, causing her to stumble in her three-inch wedges. She threw out a hand to catch herself and landed against something muscular. LeRoy. "Oh!"

"Hey there, little lady. I've got you." His voice was strong and low and close enough he could have swallowed the diamond studs in her earlobe.

Charlotte twisted away from the two sure and steady hands that gripped her and brought her close in an embrace. Wondering at their shakiness only a few moments before, she shoved LeRoy, which propelled her backward onto the ottoman. She landed on it, bounced, and her head rocked back. Before she could blink, he straddled the ottoman—and her—with his long legs. And that's when she saw his grin.

"You've been playing me, haven't you?" Charlotte barely could speak over the sudden glob of cottony spit lodged in the back of her throat. It was more anger than panic. "You've been playing me like a fiddle."

LeRoy's shoulders shuddered with his laughter. "Little lady—"

"Don't call me little lady." She forced herself to calm down and breathe slowly, much as she had thought she was teaching her client—no, this charlatan—while keeping her chest from heaving. "What do you think you're doing . . . Lee-roy?"

His lip curled. "What you've wanted me to, *Doctor.* You say you want to help me. Well . . . I can think of a way you can help me."

Charlotte couldn't make her body move as he started to crouch. But then her office phone rang, and he froze.

She used her elbows and feet to scramble backward from under him. Then she spun, popped off the ottoman, and strode around the back of the chair opposite him. *Her* chair. The nails of one hand dug into its nubby fabric, and the index finger of the other pointed at the office door. "If you touch me, I'll make sure you don't *help* anybody else. And I mean that. Do you understand me? Get out. We're done."

The phone rang again, and she marched to her desk and lifted the receiver. "Becky? . . . Oh, yes! She's right on time. Please, could you show her in and my 10:30 out?"

LeRoy stared right at her, unblinking, as he thrust his hands into the front pockets of his slacks. His unbuttoned vest hung open, and his black checkered suit jacket flared out like a cape.

Charlotte buttressed her weight on the five fingertips pressed to her desktop. When her assistant tapped on the door and opened it, she managed to keep her voice steady. "Becky, we need to close his file. If I was a bettin' woman, I'd guess his wife's too."

"You know, Doctor, your wig's crooked," he sneered, and nudging aside the tufted ottoman with his toe, he sauntered from her office, forcing Annabelle to press against the door to make room for him.

Charlotte backed against her desk to support her shaky legs and shrugged at her wide-eyed sister. "You don't know how glad I am to see you! Never thought you'd hear me say that, did you?"

Chapter Nineteen

"ARE YOU OKAY, CHARLOTTE?" Max reached around the copper vessel centered on their table at Biscuits & Boogaloo and squeezed her wrist.

She twirled her braids together and secured her hair with an elastic cloth band. "Yes. No. Well, I will be." She braced an elbow on the table and propped her chin on a fist. Managing a smile that was much tighter than the bun at the nape of her neck, she tried to focus on the soft music emanating through the small restaurant as she toyed with the knife balanced on her bread plate. As much as she usually enjoyed jazz, the live band did nothing to loosen the muscles at the top of her shoulders. In fact, the harder Charlotte worked to relax, the more her deltoids tightened.

Her knife clattered against the empty glass, and the foursome on Charlotte's left briefly looked her way before returning to their animated discussion.

The candlelight flickered off the barely-there silver strands at Max's temples, the only hint that he had her by nearly ten years. "Need me to take care of him? I will, you know. And I have three brothers who're much bigger than I am, and older and wiser too. They could fly over like that." He snapped his long fingers, obviously uncaring about the sidelong glances cast their way. His eyes were only for her, as usual. "We won't leave a shred of evidence."

Though he delivered it lightheartedly, Charlotte detected the serious edge in his softly accented offer. She laced her fingers together and rested her hands beside his, admiring the way their complexions complemented each other, standing out against the stark white damask tablecloth. "I bet you wouldn't, Maximilian, but you don't even know this dude's name."

"That is correct. But you could change that. Just say the word." The serious look in his eyes belied the curve that played with his soft lips.

"And break every rule in the book? No, thank you. As much as I'd love to wipe the smirk off that man's face . . ." She sighed, knowing she'd probably already revealed too much by the rule of professional ethics. Not only was she angry; she was ashamed she'd fallen for LeRoy's deception. And she refused to add *unlicensed* to the list of adjectives. Charlotte shook off his expression and his comment about her hair.

"Let it go, darling. From what you've told me, which wasn't nearly enough, your sister saved the day, and you had the opportunity to have a decent talk with her. You did nothing more than trust your patient—" he held up his palm, his way of quieting her—"I mean, client. What he did with your trust was all on him."

But it wasn't, not as far as Charlotte was concerned. She had a duty to protect herself, to guard the heart her mama had done her best to break. Thanks to Mayhelen's open-door policy, one man after another had tramped at will in and out of their lives, but Charlotte had more sense than that. More pride. More determination. She didn't need to see her value reflected in another man's eyes to convince her that she had any. No way would she become a victim of any person—whether it be a client or a sister—and become a star in her own personal *Lifetime* movie.

Her eyes lingered on Max's angular jawline and the five o'clock shadow that grew in by three. *Not even if that man is as cute as the dickens and is like no man I've ever known.*

Max ran a tapered, manicured finger along the side of her face. He gently tugged a braid that must have escaped her hair tie. "What is it? You're thinking about something."

"Me? I'm thinkin' about how hungry I am. Where is our server?" Charlotte made a show of craning her head to peer around the room, thereby escaping his touch. Men and women in black shirts and pants, white aprons tied around their waists, visited tables around them. A jazz ensemble on the far side, opposite a wall of windows, launched into an instrumental version of an Anita Baker tune, and three couples strolled to the dimly hardwood square that settled for a dance floor.

"Does that mean you plan to eat tonight?" He crossed his arms and leaned on them, putting his face a foot or two away from hers. The sparkles in his eyes mirrored the candlelight on the table.

Charlotte reared back in her seat, brows raised over her glasses. She'd had about enough of a man thinking he could invade her space.

Max matched her look. "If you're trying to look innocent as well as beautiful in that orange jumpsuit, I should tell you you're only half-successful. Guess which side is working," he chuckled. "I don't think I've seen that outfit before, what I can see of it under that sheer thingamajig you're wearing."

He was so perceptive it hurt sometimes, especially when she was trying to hide in plain sight. "I went shopping the other day and came upon this sleeveless number." She pinched the sheer fabric of the pale duster she wore and held it open to show off the pantsuit underneath. "You like?" The jumpsuit hugged her in all the right places but the last thing she felt was innocent. Not after the fiasco this afternoon. There had to be a reason LeRoy thought she was either weak-minded enough to fall for his schemes or desperate enough to be amenable to his advances. What made it worse was getting rescued by Annabelle. *Ever the baby.*

"I do like. It was made for you. Too bad it doesn't lift your spirits the way it brightens your face—since I haven't been able to do that tonight." Again, Max rested his hand on hers.

Charlotte slid it out to reach for her ice water. Condensation was running down the sides of the glass. "That's not your job, Max."

"What's not my job? Making my girlfriend feel better?" He sat up straighter and signaled to someone behind his date. When the server approached the table, Max asked for more tea. The two of them sat silently while the woman refilled his glass.

Charlotte's heart pounded, watching his mouth on the rim, and she turned away for a second and gathered herself. "What's up with the label?"

Max set down his tea and licked the moisture off his top lip. "I'd prefer fiancée or wife, but I'll settle for girlfriend . . . for the moment."

Her stomach flip-flopped. She'd sensed such a prospect loomed on the horizon, the opportunity to trade up her watch for a ring. "Max, I'm serious! Mama gave me the only title you have the right to use, and that's my name: Charlotte Winters. I don't need any other designation." She closed her duster.

At first, his response was to offer his profile. His nostrils flaring slightly, his eyes followed the men and women swaying across the room as the saxophonist leaned into his solo. When Max faced her again, his expression had softened but revealed nothing. "Did your mama pass down any dance moves along with that beautiful name, *Charlotte Winters*?" He stood and waited beside the table, his fingers playing the tablecloth like a keyboard.

It took five heartbeats for her to scoot back her chair and another for her to decide to tuck her arm through his. They eased around other tables and did the two-step with the waitstaff as they wound their way to the dance floor. When he drew her to him, only a breath could fit between them as they moved to the beat of the percussionist's brush swishing the cymbals.

This is where they'd met, at Biscuits & Boogaloo. Max was sitting amidst his three brothers, two sisters, parents, and his grandmother, celebrating a real estate deal. Charlotte was sitting alone that Saturday morning, eating brunch in the corner spot he'd come to call theirs. She'd watched the group toast and sing, taking over the restaurant with their effusive laughter and noise and joy. Max had implored her to join them after he'd spotted her solitary figure nursing what he'd called "sweet tea."

"It's just tea," she'd corrected him after he'd crossed the room to order her a refill.

His thick eyebrows had questioned her without his mouth uttering a word.

Charlotte had squinted up at the handsome man whose smile competed with the light shining behind him. It was hard restraining an answering smile, but she just couldn't give in to it. "You're in North Carolina. Saying 'sweet tea' is redundant, like calling it pork bacon or a beef burger. You wouldn't order me wet water, and you don't need to call it sweet tea, especially not when you're throwing down on soul food."

She'd started feeling rather contrary the moment he introduced himself, and she couldn't explain why. But Maximilian Demos seemed to enjoy rubbing up against her sandpapery personality, as did the rest of his family once he'd convinced her to sip her tea at their table. Maybe it was his confidence, the authority he exuded, and how something inside her had yielded to it. Or maybe she'd sensed from the beginning how difficult it would be to extricate herself when the time came. Because the time had to come.

At the final tinkling of the piano keys, Max whirled her away from him until their fingertips barely tickled each other. Breathlessly she shimmied back into his arms, the shimmery featherlight fabric swinging wide behind her, and kissed him on the cheek. "You're good at that."

He cupped her face and pressed his lips to hers. "You make me good at that."

This time, she snuggled close to his side as they followed the other dancers from the floor. As soon as he'd slid her seat under the table, the server set a basket and a dish of melting butter between them. Max peeled back the cloth and withdrew half a biscuit, the way B & B served their standard appetizer—presliced and ready to share.

She shook her head. "No thanks."

He inched the dish toward her side of the table.

Charlotte pushed it back. The girl inside her who'd eaten at Miss Hattie's table wanted to dive into the butter pooling in the dish. It appealed to her Southern tastes more than any puddle of olive oil other restaurants served.

He placed a circle of house-made bread in his palm. "Why not? It's good. Still warm, fresh." Max wiggled his eyebrows. "Like a certain Greek man I know."

"I'm well aware, Max," Charlotte chuckled. "But a moment on

the lips . . ." She murmured before she gulped down the rest of her words along with some of her ice water.

"Is a lifetime on the hips. Is that what you were going to say?" He slathered herb-seasoned butter on what remained of his piece.

She watched his slow, deliberate movements. "Yes, but a gentleman wouldn't point that out."

He pierced her with his deep-set eyes. "A man who loved you would, a man who knew you. That man would also tell you that you need the bread more than you need that jacket thingie you're wearing."

"If my mama was here, she wouldn't say that. I suppose she loved me and knew me, though my sisters debate it." Charlotte swallowed. "According to Frankie, she thought girls should order a salad and take their time with it, then order something small but expensive and eat most of it at home. Mama would say, 'You better keep on that fancy jacket because it covers up a multitude of sins. And if you don't do nothin' else, stay away from the bread.'"

"Are those your memories, or your sisters'?"

"One and the same, if they're to be trusted. And since they've been in my life longer, then . . ."

The music played in the silence before he spoke. "If that's the case, darling, it's a good thing your mama isn't here."

Charlotte snorted and murmured, "You ain't never lied." Louder, she averred, "But I'm still not having any of those biscuits. I don't care if B & B is famous for them."

Max tucked the cloth around the rest of the bread and brushed his hands together. Then he tapped the bump on the bridge of his nose, the barely-there hump that made his face a little less perfect and a lot more attractive to Charlotte. "What would you say if I told you I was thinking of getting this straightened?"

"I'd say that's all of your business and none of mine." She

shrugged. "I don't know why you'd want to do that since you wear it so well. Your nose is perfect on you."

"Because when I see it, I think of the day it got broken. It started with me losing my temper and getting in a fight in high school. Which meant the headmaster had to call my parents. They weren't at home, so he had to contact my *ya-ya*." Max bobbed his head to show how each event led to another. "Because she was at the restaurant, she sent my *pappouli*." His voice grew husky. "Who was hit by a truck on the way, and he never made it to the high school to pick up his hardheaded grandson."

Charlotte sucked in a breath. "Max . . ."

Eyes wistful, he seemed to leave the present, but in a blink he traveled back to the restaurant, to her. He pressed a thumb to the outer corner of an eye. "So, this bump isn't so perfect, is it? It does remind me that nothing . . . no one . . . ever is, and that the past can't be changed as much as we want it to be so. However, we can learn from these bumps and bruises, because they are part of our God's perfect design for us."

"Max," she repeated, in a different tone, looking about her. This wasn't the right time and place for a sermon, however aptly delivered.

"Speaking of *perfect*, I think your curves are quite perfect on you." He played with the hairs on the back of her arm. "So, too, your prickliness and your independence. Your boldness. I love all those things about you . . . and the you that's in all those things."

Mmm, that was good. Mama would have fallen for this smooth talker, no doubt, and had a gorgeous little baby with dark hair. Yet Charlotte's skin tingled, and her heart felt all melty, like the butter filling the center of the dish. No part of her believed Max was using his words to wind his way past her front door, about as far as he'd gotten in her townhome. She'd dragged him to every spot in eastern North Carolina, and he'd gone willingly, no questions asked, without demanding more.

"Remember that friend of the family I told you about?" Her fingers danced near his.

"Miss Hattie?" Max's pinkie looped around hers.

"She was as skilled as you are about simultaneously tappin' my hand and kissin' my cheek." Charlotte adopted a subtle Southern drawl.

"I wish I could meet this Miss Hattie because she sounds like my *ya-ya*. Wise women, those two. I'd rather serve up a gentle rebuke from this bread basket than carefully conceal my love in a bouquet of roses."

The familiar-sounding words eased the tension in Charlotte's shoulders, something the music hadn't accomplished in the forty-five minutes they'd huddled together in their favorite corner of the restaurant. "Well, I don't like thinking of my hips . . . my curves. And I don't know how I feel about you looking at them."

He interlaced their two hands. "In time, I hope you get used to it."

Actually, Charlotte was starting to think she could. Before she could respond, the server appeared at the side of their table, pad and pen in hand. Having not even peeked at the menu, she grimaced as she listened to Max order chicken-fried steak without gravy and a side of succotash.

Once he finished, he threw his head back in a boisterous laugh that ran in his family, his teeth glinting in the muted overhead light. "Why are you pretending you need more time? You always order the same thing!"

Her teeth clicked together once, twice, and she closed her eyes and pressed her finger to the menu. When she opened them, she read, "The half honey-fried chicken is what I'll order for my entrée.

And for the table we'll have the sweet potato casserole, greens, and mac and cheese." Charlotte lifted the basket along with her menu, her lips a smug, flat line. "We'd love a fresh order of biscuits too. Thank you." *That oughtta shut him up.*

The server padded away in her black loafers. To Charlotte, the burgeoning silence between them sounded louder than the surrounding conversations and muted the horn accompanying the double bass. She brushed at the crumbs on the cloth as she searched for something to say.

Max beat her to it. "So, does your mama have any other wise words you'd like to share with me? I feel like I know your sisters, but this is the most you've talked about your mama."

Charlotte liked the way he said *mama*, but how she felt about the word—and the woman—confused her. "You know more about my sisters than they know about you," she admitted. "And what I said earlier pretty much sums up her parenting." She moved her hands when the server set down a new basket.

"I haven't wanted to pry, and frankly I've made some assumptions when it came to your parents. But I think it's time I got to know more about your family."

"Oh, you do, do you?" Charlotte's mouth watered as she folded back the cloth and grasped one of the fluffy, warm pillows of bread. She loaded its crevices with butter and took a bite.

"I do." Max watched her savor her first biscuit in months. "One of my assumptions is that you didn't talk to her much before . . ."

Watching him flail about, searching for a word easier on her ears, Charlotte decided to throw him a life raft. "Before she died, you mean. *D-i-e-d.* Maybe if our memories of Mama weren't so hard for us to live with, that word would be easier to say. We could finally lay her to rest."

He dabbed at her lip with his napkin.

Before he could withdraw, Charlotte clutched his hand and let his cloth fall to the table. The candle flickered and nearly blew out. She spanned the table with her other arm.

His lips immediately parted when her fingers reached his mouth.

Charlotte gently popped a pinch of bread between his lips, and she watched him slowly chew it. "You know, I hadn't spoken to my mother for almost three decades, and then she reached out to me a few months before she died. I decided to tell Annabelle earlier today when she stopped by, which means that now I need to tell Frankie. I thought Annabelle would be jealous or, I don't know. Something. She did remind me that Greg . . . my baby brother . . . he would've been twenty-seven now. When I decide it's time for you to get to know my sisters, they'll probably have plenty more to say about him."

Chapter Twenty

Then

THE RAIN WAS WORSE THAN THE DARK. Most nights, Charlotte would lie in her half of the double bed Annabelle kept empty for her, peering into the inky blackness of the large center hallway outside her room. Sometimes, there was a crack of light under their mama's door, and she'd focus on that until she could no longer fight the weight of sleep pressing on her eyelids and they finally closed. But not that night.

Heavy raindrops were pummeling the roof and tiny hailstones were pelting the thin windowpanes. Annabelle had mumbled reassurances to Charlotte before drifting off herself, her arm a dense blanket draped across her little sister's chest, but Charlotte would have no part of that meager comfort. She'd convinced herself that the end of the world was upon them, and all the patters and thumps were the sounds of the devil and his legion landing on their house. And he looked just like Old Red Slewfoot, the name Miss Hattie gave him when she pointed to him in her giant, illustrated family Bible.

The sliver of light under her mama's door didn't help a bit that night. The shouting traveled farther down the hall, past Frankie's room. How her big sister slept all alone, through the name-calling and swear words, Charlotte couldn't fathom.

"I told you before we got married, I didn't want no more children runnin' 'round here," their newest uncle growled.

Somehow, his voice sounded deeper in the dark. Charlotte could feel it even deep in the pit of her stomach, that hungry place that Frankie's thin peanut butter and jelly sandwich hadn't satisfied. She turned on her left side and her sister's arm flopped to the bed, allowing Charlotte to pull up the checkered blanket so that it met her nose but didn't cover her eyes. That way she could keep staring . . . at whatever might come through the doorway. She and the long-legged girl snoring softly beside her were two of those "children" they were fussing about; Frankie was another. *But who is the "more"?*

"I know, honey." Her mama's voice was smooth as silk.

No. Satin. Charlotte had read about silk in the *Ranger Rick* magazine at school, and it talked mostly about the worms. She didn't like to spend time picturing their fat, squirmy bodies, so she decided that Mayhelen's voice was soft like one of those satiny nightgowns Charlotte played dress-up in when her mama wasn't home.

Should I wake up Annabelle? Since he doesn't want kids around here, are we gonna get kicked out the house? Charlotte pictured herself having to face all those waterlogged demons dancing on their roof that very minute and started to shake. She had to forcibly hold herself still under the sheets and the coarse blanket that made her itch when it touched her bare skin, so she could concentrate on the conversation across the hall. Frankie called it "ear droppin'," but Annabelle said sometimes listening in wasn't rude if it was for a good reason. Charlotte thought this time, keeping her and her sisters safe was one of the best reasons in the world.

"Don't 'I know, honey' me. If you knew, then how'd this happen? It don't make sense. As if there's not enough mouths to feed up in this house." His voice was gruff.

"But we've got plenty room, and we're not hurting for money. Where are you going? Come on, honey, don't be like that. You won't have any problems, I promise. This baby won't change a thing between us . . ."

Upon hearing Mama's wheedling voice, Charlotte relaxed her grip on her blanket and sat straight up in bed, causing the covers to slide down to her waist. From the sounds of it, nobody was going anywhere, at least not the girls, but did Mama just say *ba—*

"Charlie!" Her sister's hiss sliced through the dark. "Lay down before they come out and see you. Then there'll really be trouble. Next time, I'm-a make you stay in your own bed in your own room. I see why Frankie doesn't sleep with you."

Charlotte slowly sank onto the pillow they were sharing and lay still, allowing Annabelle to yank the blanket up to her chin and tuck it around her shoulders before she spoke. "Did you hear—?"

"Shh. What'd I say? I didn't need to hear it 'cause it wasn't news to me. You know how Mama is. He needed a reason to stay and she gave him one. Same as with you, and probably same as me and Frankie. We just weren't old enough to know anything about it then."

Bewilderment shooed away Charlotte's fear and took up residence in the empty space it left behind. "But . . ."

After a silent moment or two, Annabelle shifted to her side, in her younger sister's direction. The older girl seemed to be holding her breath, as if she expected Charlotte to fill the hole her three-letter conjunction had dug.

Yet the dark only held questions now, not answers, bigger questions than Charlotte's immature mind could squirm around and get a grip on. And the conversation growing in volume around the corner from their room only heaped more confusion onto the growing pile in her head.

"What did you expect? It takes two to tango."

"What I expected was for you to make sure this didn't happen, that's what. In fact, you told me it couldn't. That's why we decided to *tango* in the first place."

"Well, everybody makes mistakes."

"Not ones that cost this much. Get your hands off me, Mayhelen. I mean it. That's not going to work this time."

Charlotte jumped, and she squinted at the doorway. *What was that?*

Annabelle shook Charlotte's shoulder. "Shhh. I bet it's Frankie."

The faint moonlight peeping around the window shades revealed the bumpy outline of the scarf tied over their oldest sister's hair rollers. The wood floor creaked as she skittered across it and climbed in the bed, taking up what little room Charlotte and Annabelle had left. She snuggled the youngest Winters girl. "I knew you'd be in here, ear droppin'. It won't do you no good since you can't change nothin'. Mornin's gonna be here faster than you know it, and you're not gonna want to get up for school. If you miss the bus, you'll have to walk, and you'll do it by yourself."

Frankie's warm, slightly stale breath tickled her nose, Charlotte was curled up so close to her, and she took comfort in her oldest sister's steady presence. Something inside Charlotte recognized that Frankie cared enough to fuss at her, not about her. And she most definitely didn't want to walk the long way to school because there were sure to be deep puddles after that night's rain. Charlotte scooted low in the bed as the late-April storm picked up in intensity, drowning out all the talking coming from their mama's bedroom.

"Girl, you better be glad for all this rain and the dark you claim to be afraid of." Annabelle's arm encircled Charlotte from the other side, and the three girls settled into the embrace. She didn't move when Charlotte's head bumped against her own. "Otherwise, we might find ourselves at the park."

Chapter Twenty-One

Now

"ARE WE THERE YET, MOMMY?"

Annabelle closed her eyes and counted to ten before turning to study the small, scrunched-up face in the back row. "Henry."

Oliver squeezed her knee and glanced in the rearview mirror. "Almost there, son. Closer than we were when you asked . . . let's see—" he peered at the clock on the dashboard—"about five minutes ago."

She laid her hand on top of her husband's to get his attention and lowered her voice to a near whisper, making it for Oliver's ears only. "You're so patient. Every time we get in the car for more than ten minutes, it's the same thing. I don't know how you do it. Talk about love suffering long." Annabelle flicked imaginary sweat from her brow.

"Good thing. Sometimes it takes people a while to get the picture, to understand we're all going somewhere together and we'll get there in time, so to speak." His dark-brown eyes met hers for only a second before returning to Interstate 40 and the traffic zooming by them.

Ouch! Chagrined, she took a deep breath. Their conversation about the rescheduled doctor's appointment had adhered to them both; it would be a long time before she wiggled free from its clutches. Not that she wasn't grateful Oliver had spoken up. If he hadn't, he wouldn't have been there to take the fetal Doppler from Dr. Nagele and press it to the small, rounded hill of her abdomen. The wonder in his eyes upon detecting the whoosh-whoosh of their baby's heartbeat . . . ! She'd never forget it.

Grateful for Oliver's patience, Annabelle flipped her hand palm up and interlaced her fingers with her husband's, absently studying the squiggly lines on his knuckles and the broken fingernails. She couldn't wait to play the recording for Henry, now that she was into her second trimester and wasn't so worried about miscarrying. They were planning the right moment to tell their little boy and Oliver's parents. Once they did, she and Oliver would have to prepare themselves, knowing Henry would blab their family's news to random strangers. *Lord knows, that boy can't walk through the grocery store without telling the clerk spraying the vegetables about the new dog he's asking for, let alone keep the news of a baby brother or sister to himself.*

Oliver squeezed her hand. His eyes crinkled at the corners, as if he was ready to laugh along at whatever was secretly tickling her. "What?"

"Chicken butt," Henry piped up from the back, giggling.

Annabelle peeked around her headrest and aimed an index finger at him. "Oooh, that's a quarter! You said b-u-t-t!"

"But I—"

"Ah, you did it again. Ch-ching! That sounds like money in the bank. More pizza for me!"

"Daddy, isn't that cheating?"

"That's fifty cents, buddy. Rules are rules. But—" She clapped a hand over her mouth, which elicited a peal of laughter from the back seat.

Lips pursed, Oliver mouthed *poor sport* in his wife's direction but directed his comments toward Henry. "We'll work something out. I'm sure Mommy will compromise. Everybody makes mistakes, right?"

Annabelle used their tethered hands to shield her face from their five-year-old, then stuck out the tip of her tongue and crossed her eyes. That was what she thought of Oliver's question that wasn't a question.

For the next mile or two they rode in silence, but Annabelle couldn't keep her mind from racing from one momentous life event to the next. Some of those thoughts wiggled through her mind and squeaked through her lips before she could contain them. "Let's hope she made a mistake about the sex of the baby. Can you believe that Dr. Nagele is relying on some folkloric nonsense about the baby's heart rate to determine the sex?" Hoping it wasn't too late, she glanced back to make sure Henry was occupied with his coloring books and crayons, then blasted the volume of the Brooklyn Tabernacle Choir playlist they were listening to.

After her one-on-one with her obstetrician that day, Annabelle had finally changed into the blue paper gown and hopped up on the examination table. Arlene had given her a moment to dry her eyes before calling in Oliver so she could perform the ultrasound and use the Doppler. Once she took a few measurements and listened to the baby's heartbeat with her own stethoscope,

Dr. Nagele had pronounced that as far as she was concerned, the baby was a girl.

"I know you want a boy," Oliver said now, the volume of his voice several notches below hers. He withdrew his hand and wrapped it around the steering wheel as he navigated around a large tire retread spinning in the middle of their lane.

The spot on Annabelle's thigh immediately felt bereft and cold, and she missed the pressure of his palm on her skin. "I don't know, Ollie. I think I've had more than my share of estrogen, what with growing up with four girls under one roof. I guess we'll have to see."

"You do know having a son won't replace the baby brother you lost."

Annabelle pictured a suspicious buzzing object hanging from a tree. Deciding it was best not to poke the thought to investigate further, she nodded and counted the dashed lines separating the lanes on the highway.

"Welp, let's see what the Lord says." Oliver was holding out for the big reveal that came after hours of eye-bulging pushing, screaming, and sweating—the way Annabelle visualized herself as a laboring mother. "I feel the same way about that amniocentesis. I've been researching it since the moment I was banished to the waiting room before you called me back for your exam."

Annabelle laid an arm across the back of his seat and played with the fine bristles of hair at the nape of his neck. "I agree. No need to take unnecessary chances with our little guy."

Oliver scrunched his shoulders and smiled a little when Annabelle hit a sensitive spot low on his hairline. "You'd better watch it. I'm trying to drive safely, young lady."

She thought about her private conversation with her obstetrician. "Are you worried about our genetic counseling? I don't have much to share when it comes to my family background."

He pressed the accelerator and zoomed by a car. "Not at all. Our Father God is faithful, and He knows how to fill all the blanks in your answers. We have to trust everything's good with Baby McMillan, but if it's His will that we need to prepare ourselves . . ." This time, his shrug had nothing to do with being tickled.

"Prepare ourselves for a girl?" she teased. Annabelle sensed he was talking about more serious matters, but she opted to reroute the discussion from veering off on those alarming roads. "From my experience, the best place for sugar and spice is in my chai tea." While she was of the opinion that learning she would deliver a baby as a forty-year-old was enough of a shock, she'd agreed to let Oliver have his way and let the baby's sex remain a mystery. For now.

"Huh? What is that supposed to mean?" Brows furrowed, he raised the turn signal and navigated the car toward the next off-ramp. "We'll be at the stone yard in about ten minutes, Henry."

Annabelle matched his normal speaking voice, signaling their private discussion was over. "You know, the old adage promising that girls are 'sugar and spice and everything nice.' Give me some puppy dog tails any day." Annabelle decreased the volume of the music playing on the speakers so the choir's rendition of "Psalm 34" no longer masked their conversation and looked around her headrest. "Right, Henry?"

"Right, Mommy."

"Awww, you'll agree to anything that has somethin' to do with a dog. That's a lot of trust you're putting in your mom. I bet you don't even know what she's talking about."

"Yes, I do!" The child bounced in his booster seat, making it rock so hard it nearly tilted over on its side. "We read a book of poems at the library, something about a goose."

"Mother Goose?" Glad that he remembered their time together, Annabelle's prompting was gentle, not corrective.

"Nice. The library, huh?" Oliver's eyes posed an unspoken request, hinting at the long-standing discussion between him and his wife.

She crossed her arms and looked out her window, noting the signs marking the upcoming exit. This way for Bojangles, Krispy Kreme, Chick-fil-A; that way for McDonald's, Popeyes, and Sheetz. How to avoid their discussion wasn't so clearly marked. "I know you and Frankie have put your heads together on this homeschooling business, but don't get your hopes up, Oliver. That's for my sister and her family. I can teach Henry plenty of important things without adding math and history and science experiments. Sometimes a library trip is just a library trip. We were signing up for the summer reading program that'll get kicked off in a couple weeks. That's all."

"But he doesn't know how to read yet." Oliver turned on his signal and took the exit. He slowed the car as he approached the stop sign at the top of the ramp, then turned right.

"But you can read to me, and that counts too!" Henry had danced in the aisle between the book stacks when he heard that even running around outside, playing board games, and other fun activities were included in the program.

Helping Henry learn to read was like using her hand to separate the egg white from the yolk. It was certainly possible; people did it all the time. Still, Annabelle often made a mess of it, inexpert teacher that she was and sensitive student that he was. Processing the English language was much different from relishing it, reading it, and consuming it. As she witnessed him wrestling over letter recognition and all the sounds associated with his ABCs, she ached to say the words—but not out of impatience. She considered

Henry the next leg of the relay, and she desperately wanted him to grasp the baton she set in his hands and watch him race away with it. To cheer for him when he won. Reading was one of her favorite things to do; it had helped her escape the realities of her childhood.

"And he can earn fun prizes just by trying." Annabelle lightly clapped her hands together to convey her excitement. The fact that her young son considered a book a hurdle to cross pained her, and she realized she'd communicated her frustration to him, something she was trying to fix by applauding his efforts instead of his accomplishments.

Oliver's eyes flicked to the rearview mirror and briefly locked with Henry's, unaware that beside him, Annabelle hungered for just as much encouragement. "That's great, Henry. I'm proud of you. Your grandma set aside an hour every night to read to me before bed, and then we'd say the Lord's Prayer together. I'd have you know I didn't read on my own until I was in third grade. Mama helped me with all my homework so I'd understand the directions. And that's okay. When I finally did it solo, it was in my own time, and to hear her tell it, I went from singing the ABC song to reading *War and Peace*."

Annabelle eyed Oliver. "Baby, you don't read *War and Peace* now."

He thunked her knuckle.

"Ow!" She shook her fingers and rubbed them.

"What about you, Mommy? Did your mommy read to you too?"

Annabelle let her hand fall into her lap and took in the changing landscape. When they'd first pulled off the interstate, they'd passed restaurants and strip malls and a Dollar General every two miles or so. Then came empty stretches between those small businesses. Now they were driving by a large high school with a stadium rising behind it, a nest of mobile homes surrounded by fields, and a large white house fronted by columns with horses and cows grazing to the right and left of it. Evenly spaced rows of ripening corn and alfalfa stretched for acres with swaths of newer, homogeneous houses sprouting side by side in the distance beyond them. Oliver slowed down as they approached a blinking traffic light.

Annabelle wasn't searching for the answer in the quiet; she knew what she could say—but she *wouldn't* say it. Not to the immature set of ears in the back row of Oliver's truck. They'd pick up on the hurt threading through her words, and his young mind would be unable to figure out that he had nothing to do with putting it there. Maybe one day, she'd sit him down alongside his little sister—that is, if the doctor had her way—and explain, *My mama didn't read jack diddly-squat to me, Henry. Except maybe the riot act. She didn't teach me my letters or show me how to write my name or braid my hair. She was too busy to help us do anything of consequence. Busy seeing to her own needs, reading up on how to catch a man in those fashion magazines she sold in her store, and leaving my sisters and me behind.*

She thought about the conversation in Charlotte's office. *And when Mama finally reached out to somebody, there still wasn't room enough in her heart for me. I learned to read because I had to, Henry. That was my only way out.* One day she might tell him some of that, but not this day.

"Mommy?" Henry's voice sounded faint, like it had to travel miles and miles to reach Annabelle's ears.

"Bella, are you all right? Is it my driving? Are you feeling nauseous?"

Miss Hattie would be too persnickety to let you get away with that. She'd say, "Oliver, the proper word is nauseated.*" I only know that because of all the hours I spent with her, learning what to do rather than what* not *to do. And I'm not talking about grammar.*

"Honey? Where'd you go?"

Annabelle twisted her body away from the window. "Sorry, I'm right here. I kinda got lost in the weeds for a minute. All this talk about reading has me thinking of a couple of games we could play on the way home that Henry might find fun, the ABC game or perhaps the 1-2-3 game. I can't believe we've never played them. In the first one, we try to find the letters of the alphabet on buildings or other cars, anything outside this one we're driving, and the first person to 'Z' wins. What do you think?"

She knew she was rambling, that her mouth was moving faster than the forty-five miles per hour Oliver was driving at the moment on that stretch of two-lane road, but Annabelle couldn't slow herself down. Of their own accord, more words fell headlong from between her lips. "If you don't like that one, we can try the numbers? It's kinda similar, but we can play as long or as little as we like. As I said, we do the same thing as in the ABC game, but we'll have to select a winning number like twenty-five or something like that? Nothing too high. Henry and I could team up and you could form your own, Oliver? Or we could play boys against the girl and make it a battle of the sexes. What do you think?" Even to her own ears, she didn't sound herself—too lighthearted, too many declaratives turned into interrogatives, too much effort exerted to make believers out of her audience.

At first, the only noise in the car was the *chu-chu-chug* of the F-150 lumbering to a stop on the blacktop and the click of the truck's signaling arm as they waited to turn left into the fabricators. Traffic passed them, headed in the opposite direction, back toward the interstate. On their right, a green sign pointed out that if they drove another twelve miles, they'd land in the heart of

Jasper, where Frankie and her family lived. Where Annabelle grew up and where her baby brother didn't get to.

She wondered if Oliver would call her bluff and ask her what she'd really been mulling over. She wasn't lying; she hadn't answered his question—*Where'd you go?* She'd used the present tense, not the past—*I'm right here*. Here. Now. The answer was never in the past as far as she was concerned.

Oliver reached across the console and squeezed her hand, and he didn't let go. His long look told her all she needed to know: she hadn't fooled him for one minute. Not one. "Both sound fun, Bella. What do you think, little man?"

Annabelle looked around her headrest to see if Henry was nodding or shaking his head instead of answering out loud, a habit of his. She squeezed Oliver's hand and tilted her head toward the back seat. "You can see for yourself what he's thinking. Or should I say, dreaming?"

Her husband again glanced in the rearview mirror, then smiled.

Henry must have given up hoping that his mother would respond to him. Head bobbing against the back of his booster seat, his eyes were closed and long lashes splayed across the tops of his cheeks. His mouth hung slightly ajar. He dropped into the world of dreams the way that only children and pregnant women could, going instantly from awake to asleep, without even intending to.

"My boy's worn out before we've even started tromping through this stone yard." Oliver crossed the road, and they heaved up and over the craters and humps marking the entrance of the gravel lot.

So's your girl, Annabelle thought to herself as she read the hand-painted sign, J & J Fabricators, and took a deep breath.

Chapter Twenty-Two

"SO, I DID SOMETHING, and I wanted to talk about it." Frankie set her baby in the bouncy swing hanging in the doorway between the kitchen and the dining room.

Was this 'something' to me or for me? Charlotte kicked off her shoes and shed her purse and keys, ignoring the twinge of suspicion about what lurked behind door number one, and opened door number two. "You did? Something good, I'm sure. Actually, I did something too, and I should talk to *you* about it."

Frankie bobbed the swing with her hand and threw a smile at MJ first before wrapping it around her sister. "My 'something' is pretty important. May I go first?"

"Does your 'something' have to do with Annabelle?" Frankie was doing her best to reestablish the sisterly bonds, stretched so far they threatened to snap. Feeling a bit peckish, Charlotte nudged the fruit around in the bowl on the bar to find a bruise-free apple.

"Annabelle? No. Why do you ask? She and Oliver are shoppin' for granite today." Frankie donned a stained apron and looped its long remaining string around her waist and knotted it.

"I thought they did that a couple weeks ago. Isn't that what you told me?" Charlotte had come at her sister's request but didn't have time for lollygagging while Frankie did dinner prep. Plus she wasn't in the mood to discuss a reconciliation or work through some nonsense over Annabelle. *It's not like she's planning to stick around anyway. No need for me to get attached when she's probably already planning to move on, like she always does. Poor Oliver. Or maybe this time, she'll take her family with her.*

"They were supposed to, but it conflicted with her prenatal appointment, and then there was a delay with the cabinets or something or other. That's for them to worry about though. Now, stop distractin' me. Don't you want to know what I did that was interesting?" Her voice was nearly lost in all her riffling through the pantry.

"Excuse me." Having rinsed her fruit, Charlotte bumped Frankie's backside to get a knife. "Actually, I'm more curious about what you're doing right now."

"Gettin' ready to fly an airplane." Her sister emerged, toting what appeared to be a sack of sweet potatoes. She held them aloft. "What do you think? I'm about to make dinner."

"Ugh, always with the jokes. I can see you're cooking. You said you wanted to talk, so . . ." Curiosity took over as she watched Frankie retrieve a large pot from the cabinet and set it beside the sink. "I thought you baked your candied yams? That requires an oven and a thirteen-by-nine dish, unless I'm crazy."

Frankie rinsed two of the potatoes and set them in the tall stainless steel pot before she answered. "Well, you are crazy, but yes, eventually, I'll put them in a casserole."

Charlotte's mouth dropped as her sister prepped what was left in the bag and filled the pot with water. "So, you boil the dickens out of the sweet potatoes and then stick them in the oven?" While the same electric stove had reared them all, Charlotte hadn't paid much attention to how things made it from the pantry to the plate. Her sisters always accused her of turning up her gentrified nose to their childhood recipes, but Max's love of soul food led her to risk Frankie's scorn. She couldn't believe this man had her thinking about domestic activities like cooking.

"That's so the syrup, butter, and sugar will candy." The clanking of the lid punctuated Frankie's answer.

"And you add syrup to the processed sugar? But aren't yams or sweet potatoes—whatever you call them—naturally sweet?"

Frankie planted a hand on a hip. "Maybe you need to take notes. Are you askin' for a friend?"

Charlotte didn't respond.

"Which reminds me . . . the something I did and saw. Remember me mentionin' that?"

Before Charlotte could say, MJ called out and snagged his mother's attention. Frankie danced over to the baby to make him laugh, a routine Charlotte had witnessed many times over. Her sister reset the dial and "Mary Had a Little Lamb" started playing again. She hurried back to the sink once his gurgles seemed to reassure her.

"Let's get out of the kitchen where he can see me. He'll never be satisfied seeing his food source busy doin' something else. I'm nothin' but a chicken wing to him. And you . . ." Frankie shook her head at Charlotte, "you don't have any business in here anyway. I can see why Miss Hattie always had you set the table at Thanksgiving. It kept your eyes busy and your mouth shut since you weren't much good around the stove."

Obviously satisfied that MJ wasn't about to hop from his bouncy seat and run through the house on stubby legs that had squishy rolls from his hips to his ankles, Frankie led the way toward the family room, her shoulders hunched as if she was trying to make herself as unobtrusive as possible. Two steps through the doorway, she snapped her fingers and half turned toward Charlotte. "Oh, I forgot to start the potatoes. Could you do that so the baby doesn't see me? Put them on low, and they'll come to a slow boil." She shooed Charlotte toward the kitchen.

Is that your attempt to whisper? Charlotte restrained a snort and did as she was told, yet she couldn't resist caressing the baby's cheek that was as juicy as his thighs. So scrumptious were they, she pursed her lips and blew a raspberry at the top of his leg, making him squeal as he sucked on his fists and beat a rhythm on the vinyl floor with his bare feet. While she wasn't one to bow the knee, MJ looked like he'd be the answer to anybody's prayer. She gave his foot a goodbye tickle once she'd completed her assignment, and hoping he wouldn't protest, she followed Frankie into the next room.

Charlotte found her balancing a hip against the back of the sofa, her arms crossed. "I can't believe you're takin' your eyes off him."

"I'm tryin' to get better about all my worryin'. I can hear him, and Leah'll be close by because she's comin' to the table to take a timed test."

Charlotte figured there was a catch to MJ's sudden independence. This mother was never far from her babies, which Charlotte of all people understood.

Frankie went on. "So, since you asked . . ."

"I didn't ask—"

"I went on a field trip." Frankie grinned. "And I felt like I was playin' a game of I spy."

Are her eyes twinkling? "O-k-a-a-y. Y'all went shopping at the new Walmart?" Charlotte was well acquainted with the homeschooler extraordinaire's one-word, four-letter mentality for spending money: don't. This family lived a relatively simple life and probably found a trip to the discount giant an adventure.

Frankie poked Charlotte's shoulder with her index finger. Not hard, but with enough force that said, *I know what you're thinking, and I don't appreciate it.*

"What? I appreciate your gift for . . . how do I say it . . . ? 'Building your savings.'" She puckered her lips as she made quotes in the air. "Which works for a large family, but . . ." Charlotte tried and failed to cloak her guilty tone with laughter. Frankie and Melvin Senior had always wanted a large family. Their mutual desire had drawn them together in their church's singles ministry twenty years ago.

"*But* you'd better take notes on how this large family gets things done is all I'm sayin'. One day, you'll be workin' on your own, little sister. At least, that's the feelin' I get based on what I saw on our field trip." Frankie sidled around the sofa and knelt at the coffee table in the middle of the area rug. She cupped her hand and used it to gently sweep the circles and pie slices off the Trivial Pursuit board before folding it up and setting it in the box. "Believe me, Melvin has to do a heck of a lot more than look at me to give me one of those." She aimed a finger in the direction of the baby cooing in the kitchen. "So, I know what I'm talkin' 'bout."

"Frankie!" Charlotte wasn't a prude, but her sister's frankness always took her aback.

"You know what I mean." Her voice matter-of-fact, she seemed preoccupied with fitting the small pie slices into the circles. "Sure, we may get pregnant pretty quickly, but it's much harder for me to carry the baby, to stay pregnant. If we hadn't wanted him to be a junior, we would've named MJ Samuel."

Charlotte hoped Frankie would assume that her noncommittal shrug communicated *I can see why you'd do that,* and not *I don't know why you would've named him that* because in fact, she had no idea of its significance. She had invested so much energy distancing herself from all things church-related that she hated to admit she'd succeeded.

"Samuel. Samuel? You know, Hannah's Samuel." Frankie froze before she could set the completed game pieces inside the box. "Charlotte, please tell me you know the story of Hannah and Eli and Israel's first prophet . . . ? Okay, never mind. You are the most unchurched person to ever sit in the pew." She rolled her eyes. "Oh, that's right. You don't sit in one now, despite all Miss Hattie's efforts."

Charlotte pursed her lips and waved a hand in her sister's direction. She aligned the magazines on the side table. The dog-eared copy of *Southern Living* reminded her of the sisterly meetup in the room a few weeks ago.

Frankie sighed and continued working on the game. "We prayed that baby into the world, believe me. All the bleedin' and crampin'. Early contractions. Bed rest. He took us on a journey from the moment we found out I was carrying him until the moment I pushed him into the world at thirty-four weeks along. He was our gift from God, and from the minute we locked eyes in that delivery room, I promised to give him back to Him.

"Most of what Mama gave us could fit in that pocketbook hangin' on the back of that chair over there, and the only person she ever gave us to was Miss Hattie. Certainly not the Lord or anything of any faith. We were burdens, not blessin's."

Charlotte ran her fingers along the books on the shelf, sliding a few into place. "Don't y'all get tired of all this rigmarole about what a terrible mother we had?"

Frankie's mouth dropped open and she fell back on her haunches. "What?"

"I don't mean any harm, Frankie, but Mama went through a lot—"

"You mean, she put us through a lot. One husband after another. Usin' me to parent. Abandonin' us."

"Or did you jump in when you didn't need to and push her away?"

"Jump in—?" Frankie's throat worked so hard she could've been swallowing a full Trivial Pursuit pie. "And if I hadn't, who would've helped you get ready for school, or make you dinner, put you to bed, take care of life's basic necessities . . . ? Or should I have stepped aside so you could've ended up like Greg?" She began tossing pastel-colored triangles into the box willy-nilly.

"I can't believe you'd say that." Though she very well could. It was just like Frankie to spout such thoughtless words without compunction.

Frankie closed her eyes and rubbed her forehead. "Maybe you think I'm makin' light of what happened, but heaven knows that's the last thing I'm doin'. And I'm not dwellin' in the past, if that's what you're tryin' to say." Her chest expanded then contracted. "I own *now*. Child, I downright own it. I'm not blamin' Mama for any of the choices I've made since then, but she's plenty responsible for the choices she made for me. Me, you, Annabelle, and yes, our little brother. And she won't ever own up to it, Charlie. How we were raised has affected our whole life. Where we lived—"

"Or didn't live." Charlotte couldn't help but draw an absent Annabelle into their conversation.

"Who we married . . . or didn't marry." Frankie nodded at her baby sister. "Whether or not we had kids—"

"And how many." Charlotte ducked at a stuffed animal chucked at her head. "Hey!"

"You want to be funny, but I'm serious!"

Charlotte tossed the bear into a bin in the corner, frustrated. She'd lost the gumption to bring up her conversations with their mother. "You're right," she conceded, tired. "Mama and all her shortcomings changed the trajectory of our lives. However, isn't that the way of any parent? Everybody's yes or no and absence or presence impacts someone or something else, to a greater or lesser extent."

"That's a lot of twisty-turny hogwash. You're sayin' a lot but not much of nothin'."

Charlotte balanced a hip on the arm of the leather chair. Her foot swung slowly. "Okay, I'll put it this way. You say God is in control, that He knows everything. What's His role if Mama had the power to completely ruin our lives?"

Frankie extended her legs under the coffee table, looking like she was going to be there a while. "I didn't say Mama had the power to ruin our lives. God is the only One with that kind of power. He's in control . . . over your life and mine. Over everything and everybody. How does the Proverb go? 'The king's heart is like a stream of water directed by the Lord; He guides it wherever He pleases.'"

Her eyes scanned the room, as if contemplating where the river's flow would carry her next. "But when it comes to His children, He uses everything that happens for our good."

Charlotte harrumphed. "Everything?"

"Everything, Charlie. Even Mayhelen's exploits."

"Even—"

"Yes, Greg's death too. Unbeknownst to my new homeschool friend, she's helping me understand that maybe we can't see it or don't know how, but that's where faith comes in. Trusting that He will use all the hardship, all the lack, all the pain . . . for our good. That He will provide for us and meet our deepest need." Frankie seemed to come back to herself. Her eyes, now moist, met her sister's. "He remains our Abba Father even when our earthly fathers and mothers abandon us, die, move away, or plain don't care."

"Well, if that's the case, then why are we still talking about all our dysfunction? If God took care of it?" Charlotte held out her hands, palms up.

Frankie shrugged, and her flattened lips responded, *I don't know.* "She didn't cover that. Too little time."

Charlotte laughed. "What? I know I didn't render *you* speechless, not the great Frances Mae Winters Livingstone. I would say we've reached an impasse."

"For one thing, you can drop the Winters. And for another, the Scripture says it all works to the good for God's children, for those who love Him and who are the called according to His purpose. I wouldn't call that an impasse."

Here Charlotte was, doing the very things she didn't have time to do: rehashing the past and debating matters of faith with this Holy Roller. "Listen, Frankie, there are two places I'm not goin' with you—and that's back and forth. Call it whatever you want. I have plans this evening."

Frankie looked like she wanted to say more. Typical. As the oldest, it seemed that was her purview. The second hand in the clock over the mantel traveled around its face one rotation before she spoke. "Let's say we've reached a crossroads, not an impasse. A junction of sorts. Maybe we've reached a place where we need to make some important decisions. I can try to let it go, as difficult as that may be. But what about you? Where do you go from here? I can think of two places myself." Frankie paused a beat before she pointed up and then down.

Charlotte cocked her head, trying to figure out what she meant. *North and South? Up or down?* Oh! Understanding dawned, and Charlotte narrowed her eyes. Her sister and her proselytizing. Charlotte's faith was her own, including the lack of it. Rubbing her thighs covered by her orange rayon sweatpants, she growled, "Frankie . . ."

She waved off the warning. "I know, I know. But I'm not your mama, and I love you too much to leave your life to chance."

MJ started to fuss.

"I've got him!" Charlotte threw her leg over the arm of the chair and hurried from the family room. She squatted to lift the baby out of his swing. "How do you get him out of this contraption?"

"You're the one with the PhD. You tell me." Frankie, a few steps behind her, edged by and continued around the bar into the kitchen, leaving Charlotte to fiddle alone with the straps. "I guess we might as well move onto touchy subject number two, since we've gone as far as we can with touchy subject number one."

MJ let out another squawk, obviously ready for freedom.

Charlotte squeezed and tugged before finally unlatching the safety harness. As she lifted him from the swing, she caught a whiff. "Ooh!"

He wailed. Either his auntie had startled him or he'd realized Charlotte wasn't his mommy.

Frankie made a move toward them, arms extended. "What is it?"

Holding her five-month-old nephew to her shoulder, Charlotte patted his back and murmured, "It's all right, baby boy. Shhh, come on, now. Mama's coming." She looked at Frankie. "Why haven't you taken him? I think he needs a change."

Frankie, who'd stopped a foot or two away from her younger sister, propped an elbow on the bar. "You know where the diapers are." She indicated the room they'd just exited. "In the cabinet to the left of the TV. If we're out, check his room. I've changed your diapers before; you owe me."

Charlotte's head shook slowly at first, but as her panic grew, it turned side to side more vigorously. "Nope, uh-uh. If anybody owes you, it's Mama."

"I thought we weren't goin' there anymore."

"You made that promise; I didn't. I'm the fun aunt. Leave this part to Annabelle. She needs the practice with poopy diapers that shouldn't stink, according to you. All that bragging about breastfed babies." She held out the wiggly infant, hoping his mother would take the hint—and him.

Instead, Frankie arched an eyebrow and resumed her position in front of the stove. "From what I could tell, you may need the practice too."

Charlotte gritted her teeth, held the baby closer, and stalked away. "What are you talking about, Frankie? I'm tired of all the teasers. You're worse than a movie trailer." Her voice trailed behind her, along with her anger. She enjoyed being with her nephews and nieces, but what she did with them was up to her, on her terms.

"That's my second thing . . . well, the *first* thing I mentioned, and you're now gettin' around to ask me. Your lack of curiosity isn't normal."

Her voice carried easily through the kitchen and into the family room where Charlotte was busy ransacking the cabinet for baby wipes. *How does Frankie do this with one hand?* MJ's fussiness became outright screams. Charlotte found what she was searching for and stomped back to the kitchen, clutching the baby, a diaper, and the box of wipes. "Do you know what else is abnormal?

Doing what you do twenty-four seven, plus teaching the kids, and keeping Melvin happy. I'm hiring you a nanny because *this* is abnormal."

"Abnormal? What's abnormal about takin' care of a family?" Frankie used a long spoon to shift the potatoes around in the bubbling water.

Charlotte plopped into a seat at the table and laid MJ on his back across her thighs. She held him down with one hand as his arms and legs flailed and his head thrashed. "Most people don't do what you're doing, Frankie."

"Maybe not. Nobody did what Jesus did for us, when He chose to die on the cross to take away my sin. So, honestly, I'll take that kind of abnormal over the way we used to live and the way we were loved." She set down the spoon and moved about the kitchen, collecting items in a large bowl—vanilla extract and salt, eggs, butter, and milk. She placed them beside the stove and revisited the pantry.

There she goes again. "I thought we weren't complaining about our childhood anymore, Frances Mae. We've stopped blaming Mama for what's wrong with our world." Charlotte taped closed MJ's diaper and snapped his onesie. She couldn't keep herself from smiling back at his contented face. *I guess I'd cry, too, if I had all that goin' on.* She shivered, picturing the smushed green-and-gold contents in the soiled diaper by her feet.

"I'm still at that junction, dear sister, between hurtin' and healin'. Give me time." Frankie opened a container, unleashing a puff of white. "And now that we're finally back to my original subject . . . my something interesting." She faced Charlotte, flour dotting her forehead and sprinkled all over the front of her apron. "I'd say not tellin' your bestie about the man in your life is pretty interesting and rather *abnormal.* Wouldn't you say? Y'all looked mighty cozy at the Museum of Art."

Chapter Twenty-Three

"WHAT ABOUT THAT ONE, BABE?"

Oliver's eyes followed his wife's rosy-tipped fingernail. "Nah, too much of an ocher vein. You'll get tired of that."

"Really? I thought it was more gold than ocher. Maybe it's this light, what there is of it." Annabelle had hoped they'd outrun the clouds when they set out that morning, but they had chased them all the way from their house.

She and Oliver were standing at the end of a row of granite slabs, one of the many lines of stone the two of them had explored over the past hour and a half. Jim, half of the "Js" who owned the twenty-five-year-old business, had excused himself from the search about forty minutes earlier, presumably to give the couple an opportunity to discuss their selections in private. The other half of "J & J"—Jackie—had absconded with Henry right from the start, as if she'd taken one look at the couple and sensed the process was going to take more than a little while.

"Hey, at least we're making headway!" Oliver declared, his smile a bit droopy at the edges yet still wedged to his face. That was his way, his perpetual glass-half-full manner of looking at life, even if he had to tilt his head—or the situation—to find its bright side. "We've ruled out more slabs than we have left to inspect, so we must be close to finding the McMillans' special piece. If J & J doesn't have what we want, then the granite must not exist." He nodded at the metal trailer that housed the office, where his son was probably stacking wooden blocks at that very moment. "Trust me, Bella. They've never let me down in all the years we've done business together."

"Then why didn't we start with them in the first place instead of going to those other places?" Annabelle grumbled. She adjusted her glasses and peered at the other side of the yard they'd covered earlier, and her shoulders slumped. For her, hope might trickle, but it certainly didn't spring eternal. "Oliver, come on. There're only two rows left. There's no way in the world we'll find the right granite for both the kitchen and the bathrooms this afternoon. No way."

He enfolded her with his long arms and rocked her from side to side. "Buck up, oh, you of little faith."

She thought about it then concluded, "My faith isn't meager. It's only a little wet behind the ears."

"Like our marriage, Mrs. McMillan. Now, let's go find our stone." He shuffled toward the next-to-last row of slabs, dragging her with him. "Start here while I ask Jim about new stock."

As Annabelle waited for her husband to return, she ran her finger along a wide black vein in a slab with a gray background and purplish splotches and swirls. Beautiful, but the coloring had a melancholy feel to it. And that was the last thing she wanted to feel—sad or depressed—when she walked into her kitchen.

Tomorrow brings enough cares of its own, and so does cooking, she concluded. The passage from that morning's devotional had stuck with her.

No, what she needed was warmth. Gold . . . cream . . . that was what she was looking for as she gazed down the row, rejecting one style after another without having to study any up close. *Seen it before. Ooh, way bold! Too much yellow.* Leaving her hand splayed against the smooth stone, her ears picked up on the familiar sound of Oliver's gait, crunching her way.

"Oh, I like that one too. Isn't that purple?"

Annabelle rotated toward him, a little afraid to hear what he had to say. "Uh-huh, that's purple. Are you thinking—?"

"That it's an interesting color? Yep. But it's too dark for our kitchen. Too . . . what's the word? Melancholy. I think that's what I'm looking for. Depressing. Okay for some, but I'm looking for a kitchen we can cook in, not look at." Oliver snorted, "Or encourage Henry to whine in. We need a happy hue so we can make happy food like chicken nuggets, hot dogs, and the occasional steak and baked potato." He linked his fingers with hers and began to stride down the aisle in his scuffed black boots.

Their locked arms stopped Oliver's forward motion, and he shuffled backward until they stood side by side. "What is it?"

Annabelle bumped his arm with her shoulder. "Nothing. I . . . sometimes it's clear we were meant to be."

Her smile found a twin on her husband's face. "You're just figurin' that out? Now, let's go. Jim said he has more inventory on that back lot he saves for his special people."

She fell into step with him. "Special, huh? So you've been there before?"

"Uh . . . yeah."

Annabelle noted the way he averted his face as he helped her around an iron frame anchoring a slab in place. "Oliver? I take it you're not talking about a client. Was Eleanor one of those 'special people'?" Eleanor, as in the first Mrs. McMillan. "Did you bring her here?"

His brisk pace slowed. "Not exactly."

"Then what exactly?" As if the weather forecast wasn't gloomy enough. Now, talk of his ex-wife was casting its own pall over the day.

"Jim and Jackie . . . he's her cousin. They're Eleanor's family."

She yanked on the cuff of his short-sleeved polo shirt, and Oliver's crawl came to a standstill. "Are you telling me we're buying granite from your in-laws? No, please don't tell me that. Please." A miniscule ball of saliva flew from her mouth and landed on his upper arm.

"They're not my in-laws, Bella—"

"Don't 'Bella' me. And stop splitting chin hairs, Oliver McMillan. You know what I mean."

He grabbed the tips of her fingers as she took a step back in the direction from which they'd tromped a few seconds before. "Wait. *Annabelle.* I'm sorry. Hey . . ." Oliver brought her close. "Yes, they *were* kinda like my in-laws for a couple years, but they've been my friends for decades. I was escorting clients through here long before I met Ellie . . . nor. Eleanor." His tongue tripped over the overly familiar version of his former wife's name. "They know what she was like, why she left me . . . us."

"Uh-huh. So you're saying at this very moment, they're hanging with Henry, a member of their family?" Her mouth and her brain had some catching up to do. "Which explains why you didn't start out with J & J, the 'best.' Did you think maybe I should've known that before we drove all the way out here?" Annabelle tried to stalk away, but tripped over that same iron frame Oliver had helped her over.

He caught her just before she landed in the mud. "Whoa! Annabelle, be careful. Don't let your anger make you forget you're carrying a baby in there."

His reminder brought her up short. Her mother was good for letting her emotions make her forget about her babies, and no way was Annabelle going to behave anything like Mayhelen Winters. Annabelle marveled at the way life continued around them, unaware that they were at odds with each other—not over color samples or backsplashes, but over old family business. People continued to mill around, by themselves, with quarrelsome children in tow, and as couples—like Annabelle and Oliver—while the slow, high-pitched *beep . . . beep . . . beep* of a delivery truck warned customers that it was backing up into the lot. She wished someone had provided a similar warning that this moment was coming.

"I get why you're uncomfortable, Annabelle, but there's almost no way to avoid family in this part of North Carolina. I'm probably kin to every other person in this county, one way or another. The same is true for you, too, for that matter. I guess you've been away so long you forgot about small-town life in the South."

"I get it, Oliver. Everybody and his mama could be our second cousin once removed. But that's different from letting your ex-wife's family babysit our boy while we shop for granite at the family business. Technically, Henry's more their relative than he is mine! Having a say in the matter is one thing, but you took that say away from me. You didn't give me a choice."

"I just don't think of them as family like that. Not anymore. That life is behind me."

She swallowed. The truck driver had climbed down from his cab and was ambling back to his trailer to raise the door. "At one time, life with me was behind you too."

"What are you talkin' about, wife?" His impatient tone announced he was about fed up with her shenanigans.

"I might be special enough for this secret stash of granite you were dragging me to, but not so special you wouldn't have let me go. 'Been there, divorced that.' Remember?"

A man wearing a white baseball cap with a Duke University insignia scrolled across it scooted by in the narrow aisle. He tipped his hat to them, and the ever-polite Oliver nodded back, though it was obvious to Annabelle her husband didn't see him. Like Annabelle, he was probably picturing himself ankle deep in the chilly waters off the Outer Banks, his pants rolled up to his knees.

On that early-November day more than two years ago, Oliver could've been tearing up from the brisk wind blowing sand into his eyes or he was already mourning the loss of what could've been between the two of them. He had professed his love for Annabelle a mere month after they met, but standing there in the cold surf, he was explaining why marrying her was out of the question:

"How does that saying go? 'Fool me once, shame on you . . . ?' I thought I could change my first wife by being good ol' Oliver, smiling at everything, not being pushy, waiting for things to get better. Praying. Going to church by myself. But do you know what, Annabelle? Even though God loved me, Eleanor sure didn't, and she left Henry and me to prove it. And I'm not going through that again, as much as I love you. Been there, divorced that."

According to Oliver, faith was the last thing his first wife thought she needed. When she left him to find real happiness—"Her words, not mine," he'd pointed out to Annabelle that day on the beach—he'd vowed never to make that same mistake of committing himself to someone who didn't share his belief in God as well as his love of family. He had Henry to think of. "So if you don't want that—and I don't mean to please me but for yourself—then we can't be a 'we.' The Lord has to be first in both our lives if we're going to move forward."

The memory of that scene around them—the surfers riding the waves of the Atlantic; the gulls squawking overhead, urging tourists to give them bread; the passing chatter of a couple running by with their wet dog—faded into the background. Planted in the muck at the fabricators, Annabelle relived their two-month "hiatus," what she called the period when they only communicated by telephoning each other once every week or so. Enough to make her yearn for him and develop a curiosity about this God Oliver loved more than he loved her. Annabelle knew he was weaning himself away from her, and the thought of losing him frightened her. Yet she resisted, refusing to get coerced into adopting a faith that belonged to someone else.

It wasn't that she didn't know who God was; in her mind, He belonged to other people. Miss Hattie had taken Frankie, Annabelle, and Charlotte to church with her sometimes on those Sundays when they were serving fried chicken, macaroni and cheese, and green beans between morning and afternoon service. In those days, the women in the church passed Charlotte around like she was the collection plate, showing her more attention during those three-hour services than she ever got within the walls of her own home. God looked like the missionaries wearing the white caps and long-sleeved blouses tucked into their knee-length skirts to Annabelle's immature eyes. They called each other Sister So-and-So and covered women's bare knees with shawls if they sat in the front row.

In the life-size chunk of time she and Oliver spent apart, however, God came to look like someone else. He came to sound like something more. While Annabelle was working full-time at a jewelry store, a customer walked in right before closing late one Monday afternoon and asked her to personalize a cross that belonged to her grandmother. Something about the woman's way led Annabelle to ask questions she'd never considered, to look inside herself and see the hurt as something she could lay down, if only for a minute or an hour. Hadn't this Jesus the customer was talking about carried His cross and left it behind . . . for good? If He could, then maybe she could too.

That "maybe" marked the beginning of her faith, not its limits, and during that time apart from Oliver she spent time drawing near to God. Eventually she'd come to think of church as a reflection of heaven, not a building on earth.

Oliver tucked Annabelle's hand in the crook of his elbow. He had to tug a bit to coax her into shuffling along beside him, albeit slowly. "What are you thinking about, or do I have to ask?"

She shrugged. "That . . . as perfectly made for each other as we seem to be, if I hadn't promised 'your people shall be my people, and your God, my God' before we exchanged our wedding vows, you would've walked away from me too. Isn't that the truth?"

"'Seem to be?'" He stopped and faced her. "I think the Lord has made it clear that He did join us together. You're stuck, baby, no doubt about it. You said "I do" to Him before you married me, and willingly, because He called you by name. Not because you wanted to change your last name to mine."

Annabelle peeled her gray eyes away from his. She wasn't sure she saw the truth, though her heart tried to assure her she'd heard it somewhere in that answer that wasn't an answer. A car lumbered through the open gates of J & J and crept through the parking lot that was nearly full with a minivan, a few SUVs and pickup trucks, and what looked like a Hummer. People hoping to remake their lives as they redid their kitchens, people like her.

"Bella. I don't know what's bangin' around in that mind of yours, but the look on your gorgeous face gives me some idea. Your mama really did a number on you." He started walking again. "Keep in mind that I'm not Mayhelen Winters."

Annabelle's chuckle was so dry it sounded more like a cough. "You'd best believe I know that. It's . . . well, I've learned from past experience that the death of a marriage is hard on everybody involved. And moving on doesn't mean you forget. Mama referenced her husbands' names countless times, and I don't think she loved any of 'em. Not a one."

"What does that have to do with me?" Apparently, Oliver struggled to see the connection.

They were crossing to the other side of the grounds, approaching the trailer where Jackie was watching their son. Eleanor's son by all respects. Sitting in the lap of the woman's family. Annabelle bit a dry, cracked corner of her lip, hating how small she felt at that moment, having to append *step-* to the *mother* she had embraced—like the *half-* she'd attached to *sister*. Would her life be punctuated by hyphens and brokenness?

"You actually loved her; you love the child your marriage produced. I imagine you're grieving over what you lost with your first wife as much I grieved over the lack of a family unit growing up and when I thought I'd lost you." *Is he still mourning that marriage?* She injected an offhand tone when she asked, "How often do you think of your first wife . . . Ellie? She had to come to mind the minute we planned this trip, and if not then, surely, the second we drove through the gate."

"Oh, I don't know. Not that much."

Not that much. How much is that? She trailed her fingers along a slab as they passed it.

Oliver squeezed their clasped hands with his free one, drawing her attention. "I'm sorry, Bella. You're right: I owed it to you to tell you about Jim and Jackie. That I met Eleanor here one day when I brought some customers out. They introduced us—quite reluctantly, I might add—because they could tell I was attracted to her. Right away they warned me she wasn't the one for me and told me from the very beginning that it wouldn't work out. They knew what I believed and what she didn't believe. By now, you know they were right."

Moving ahead of her, Oliver helped her navigate around the dips in the path and rough-edged slabs that jutted into it. His voice carried over his shoulder. "Getting married didn't keep me and Ellie together, and neither did getting pregnant right away or having our son. And I bet delivering the forecast all the way over on the West Coast ain't cuttin' it for her either, Bella. Only a love for Jesus could have changed Eleanor's heart for me and Henry, as well as for herself. To make Him and us what she wanted most in life. He was the third Person missing in our marriage—not a baby."

"I wonder what, or who, you think is missing in our marriage." Annabelle's voice was small enough she barely heard herself. Surely he hadn't, with all the activity in the yard around them.

Oliver's sigh had weight to it, and he gripped her fingers hard enough to hurt. Maybe that was the point. "Nothing is missing in our marriage, Annabelle."

Not now that I'm pregnant. This time, she made certain to keep that thought safe within the confines of her mind since he'd obviously heard what she thought was her heart's whisper. As she watched the muscles in his back ripple under his fitted ice-blue T-shirt, a little voice reminded her, *He never answered your question, did he?* What if the Lord up and told Oliver that Annabelle wasn't the right one for him and Henry? What if she lost her temper and muttered one too many four-letter words one day? *Would he leave me?*

"Of course I think about Eleanor. She's a part of Henry. We all talk; you participate in those conversations. But I don't think this is about Henry's mama." He dropped her hand to loop his arm around her shoulders, and he leaned his head to rest atop hers. "This is about yours . . . and you. I'm not Mayhelen, and you aren't Mayhelen. And Henry isn't the brother you lost."

"The brother she killed." His words were two major tectonic plates bumping against each other. She couldn't stop the hot flow of tears and emotion. "She was so addicted to herself, to what she wanted, she didn't care about who she hurt. Who got left behind. She stole from us to make sure she had all she wanted."

"No, she didn't seem to care, but we can't know what was going on inside of her. She didn't share that with you." His voice was solemn, contrasting with their little boy's high squeals coming through the windows of J & J's office. "But God didn't leave you behind, or your brother. God was with you and Frankie and Charlotte at that house when y'all found Greg. It wasn't your fault. The only responsibility you have right now is to forgive your mother. Otherwise you'll never be free from your anger toward her, the grief over losing your brother, and the fears over our marriage. If I'd never forgiven Eleanor for leaving us, our hearts wouldn't have been available for you."

Pressed together, his hip and her thigh were one as they passed the trailer that reigned over the parking lot. "You need to make room for our baby, Bella. For us and for Henry."

They trooped slowly toward the other side of the granite yard as they both dove deep into their own thoughts. After a couple minutes, he dropped his arm and again took her hand and looped her arm through his. "I don't want this to be a wasted trip out here, so let's hotfoot it over to Jim's secret stash. Watch yourself." He pointed to a pothole filled with muddy water.

Annabelle followed him through the muddy slab yard under clouds that looked as full as her bladder, which was fixing to burst. They wound their way past the parking lot and away from most of the other run-of-the-mill people tending to their fixer-uppers. Once Oliver dragged Annabelle around the back of the warehouse, located on the left corner of the property, they reached another area holding several rows of granite slabs.

"Now we're talking." He grinned and did a little dance, disregarding the squelching of his boots.

Annabelle glowered at him, sure she'd felt the plop of a raindrop on her forehead. "Why did you decide today was the day to come all the way out here? You should've checked the weather. Yesterday was beautiful."

"What? You're not having fun?" Oliver attempted to lift the corners of her lips with his thumb and index finger, but no amount of pinching was working. Her growl seemed to make him think better of his attempt to literally lift her spirits. "I did check the weather, Bella. Today's trip was brought to you especially by yours truly." A rumble of tires caused them to pivot one hundred eighty degrees. A forklift was traversing a wide patch, its metal arms wielding a rough-edged rectangle of stone. Oliver edged her further down the aisle and from their safe spot, they watched the machine set the slab in place.

Another heavy drop landed on Annabelle's shoulder, and she whirled back in Oliver's direction. She held up her palm to catch the next one. "And I suppose you arranged for a thunderstorm."

He had the nerve to grin. "No, that's all God's doing. But that's only a bit of a cloud passing over. It's not going to rain, I promise. It's like I tell all my clients: you want to go to the yard when it's overcast, on a day exactly like today. Bright sunlight washes out the colors of natural stone. Once we see something we like, we'll ask them to move it into the warehouse over there —" his eyes glanced toward the large metal building behind them—"and we'll see how the stone looks indoors, under artificial light. Do you still have our measurements?"

Concentrating on the skies, she nodded.

"Good, and I have our cabinet samples in the car. When we find what we're looking for—and I do mean *when,* not *if*—I'll get them, and then we'll take a look in the warehouse and see if they complement each other." Oliver wrapped his hand around hers, which was still elevated, and clasped it tightly. "It's not going to rain, baby."

But it did. The skies opened up. Oliver covered her with his arms the best he could, and they dashed back to the trailer. Standing under the overhang in front of the door, he hugged her. "Obviously, this is a sign we should go with quartz instead. I know the perfect place that specializes in it. And I'm not related to a single soul there."

Annabelle grabbed his collar and kissed him, her half-empty heart overflowing.

Chapter Twenty-Four

Then

ANNABELLE THREW A ROCK and it landed on square number four. She lifted her left foot and set to hopping. After making it all the way to the semicircle marked with the number ten, she put both feet down and spun to make the return trek.

"Nuh-uh!" Six-year-old Charlotte pointed at Annabelle's sneakers. "You have to keep your foot up when you land and turn around. You're out. It's my turn!" She'd been squatting at the edge of the cement pad in the middle of their backyard, keeping one eye on her sister to referee her play. Her fingers were dirty from using her rock to scratch pictures on the ground in the space between her widespread ashy knees.

"Uh-huh. You can so. You just don't play right." Annabelle wasn't actually aware of the rules of hopscotch, but the girl who once dashed into the street after baby Charlotte was tired. In more ways than one. There was no way she was going to make it all the way to ten, hop back, and stop to pick up her pebble without standing on both feet somewhere along the way. She decided to go with how she felt, not with what she knew. And at twelve years old, she was way too big to be out here playing hopscotch. Charlotte had better keep her mouth shut if she knew what was good for her.

But the younger girl seemed to think and feel otherwise. Scrambling to her feet, she waved her sharp stone in one hand and aimed a finger at Annabelle with the other. "You're cheatin'! You're cheatin'! That's not fair. I'm gonna tell on you."

Annabelle slowly tossed her rock back and forth from one hand to the other and shrugged. That would mean she could quit playing, at least for the amount of time it took for Charlotte to report on her supposed misdeeds and come back with a directive. "Go 'head. I don't care."

Charlotte shuffled toward the steps leading up to the back porch. On the second tread she cut an eye back at Annabelle. "I mean it. I'll do it . . . You can't stop me from goin' inside . . . I'm gonna tell on you."

Annabelle turned her back and rubbed at the chalk outlines with the tip of her sneaker. She listened to the press of feet on wood, and then the screen door squeaked open and slapped shut.

She did it! I can't believe she's telling on me. She always goes whining when she can't get what she wants. Well, I don't care. I'm still gonna put both my feet down when I get to number ten. No matter what she says or does to me. Why should Charlotte get special treatment just 'cause she's the baby?

The door opened and shut and two sets of feet clomped across the porch, cutting short Annabelle's internal rant. Her heart thudded in her chest, but she gave place to her anger, letting it smother

her trepidation, which was just how mad she was. With deliberate casualness, she dropped her rock on number four, deciding this would be as good a time as any to practice.

"You know you can't put both your feet down in one number." Frankie appeared, flanked by a triumphant-looking Charlotte. "The rules are the same as when I played with you. Why you always messin' with Charlotte, tryin' to take advantage?"

Annabelle kept jumping from one square to the next, landing right smack dab in the middle. She did an extra wiggle in each one to rub out the number. "Why's she always messin' with me? It's only a stupid game." She made it back to the square with the four—or rather, that *used to* have the four drawn in pink. Wobbling, but determined not to fall in front of her audience, she leaned down and retrieved her rock, straightened unsteadily, hopped-hopped-hopped, and landed on both feet, free of the hopscotch frame. She brushed away the dusty pink smudges from her fingertips before she cocked an eye at her older sister.

Frankie adjusted the leather purse strap on her shoulder.

Annabelle dropped her bravado along with the stone she'd been holding. "Where are you going?"

"Me and Mama are goin' to the store." Pride adorned her otherwise simple announcement. Her hand played with the flap of her purse.

"To do some shoppin'? What kind?" Annabelle pictured the squiggle of milk left in the jug on the otherwise-empty top refrigerator shelf and the crumbs and sugar left in the bag of Frosted Flakes in the cabinet. It had made a terrible lunch. Somehow, Charlotte always found something to eat in their kitchen. "Can I go?"

"Somebody has to watch Charlotte." Frankie adjusted the waistline of her jeans, making them ride lower on her hips. She detested high-water pants and made sure everybody knew it.

"But why does that somebody have to be me?" Annabelle never got to go with Mama. Usually, none of them did. Her mother might press a ten-dollar bill into one of their hands and send them into the store to pick up a few things she wanted for herself, but they never went shopping together. Annabelle could picture herself strolling up and down each aisle, asking for SpaghettiOs and Mr. P's frozen pizzas.

Frankie jutted out her chin. "Because I'm goin' with Mama to McNair's."

That was why Frankie had her purse! "Whatchy'all goin' there for? I thought you were off to Food Lion."

Their mama's business was a large two-story department store near the creek running through downtown Jasper. It had started out as a small shop owned by the McNair family that provided locally grown and made goods downstairs and rented rooms to tenants upstairs, mostly unmarried people who helped out in the store. After working there for years, Mayhelen had bought it from the original owner during the seventies, and had put in long, hard hours to expand the business. It now sold clothes and shoes for men, women, and children on the first floor and all manner of household goods on the second. Their mama brought home most of their clothes from there, but Annabelle couldn't recall ever stepping foot in the store with her during the light of day. Annabelle felt like her mother dressed her to play a part in life she'd never rehearsed.

"Did you hear me say anything about the grocery store? If that's what I meant, I'd-a said it." Frankie seemed put out, as if she'd been forced into a bad position. "You're always thinkin' with your stomach. I get to help her with some work, and then I'm lookin' for a dress. I'm goin' to the formal next week, and I don't have anything to wear. Mama was gonna let me borrow one of hers, but none of them fit." At fourteen years old, Frankie's legs came up to their mother's chest.

She stomped past Annabelle, heading for their Oldsmobile Cutlass glowing like a penny out back, by the oak tree whose limbs nearly hid the telephone and electric wires traversing the yard from the pole to the house. Frankie opened the passenger door and crossed on all fours over the seat to insert the key in the ignition. The car chugged to life and belched a plume of grayish smoke from its exhaust pipe.

Figuring if she couldn't go, nobody should, Annabelle almost wished one of the dry, leafless branches casting long shadows over the car would crash onto its hood. Almost. But she'd hate for them to be stranded at the house, all for a can of spaghetti her mama probably wouldn't buy her anyway. Hadn't Miss Hattie taught them, "You dig one ditch, you'd better dig two"? Still, Annabelle had no intention of spending her Saturday afternoon throwing rocks at numbers behind her house. She trailed after Frankie, and Charlotte shuffled behind her. "I want to go. Why can't we all go?"

Frankie looked up from the purse she was rummaging through. "'Cause you weren't invited. It's a ninth-grade dance, and I'm the only one livin' here who's in the ninth grade. You don't need a fancy dress, and when it comes your time, you can borrow mine. Besides, this is really about me helpin' Mama at the store. One of her workers didn't show up, and she trusts me to manage the register."

"I'm not askin' for some clothes; I'm just askin' to go. I'm tired of stayin' here with *her*, doin' Mama's job." She directed a thumb behind her.

"Hey! Mama said don't point!" Charlotte's feet kicked up dust as she circled Annabelle and stood in the shadow of Frankie. Her eyes were like pistols aimed right at her middle sister.

"Mama also said don't get anything on your clothes, and that looks like mustard to me." Annabelle waved all ten fingers at the front of Charlotte's shirt.

"Anna, stop fussin'. You're actin' like you're goin' on three, not thirteen." Frankie took out a rectangular pack of tissues and snapped her purse shut. "Now I see why Mama said I shouldn't tell you where we were goin'. She told me you'd be as green as that crabgrass growin' over there. Charlotte, come here."

Charlotte turned around without a murmur. When Frankie tilted her chin, she stood still to let her oldest sister dab at the food in the corner of her mouth.

Annabelle curled those same fingers she was wagging a second ago into frustrated fists at her hips. "I'm not jealous! Jealous of what? Of who?"

"Whom," Frankie muttered, intent on cleaning her baby sister's face.

Annabelle watched Frankie fussing over Charlotte, who was big enough to wipe her own mouth and get her own stains out of her clothes—or to avoid dropping food in the first place. Then she began to wonder what the girl had found to squirt mustard on in their bare cupboards, and she could feel her temper rise another degree or two.

"I see you've finally been payin' attention in Mrs. Chestnut's class," she scoffed. A hard worker, her sister, and smart, though it didn't pay off in the highest grades, something Mayhelen rode her about. Annabelle figured that even if her mama didn't care anything about them, she, Frances Mae, and Charlotte had better act like they came from a loving home and weren't about to become another statistic. That might have been the reason Mama got married every time, even though she was too proud of her own name to take theirs. Their daddies didn't show up on Parent-Teacher Night, but at least her girls could claim they started their life with one.

"There's a lot of things I'm payin' attention to. Like what Mama says, for instance. And you should too. Maybe one day you'll learn something that gets you out of here." Frankie placed both hands on the sides of her youngest sister's face and gave her a big smack on the forehead with her lips. She bent to look Charlotte in the eye. "Did you eat all your ham sandwich?"

The six-year-old nodded.

No, she didn't say a ham sandwich! That really boiled Annabelle's buns. And here she'd only had a bowl of squishy frosted *crumbs* for lunch. "Where did Charlotte get a sandwich?"

"From Mama." Charlotte's answer was matter-of-fact.

Tears threatened—burning, angry, *ravenous* tears—and Annabelle dared them to fall. She knew she wasn't really crying about the food, but about a whole list of needs that food and water wouldn't satisfy. "Why can't we all go? Isn't that what most families do? They go places together and spend time together. Moms don't give love to some and leave the rest behind to pick up the crumbs."

"Listen, Annabelle, nobody said anything about love. This is about me gettin' my dress, something I have to do. Which means you need to keep an eye on this one right here. It doesn't matter if you hop on one foot, two feet, or if you do crazy eights across those ten squares—right, Charlotte?—as long as you play."

Charlotte looked at the hopscotch they'd drawn, at Frankie, at Annabelle, and then back at her oldest sister. She nodded again, this time more slowly. Charlotte was all about fair play.

Frankie gave her a little push in the direction of the concrete pad. "Why don't you get your rocks and the chalk. Redraw the numbers so y'all can see what you're doin'." Once she was out of earshot, Frankie sidled next to Annabelle.

"Your turn will come, Annabanana. This dance is more for Mama than it is for me. You know I sure don't care about gettin' all doodied up for some boy who's not into what really counts about me—what I think and how I feel about things. This is Mama's thing. Scared we're all gonna end up in her house is all. Then she'll have to take care of us and nobody can take over that store she loves so much. Which is probably why she rides me so hard about my math grades."

"Shoot, Mama doesn't take care of us now." Annabelle watched Charlotte, her tongue in the corner of her mouth and her eyes nearly shut, painstakingly tracing the faint outlines of the numbers her sisters had drawn for her earlier. Without looking, she swatted at the small sweat bee flying around her shoulders but didn't stop drawing.

"Okay, put up with us then." Frankie brushed her bangs back, making the hair stand out straight. Perspiration dotted her forehead and had started to make her newly pressed hair curl at the roots. "Don't worry, we won't be gone long. She'll get tired of playin' mother way before you get tired of playin' big sister."

The door flapped against the house and the planks creaked under the weight of the feet click-clacking across the porch and descending the steps. "Frankie, you ready?" Her voice low and gravelly and her stomach out to there, Mayhelen didn't bother acknowledging her other children as she teetered by on pencil-thin heels. She only had eyes for one thing at a time, and at the moment, that was her car. Its chugging had evened out to a low rumble, courtesy of her latest husband who fancied himself a mechanic during the week and a preacher on the weekends. Tendrils from Mama's cigarette chased her to the car, though her oldest daughter didn't. Not at first.

Frankie elbowed Annabelle conspiratorially. Then she walked to Charlotte and kissed her on the top of her head again after squeezing her to her side. As the Cutlass began rolling toward the street, Frankie picked up her pace. She made a running jump through the open passenger-side door as the car accelerated down the rocky drive. She slammed the door closed and threw an arm out the open window, waving goodbye to her sisters with a V-shaped peace sign.

Annabelle sighed, at twelve years old, already tired of the games.

Chapter Twenty-Five

Now

CHARLOTTE SKIRTED THE PUDDLE but couldn't avoid the crack bisecting the sidewalk. The light was too dim. When her sneaker touched it, she winced, thinking of the rhyme she and her sisters used to say. *Sorry, Mama. But Annabelle would say, that's for breaking our heart.* A vibration on her wrist encouraged her to pick up the pace—two more laps to go around her neighborhood to complete that week's exercise goal. Then straight to the shower and change for work and later, a quick brunch with Max in between appointments. A date with him should get her all jazzed up to meet with her sisters that weekend. *Exactly what a single woman my age does on a Saturday afternoon: attends a four-year-old's birthday party.*

Actually, she was looking forward to it. Involved auntie that she was, she'd ordered the balloons and would pick them up on the way to Frankie's, along with a boatload of picture books and clothes for the birthday girl, a ton of sweets for the twins, and a noisy toy that MJ could shake for his parents in the middle of the night. Charlotte giggled, imagining it, and was rewarded by a large droplet of water hitting her square in the middle of her forehead. Feeling chastised, she swiped her nose and glanced up—not at the heavens, but at the branches still dripping after the rain.

A breeze had swept away the remains of the late-night spring storm, leaving the air clean and fresh-linen crisp. Yet Charlotte's mind was all cloudy, her thoughts and feelings still muddled from her visit with Frankie. So much subterfuge, unusual for a person who let any and all words trip off her tongue. All so she could reveal that she'd spied Charlotte with Max at the museum. It had really thrown Charlotte, that confrontation. She wasn't prepared to introduce that part of her life to the other part, let alone sew the halves together to form a whole, and it had disrupted her planned conversation about their mother. Of all places and times to play hooky from the office!

Frankie had grinned like she was teaching the Cheshire cat how to do it. "Why don't you ever wear your hair down, the way I saw it when you were with the mysterious Maximilian?"

"Nothing's mysterious about Max. You haven't met him."

"Yet." Frankie had clipped the word on the end of a sentence Charlotte hadn't meant to leave hanging, as she would a wet towel to the clothesline. "Go ahead and take off your wig now," she had insisted, casually flinging a hand at her sister's head. "The kids are busy with school and won't pay us any attention if you're embarrassed for some reason."

Charlotte had begged off, claiming she was too busy holding the baby to be whipping off a wig for Frankie's viewing pleasure. It wasn't like she'd invited her baby sister to doff her sweater because it was warm in the room; Frankie had asked her to disarm. Charlotte felt more comfortable—more able—in her synthetic curls when she was around family. With them, she needed some protection, a uniform; she adopted a tougher persona that helped her bear up under their pain. Not that she didn't have any. Only, it was hard to tell sometimes which scars were hers and which were theirs.

When Charlotte closed her eyes to that conversation, she nearly missed one of her favorite parts of the walk—the crest of the hill. After laboring to climb out from under the leafy bower that sheltered most of her walk, she was rewarded by the pinks and purples of the early morning haze hovering over a field sprinkled with wild daffodils and dandelions. The gold-flecked grass stretched far to her right and ended at a copse of scrawny evergreens where her "friends," a group of deer, stood poised, ready to run. Charlotte, her face scrunched, barely noticed the animals she routinely waved to, her only company.

She'd settled on her home's rural location to have somewhere to retreat to when she left the office; like her mother, she labored long and hard. Unlike her mother, however, she refused to ramble around in a large home that didn't know what to do with itself or the people living in it. Her brick town house was cozy in size and had a traditional facade, even if her decorating style was more modern and cool. And lately, she'd begun to hanker for a warm body to help her fill it.

One body in particular—Max. When she was with him, she was all Charlotte, warts and all. Hairy ones that he hadn't hesitated to point out the night before.

She'd finally allowed him to venture farther than the entryway or the powder room in her townhome, to do more than escort her to the door or meet her there as he jingled his keys and peeked around her to learn more about the woman he'd hinted at loving. They'd squeezed next to each other on the middle cushion of her cream-colored sofa that no child of Frankie's would ever touch.

"It always feels like you'll leave me—or ask me to leave you—at any minute," he'd confessed in his sweetly accented voice. "Here we are together, but you hold yourself separate from me. Is that because your father left your mother, you think? Because you had to grow up without a man in the house? I can tell you're afraid, ready to, to . . . to bolt."

She'd suppressed a cackle that had bubbled up from her belly and threatened to erupt. Charlotte wanted to ask, "Are you kidding? It's because of all the men in the house! Not one stayed for more than a minute, including the youngest man of all, my baby brother." All she could do was nod slightly, however, and burst into tears. He'd held her for a good long time. Much longer than she'd patted and cooed over MJ before handing him off, quite thankfully, to Frankie.

Power walking toward the light post, her next marker, Charlotte shook her head at her weakness, a first for her with any man. At least it wasn't over just any man.

"Ready to bolt . . . like those deer back there," she huffed, pumping her arms and raising her knees to her chest. At this point in her trek, when she reached the park near the corner, she high-stepped the rest of the way. Charlotte's body must have remembered though her mind was otherwise engaged. She didn't flinch when a pickup truck rumbled by, pulling a trailer loaded with lawn mowers and weed eaters. It passed so closely to her, a loose braid fluttered and stray leaves blew about the sidewalk in its wake.

Last night, she'd eased a hand around Max's waist and pressed herself to his chest as he'd enveloped her in his arms, and she'd wondered, *Is this how MJ feels when I hold him?* So close, she could smell his cologne on her shirt after he left, just before midnight.

"My Cinderella." He'd smiled and nuzzled her ear.

For the first time, it was hard to let him go. *That's why I know I need to,* she resolved. *For good. And there's no time like the present.* Charlotte pushed the button at the crosswalk, readying for the slow, three-minute cooldown from the gate at her neighborhood's entrance to her front door, and slid her iPhone from the side pocket on her leggings. She pressed the ten digits of Max's number; old-fashioned, she typed in telephone numbers to commit them to memory. But his was a number she determined to forget.

He answered on the first ring. "Hello, love."

Charlotte stood there on the corner, the blip . . . blip . . . blip signaling she could cross safely, and cried, something she'd vowed never to do with a man. "Max."

"Yes? Calling to cancel brunch, are you?"

Ready to bolt. "Yes, I mean no. I-I just called to tell you I can't . . . I-I love you too."

Chapter Twenty-Six

Then

"SHE OWNS MORE HOUSEDRESSES than I can shake a stick at."

Though Charlotte had no idea what Annabelle meant, she nodded and blew on her cookie before taking a bite of it. Miss Hattie had taken them straight from the oven and put them on a plate in the middle of the table. When she told the girls to help themselves, Charlotte, Frankie, and Annabelle had set to it. Eight-month-old Greg had scrambled for what he could reach from the vantage point of Frankie's lap. Now the woman had taken the baby into the next room to clean off the chocolate that had melted on his hands and cheeks.

"Somebody should tell Miss Hattie none of her scrubbing and spit shining is gonna do any good. That boy will get messy eating something else, probably the next batch of cookies."

Greg was always getting something on his clothes, probably because he liked to snatch up food with both hands that they had to wrestle away from him. "Why'd we bring him anyway?"

Annabelle plucked a gooey cookie from the top of the pile. "Like we'd leave him by himself. Anything could happen to him!"

"But Mama is home." Charlotte counted the brown dots in the ones she could see, making sure she wasn't getting shortchanged.

"A-n-n-d?"

She hated when Annabelle slowed down her words that way. Charlotte wasn't an ignoramus, although it should've been obvious why they'd trooped across the field with the baby in tow. "Oh."

After a few seconds of munching, Frankie licked her fingers. "What does that even mean?"

"Ooh, ah, ooh . . ." Annabelle's mouth contorted as she tried to talk and keep the cookie from burning her tongue and the insides of her jaws at the same time. "What does what mean?"

"What you said . . . about shakin' a stick."

"Ew, don't touch all the cookies!" Charlotte pinched a napkin from the stack Miss Hattie had set beside the plate and tossed it at Frankie and waited for Annabelle to answer the question. It always knocked Charlotte for a loop when one of them knew something Frankie didn't, since her oldest sister seemed to know everything. She sensed Frankie didn't like it, that she felt at a disadvantage somehow. And she could tell that having a slight edge made Annabelle take her time explaining.

"You know—" *smack, smack, swallow*—"it's an idiom."

Frankie's stare communicated nothing.

Charlotte reached for another cookie and wondered if she should leave some for Greg. Miss Hattie sure was having a time with him in the other room, based on his screeching.

Annabelle leaned her head from one side to another and took a third bite. "You know, like the words don't mean exactly what they say. Not literally. But once you put them all together, they mean something else. Something everybody recognizes. They create a picture you can see in your mind." She chewed.

Frankie's mouth formed a flat line.

"You know, like . . ." Annabelle shrugged and surveyed the kitchen. "Hmm . . . 'spill the beans.' I don't really want you to knock over Miss Hattie's beans. It means tell the truth." She scrutinized her little sister's face. "As in . . . okay, Charlotte, spill the beans. What were you doing in my room, and where's my hat?"

Charlotte nearly choked on a chocolate chip. *How'd she know I took it?* While Annabelle pulled weeds by the walkway the other day, she'd tiptoed into her sister's bedroom and played dress-up in the closet. A big no-no. When Charlotte heard Annabelle troop into the house, she'd pilfered a soft gray hat stuffed behind a box of old toys and books. It was probably a prized possession.

Annabelle glared from across the nicked Formica table that had to be as old as Miss Hattie.

Thunder shook the house and streams of water ran down the front window. Charlotte pointed, trying to buy time. "Hey, I've got one! 'It's raining cats and dogs.' Do you really see cats or dogs on the ground? No. It means it's—"

"Stupid. That's what it is. Just say it's pourin', or it's rainin' so much we're gonna get soaked." Frankie didn't waste time on analyzing word pictures. She nudged cookies aside until she could pluck one from the middle at the bottom of the pile. "But if you mean Miss Hattie has a lot of dresses, you're right. She does. Maybe when we get her age, we'll wear 'em too."

Annabelle rolled her eyes. "Ugh! I mean it, Charlotte. Give me my hat."

"Maybe when you get to be my age, you'll also be blessed

enough to have three—excuse me, *four*—crumb snatchers sittin' at your table, keepin' company with you. Then you'll realize you need some room in your clothes to get some work done."

Charlotte scooched around in her seat and found Miss Hattie standing there with Greg on her hip. His meaty hands kept scrabbling for the woman's glasses dangling on a chain around her neck. Charlotte shifted under her piercing gaze but couldn't escape it.

"Now, what hat are y'all talkin' 'bout? Miss Charlotte, did you take somethin' of your sister's?"

Annabelle shouted, "Yes!"

At the same time Charlotte muttered, "No," but changed her mind at the look on their neighbor's face. "Well . . ."

"Give me some sugar, some of that brown sugar." Miss Hattie pretended to nibble on the baby's neck and he squealed, showing off his four tiny teeth. She shifted him to her other hip. "Out with it, child. Stop sittin' on the fence—and I believe that's another idiom. It means—"

"Make a decision. Choose one or the other. Yes or no." Frankie broke a large cookie into smaller chunks and plopped one onto her tongue.

"That's right, dear. Very good." Miss Hattie applauded the teen with a grin before pinning the youngest girl to the spot with her full attention. "Now, little Charlotte, did you take the hat?"

"She stole it! She's always goin' through my things!"

"I didn't steal nothin'! I was only lookin' at it!"

"How were you looking at it when it was under a box in my closet?" Annabelle smirked.

Three pairs of eyes trained themselves on the six-year-old bull's-eye sitting at the table.

Out of excuses, Charlotte hung her head and shuffled to the porch. Humid air oozed through the open door as she unzipped her backpack and freed the hotly contested hat. Charlotte knew better than to play in her sister's room. Annabelle was a teenager, a fact the girl emphasized every other day in response to her sister's requests. Still, the child couldn't help it. There were so many goodies in both older girls' spaces, and nobody paid her a bit of attention except when she cried. Frankie giggled with some boy on the phone every chance she could—*ew!*—and Annabelle stayed hidden with her pile of books and doodads nobody knew where. Miss Hattie had warned them all about the dangers of idle hands and idle minds, so shame on them. They should've known better, same as her.

"Charlotte, Miss Hattie is talkin' to you. Frankie says we're supposed to listen to people bigger than us, which mean you're supposed to listen to me." Annabelle crossed her arms and sat back in her metal chair.

It's 'cause you're older, not bigger, you dumbbell. Otherwise Miss Hattie will have to listen to you soon. Squinting at Annabelle from the kitchen door, she fiddled with the hat her fingers gripped behind her back and considered all the alternatives: If she mocked her sister, Annabelle would smack her and take the hat, Miss Hattie or no Miss Hattie. If Charlotte pitched a fit, they might all get sent home, and Mama would take the hat. If she held on to it, she'd disappoint Frankie and she'd still end up giving Annabelle the hat. Charlotte's arms fell to her side. "I didn't want this stinky ol' thing, smellin' like it's been left out in the rain."

"Let me see that, and shut that door." Miss Hattie extended one arm; the other encircled Greg, whose head bobbed drowsily against her shoulder. When Charlotte dropped it in her hand, the woman's mouth formed an O and she nearly let go of the baby.

In one giant step, Frankie caught Greg and cradled him to her chest. "What? What's wrong, Miss Hattie?"

"Where'd you get this?" Miss Hattie turned the hat this way and that. When nobody answered, she inspected each face. "Charlotte? Annabelle? I asked you both a question, and I'm bigger *and* older, so you'd best answer me." She twirled the gray felt cap on one finger.

Charlotte stretched an arm toward Annabelle. *You're in trou-ble!* Her heart sang the words.

Now it was Annabelle's turn to squirm in her seat, like she was perched on a hot potato. "I found it . . . in Mama's room. I needed to look like a hobo in a play."

Again, everyone watched Miss Hattie, who couldn't get enough of her new find. Charlotte wouldn't have been surprised if the woman sprinkled hot sauce on the hat and took a bite, the hat looked so good to her.

Frankie coughed a little as she swayed side to side, Greg asleep on her chest, the way she'd held her baby sister too. Or so she'd told a jealous Charlotte. Once she snagged Charlotte's attention, she mouthed *What?* and threw her head in the direction of Miss Hattie.

Charlotte shrugged and turned to Annabelle, who shook her head so hard her earrings jingled.

"Did you say a hobo? Woo-hoo!" Miss Hattie's shoulders jiggled. "A hobo. Heh, heh, heh."

Charlotte didn't know if this was one of those adult jokes her mama didn't let them in on, so she wondered whether to ignore Miss Hattie and eat another cookie. She could tell Frankie and Annabelle were confused too. *I guess Annabelle's not in trouble.* She sighed.

"I suppose it's your right to do what you want with this. It's yours now." Miss Hattie stepped forward in her slippered feet and lowered herself into an empty chair. She pushed the hat across the table to Annabelle, whose fingers crawled over it like a spider.

"I'm surprised your mama kept that. Maybe it's a reminder, the way somebody holds on to the first dollar they earn." She tapped the table near Annabelle's fingers. "That, children, is called a fedora, and it looked 'bout the same way when I saw it the first time. The man it belonged to never let it out of his sight. He wore it come rain or shine."

Charlotte couldn't make heads or tails of Miss Hattie's soft words, but they held sway in the warm room that smelled of chocolate chip cookies, rain, and a baby's full diaper.

"What do you mean, Miss Hattie? Is that another idiom?" Leave it to Frankie to get right to the point.

The woman chuckled, more to herself this time. "No, baby. I meant exactly what I said. That hat belonged to Annabelle's daddy. Dang if I know how your mama got her hands on it, or him either. But I would've bet my eyeteeth he would've been buried with it before he let it go."

Chapter Twenty-Seven

Now

FRANKIE LIGHTLY RUBBED the soft skin of MJ's back. He was stretched out, arms akimbo, on her lap, panting in the way of babies. She wished she could bend down and smell his milk-sweet breath, something she might not want to do in another eighteen months or so, once that precious part of his infanthood was over. There was no way she could manage to do it, however, not while she was cradling her Bible in the palm of her other hand.

The lamp bathed the closet in a soft glow, contracting the walls of the baby's room. It was unusually quiet at this impossible hour of nine-thirty on a Friday night. Her husband had to cover the late news for another cameraman, and MJ had conked out after a feeding and before she could change him for bed. Thanks to an overlong family movie and a timely reminder of tomorrow's shindig, the twins and Nora had scampered off to bed of their own accord. An exhausted Frankie, grateful for a moment to actually hear the soft snores of her infant and think about all the family's goings-on, relaxed her head against the back of her cushioned seat and allowed herself to close her eyes for a half second.

The plans for the birthday party . . .

Charlotte flying out of there after mumbling about some Greek man named Max who didn't mean anything . . .

Then why was she so flustered when I told her I'd seen them, if their relationship was of no consequence? The sun rising on her face when I said his name.

What did she say about Mama?

Buzz. Buzz.

Frankie jolted awake and MJ nearly rolled from her lap. She caught him as the phone thunked to the carpeted floor and landed on top of her Bible, which she must have dropped while she dozed. *Buzz. Buzz.* After wedging the baby—miraculously, still sleeping—into the nest between her shoulder and jawline, she fumbled for her cell. Missed call from Miss Hattie.

Should I call her back? What will I tell her? Charlotte and Annabelle would be here tomorrow to celebrate Nora's fourth birthday, and she'd extracted a promise from each of them that they'd come prepared to render a decision about their mama. No way could they look Miss Hattie in the eye and shrug. But she didn't have an answer yet about the issue their old friend had brought up weeks ago. She caressed the back of MJ's silky head and prayed about her path forward.

Resolute, Frankie scooched to the end of the seat and rose stiffly, willing her hip joints to do as they were told. Sleeping in a chair that wasn't intended for that purpose would do that to a forty-two-year-old's body. She laid MJ in the middle of his crib, and after a moment's thought, took a light blanket from a drawer and covered his bare tummy with it. Leaving the door open provided her some reassurance that he wouldn't smother or entangle himself in the few minutes she'd be away to return the call. She padded to the kitchen.

The older woman answered after the second ring.

"Hello? Miss Hattie?"

"Hey, baby!" The voice, not as strong as it used to be, still radiated warmth and love. It sounded like home, though the "home" the woman represented looked into the backyard of the house Frankie had raised herself and her sisters in. "I just rang you on your phone."

"I know, I know. I was holding the baby and couldn't get to it in time. You remember how it is, Miss Hattie."

"Huh, it wasn't like this when I was comin' up. Folks can reach out and touch too much in my opinion. I thought you might have been screenin' your calls, which is a smart thing to do these days, what with these strangers acting the fool, tryin' to get you to buy everything and his mama."

Aren't you doin' the same thing, sellin' us a bill of goods about our own mama? Out of respect for the older woman, Frankie knew better than to pose such a question. "How are you?" Frankie reached for the teakettle and listened to faint rustlings on the other end of the line.

"Stop it!" the ninety-two-year-old commanded someone, her mouth moving away from the receiver. "I told you I could do it myself."

"Miss Hattie? Everything okay?" Frankie filled the copper pot, affixed the lid, and set it on the back burner of the stove. The heating element glowed red.

"Yes, honey. Your Aunt Suzy over here thinks she knows better than I do. She must not see all this white hair on my head . . . more than she has, heh heh." More rustling.

Aunt Suzy was Miss Hattie's daughter, the older of her two children. When the Winters girls were younger, they'd paid no attention to the rest of Miss Hattie's world that spun outside of their line of sight—her son and daughter, in-laws, and friends. As far as they knew, their neighbor existed only to share contraband goods and provide a soft place for them to land. At first. Once they matured, they paid more attention to the photographs on her walls, the Christmas cards on the table, the cars that came and went, and the telephone calls. Of course, later, her family became their family, and her God, theirs. But unlike Naomi in the book of Ruth, Miss Hattie never tried to send the girls away.

"Tell Aunt Suzy I said hello and to leave you alone," Frankie chuckled, then glanced at the clock on the microwave. *10:45.* "What's she doin' there in your bedroom at this hour? Shouldn't you be in bed? It's not like you to call me at this time of night." Ten years ago, Suzy had moved her mother to Raeford, North Carolina, to live with her family after selling Miss Hattie's house. *She knows how to honor her mother,* Frankie thought. She riffled through the box of tea flavors, looking for one that would settle her spirit. Seeing nothing marked "Jesus," she opted for chamomile with lemon.

"Why are you asking me all these questions, Frances Mae? Are you tryin' to avoid me?"

The indomitable Hattie Mason. Nothing could get by her. Frankie sighed. "You got me. We need more time. We have a lot to talk through, to sort out." Frankie didn't have to explain that "we" meant Charlotte, Annabelle, and her. "You're not Mayhelen Winters, Miss Hattie. It's not as simple as one, two, three." She flapped the paper square of tea leaves against her hand for emphasis.

"Are you clapping your hands at me?" Suddenly, the volume of Miss Hattie's voice rose by several decibels. "I know you're not bowing up—"

Frankie heard a low murmuring on the other end, encouraging Miss Hattie to calm down. Aunt Suzy was reassuring her mother that "Frances Mae was doing no such thing as being sassy or bowing up."

"Hush, Suzy. This girl better act like she knows better. She doesn't want me to come up there." But Miss Hattie sounded more like her old self. Not the newly retired woman who'd helped them cover every centimeter of their rolling pins with flour, but the woman with more years behind than ahead who brooked no disrespect from people who hadn't traveled the earth as long as she. "You're right, Frances Mae: I'm not your mama. But y'all know what's right, just like my Suzy. There's little to debate over, even less to decide. You just have to acknowledge what's right, and then set your minds to doin' it."

The kettle whistled, and Frankie shuffled to the stove in her worn slippers and turned off the burner. Too tired for this verbal spanking, she leaned against the edge of the counter, her arms crossed and her eyes squeezed closed. Charlotte would've evaluated her body language as "noncompliant." "Do what's right? What's right in your eyes may not be what's right in ours, Miss Hattie."

"Hold on a minute, Frances Mae." She grunted, and there was a fair amount of shuffling on her end. The tone of her voice lightened, and she became the woman who'd introduced herself to Frankie and Annabelle many years ago. "Thanks, Suzy. I'm comfortable and won't be movin' much. You can go on ahead to bed, baby. *Mmm-mwa.* Share that hug with my son-in-love, but don't get in any trouble." Miss Hattie giggled.

Frankie ran her hands through her hair that she hadn't taken the time to roll or stuff under a silk cap and waited for the conversation to resume.

When it did, Miss Hattie sounded like she was back to business. "Now, Frankie. I take it you think right travels in two directions? No such thing as two-way traffic in such matters that pertain to God."

Frankie sighed. Based on her history with the woman, she knew Miss Hattie had more to say, and she figured she'd wait and respond to all of it rather than piece by piece.

"I was there, Frances Mae. That middle-aged lady in the flowered dress? That was me. For years, I watched the comins' and goins' at that rambling old house across the way. Saw you girls as you appeared one by one, year after year, and stood guardin' that yard as the men did the opposite. I took it upon myself to do something and invite myself into your lives, even when you weren't sure you wanted me there and when your mama tried to kick me out. I was there.

"And yes, I was a few minutes too late to protect you from being the one to find your brother, but I was there for you, wrappin' you and Charlotte and Annabelle—and even your mama—in my arms after Greg died. Takin' care of you the best way I knew how and sometimes havin' to fight you to do it. I know how hard you had it. How hard you *still* have it."

"But my baby brother didn't just die, Miss Hattie. That's what a plant does. It just dies when somebody leaves it to itself in the dark or because they don't give it water or clip its withered leaves. But Greg . . ."

The gargantuan lump in Frankie's throat only appeared when she talked about the circumstances of her brother's death, and it seemed to have grown over the years. She willed it to shift so she could get a word out. "I'm not sayin' Mama killed him on purpose.

As selfish as she was, I don't believe that was the case, though that's the way Annabelle sees it and will until her dyin' day. And it wasn't 'one of those things,' the way Charlotte views it. The truth is in between, at the junction of those two lies. Yet and still . . . all Mama's years of doin' wrong by the three of us . . . the *four* of us . . . led to that night. And the sad fact remains that, because of her neglect, my baby brother never saw his first birthday. And now we're supposed to forgive and forget and simply absolve her of any part she played in his death."

"Nobody's sayin' you're supposed to forget. Only God can absolve our sin and put it as far between us as the east is from the west. I'm talkin' about lettin' go, Frances Mae. After all, what are you holdin' on to—and I mean *you*, Frances Mae Livingstone? Annabelle's stewin' over her accusations and the plain not knowin'. Charlotte's keepin' hold to her confusion and suppositions and the stories y'all pass down. Maybe you're keepin' company with your doubt and anger, your fear, the inability to forgive yourself."

Frankie withdrew an oven mitt from the drawer to the right of the stove and wrapped it around the handle of the kettle. She never trusted those mitts enough to stick her hand in one. In fact, she didn't much trust anything or anyone, after getting burned more times than she could count in her lifetime. A full minute passed before she felt able to string some thoughts together that made a little sense.

"Remember the day you took us to church?"

Silence answered her. Miss Hattie may have been trying to figure out which route Frankie was taking to get to her point. "What time? I took you more than once."

"I'm talking about Mother's Day, Miss Hattie. Mother's Day. That's what we're really talkin' about, isn't it—Mama?" It was Frankie's turn to swallow her impatience. "I'm sorry, I don't mean to be disrespectful." She sighed and began again. "You and Mama had finally come to some kind of terms once she realized your presence in our lives helped her even more than it helped us. At least, that's the version I'm *holdin' on to*. Anyway . . . you asked if we could go with you to church, and Mama actually let us. We didn't have to hide or wait until she was otherwise occupied."

Mayhelen had pronounced that every day was her day and she didn't need a special Sunday in May to prove it. To prove her point that it was just another day, she decided "she wasn't doin' nothin' for nobody" and sent them on their way with the older woman.

"After that Sunday, you took us to Wednesday night Bible study, a Saturday potluck, church again. Then Vacation Bible School."

"Frankie."

Miss Hattie rarely used her nickname, so she must have meant business; she wanted the younger woman's attention.

But there was no stopping Frances Mae. "Okay, about that day. You volunteered to drop me off at the movies and take the girls to VBS. You wanted to give me a break, you said. A chance to hang out with my friends and stop motherin'. But Greg had a bad cold, and he needed tendin' to." Frankie peered through the window over the kitchen sink. The darkness revealed nothing, but what she was looking for wasn't out there. It was inside. "At the last moment, lo and behold, Mama decided she'd step up and babysit—yes, *babysit* her own son. What made her do it? Why, that night of all nights? She was alone for a change because her last husband was long gone. No man in the house and no prospects. Only that daggone store that claimed the rest of her attention her love life didn't consume, and I guess she had nothing better to do.

"So, we left my nine-month-old brother in his dear mother's care."

"Don't be sarcastic, Frances Mae." Miss Hattie's voice had grown weary.

Frankie marched on, to the painful throb of her heartbeat. In her mind, however, she had retreated to that moment; that long-ago *then* felt so much like *now*. "And ironically, I have the most fun of my teenage life. I don't think of Charlotte or Annabelle. Or the baby. Probably for the first time since Mama started bringin' babies home like a carton of eggs or a gallon of milk from the grocery store or the cast-off clothes her customers didn't buy. When we get home that Friday night, me with my leftover popcorn, and Charlotte and Annabelle with their extra crafts and lessons about the fishermen and bags of Goldfish—all for Greg . . . when we get home, we discover Mama has fallen asleep after one of her *constitutions* and he is burnin' up with fever. Unconscious. *'Only sleepin','* Mama says. *'Only sleepin'* . . ."

Somehow, the tears that fell unclogged her throat, and Frankie was finally free to utter the word without choking. "With the Lord? Or some such euphemism that only means 'dead' . . . by the time we get him to the hospital. And Mama is gone not too long after. All I can think is how could we have left him? How could *I* have left him?"

"That wasn't your fault, Frances Mae."

Fully present, Frankie closed her eyes. She had heard it before because she'd comforted herself with those very words. "Maybe not. Okay, no, it wasn't. In my head, I know that. But in my heart? Still workin' on it, Miss Hattie. It took me a long time to accept that it wasn't God's fault either. I almost didn't believe in Him after that. If He could take my baby brother and let Mama get away scot-free, what kind of God could that be? How could I serve Someone like that? It took me a long time to see that He didn't do it. That Mama didn't do it, though she didn't prevent it.

Annabelle doesn't see that yet. As I told Charlotte, I'm at the junction of healin' and hurtin'."

Miss Hattie didn't—or perhaps, couldn't—respond; Frankie didn't know which. She pressed the speaker button and listened to the woman breathe as she retrieved her favorite cup from the drying rack in the sink. Frankie poured the boiling water over her tea bag and watched the tendrils of steam dance and drift away.

Finally, the nonagenarian stirred. "Frances Mae, I can't tell you what to do or paint a pretty picture of how your faith should look. You felt forsaken, but God showed you He never left you. And He'll help you make the right decision now if you'll seek Him. You've done right by your sisters all your life, and I know you'll do right by them now. I'm here for you . . ."

Distant murmuring in Miss Hattie's room seemed to distract her. "Believe it or not, I called to tell you I wasn't up to travelin' to little Nora's party, but God has a way of redirectin' our ways and our words. Now, I'll let this girl—I know, Suzy, you're feelin' about as old as your mama but you're still a girl to me—as I was sayin', I'll let this *girl* help me into bed because you're right: it's high time I was asleep. I love you, Frankie. You and Charlie and sweet Belle. Good night, love. Call me when you know something."

Frankie watched the light on her iPhone fade to black after Miss Hattie disconnected. She found a spoon and slowly stirred two teaspoonfuls of sugar and a few drops of cream into her cup. Neither one would help her lose these pesky twenty pounds that had come to visit during her pregnancies and decided to stay a while. But then again, extra sweetener might help with the bitter pill her former neighbor was encouraging her to swallow.

She raised the tea to her lips, but before she could take her first sip, MJ cried out.

Chapter Twenty-Eight

THERE WERE MORE TREES THAN people living in Frankie's wooded neighborhood. Towering elms and sugar maples stretched their arms over the low-slung, ranch-style houses that spread over their one-acre lots the way softened butter covered warm toast. Annabelle figured the homeowners association must have worked overtime years ago, because evenly spaced flowering trees such as Bradford pears and dogwoods grew all along the edge, in the mossy space between the wide residential street and the sidewalk. Sunlight played peekaboo through their spindly branches.

Annabelle and Henry eased toward the birthday girl's house, curving past the diamond-shaped yellow sign near the corner that warned drivers that children played in that neighborhood. She waved at neighbors she didn't know because that was what folks did in North Carolina, smiling when they flicked a hand in return at the strange woman and child in the 2018 red Mustang who could've been there to purloin packages from their porches. She coasted to a stop a few feet away from Frankie's bricked-in mailbox into the same spot at the curb as she had last time and turned off the ignition. The window retracted with a soft whir, and cool evening air wafted inside—bringing with it a faint whiff of fish from the Bradford tree's delicate white blossoms that an unprepared Annabelle sucked in. Holding her breath to prevent another assault, she wondered at the dichotomy of God's natural design.

Families are part of that same design, murmured a small, yet powerful voice. Beautiful, yet flawed.

"Are you okay, Mommy?" Henry's Spider-Man action figure took a dive from the window well straight into his lap.

"Yes, baby." Sighing, Annabelle fought with her spirit and her stomach to settle as she unclicked her seatbelt.

Her son popped up between the front seats. "May I get out and see my cousins? I want to take Nora her gift."

"Sure, go ahead. I'll watch you. When you get inside, tell Aunt Frankie I'll be there in a moment."

Henry grabbed the handles of the pink-and-yellow polka-dot gift bag and flew from the car. Annabelle watched him skip up the steps and ring the bell. Once he was safely inside, she closed her eyes and felt herself sink into the seat.

Hearing voices blending and dancing together a few blissful minutes later, Annabelle blinked slowly and opened her eyes. She adjusted her rearview mirror to see who was approaching. Engaged in an animated exchange punctuated by one-handed motions and open-mouthed laughter, a boy in his teens and a girl around seven or eight years old pushed their bicycles along the sidewalk past Annabelle's car. Trailing a few steps behind the boy, the younger child raised her voice as she started counting the squares created by the lines in the sidewalk, drawing out each number in an exaggerated, "I-really-need-to-concentrate" fashion.

"Onnnnnee . . . twooooo . . . threeeee . . ."

Every few rotations of their wheels, the teen glanced down at the girl's bike until at last he pointed at her spokes. After saying something to his little sister—or so Annabelle had convinced herself upon comparing their similar wispy, sun-burnished curls and matching round faces—they paused beside a painted Little Free Library someone had erected on the strip of grass between a pair of those noxious pear trees. Instead of opening the small door to borrow a book, the teenager propped the bulky wheels of his dark-blue mountain bike against the wooden post and dropped to one knee. He studied his sister's bike and then jiggled the chain, tugging this way and that, while she twirled the green and white streamers dangling from her handlebars. One yank too many caused her bicycle to teeter and crash to the concrete, nearly taking the girl with it when the handlebars grazed her shin.

"Oh!" Annabelle pulled up on the Mustang's steering wheel to get a better view. When the little one threw her head back, wailing to high heaven, Annabelle wrenched open her door. But before she could step from the car, the boy murmured something which seemed to calm his sister by small degrees; her chest hitches slowed, like far-off thunder that assured the storm had passed. Within minutes, after he examined her leg and brushed off her apparently uninjured skin, the little one was wiping her face with her sleeve and trading another word or two with her sibling. Annabelle eased her door closed and settled into her tufted leather seat. "This is better than a movie," she murmured, wishing she had some buttered popcorn and a box of Milk Duds.

Big brother returned his attention to whatever he was doing

with the bike. He righted the two-seater and steadied the kickstand while his sister squatted beside him, pointing and laughing at something as he untwisted the chain. Once he'd tested the links by moving the pedal backward and forward, he tucked his hands under the girl's armpits and lifted her high in the air, sending her squeals trailing like stardust behind her. Grinning at her, he set her on her sneakered feet.

"That's some love right there. That's how your big brother Henry is going to be with you, little one, whoever you are." The sides of Annabelle's oversize, unbuttoned shirt parted to reveal a tightly fitting peach camisole. It stretched over the nearly sixteen-weeks-and-counting-size bulge under her splayed fingertips. *Yes, he's treating her the way Frankie was with you, and how both of you were with Charlotte,* a nearly audible thought reminded her. *And how none of us got to be with—*

Knock-knock!

Annabelle jumped and her right hand clutched the shirt she'd borrowed from Oliver that morning. What felt like her heart wedged itself in her throat and pulsed frantically there. Its painful *bumpa-bumpa-bumpa* shushed the memories peppering her subconscious, and she swiveled toward the window on her right.

Charlotte's sandy-colored knuckles hovered an inch from the glass. She looked about ready to rap once more, but then her light-brown eyes met her sister's silver-flecked ones and the sharp impatience in them softened in greeting. Her hand seemed to inside-out itself and she went from curled, bare knuckles to palm out. Charlotte waved and her lips relaxed in a smile. She mouthed, "Hey!"

Annabelle's chest and belly rose in a deep inhale and exhale to ready herself for this talk with her two "What Do We Do with

Mama?" confreres, though they were ostensibly gathering to watch Frankie's middle child blow out her candles. This was the second time in about a month she'd found herself at her older sister's house, and she was no more comfortable there than at the last visit. Quickly, she buttoned the last three buttons of her shirt, retrieved her purse and the bag of sweets from the floor next to her, and climbed from the car. The brother-and-sister duo were again wending their way around roots that had broken through the concrete and rounding the corner at the four-way stop.

"Hey there, Charlotte. Good to see you." The words trickled from her mouth out of habit, the way a stranger automatically muttered "bless you" when someone sneezed. It was the Southern way and would never be wrung completely from her, much as she couldn't completely squeeze all the juice from a lemon. There would always be a drip of it, no matter how far and wide she traveled from North Carolina, how long she stayed away.

At that moment, one of the balloons in the bouquet Charlotte held freed itself and floated away, taking her sunny expression with it. While it may have taken time for her to hear and understand what her sister hadn't said aloud, eventually, the message came through loud and clear. She parroted both her sister's words and sentiment, responding dryly, "Next time, say it like you mean it. Good to see you too. Or should I say *y'all*, since you're eatin' for two these days?"

All the goodwill from their recent visit dissipated. Annabelle locked the car with a click of her key fob, wishing she could find a way to recover the peaceful ground she'd willingly ceded before their time together had even begun. She stepped onto the curb and followed Charlotte's dark-brown curls as they bounced up the driveway toward the front door. The glass reflected the images of the two women as they mounted the three steps, one behind the other, neither of them looking particularly happy to be there.

At least we do have something in common, Annabelle consoled herself.

"I used to think all Melvin has to do is look at her, and she'll get pregnant. Ugh . . . 'baby-making machine.'" Charlotte cringed, hearing her own harsh words ping-ponging in her brain. After her conversation with Frankie about her pregnancy struggles, she wished she could retract all her snarky innuendos and snide comments. To sweeten the sour taste of guilt on her tongue, she licked the chocolate icing off the flat side of the cake knife she clutched.

Annabelle's mouth fell open at Charlotte's audacity, apparently hearing the content but not the spirit behind her words, much to Charlotte's shame. "Only you would have the nerve to insult our sister in her own home! Teasing is one thing, but that's downright rude, Charlotte." She sat directly opposite Charlotte on one of the shorter ends of the eight-by-four-foot acacia wood table on the deck behind Frankie's house. The two women rarely found themselves on the same side of anything. "Don't take out your problem with me on your favorite sister. Frankie doesn't deserve that."

Charlotte set down the knife and scanned the den, visible through the glass double doors to her right. *No sign of Frankie, thank God. Maybe I'll have time to clear up this misunderstanding.* "You may not believe it, but that's not what I meant. What I said about Frankie. I mean, I meant it at one time, but . . ." She cleared her throat. "I know you think somebody needs to defend her, and maybe so. But not from me."

The three of them had been watching the cousins play in

the backyard. Filled to the brim with snacks—Auntie Charlie's lemon-lime soda, Auntie A's gummies, and the chocolate layer cake Frankie had whipped up—the four youngsters were burning off sugary energy, playing hide-and-seek behind the azaleas and darting among the cherry laurels that lined the back fence. Every now and then, Frankie yelled, "Watch out for snakes!" and "Don't swat at bees!" but then a sound from the baby monitor had sent her and all her precautions scurrying across the threshold into the house.

"Who knows how many children you might have yourself if you'd only be still long enough for a man to find you." Annabelle's lips clamped shut around the tines of her fork after her not-so-gentle verbal slap. A few words too late.

Charlotte glanced down at the red bars moving on the monitor's screen. She could hear the baby's whimpering and Frankie murmuring, unaware of what was taking place outside, a conversation that was getting her dander up. She had to work to show little to no emotion. "Well, at least I'm not afraid to have a family. You acted like wife- and motherhood was a disease you could contract. Maybe you've learned at last that it won't kill you to nurture something besides your bad memories and inability to forgive. I hope you appreciate it."

Annabelle grabbed the hem of her shirt. "I have half a mind to stand up, lift my shirt, and show off what I've been 'nurturing.'"

Girl, if you know like I know, you'll keep your butt in that chair. Charlotte picked up her own fork, shoved a bite of cake into her mouth, and choked down both the desire to avenge herself and the dessert she'd lost her taste for. She'd hate for Henry to find his auntie and his mama tussling, and she'd promised Max she'd strive to keep the peace, even if it killed her. Even if she had to kill Annabelle. A promise was a promise.

Annabelle's exultant face claimed a false victory over their brief skirmish. She pointed the stainless steel at Charlotte. "Mmm-hmmm. That's what I thought!"

Frankie slid back the glass door and stepped onto the deck, balancing MJ on her right arm and dragging the door closed behind her. "Annabelle, I'm going to stop invitin' you to my babies' birthdays if you're gon' cut up like this. An expectant mother at that! And you, Charlotte, I thought you stopped showin' out when it wasn't your party?"

"What?" Charlotte spun with such speed and force, her wig threatened to fly off into the hedges beside the deck. She tugged at the curls above her ears and readjusted its position.

"Girl, I'm just messin' with you. Annabelle must have tried to get you to take off that wig because you're glarin' at her the way you glared at me the other day." Frankie laughed. "Or were y'all talkin' about Max the Mysterious?"

Charlotte could've throttled her so-called favorite sister. "Would you please stop calling him that?"

"Well, when you introduce him to us, I will. Look at you over there, turnin' red and breakin' into a sweat at just the mention of his name. Max . . . Max . . . Max . . ." Frankie danced toward her seat.

"Calling *who* that? Who in the world is Max?" Annabelle threw herself into the middle of the back-and-forth volley between the two women.

"The new man in her life, that's who."

"Uh-uh," Charlotte fretted. She'd hoped to protect the beautiful, fragile "us" formed by Max and her. Like a baby bird with untried wings, their relationship felt too new and too precious to withstand a Winters examination. But there was no avoiding it: she couldn't let him go. She had to yank off the Band-Aid sometime and throw him to the wolves.

Frankie's laugh was boisterous enough to make up for Charlotte's discomfort. "But we can talk more about that later. First, you need to tell me what you did to Annabelle to get her so riled up. She's lookin' mighty suspicious down there, pointin' that eatin' utensil. Okay, ladies, what'd I miss?"

"Only another episode of *As the Winters Turn*," Annabelle remarked, knowing they'd get the reference to the old soap opera. "Stuff like the age-old chocolate-versus-vanilla debate. I might get left out of all the juicy talk—" she eyed the two of them—"but you know we'd wait for you before fussing about something that really mattered." She stood and began gathering empty plates belonging to her nephew and nieces and scraped cake remains and cheddar Goldfish into a trash bag conveniently taped to the edge of the table. *That Frankie certainly knows how to run a tight ship. I'd better take good notes before Baby McMillan makes his debut.*

"There you go again, grinning at some story you're telling yourself," Charlotte grumped. "Come on, share. Is the joke on me, or what?" As if refusing to be outdone by Annabelle—as usual—she plucked the used candles from the cake and dropped them in the pile headed for the trash.

"Oh, no! Don't get rid of those. I'll certainly be using that number four again." Frankie snatched up the candle and licked the chocolate off the end that'd been wedged in the cake. "The twins used it, and now Nora, but the wick is still good. Little Melvin Jr. here will get a turn soon enough."

Annabelle laughed, mostly at her baby sister's wide eyes and her mouth that matched. Unlike Charlotte, she could relate to

Frankie's miserly ways, in more ways than one. Her older sibling practiced good stewardship over their household's single income—almost too good. On the other hand, Annabelle managed her money so she'd never become a slave to it or her work, something else she could thank Mayhelen for. *Note to self: buy our birthday candles from Family Dollar each year. Oh, and never eat the cake near the candles when we're at Frankie's house.*

"Anyway, sit down. Y'all are gonna need all that energy for our talk about Mama, not to mention this girl's new boyfriend. Annabelle, you should get off your feet. Avoid swelling at all costs." Frankie walked to the railing and snapped her fingers two times, and three sets of young brown eyes swung her way; Henry, paying no attention to his aunt's signal, did a series of cartwheels in the opposite direction. Frankie pointed at the toys sprinkling the lush, ankle-high grass, and immediately her children set down their bottles of bubble solution and collected the balls and hoops they'd discarded.

"Must be nice, not having chores at his age." Frankie cut an eye at Annabelle.

Annabelle plastered a pleasant expression on her face and continued clearing the mess. Internally, she ranted at the snide comment about her son and willed Henry to join his cousins of his own accord, so she didn't look like the lame stepmom of a lazy, disobedient child.

After watching Paul, Leah, and Nora work for a minute or two more, Frankie took the advice she'd offered her sisters and flopped into one of the empty seats on the longer side of the table that faced the yard. She transferred the infant to her shoulder and ran her hand in a swirling motion on his back.

"So, what's left to say about Mama, Frankie?" Charlotte squeezed her hips back into her rattan chair.

"Everything! We still haven't made any decision about what to do."

"What about Miss Hattie? I thought she was coming." Annabelle brushed the crumbly bits of cake and crunched-up crackers into her hand and threw them into the grass to feed the ants and birds, hoping their hostess wouldn't mind; Frankie's husband was a stickler when it came to his yard. As she slapped together her palms to clean them, her eyes narrowed in the strange silence in response to her question. Those two always had something to say. And what was that look that passed between them? "Is there something y'all need to tell me?"

Charlotte cut her eyes at Frankie and back at Annabelle. "Well . . ."

Frankie wiggled into a comfortable spot, braced her elbows on the table, and let her eyes do the talking for her, clearly willing Charlotte to continue. But sure enough, Frankie jumped in anyway. "Charlotte and I—"

"Wait, *Charlotte* and you what?"

"Well, if you let me finish, I'll tell you!"

Annabelle felt herself bristle like a porcupine. "Now, wait a minute."

"Anna." Frankie's tone could've sliced the birthday cake all by itself. "Hear me out. Please."

With a huff, Annabelle complied.

"Miss Hattie isn't feeling up to snuff. We were really hopin' we could hash all this out today, but we weren't sure you'd show." Frankie kissed the baby's cheek, then began to bounce him on her lap with his face toward his aunties. His arms beat the air like tiny windmills.

"'We,' meaning you and *Charlotte*." Annabelle didn't flick an eyelash in her sister's direction when the younger woman sniffed at the other end of the table.

"Regardless, Anna. For the longest time, you separated yourself when things got sticky." Frankie cleared her throat and adjusted the position of her seat to peer around the hedges. Seemingly satisfied that the children were safe, her gaze turned inward as she gathered her thoughts, much the way her son and daughters were sorting their toys into organized piles in the yard.

Annabelle jumped in before Frankie could formulate her words. "And when would that be, exactly? As you very well know, things have always been . . . how did you put it, '*sticky*' . . . when it comes to this family."

Charlotte's chair squeaked, but that was the only noise from that end of the deck.

"True. And rather than deal with it, you've been on the run ever since you had the wherewithal to do so. I don't need to remind you that you dropped out of UNC and disappeared for over a year. When you finally popped up, it was only to send a postcard from . . ." Frankie made a tapping motion in the air, searching her memory. "Where was it?"

"Arizona." Charlotte's voice was as dry as the climate in that southwestern state.

"Arizona. *A-ri-zo-na.* You wrote me five hard-to-decipher lines, tellin' me you were alive and well and learnin' how to bend metal at some school down there."

"Fabricate," corrected Annabelle. Obviously, there was no use denying the truth, and that was all she could offer.

"Whatever. Then from there you went to . . ." Again, Frankie's attention veered off toward the yard, though she didn't focus on the youngsters dousing each other with bubble solution and laughing hysterically.

"Seattle, wasn't it?" Charlotte's chair cracked and squeaked again as she inched closer to the table. She propped her feet on the ironwork below the tabletop and crossed her ankles.

Frankie squinted. "Are you sure, Charlotte? Maybe you're right, but I thought it was New Mexico. Hmm."

Sitting still as stone, Annabelle didn't chime in. She didn't have to tell them no, it was neither New Mexico nor Seattle, because Frankie eventually remembered it was Colorado, and following that, Annabelle went to New Mexico. She never made it to Seattle because she'd returned to the East Coast to live closer to family. Just not too close. If she hadn't moved back, she might never have met Oliver and Henry—and wouldn't be here, held hostage across from her sisters at that very moment.

Frankie snuggled the baby to her chest and played with one of his tiny fists. "Anyway, that's not the point, where you've been, because you're here now. But when you think about it, you talk about Mama like a dog; however, you left too."

Chapter Twenty-Nine

Then

SMACK! **"FOR THE FIFTY-ELEVENTH TIME,** I said, sit still. Don't make me tell you again. You're the oldest, and you should know better."

Her mama's words sounded hot in Frankie's right ear, almost as hot as the spot on the back of her hand. *What about you, Mama? Do you know better now?*

"And you bet' not cry." Mayhelen sat straight and tugged the hem of her daffodil-colored dress closer to her knees. The material didn't quite make it. Her outfit looked too . . . much somehow for church, and by the way she kept shifting and pulling, she seemed to know it. She also needed to take her own advice about not crying, something she'd been doing more and more. Uncontrollably at times. To Frankie, her mama looked like the woman Miss Hattie's

Bible talked about. Not the one in Proverbs dressed in purple who got up when it was dark to feed the poor and buy fields and such, or something like that. Mama reminded her of the other woman whose husband had to keep searching for her and bringing her back home, the kind Miss Hattie warned them about. Frankie didn't understand what a generational curse or a harlot was, but neither sounded good.

Frankie's own dress was itchy, and she had to fight like the devil—*Oops, I'm sorry, God*—not to scratch her thigh. Her stinging hand should've served as a good reminder. It wasn't her dress, not really. Up until that morning, it had hung in the closet in Annabelle's room. When Frankie couldn't find something appropriate for the cooler weather to wear to church, her mama had stomped into her sister's room, hair flying and mascara running, snatched the striped, long-sleeved dress with the wide blue belt off the hanger, and slapped it against Frankie's chest.

"Here, put this on. Nobody's gonna be lookin' at you anyway. It won't matter how it fits."

That was where her mama was both right and wrong. Most eyes had indeed followed Mayhelen as soon as her high heels hit the pavement; she'd commandeered nearly all the attention as she strutted across the parking lot. But the gaggle of girls in Sunday school had snickered when Frankie had slipped in all late and wrong, right before it was time to take up the offering. She'd pretended she couldn't find her quarter, that it had fallen out of the one pocket on the left side of her chest, but Frankie could tell the rest of the group knew good and well she hadn't brought money in the first place.

And in the second place, the dress was noticeably too small. They'd had to unfold the cuffs, revealing the raw hem. The knit fabric stretched too tightly across her—what did Miss Hattie call them?—bosoms. Where her mama's were making her own dress gape and strain. Frankie sat taller and drew back her shoulders and blinked back tears, unaware that she was drawing undue attention to the very area she wanted to hide. Crying in church would only earn her another slap on the hand, worse than the first. At nearly sixteen, she was too big for that.

On Frankie's left side, Annabelle shifted. Her younger sister had trained herself to sit through church without moving a muscle. Their baby sister hadn't figured it out yet, so some woman from the missionary department was rocking the fussy child to sleep in what the church called "the cry room." The God-lady must have thought that Mama needed to stay and hear the message. *Whole lot of good that's doing. Anybody with half a mind can see that Mayhelen is holding the red hymnal upside down and is only pretending to sing along to "Amazing Grace."*

During the early part of the service, when they were supposed to turn to their neighbor and greet new worshipers, Annabelle had shared her secret for staying out of trouble. "I go to sleep in my mind," she'd confessed over the head of a whimpering Charlotte, who hadn't yet been swooped up by the watchful missionary circle. "My eyes may look like they're wide open, but in my head, it's a Saturday morning, and I'm in my bed, wrapped up tight under the covers."

Ever practical, Frankie had considered and discarded her advice in one fell swoop. "But where's Mama? She'd never let you sleep in on a Saturday."

"Girl, this is a church dream. Nothing bad can happen when you're dreamin' in church, not with Jesus watchin'! Mama goes out to buy donuts for us so when we wake up, we can eat as many as we want," Annabelle whispered behind her hand.

"Mama's in it too?" Frankie could have swallowed a fly, her mouth had opened so wide.

"Only when I dream here. When I'm home, sleeping in my bed, y'all are nowhere to be found. Especially Mama. Mmm-hmmm. You know it. But somebody's gotta bring me my breakfast, right?"

Thinking back on it, Frankie fought to hold back her laugh. She should've known better, because holding in a laugh in church was near to impossible. Everybody and their mama knew that—including hers. When Frankie snorted, Mayhelen reached over and pinched her thigh, right through the thick fabric of that polyester dress.

"I should tear you up when we get home, drawin' all this undue attention to me. As if we needed any more." Somehow, Mayhelen managed to keep her face straight for the rest of the church while looking all cross-eyed at her daughter.

Mama never seemed to expect as much out of Annabelle and Charlotte as she did from her oldest daughter. Frankie felt like she was that lone runner carrying the Olympic torch. If she dropped it, the flame would go out—and who would relight it? Not her mama. Her mama's breath a blow-dryer against her inner ear, Frankie fought to keep her eyes from overflowing. The prospect of crying in front of everybody . . . The shame of it was too much to bear.

As if she could sense her sister's agony, Annabelle slipped her hand into Frankie's and gripped it down low so their interlocked fingers rested on the pew, squeezed between their two thighs.

Yet, Frankie didn't glance her sister's way because tears were even harder to hold back than laughter when they really got cranked up. To combat the threatened overflow, she widened her eyes and stared at the preacher shaking his Bible in the air with one hand and gripping the microphone with the other. Frankie wondered if God would sound like this man, huffing and puffing and yelling through a speaker that was turned up way too loud. He seemed to be mad at everybody for some reason. *Is he looking at Mama? Does he know what Mama did and that she pinched me?*

Frankie had a feeling that man wouldn't care one bit about her sore leg, so focused he was on their "dirty rags." As he strutted around the red-carpeted stage, his eyes seemed to find them in the middle of the third row, prowling like the lion he was preaching about. Nothing about him and all his yelling reminded her of the peace-seeking Good Shepherd in that Book of Miss Hattie's, although whatever her mama had heard had her craning forward in her seat.

As they edged down the row toward the aisle after the service, Frankie watched Mayhelen stop at the double doors of the church. That same preacher who'd been fussing at the people sitting in the red pews was smiling and going on, chatting it up with those same sinners as they milled past him. She wondered if anyone else thought her mama held the preacher's hand a little too long. If they also wondered why she was speaking so earnestly and what he said with his hand on her shoulder. Knuckles rapping between Frankie's shoulder blades drew her attention to her sister's voice at her ear.

"Miss Hattie never waved her Bible like that preacher was doing. It looked like a weapon." Annabelle's breath smelled like Alexander the Grape, her favorite candy. "She shows us pictures and all those words printed in red. Charlotte says she talks in her sleep with the Bible in her lap."

"Miss Hattie doesn't sleep-talk with her Bible. She calls it havin' a conversation with God. Prayin'. So God will keep us safe. She says He loves us."

"Do you think she prays for Mama too? I hope so."

"She must be. Mama's here, isn't she?"

This time it was Annabelle's eyes that welled up. "I guess she didn't pray for Greg."

Once they reached the carpeted aisle, the two of them trod side by side to retrieve Charlotte from the cry room, aptly named for their baby sister's favorite activity. "So, did you do that church dreamin' like I told you about?" Annabelle briefly closed her eyes and put her head against her closed hands.

Frankie was grateful for those prayers of Miss Hattie's. Only God could've kept Mama from seeing her lean her head on Annabelle's shoulder and close her lids that had grown heavy from crying. She nodded curtly, trying to shed the vestiges of her unsettling "church dream" she'd had while her hand got all sweaty in Annabelle's.

It was about a white rose that looked like the one Miss Hattie had asked her to pluck from the hedge between McDonald's and Popeyes. They were on their way to a Mother's Day service, and their neighbor had explained how she couldn't wear a red rose, the color of life and love, since her mama had gone on to meet her reward. That long-ago day, Miss Hattie had affixed that stark-white rose high up on her bosom and strode into Macedonia Baptist with somebody else's children to keep her company.

Now that she thought about it, Frankie thought it'd be fitting if she pinned one to her own chest. Aching to snuggle her baby brother, Frankie wondered about affixing a white rose to the collar above her own bosom. As far as her heart was concerned, her mama was long gone.

Chapter Thirty

Now and Then

BIRDS SWOOPED IN SILENT PAIRS in the sky over the house. Annabelle wished she, too, had such a friend in her family, someone who supported both her flight and her eventual return. "I don't set out to disparage Mama; I speak the truth about her. I can't help it if those words sound like one and the same. That's more her fault than mine. *She* was the reason I left."

"But why *then*?" Frankie asked. "Mama was long gone by the time you packed up and took off. Charlotte was in high school, and I wasn't ready to be Mama and Daddy by myself."

"Why not? We'd been playing those roles our whole lives, Frankie. We were the only real parents she'd ever known, other than Miss Hattie."

"Why are y'all talkin' about me like I'm not here?" Charlotte's seat scraped against the Trex deck when she pushed back from the table. She positioned herself by the railing, drawing their eyes her way. Her lemony pantsuit stood out in stark relief against springtime's vibrant green shades and the pink petals of the camellias. "I can speak for myself."

Annabelle gasped, Charlotte's words an unexpected trigger. "You know, that's what I remember most about the night we found Greg unresponsive in Mama's bed: your silence. All that you *couldn't* say, Charlotte. All the words she took from you."

"And I had to start speaking for you." A tremor ran through Frankie's normally confident voice.

It's probably about time we stop, Annabelle realized.

Stricken, Charlotte covered her mouth.

Frankie went on. "I remember leading the way onto the back porch when Miss Hattie dropped us off. And I was tellin' y'all about the movie. How my friends kept throwing popcorn at the sad parts. What was the name of it?"

"Whatever it was, that night you said the movie was funny, and you had the best time," Annabelle reminded her. "You were positively giddy because you never got a night out with your friends. You were always mothering us." For that, she was grateful, and she could admit it now. "Charlotte was fussing—"

"No, I wasn't," Charlotte whispered. "You had the cheese crackers, and Frankie and I were wrestling over the tub of popcorn she'd brought us. I loved buttered popcorn. Still do. But I wasn't crying. We were playing and laughing—"

"At least until we stepped inside." Annabelle had dragged her feet, dreading the moment they had to enter the house and shut the door behind them. The VBS leader had explained the difference between being *in* and being *of* the world. The Winters family dealt with both within the walls of their home.

"When we stepped through the door, we got quiet," Annabelle continued. "That came second nature to us. Frankie set the half-full tub in your hands, Charlotte, and I waved goodbye to Miss Hattie through the glass because she always waited for us at the top step, to make sure we were safe." *But to do that, she should've taken us home with her long before that night.*

"That window in the door was shaped like a diamond, wasn't it?" Charlotte smiled a little.

"Yep. And it was beveled, so when the sun shone through it, it created a pattern on the floor and you danced in it." Annabelle smiled with her, briefly. "But it was dark that night. The clouds covered the moonlight, and I could only see Miss Hattie's silhouette."

"It wasn't cloudy. You didn't want to turn on the porch light in case Mama noticed it." Charlotte looked at Frankie, as if for confirmation.

"Maybe so," Annabelle conceded. "I was about to lock the door—"

"When I tugged on your hand and asked if you thought they were asleep," Charlotte finished.

The three had listened to the house, Charlotte hugging the popcorn. Annabelle knew her sister actually wanted to know if Mayhelen was in bed. If Greg was awake, he would've made himself heard by one and all.

"It was 9:30, and I figured she was probably watching *Law & Order*." Frankie pointed at Annabelle. "And you said something like 'Planning her next victim.'" She *tsked-tsked* and shook her head.

"'*Anna!* Don't say that. You'll scare Charlotte.'" Annabelle did her best imitation of her older sister as a teenager.

"Yep, I fussed then almost as much as I fuss now," Frankie admitted. "I didn't put up with mess like that because I was the one who would have to get up with Charlotte during the night if she cried out from a nightmare."

Annabelle rolled her eyes. "Charlie, you were such a baby, even at six years old."

Charlotte shrugged. "I didn't get much attention in those days."

"Max is changin' that." Frankie patted the area near her heart that MJ wasn't covering.

Their mama's scream had scared them all. Annabelle's legs carried her up the wide staircase ahead of her sisters, and she burst into Mayhelen's room and then froze in the doorway. Frankie thundered in behind her, and she had to catch Annabelle when she plowed into her. Charlotte's small feet brought up the rear; she had to crawl under their legs, one arm still clutching the cardboard bucket.

"You never let go of that popcorn." Annabelle always wondered at that.

"Miss Hattie heard the commotion and came runnin' in because Annabelle hadn't locked the door yet. I heard her tell one of her friends from church that she finally understood what 'blood ran cold' meant when she heard it." Frankie always seemed to be nearby when grown folks were talking.

"And she crushed all the kernels that I'd spilled." Charlotte seemed to be picturing it.

Mayhelen, her hair a spiky, matted, off-kilter crown on her head, was sitting in the middle of her king-size bed, shaking a limp Greg. She was screaming, "Only sleepin'. He's only sleepin'" and "Wake up! Wake up!"

But he wouldn't. Turned out he couldn't, and he never did. And in all the noise and confusion and tears, between the questions from the EMS workers and the police and the social workers, the youngest Winters female never said a word about what she'd witnessed.

"Until now. Right, Charlotte?" Annabelle's eyes met and held her baby sister's. At first, only the children's distant yelling drifted their way in the silence that settled on them like the cooler evening air. Then the faint sound of a music box playing "Turkey in the Straw" swelled as it approached the house and lingered there, its volume floating around toward the backyard. *The ice cream truck,* Annabelle recognized, as Henry ran toward the steps. Slowly, she shook her head from side to side until he hung his head and ran back to his cousins, who obviously knew better than to ask. Frankie probably never gave in.

Charlotte's lips pinched together as the music box faded, and the ice cream truck took its wares elsewhere.

Annabelle shrugged. *So much for speaking for yourself.*

"We could've used your help, you know, your company. Your presence." Frankie picked up the thread of their earlier topic: Annabelle's desertion. "Charlotte and I would've loved to have had the opportunity to spend more time with you, to get to know you as an adult the way we knew you as a child. But instead, you left us. For the longest time, we three were all we had . . . but you up and *left* us." Those last words barely made it around the table.

"I didn't break up our family. That was Mayhelen's doing, something she accomplished single-handedly before she ever made her great escape." Annabelle sounded weary. "Maybe you don't ever plan to live somewhere else, Frankie, but it's what a lot of people do. They grow up and move away all the time. Explore.

Change. And unlike Mama, I always told you where I was going." Her eyes landed on the two middle shelves of a wrought iron baker's rack to the left of the glass doors. "You see those plants?"

Charlotte followed the direction of Annabelle's finger. But Frankie didn't have to. She knew her own yard. "You mean those bougainvillea cuttings? Melvin clipped those when were in Florida and thinks he can grow them here. I told him they won't do well in this shady backyard, that it gets too cold, but—" She sighed. "Sorry." She could tell by the look in Charlotte's eyes, her sister was following Annabelle's words closely, listening to what was said and unsaid, though she might never admit it. Frankie hadn't meant to go on and on about her husband's project, unraveling the thread of the conversation.

Annabelle ran her hands through her hair. "No worries. My point is that sometimes we outgrow our pots or need a change of scenery. I wanted to see if I could flourish in different ground."

Charlotte stalked over to the baker's rack and yanked up a fledgling plant. "See this?" She flung water on the baby's arm when she waggled the limp stalk and pinched the bottom of it. She had at last found her voice. "No roots to be seen. As Frankie suspected, I'd say things aren't going so well for this transplant. All that moving from its natural habitat. How'd it go for you, Annabelle, all that gallivanting about the country, being blown by the wind? Did you put down roots?"

"If that's not a root, then I don't know what is!" Annabelle pointed at Henry, trying to hit his cousins with the tire swing. He'd pull on the rope looped over a tree branch and let it go in their direction, as if they were a row of pins at the end of a bowling lane.

"That boy out there is sweet as pie," Charlotte agreed, "but I'd say the roots I'm talking about are pretty bitter, for all your churchgoing." She threw down the plant, and it landed with a quiet splat on the deck at her feet.

The baby startled. He raised his head suddenly, bopping it under Frankie's chin, and let out a wail.

"Great," Frankie huffed, then ran her fingers lightly over the top of MJ's head and through his hair. "Shh, shh, you're all right, sweetie." Eyes half-closed, she pressed her lips to his crown.

Annabelle flopped back into her seat, her arms hanging on each side. "See? Just talking about Mama causes trouble."

"We were talking about *you*." Charlotte squatted to retrieve the bougainvillea. "Don't think we're finished either."

Frankie stood so she could rock MJ. "And speaking of Mama, what are we gon' do? She wanted to come back home, and it's up to us to make it happen."

"That's where you're wrong. Mama didn't want anything; Miss Hattie is the one who asked us. Mayhelen Winters never gave a hoot about being close to us, remember? As much as we tried." Instead of making eye contact, Annabelle teased an ant that was crawling across the table by continually moving a tiny piece of cake a centimeter out of its reach. Like that crumb, Annabelle's problem with their mother was five thousand times heavier than her ability to carry it herself.

"Anna." Frankie's voice was soft but demanding.

She flicked the cake off the table and smushed the ant with her thumb. Then she looked up.

Charlotte felt Frankie sway side to side between her and the empty chair. Both her arms were wrapped around the infant who was pressed against her breasts, providing shelter, comfort, love. *Did I ever get those things?*

Frankie bumped her hip. "Despite what you may think, Annabelle, we're all on the same side. Aren't we, Charlotte? We're still the three muskrats . . ."

Charlotte nodded peremptorily, obediently. "Three and a quarter."

"Quit that, Charlotte. We need to act like it—be open and honest with each other about what we're thinkin' and feelin'."

Annabelle crossed her arms. "You don't want that. Neither of you do. In my experience, the very people who say the most to others are the most sensitive themselves. They can't take hearing the same frankness they're always laying on somebody else."

"Well, we're not 'people.' We're family. So bring it on." Seemingly satisfied that she'd soothed the baby, at least for the moment, Frankie eased back into her seat.

Charlotte waved off a large mosquito hawk. Its long legs dangled below as it fluttered about the table. "Speak for yourself, Frankie. I don't want to get my feelings hurt. Maybe you need to lie to me."

"Charlotte, maybe you should speak now or forever hold your peace." Annabelle nodded toward Frankie. "Seems like as good a time as any, since Mama is on the menu."

Charlotte sighed. *Why didn't I lay it all on the table last weekend when I was here?* It wasn't getting any easier to tell Frankie about her conversations with their mother.

"Are y'all fighting again?" Frankie fanned herself, misunderstanding what was going on between her sisters. "You know, we spent too long all up under each other to waste another minute living at odds. It matters not if it's Miss Hattie's request or Mama's. If we're goin' to honor it, we need to agree to it. And the same goes for turnin' it down. Because I won't do anything unless we're *all* doin' it or we're all *not* doin' it." Her head rotated toward Annabelle, and then they both turned to Charlotte.

She closed her eyes in a long blink and opened them in the direction of the evening sun, an orange glow above the treetops. A moth fluttered around the light mounted on a wood post at the corner of the yard that had flickered on a few minutes before, reminding Charlotte that Annabelle and Frankie were allowing the children to run around in the dusky half-light. Darkness was nearly upon them. At last, she whispered, "I'm in. Anna, in or out?"

"I guess . . . I'm in." Annabelle glared at both her sisters, showing how much she resented the corner she felt pressed into. "If you two insist on doing this, even though I don't think she deserves it one bit."

"It's not about Mama, what we think she deserves. That's for God to worry about. This decision is about doin' what's right. We're not tryin' to make peace with Mayhelen Winters. We have to have peace within ourselves, with God. When He commanded us to 'honor our father and mother,' He didn't say how long or under what conditions. We're supposed to do our part and let Him take care of the other part that doesn't belong to us."

"Okay, okay, Frances Mae. Don't go full Bible and use it against us." Charlotte hadn't stepped foot in church since Annabelle's wedding. That would change tomorrow, thanks to an invitation from Max. She planned to sit in the back near the door.

"I'm not using it against you, Charlotte. I'm using the Word to help us. Do you think I want to do this? When Miss Hattie called me all those weeks ago, my first thought was to hang up on her—well, okay, not exactly hang up on her. I did want to tell her, 'I'm sorry, no can do.' And you know I love myself some Miss Hattie. We had another good long conversation last night. As much as I didn't want to hear what she had to say, she probably didn't want to say it. But I—*we*—needed to hear it."

"Why, Frankie? Why do we need to hear it?" Annabelle banged

a fist on the table, making the plates jiggle. "I don't need convincing that it's the right thing. I know we owe a great debt to Miss Hattie." One she'd never claim they owed her. "Why is she doing this for Mama?"

"This is more than bringin' Mama home and honorin' her . . . or some such nonsense."

Charlotte smirked since she could tell that Frankie had appended the last part of her statement for her. "What more can there be?"

Frankie was tired of going round and round about it. "It's about forgiveness, for goodness sakes! Diggin' up that bitter root Charlotte alluded to. We need to forgive ourselves and let all the pain and anger go, but we can't do that—"

"Without forgiving Mama, even if she's not here to accept it. Or ask for it. I know the answer to that, Annabelle." Charlotte's chuckle lacked an ounce of humor. She slapped her bare arm and flicked off something black.

Annabelle sighed. "I'm all for burying Mama, for letting her go. But why bring her closer and deal with the house? None of those go together."

"Frankie, I should tell you—" Charlotte began.

"Speaking of proximity—" Frankie peered into the yard—"I don't see the kids, and I want to get the baby inside, out of this night air. Nora! Leah! Paul! Henry! Time to go in!" *Sometimes I sound like Miss Hattie,* she thought. So old-fashioned. *I bet she's not afraid of the dark though.*

Charlotte moved closer to the rail. She put her hand on her brow and stared toward the sun as it said its goodbyes for the day.

Frankie paced the deck. "It's not about proximity or location.

Annabelle, you of all people know that. It's the state of the heart and mind. But we've agreed, correct? We'll meet with Miss Hattie and move forward. Take the burden off of her." She glanced back and took each barely there, reluctant nod as the only *yes* she was going to get because the conversation was no longer her priority. "Then I'll set up a meetin' and get things movin'. See what's involved in puttin' the house on the market and buryin' Mama here in Jasper. I guess she's finally comin' home."

"Whether she wanted to or not," Charlotte mumbled.

"Charlotte, what are you—?" Frankie questioned before a scream pierced the backyard, followed by sobbing. She sprinted across the deck. MJ's tiny arms flailed, and he added his screech to the noise, his eyes stretching to large circles over his mother's shoulder. At the top of the steps, Frankie turned and thrust him at Charlotte, who caught him right before his mother dashed down.

Annabelle was so close behind Frankie, she stepped on the back of her foot, pulling down the heel of her sister's canvas espadrille.

Chapter Thirty-One

Now

ANNABELLE LOCKED THE LAST SEATBELT into place, not trusting the children to do it themselves. Nothing would happen to either Frankie's children or hers, not on her watch. She edged out of the car on her hands and knees, pushing herself upright once her sneakers hit the concrete, and studied the three in the back seat of her Mustang. Annabelle forced a smile that trembled at the edges, hoping to convince them she had the situation well in hand. From the looks of their wordless stares, Frankie's twins knew good and well she didn't; her own child appeared to hold out hope. Still, she offered a thumbs-up for reinforcement. "Y'all good?"

Leah and Paul nodded slowly, though they probably felt anything but good after witnessing their little sister's accident in their backyard. The last place they wanted to be was with their Auntie

A, what they'd called Annabelle since before they were old enough to manage her name. Maybe they would have been more comfortable with their other auntie, who'd been more involved in their lives since they were born. Instead, they were going home with Annabelle, who had stumbled into motherhood after falling in love with Oliver.

Gazing at Henry holding a box full of jewelry-making tools and her niece and nephew smushed beside him on the leather seats, Annabelle realized what she'd suspected all along: she needed to trade in her sporty car for a more family-friendly vehicle before Baby McMillan made his appearance. *Or her appearance,* that pesky voice reminded her. *You'd better get used to the idea before you get a surprise in the delivery room.*

Obviously thinking she wouldn't stop staring at them until they gave her a sign, Henry slowly raised his thumb, sensitive enough to his mother's feelings to help her feel better. Leah, belted in the middle seat between the boys, tucked her arm through Paul's, and they both nodded.

"Okay. Then let's go see Uncle Oliver, I mean Daddy. You know what I mean. I've already called him and told him we're coming. He's probably making burgers or hot dogs or something like that. Do you like hamburgers . . . or better yet, cheeseburgers? Tell them how yummy we make them at our house, Henry." Annabelle set the driver's seat into position, climbed in, and slammed her door. With a turn of the ignition, the Mustang roared to life. She adjusted her rearview mirror so she could make eye contact with the three behind her. Mistake. Leah was crying, and that only sent Annabelle's running commentary into overdrive. She didn't want Paul to take his cue from her, and Henry was too young to take on the role of not only pacifying his mother, but also consoling his cousins.

"Would a grilled cheese be better? Or soup? What's your favorite food? Uncle Oliver is a whiz in the kitchen. Tell them, Henry! Well, not really a whiz. Your dad doesn't know that I'm the true magic-maker, although he's great at following directions. Oh, don't tell him I said that, Henry. You know where he's the true chef? On the grill. I'm afraid of building a fire, even if it's easier now that we buy the kind of charcoal that includes lighter fluid. You can basically throw a match, and *whoosh*! Did you know grilling is my favorite way to cook a cheeseburger? I could fry the burgers inside on the stove—at least, I *could* have before we started the renovation—but there's nothing like the flavor of a bacon cheeseburger cooked on charcoal. Yummmmm-*my*. That first bite—" Annabelle swallowed the rest of the words she was about to regurgitate into the otherwise silent vehicle.

Bite. Did I have to use that word, of all the words in the dictionary I could've said? Sink my teeth? No, definitely not that. Taste, yes. That would've sounded tons better. She risked a glance in the mirror when she turned right at the corner after curving to the top of Frankie's street. Leah's head had dropped onto her brother's shoulder and her eyes drifted closed.

Great. She can't cry in her sleep, can she? Another peek informed Annabelle that yes, indeed, Leah was able to cry quite well with her eyes closed. Paul, on the other hand, was certainly wide-awake. And not a tear to be seen. Annabelle nearly missed a four-way stop sign and braked hard, making the car lurch forward and rock back a few times until it was still. Leah was awake again.

Annabelle winced. "I'm sorry. I promise I won't kill you." *Shoot, there I go again. Bite, kill . . . Batting a thousand tonight.* Eyes glued to the road, she eased through the intersection and resolved to keep quiet the rest of the way home. At least for the next five minutes. Long enough for her to replay the evening's events a gazillion times, to push her mental fast-forward and rewind buttons and play an unrewarding game of "what if."

She'd heard Frankie murmuring, "Nora-Nora-Nora-Nora" under her breath as the women tore through the yard in search of the children. Annabelle had known it was her sister's God-given heart for her little ones that had led Frankie to rule out Henry altogether and identify which of her own three was screaming. It certainly hadn't been a learned or inherited skill. When they rounded the corner of the house, heading for the front yard, she spotted Frankie's twins huddled around their baby sister. Henry shivered off to the side by himself. As soon as Paul and Leah laid eyes on the women, they both sprinted in their direction.

Paul reached them first and shouted, "A snake bit Nora!" and he launched himself at Frankie.

"It was a copperhead!" Leah supplied, enveloping her mother in a hug.

"Ugh," Frankie groaned, her breath leaving her upon impact.

From Annabelle's perspective, Henry stood like a weeping willow, feet planted, but not firmly enough to hold him. She suspected he would collapse at the least provocation.

Enfolded by her children, Frankie had to lumber the remaining few feet and drag them to the birthday girl, so Annabelle reached her niece first. When she knelt on the ground by Nora, who was still screeching to high heaven, Annabelle gently, yet firmly, moved aside the small arms the child was using to protect her leg. Immediately, she noted the two punctures right below Nora's knee; her lower leg was swelling and becoming discolored. Even in the fading light, she could tell the girl's honey-colored skin had turned pink, gray, and blue, like the colors of the evening sky.

"Shh, shh. Calm down. It's gonna be okay. Y'all, we have to

settle down." Annabelle lowered Nora's leg, flattening it on the ground. She looked over. "Henry, what happened?"

Frankie finally peeled off her older children so she could see to her four-year-old. "Baby girl, baby girl. It's okay. Mama's here. Somebody help me make a tourniquet!"

"No." Annabelle kept her voice low and even. "You'll restrict blood flow, and that could cause more damage. "Let's get her up . . ." She grunted a little as she scooped Nora up, feeling a small pull in her abdomen as she did so. "Uh-uh, no, don't lift her leg. Let it hang so it's not raised higher than her heart." Propelled by adrenaline, Annabelle held the little one close to her as she moved toward the garage.

"Henry, baby, are you okay? Yes? You're sure? Then walk with Aunt Frankie. Paul and Leah, let go of your mama. Come on, now, let go. Leah, be a big girl and run inside and push the button for the garage door, and Paul, get your mama's keys and her purse so she can drive Nora to the hospital. And bring a snack!" she thought to call after him as he scampered off.

Her son, still silent, inched close to her elbow. She felt him clutch the long tail of her shirt.

"Henry," she panted, "while you're walking with me, how about you tell Nora some of those poems we read in the Mother Goose book." She whispered to Frankie who was keeping pace with her on her other side, "She needs to calm down so the venom doesn't spread as quickly." *And so I don't lose what hearing I have left.*

Somehow, someway, everyone followed her directions, with Annabelle taking the lead, a role her older sister usually assumed. They loaded Nora into her booster seat in the second row of the Odyssey, and Frankie jumped behind the wheel. As the kids tossed her purse and two granola bars into the passenger seat, Annabelle assured her sister that Charlotte would keep baby MJ there at home where he was comfortable and could sleep in his own bed, while she'd drive Paul, Leah, and Henry to her house for a fun sleepover.

"I'm so glad you're here, Annabanana." Frankie squeezed her sister's hand as she backed down the drive. She must have forgotten to let go, for she nearly took Annabelle with her.

"Auntie A, how much longer?" Leah's voice sounded small.

"I guess they never grow out of that question," Annabelle said to herself. Louder, she responded, "Twenty, twenty-five minutes. Are you hungry?"

"No, ma'am," Paul answered.

"Just tired," Leah finished for him. Whenever they were together, they tended to split their side of the conversation.

"Then why don't you take a nap? By the time you open your eyes, you'll be looking into Uncle Oliver's." Annabelle made a right in the direction that would take them past the granite fabricators. Eleanor's people, the extended family of the precious little boy sitting behind her. The very person she was closest to in the car was the one she was technically not connected to by blood, an idea she wrestled with as the dark gathered around the car on the long, unlit road toward the highway.

Don't be ridiculous. He's your son and always will be. This time the tiny voice sounded much less irritating, much more comforting.

"But isn't it too late for a nap?" Henry's incredulity turned an oft-repeated statement into a question. Once lunchtime came, his father barely let him blink his eyes for fear it would impact his bedtime.

"This is a special occasion, wouldn't you say, Henry?" From his silence, she sensed he'd acquiesced, not agreed, and she wished she, too, could curl into a ball, thrust her thumb between her teeth, and rock herself to sleep.

"Can I get you something, baby? Are you comfortable?"

Annabelle didn't bother opening her eyes to make eye contact with her husband. She was loath to move for fear she'd break the spell the recliner had cast on her. All she could manage was an "Mm-hm."

"Is that an 'mm-hm' yes or an 'mm-hm' no, and to which question?"

Sometimes . . . Annabelle tried to swallow her growl so she didn't scare the children chattering away in the kitchen. It had taken some doing, but she and Oliver finally restored a bit of calm and normalcy after the way they'd tumbled into the house—she fighting back tears of exhaustion and spent adrenaline, Paul and Leah dazed and overcome, and Henry refreshed and eager to deliver a play-by-play of the afternoon's events. As she'd listened to his detailed retelling—including the color of the hourglass shapes on the snake and the size of its head and the way it slithered through the grass and its fangs that were "this long!"—she could see why his daddy never ever let him nap.

But for the moment, that was Oliver's problem. The chair felt too good.

Annabelle had done her duty. While he had "uh-huhed" and "wowed" and "really, that longed," helped them stow their duffels and sleeping bags upstairs, and figured out where everyone was bunking, she'd whipped up garlic-roasted potatoes, homemade meatballs, and an air fryer batch of glazed carrots. She'd even baked a few dozen chocolate chip cookies. From Oliver's expression she could tell that he'd felt hoodwinked about her supposed lack of skills in the kitchen.

That was all said and done, however. After experiencing a

maelstrom of emotions, all the leftover energy had swirled down to the pit of Annabelle's stomach, where it had pooled. Not the part of her body that cradled Baby Mac, but deeper. She'd sprawled in the recliner, feeling the effects of the day drain from her body like rain channeling through a culvert—the ordeal with the snakebite, the conversation with her sisters, the looming prospect of not only bringing Mayhelen Winters home but burying her, this little bugger who was sucking the life right out of her—until her body had shut down, completely emptied. No, she was most definitely not opening her eyes for another week.

"Honeybun?"

Somebody tell this man to leave me alone. That "somebody" was too slow in relaying the message because she heard Oliver's knees crack and felt him squat beside her. The recliner rocked gently with the pressure of his hand on the arm of the chair.

"Bella . . . Bella, *Annabelle*, Frankie is here."

Still pooped, she sighed and with great effort unglued her eyelids. When she could focus, she realized that not only was Frankie there, at her house, she was *there*, hovering at Oliver's elbow, close enough to breathe on her sleeping sister. Suddenly alert, afraid she just might, Annabelle braced her hands on the leather, pushed herself upright, and closed the footrest, all in one smooth motion. "Frankie! Wh-what are you doing here?"

Her sister's eyebrows lifted an inch. "Last I heard, my kids are here at your house." She was still wearing the chocolate-streaked T-shirt she had been wearing earlier that day but had covered it with a shapeless navy sweater that their mother wouldn't have been caught dead in.

Annabelle tried to shed the last of the sluggishness and squinted at the clock on the mantel. "But it's eleven o'clock! I thought Paul and Leah were staying the night. They're already settled upstairs with Henry." She stretched and stood.

Frankie drew her close in a hug, pinning Annabelle's arms, and rocked side to side for a long moment.

Imprisoned in her sister's embrace, Annabelle could do nothing but stare at Oliver over Frankie's shoulder, asking him *What's going on?* with her eyes. Growing up, the sisters' manner of showing affection was scrambling an egg, giving a heads up when Mayhelen was on a rampage, scooting over to make room in the double bed, or lending each other a pair of jeans or a favorite shirt. It most certainly did not involve touching or even uttering the three words "I love you."

Oliver's entire body shrugged in answer.

After another moment or so, she extracted herself from Frankie's hold and held her at arm's length. "Did something happen to Nora? Something else, I mean?" Annabelle searched her sister's face first, then Oliver's, knowing she'd recognize the truth in his deep brown eyes. Frankie's were a toss-up.

"No, no, there's nothing else. I mean, other than the tissue damage—"

"What?" Oliver and Annabelle cried together. He took a giant step closer, but she retracted.

Frankie put a palm flat against her brow. "Which is normal. It's not necrotic; it will heal. The doctor said that with treatment and in time, the tissue around the bite should return to normal and there should be no lasting damage. Dear Lord, her leg swelled out to here." Her voice fluttering like the wings of a hummingbird, she formed a circle with similarly shaking hands. "And they had to give her several shots of antivenom, but my baby girl took it like a champ."

"So . . . it was a copperhead?" Her feet seemed to have their own mind. They edged back another inch or so, putting more space between the baby Annabelle was carrying and any residual danger Frankie represented.

"Yes, it was definitely a copperhead bite. Can you believe it?" Frankie sank to the sofa and dropped her head.

"No, I can't." Annabelle returned to the recliner.

After a brief pause, Oliver perched on the edge of the sofa cushion beside Frankie and searched for somewhere to place his hand—her back, her arm, her thigh. It hovered until he finally patted the back of her knuckles that gripped her knees and nodded when she sent him a grateful smile.

Annabelle cringed and mouthed *Sorry* at the pointed look he sent in his wife's direction, over the head of his sister-in-law. There was nothing Annabelle could do about it now; exchanging seats with him would prove more awkward.

Frankie didn't seem to notice. Her voice low, she sounded like she was carrying on a conversation with herself. "After all those years livin' there, puttin' myself between them and any and every tragedy, tellin' the children to watch out for snakes . . . Not one time did I really think they'd get bitten by one. Step on a rock? Sure, the way they ran around like hillbillies. But a snakebite?"

She turned her attention to Annabelle. "How did *you* know what to do? Plus, you knew exactly what *not* to do. You didn't hesitate one second." She laughed. "Oliver, you should have seen me: I completely panicked. Frozen one minute, doin' absolutely the worst thing the next, from what the doctor told me. I was about to tear off my shirt and make a tourniquet! But not your wife. I thought she was gonna jump me to keep me from doin' that. For the first time in my life, I'm willin' to admit you knew better, and I'm grateful you told me what to do."

Oliver's demeanor transformed from frustrated to admiring.

Annabelle glowed in her sister's praise but knew she didn't deserve to stand in the spotlight all by herself. "It was Henry, Henry and the Kratt brothers or one of those other friends of his."

Oliver chuckled, but then he answered the question plainly written on Frankie's face. "*Wild Kratts*—the show Henry watches every day. Annabelle joined him in front of the TV when I made her stop painting."

Annabelle flinched from a stitch in her side. Placing her hands on the base of her back, she stretched to her right. "Yes, it's all due to your nephew. You'll have to thank him in the morning. You *are* going to let Paul and Leah stay, right?"

"Absolutely. I wanted to give you an update on Nora. I figured they'd be asleep . . ." Frankie cut an eye toward the door.

Laughing, Annabelle shook her head. "You so did not come all the way over here only to confirm the snakebite. That's what your cell phone is for! You wanted to see your babies, didn't you? Couldn't make it a few hours without laying eyes on them. What about MJ? That's who I thought you'd run to first! Charlotte is probably dancing from one foot to the other as we speak, trying to get that baby to take a bottle."

Frankie hung her head. "Yep, you caught me with one foot out the door, holdin' the stolen goods. I admit it." She looked up, her grin sheepish. "I left Melvin with Nora, and I thought I'd swing by here and then peep at the baby. But really, I came here first to thank you, and I didn't want to wait until the morning when we picked up Paul and Leah. What you did . . . it made all the difference—and you know that based on those Cart Brothers—"

"Kratt," Oliver corrected.

"K-r-a-t-t," Annabelle added, right on his heels.

Frankie blew out another breath. "Y'all are makin' it mighty hard for me to keep my cool. Aren't you quite the pair, and married only two years. But since you saved my baby's life, I can't get mad at you." Frankie pursed her lips, eyeing the two of them, and then she exhaled loudly. "Anyway, Melvin stayed at the hospital with Nora, and Charlotte and her new man are enjoying their lovefest with MJ, so I figured I had time to peek in on my babies and give you a hug. You know I don't leave my children with just anyone."

Oliver clasped his hands together. "Can I get you something, Frankie? Some food? Some iced tea? Coffee or hot tea? Your sister made a mean dinner tonight. I believe she's been holdin' out on me, pretending she can't cook."

"I never said I couldn't cook. I said I *don't* cook. There's a difference." Annabelle squeezed her thighs and rose. "I can heat up some food because there's plenty, and you must be starving. I bet all you've had is birthday cake, grape Kool-Aid, and Skittles since four o'clock this afternoon."

Standing quickly, Frankie grabbed the sides of Oliver's oversize striped shirt that Annabelle was still wearing and yanked them back, revealing the tightly fitting camisole; she hadn't had the time to change after getting home.

Frankie gasped. "Goodness gracious . . . that's what this man over here meant when he said he made you stop paintin'! How could I forget?" Her hands clapped over her open mouth. "Annabelle! You picked up Nora! And here I was thankin' you for doing that. Oh, my stars, you shouldn't have done that. I could've carried her."

Oliver got to his feet and walked to his wife. "What's Frankie talking about, Bella? You lifted Nora?"

Annabelle brushed away his outstretched hands and tried to do the same with all their worry. "Stop. Both of you. Frankie, you may have forgotten I'm pregnant, but I didn't. Oliver, you know I've lifted Henry, and Nora is nothing but pointy elbows and knock-knees. I'm all right. *We're* all right." She glanced at the open door behind her and lowered her voice. "You've also forgotten, Frankie, that we haven't told Henry. So, shush. And don't mention the baby when we go see—"

Frankie held up her palms as if stopping traffic. This time it was her turn to back away from perceived trouble. "Don't worry. That'll be your bomb to drop." She looked Annabelle up and down. "Although, lookin' at you now, you won't have to say a word."

Annabelle squirmed, uncomfortable under the lens of Frankie's microscope. "How about you go and give Paul and Leah that hug you came bearing."

Oliver placed an arm around Annabelle and rubbed her shoulder. "She had to tell y'all, of course, that whole sister thang, but we weren't telling anybody else—my parents or Miss Hattie, *nobody*—until we were out of the first trimester and until Henry knows. He'll be sick if he learns otherwise."

Confusion suffused Oliver's face when he sensed something from the looks on theirs. It was obvious he couldn't decide whether or not to be offended. "What?"

Annabelle's eye-rolling matched her sister's as Annabelle murmured, "'Until *we* were out of the first trimester, he says . . . I guess *we* and not *I* will carry this baby for the next twenty-four weeks." She walked over to slide the pocket door closed to muffle their laughter.

A sudden silence swallowed up their teasing.

"Bella—"

"Annabelle," Frankie said at the same time.

Her sister was using the same authoritative voice Annabelle had employed earlier that evening at Frankie's house. It made Annabelle think of snakebites and danger and warnings. And sure enough, she read alarm on their faces when she swung around after closing the door.

"Let's get you to the hospital. I think you're bleedin'. Oliver, I'll wait here with the children."

Chapter Thirty-Two

Then

CHARLOTTE PROPPED HER CHIN on her crossed arms and stared at the back of her house. Her old house. She didn't think she'd ever swing in that old tire again or dance in the diamonds on the floor. It had already been over six years since she'd placed one toe on that back porch.

"I know you're gon' miss her."

She answered Miss Hattie without facing her. "Yeah, but she'll be back." Her eyes left the empty, weathered, two-story house and settled on Annabelle, stowing her last suitcase in the back seat of the older woman's Subaru Outback. *Their* car.

They no longer thought of this place as their neighbor's. The kindhearted soul had moved Charlotte, Frankie, and Annabelle into her two back rooms a month after Greg "went to be with

Jesus"—or so Miss Hattie put it. That was the day Mayhelen decided the fiery preacher offered a different kind of salvation than the one he talked about so fervently in church that long-ago Sunday. Their mama was definitely in need of a rescue. When their baby brother died, the girls lost her for good.

Charlotte laid her cheek on the wrinkled hand Miss Hattie placed on her shoulder. It smelled like lilacs. "Don't worry, Anna only has two more years left at Chapel Hill, and she'll be back for fall break. By the time she graduates, I'll have my license." She searched the older woman's eyes for a confirmation of her own hope but didn't find what she was looking for. "Maybe we'll all get a house together, or move in with Frankie." Even to her own ears, Charlotte didn't sound convinced. Frankie had graduated from a community college and was dating some guy she'd met at church. Miss Hattie deemed her "a good Christian girl," so Charlotte had a feeling the two would up and get married sometime soon. *I'm never getting married, and I'm never having kids. Why hitch your heart to somebody who's gonna leave you anyway?* Miss Hattie wasn't going anywhere. She'd recently had the house painted a robin's-egg blue, and the handyman guaranteed it to last ten years. *That will take me to college easy-peasy lemon squeezy.*

"Are you okay, honey? Why don't you help your sister load the rest of her things? She'll be leaving soon."

Charlotte watched Miss Hattie walk toward the kitchen, the movement of her hips barely visible in her loose-fitting flowered dress. Her daily uniform, in one color or another, whether she was going to check on things at McNair's or piddling around the garden out back. Then she faced the window again. She knew Annabelle would reject her offer of help. Something in her sister had died with Greg, and when their mama had exited stage left,

Annabelle had heaped dirt on top of her loss, burying any need to cling to her family. No, Charlotte wouldn't offer her sister help to leave. Mayhelen had done a good enough job of that already.

Chapter Thirty-Three

Now

OLIVER BRACED HIS ELBOWS on the white sheet and clasped her right hand with both of his. He pressed his lips to her knuckles.

Annabelle could do nothing more but lay her forehead against his and then recline on the extra pillow the nurse had tucked behind her head. She closed her eyes, attempting to ignore the cloth belt strapped around her belly and the blips and beeps of the monitor against the wall.

"Can I get you anything?" Oliver asked again.

"I told you, I don't need anything. Only you." Annabelle opened her eyes and rolled her head toward him but made sure to keep still. She'd already realized that when she shifted her hips even a smidge, the monitor lit up like the Fourth of July, and they'd all had enough fireworks for one day. One lifetime. "Really, I'm fine.

No pain, and the spotting has stopped. Nearly. Arlene is just being extra careful." Annabelle's shoulders inched up a little on the bed, matching the direction of her eyebrows. "I *am* advanced in age. Remember?"

Oliver's face remained impassive. "If you're trying to make me laugh, it's not gonna happen. There's no way I can smile when my wife and child are in the hospital."

"Technically, we're not *in* the hospital, only in the emergency room. This might even be triage. We're okay. Dr. Nagele said so."

"Then why are you lying on a glorified cot, attached to that thingamajig, if everything is as okay as you say it is?" He waved in the direction of the cords connecting her to the machine against the wall.

"Oliver. Babycakes. If something was wrong, Arlene would tell me. She's taking precautions, that's all. Being super careful, for which I'm supremely grateful."

She and Oliver had rushed out of the house, leaving Frankie at home with the three children tucked away upstairs. Annabelle felt a tiny bit guilty about keeping her sister from her daughter, who was still in the hospital herself and on her birthday no less, and from the baby, who was still home with Charlotte and some man Annabelle had never met. Frankie had assured them that her husband had the situation with Nora well in hand, however, and MJ should be fine for a little longer; she had breast milk stored for such occasions as these that rarely came to pass, if ever.

"A pregnant woman doesn't mess around when it comes to blood," Frankie had told her, escorting her to the car with gentle hands on Annabelle's shoulders. "Still, I'm sure this is all a formality. You'll get checked out quickly and sent home. Then we'll all go where we're supposed to."

Within minutes of checking into triage, they were ushered

to this narrow room in the hospital's emergency department so medical personnel could examine Annabelle. She'd been counting the speckles in the ceiling tiles for the past hour, with reruns of game shows playing in the background on the television mounted to the ceiling. Dr. Nagele had swooped in and taken over Annabelle's case from the on-call physician, and she was none too happy about that night's escapades. The only good thing that had come from the McMillans' trip was getting to see their little peanut moving around in her belly, waving his arms and legs at his parents.

She wiggled a little in the bed, careful not to dislodge her hand from the shelter it had found within Oliver's. For all her bravado, Annabelle shook inside at the thought that her impetuous act had hurt her baby. Her youth had been spent worrying over somebody else's children—Mama's, her own sisters, yes; yet and still, not her own. Not the life she and her husband had formed together. *What in the world was I thinking? Why didn't I freeze the way I did when my brother died?*

Annabelle squeezed her eyes closed, so tired was she of listening to thirty minutes of *Jeopardy!* music and the click, click, click of fate on *Wheel of Fortune* that followed. Searching, searching, searching for a reason . . . That question pursued her until it ran through her lips, begging for an answer. "What was I thinking, Oliver?"

"That's just it, baby. You didn't think; you acted and did what you needed to do. That's the kind of love you have for your family. Which is a good thing. You've kept your distance all these years, but that doesn't mean you didn't—or *don't*—truly care about them. Just consider this big loving family we're bringing our baby into, all the people who're waiting to wrap their arms around this baby, just like you wrapped yours around Nora tonight. Or should

I say last night?" The thin mattress made a crinkling noise as he perched beside her and brought their clasped hands close to his heart. "And by this baby, you know I mean our baby girl." Oliver unclenched his jaw and finally, his full lips formed an arc rather than a straight line.

"Oh, do y'all know something I don't?" Neither of them had heard Dr. Nagele poke her head into the room. She widened the crack and stepped inside, wearing clogs covered in a wild pattern of glossy, colorful splotches. After the heavy door thunked closed, she leaned against it, her arms crossed over a metal clipboard. "So, how are we doing?"

Annabelle patted the top of the sheet in the area of her belly to indicate she knew the "we" the obstetrician was referring to. "Anxious to take off this gown, put on my own clothes, and get home. That's how I'm doing. This little one feels the same." She noted Arlene's eyebrows forming one bushy line across her forehead. "The look on your face is telling me we might do otherwise."

Oliver rose and greeted the doctor with a silent nod, five fingers interlocked with his wife's.

Arlene cocked her head to the side. "Tell me, Annabelle, what were you thinking, picking up that four-year-old child and running with her?"

She risked a glance in Oliver's direction, afraid if she looked away from her doctor, she'd either fail to keep tragedy at bay or miss some indication of the news to come. "That's what we were just talking about. I wasn't thinking, Dr. Nagele. I-I . . . all I could do was . . . was move. I did what I couldn't do a thousand years ago. Doing what I could to help Nora and keep her mother from hurting her unwittingly. You see, I watch—"

"Wildlife shows with your son, Henry, I know. You told the ER doc when you came in, and that dude must have been a court reporter in a former life because you'd think he took down every stinkin' word you said." Dr. Nagele's New York accent dangled like fringes off her words, not completely covering them but adorning all their edges. "But now you also have to think about your other child, Annabelle. You can't forget you're carrying a baby."

Every nerve quivered, and Annabelle ached to sit up in the bed. Yet, she forced herself to remain as still as possible to avoid setting off any alarms on the monitor. "Are you accusing me of neglect? How dare you." Her outrage didn't raise Annabelle's voice; it deepened it. She didn't have to shout to make herself heard or understood, for the timbre of her voice made her meaning clear, and she could see it in Dr. Nagele's demeanor.

Oliver shifted from one foot to the other. "Bella, I don't think Arlene was imply—"

"Then what was she saying, Oliver?" Steel reinforced every word. "Tell us, Dr. Nagele, what were you saying?"

The doctor sighed and approached the bed. "I can tell I've offended you, and I'm sorry. That was never my intention, especially . . . well, especially with everything going on right now. I definitely don't want to offend you or trigger a memory and upset you even more." The OB-GYN slipped her glasses off her head and over her eyes before squinting at the printout from the monitor. She jotted down some notes on her clipboard.

"Well, you did offend me. A false accusation will do that." Annabelle knew what neglect felt like, who it looked like. She blinked away the image of Mayhelen's face and took some deep breaths.

The doctor moved to the left of the bed, forcing Oliver to release his wife's hand. He stretched for the remote and switched off the television, all the while watching her lift the stethoscope from around her neck and press it to Annabelle's chest. They were all quiet as she listened for a moment, and then he spoke from the corner of the room. "Everybody, let's take a moment and calm down. Bella, not only is Arlene your doctor; she's your friend. Arlene, you know us. We already adore this child as much as we adore Henry. There's nothing we wouldn't do to protect her . . . him." He shrugged at Annabelle around the doctor. "From the way it sounds, everything happened so fast earlier today, and my wife did what anybody would have. It's called instinct. Don't come in here criticizing her."

Dr. Nagele put away her stethoscope and her glasses, then smoothed her hair with her fingers. "Okay, this is me acting on instinct, protecting my patient. Both of them." She looked from Oliver to Annabelle. "I told you that I believed things were okay, and I meant it. I *mean* it. The baby's heart rate is good and he or she looks good." She laughed lightly; the mood in the room weighed too much for her slight attempt at using humor to lift it. "But your blood pressure is a little higher than it has been, and you're still spotting—"

The doctor held up her hand to shush them as Annabelle propped herself on her elbow. "Though it is already lighter. We took some blood work and a urine sample when you first arrived, remember? Well, I compared your hCG levels—"

"HCG?" Annabelle expected Oliver to fill in the blanks since he was the one reading all the baby books. She wasn't disappointed.

"Human chorionic gonadotropin, a hormone your body produces when you're pregnant." He lobbed the answer to her as he gently kneaded her upper back, knowing she would catch it, while directing his full attention to the doctor.

"Ahh, somebody has been doing his homework. Yes, we measured your hCG levels at your first visit, Annabelle, and they were right where they were supposed to be."

"And now?" She wondered if Oliver realized he was squeezing her shoulder.

Dr. Nagele stood tall and clasped the chart with both hands. She appeared to be squinting at the six inches of wall visible under the raised shade, to the right of the couple, concentrating hard on the creamy lines of mortar separating each brick on the adjacent building. "They're about there, I would say. Maybe not quite as high as I would expect, but that may not mean a thing."

They're about there. About. What a small word filled with such import. On the one hand, Annabelle wanted to hold her breath, to stop time from ticking away on the large clock over the door, to keep everyone—the doctor in particular—from saying another word. On the other, she felt she must suck in as much oxygen as she could and force it into her lungs and through her blood and through the placenta to her baby. *About.* Which meant not quite. And if not enough . . . History couldn't be repeating itself.

Arlene narrowed in on Annabelle. "I can see what you're doing. Don't tell yourself stories, real or imagined. Neither does you any good. In fact, that would be one of the worst things you can do."

Oliver moved even closer to the bed, to his wife. So close, he shifted the bed, and it bumped the wall. "And what would be the best, Arlene?"

Her face relaxed, and she beamed at them, as if the crisis had been averted. "The best . . . ? Taking it easy for the next two weeks. I'll see you halfway through that period, make that a few days from now, after the weekend, and make sure all is going well. If necessary, I'll see you again, a couple days after that, and we'll see how those levels are looking. Basically, girlfriend, you're no spring chicken, and you're carrying your first baby. We don't really know your family history, so I'm treating you like you're high-risk for the moment. Is that okay with you, Dr. Dad?"

"Of course."

"What about you?" Dr. Nagele looked at Annabelle and waited.

She consented silently and with a great deal of trepidation.

"That means modified bed rest," Arlene continued, satisfied with their answers.

"Bed rest!" both Oliver and Annabelle exclaimed.

"*Modified* bed rest. Which means I'm not all that excited—*worried*—about these symptoms. Sometimes expectant mothers experience bleeding . . . throughout the entire pregnancy even. That's probably not the case here, as you haven't had a problem in the past fifteen weeks. I think there could've been some . . . stress tonight, that's all, or it could be unrelated. The levels of hCG change over the pregnancy, and they vary from case to case. I just want to get you further along into your second trimester."

Annabelle reached for Oliver's hand that was still on her shoulder. "What exactly does that mean, 'modified bed rest'?"

Dr. Nagele balanced the clipboard at a ninety-degree angle against her hip. "Well, it means I want you to take naps and actually rest, but you don't have to stay in bed all the time. When you are in bed, lie down on your left side. That's best for Baby Mac, better circulation from the heart to the baby and other organs. You can move around the house, shower, go outside, smell the roses . . . all those good and wonderful things. But I don't want you to drive, no heavy lifting, no traveling up and down the stairs throughout the day. Choose a place and stay there as much as you can. And no googling."

Annabelle rolled her eyes up toward the tiled ceiling, picturing the various stages of all the projects underway. *I knew it wasn't a good idea to renovate the house! And now look.* "You mean, you want me to lock myself up in a jailhouse that's under construction."

"Yes, that's exactly what I want you to do." The doctor was

obviously taking no prisoners. She was well aware of the work going on at their home. "For two weeks."

Oliver caressed his wife's hand. "Can she leave the house?"

Arlene moved her head from side to side, as if trying to examine a flower from various angles—the petals, the stem, the leaves. Gripping her chin with her thumb and index finger, she followed the jagged mountains and troughs on the monitor. "Y-e-s-s-s. You can drive her around . . . for short periods of time. And I mean short. No cooking or cleaning, no yard work." The doctor ticked off the chores on her fingers. "This should be a vacation, a dream, permission—no, *an order*—to do nothing. I know, I know, the very moment I tell you *not* to do these things, those are the very things you want to do. Even if you hate gardening or scrubbing toilets. Ask Paul the apostle. He knows all about that."

Abruptly, Annabelle's heart eased its painful thump-thump in her chest at the reference to her OB's faith.

"It's just for two weeks, Oliver, Annabelle. Two weeks." The V her two fingers made either emphasized the number or declared victory. "And if you do what I tell you . . ." Then she raised both her palms. "We'll see. My plan is to get you up and running before you know it. We're good?" Arlene made more notes, obviously assuming they'd answer in the affirmative. "Assuming there are no more questions . . ."

"Just one. Can I work? I can't picture myself piddling around the house in fuzzy bedroom slippers, looking out the windows for fourteen straight days." Seventeen, if she counted the weekend that might get tacked on. She had to keep her hands busy, even if she had to stay put.

"Do you even own fuzzy slippers?" Dr. Nagele held up a hand and shook her head. "Don't answer that. As long as this work is in or around the house. Your studio is downstairs, right?" She paused.

"Then sure, but no trips to a store, the post office, or to make a delivery. I expect to get a bracelet or a set of earrings out of this pregnancy. Citrine is my birthstone; I was born in November."

She winked and clomped in her thick, wide heels to the door. "I'll send in the nurse to unhook you and give you your discharge papers; they'll have everything in black and white I explained to you. Then you two can get home and start this woman's vacation. Hey, maybe you both can take some time off. Life will get busier when this baby arrives."

Annabelle closed her eyes and settled against the pillows, loving that the doctor had said "when," not "if" so offhandedly. It sounded like a foregone conclusion. Her eyes flew open at the crisp snap of fingers.

Dr. Nagele faced them, her back against the door, with one hand gripping the knob behind her. "I almost forgot. One last, very important thing: no sex. I know you're supercute newlyweds, and that's what got you into the situation you find yourselves in, but ab-so-lute-ly no sexual activity. Again, I'm aware this will make her even more appealing and vice versa. I'll set up your two-week follow-up as well as the in-between visits that'll give us a chance to take a peek at that little one again. Maybe we'll get some good photos for you to frame." With a smile, she was gone.

Before the door closed completely behind her, Oliver plopped on the edge of the bed. He ignored the activity on one of the screens. "I guess we know what this means."

"What . . . ?" Annabelle shook her head. "Sleep in separate bedrooms so we're not tempted?"

Eyes twinkling, his lips curved into a slow smile.

"Ol-iv-er . . ." She sang his name to soften the warning blow. After tonight, it was nothing but her ugliest flannel pajamas for the next six months.

He chuckled. "Believe it or not, that's the furthest thing from my mind. Well . . . maybe not the furthest." Her husband brushed her hair back from her cheek. "But what I was thinking is that it's time we tell my parents. They could be a big help if they come for a visit. While they're here, I'll work overtime on the house, and I won't have to worry about who's taking care of you or Henry. Somebody has to make sure you're behaving."

"But—"

"Those three letters cost you twenty-five cents, Bella." Oliver kissed her gently, and his lips lingered on hers. "You know I'm right, that their coming is for the best. Mama can cook, and you won't have to pretend you can't because this time, you actually *can't.* Dad can stand back and point out what all I'm doin' wrong with the house. You and Henry can watch *Wild Kratts* to your hearts' content, and you can string beads and solder jewelry 'til the cows come home, or better yet, rest while they get in some Grandma-and-Grandpa time with our boy."

Annabelle knew it would be churlish to reject his idea, not to mention foolish. Oliver was making all kinds of sense. She just couldn't imagine having James and Mary McMillan underfoot for two weeks, possibly more. How was she to act like the first lady of the house when the original first lady of the house was around? Oliver's mother . . . Annabelle was having enough trouble dealing with her own.

"I can see you're churning a mile a minute." He made circular motions around his head. "But while you're getting your mind straight, I'm going to make some phone calls."

"I have a better idea. I know two women who would love to help us out."

His eyes narrowed, and then he smiled.

The door opened, and a nurse wearing purple scrubs strode

into the room. "Ready to go? I've got your discharge papers." She waved the forms.

Oliver kissed her again. "Are you ready?"

Annabelle took a deep breath, aware that he was talking about more than her readiness to go home.

"It's time to open up and let people in, m'dear. You know my folks and your folks have been giving us space—quote, unquote—but this baby is closing the gap."

The blips on the monitor sped up.

Chapter Thirty-Four

"ARE YOU ASLEEP?"

His voice tickled her bare shoulder. Annabelle inched lower in the bed until the sheet and covers were up to her neck, then rolled onto her back. "No," she whispered.

"Why not?"

She reached for his hand and brought it down to rest on her middle. "I blame him."

Oliver's chuckle was low and soft. Something about lying in bed always made them take their voices down several notches without a warning *shush* from either of them, especially since they'd moved upstairs nearer their little firecracker. It made no difference that Henry was sleeping at his Auntie Frankie's house. Oliver touched his lips to the shoulder his breath had warmed a moment ago. "Him? You're holding on to hope, I see."

"It just feels right, that's all." She snuggled closer to his side.

He slid his arm under her and moved her until she fit against him.

Remembering doctor's orders, she rolled to her left side and draped her arm over him. "Why are you awake?"

"If he's keepin' you up, why should I sleep?"

She pulled one of the silky hairs on his bare chest.

"Ouch!" He grabbed her hand and rose from the bed.

"Shush!"

"Then don't pull my hair!" he hissed and slung a leg over the side of the bed and padded to the bathroom. When he returned, he paused in the doorway.

Annabelle squinted in the moonlight, barely able to discern the plaid pattern on his pajama bottoms. "What? Why are you standing way over there?" She flipped back the blanket and the sheet and patted his spot in the bed. The mattress was still warm.

"Am I safe?" Oliver rubbed his chest.

Chuckling quietly out of habit, she proffered a hand. "I'm sorry. I was only trying to get your attention."

"Well, you got it." He returned to the bed and climbed in.

Annabelle snuggled up to him and apologized by kissing his chest.

His hand rubbed the top of the silk scarf that protected her hair. "Now, tell me the truth. How are you feeling?" In other words, *how is the baby*?

"Fine. No more spotting, no cramping, and I feel like throwing up all the time." She felt his torso relax as if he'd been holding himself very still.

A rush of breath warmed the top of her head. "Then why are you awake?" He pressed her head to his breastbone. "What do people ever learn by staring into the dark?"

Annabelle sucked in the breath he'd exhaled and let it go as she admitted, "I'm afraid, Oliver. The dark is when all my nightmares come to life. It's easier to give in to the sadness and the fear at night, when you're alone and you don't have to face yourself." Greg's image was nearly transparent at this point. Mayhelen didn't believe in taking baby pictures or wedding photos, so Annabelle only had her fading memory of her brother to rely on. The pain, however, felt fresh. And what she couldn't clearly remember or didn't know, she filled in. She reapplied her anger and unforgiveness like fresh paint when their colors started to fade.

"Baby, it's going to be all right. The Light of the World lives in you. Right here." His hand covered the skin over her heart. "The darkness can't overcome the light, no matter how great it seems. Your childhood left a big hole in your life, but hasn't God filled it by now? Instead of thinking about all you've lost, all the what ifs and what was, think about me. Think about Henry. Baby Mac. Charlotte. Frankie. Miss Hattie."

She closed her eyes, letting his voice and the truth he spoke soothe her.

He pulled her as close as her growing belly would allow and molded her against him. "And staycations. We should be thankful for staycations. I've loved the past two weeks." His clasped hands rested on her lower back, on top of the curve of her hips.

"I have too." Annabelle kissed him again in the same spot, letting her lips linger. They'd slept in and risen in time for a quick breakfast before streaming their church service the past Sunday mornings, and Oliver had dropped off Henry at Frankie's house for a two-night sleepover. Charlotte had dropped off meals she'd purchased, including to-die-for biscuits from some restaurant she called B & B. Despite the words *modified bed rest* that had hung over them, the couple had given it their all to enjoy their time together and with their family, enjoying late starts and early nights.

"I'm looking forward to the next appointment. And your getting off bed rest." Oliver pressed his mouth to her forehead and cheekbone.

She pulled back a little as a thought struck her. "It's nice to have this time, even if it was partly mandated by Dr. Nagele. When do we pick up your parents?"

"*We* don't pick up anybody. They're grown folks who are capable of driving over themselves. That may change sometime in the future, but they're okay for now. And even if they weren't, you wouldn't be going nowhere that far, even if you get the thumbs-up." His hands traveled up and down her back.

Annabelle knew he used double negatives to emphasize his point, and she focused on the positive: the love in his words. "They're in for a huge surprise when they meet us at our next doctor's appointment." It was getting hard to focus, period, the way he was touching her.

"Thanks for rolling with my idea to surprise them. This will be the first time they've seen an ultrasound. I can't wait to see their faces when we tell them, and then they get to meet her . . . uh, the baby." Oliver's voice was husky.

Snuggled as closely as she was to him, Annabelle felt every word as a rumble within his center. It was deep and warm and real. She felt safe enough to articulate her thoughts. "Eleanor didn't invite them to her doctor's appointments when she was pregnant with Henry?"

His mouth turned upside down. "Let's just say she and Mom didn't have that type of relationship. They were never . . . close."

They rarely talked about his first marriage. She felt part of his reticence came from an undeserved stigma from being a divorced Christian. Annabelle knew he'd done what he could to stop Eleanor from leaving him and their baby boy, and strangely, that knowledge reassured her that Oliver was nothing like her "love 'em and leave 'em" mother. She hated that he'd been burned by that relationship but thanked God for the beauty of theirs, which wouldn't have been possible otherwise. *Lord, I'll have to trust You to detangle the right and the wrong of my feelings and to redeem what was lost.*

Grateful now for the dark that hid her face, she smushed her cheeks against his chest once more and shared another of her concerns. "It's too bad we can't go with our original plan to tell Henry first, but I think you're right to wait. I hope we're not telling your parents too soon."

Oliver cleared his throat. "Don't worry about that. We're doing the right thing, acting in faith." He smoothed her hair. "You know, Henry's really enjoying playing with Nora. That's a blessing that's come from this. I'm glad those two get along so well."

Annabelle sensed his relief at the change of subject in his efforts to address her fears. She never wanted to spend much time on the woman he'd loved before her anyway. "Well, based on what you said about Melvin when you drove Henry over, my sister has totally blown up the story, and Nora considers him her hero now. Those two are friends for life."

"I bet it's doing wonders for your relationship with Frankie too."

"If that's the worst thing that comes out of that whole incident with the snakebite, I'll take it."

They were of the same mind, that similar unvoiced thoughts and fears were reverberating in his head, and she marveled at the joy spilling over somehow from that half-full cup of his.

Chapter Thirty-Five

MAX DIPPED HIS HEAD AND trailed a few kisses from Charlotte's ear along her chin line, each a tiny, hope-filled promise. "I'm sure more than a few wonderful things are going to come from Friday night. God says it all works to the good of those who love Him, and I believe it. Not some, but *all*."

"I don't see much good that's come from my childhood," she scoffed, a line bisecting her forehead. "Is that because I didn't know God way back when?" Charlotte had borrowed Annabelle's title for Oliver and dubbed Max her personal Bible scholar. And her man could read it in Greek! If she ever had a question—and as of late, they were coming fast and furiously—she relied on Max for the answers. He typically directed her to ask God Himself, which frustrated her to no end.

Today was no different. "But He knew you, Charlotte. Even way back when. Let's pray He explains it all someday."

Before Max could do just that—before he could bow his head and close his eyes and pray for her, because he didn't believe in saying he'd do something; he did it—she put some distance from him, physically and otherwise, by making a long process of straightening out the belt on her soft pink dress. She retied it just above her waist and changed the subject as she returned to her desk. "What time is it? Frankie will be here before I know it, and neither one of us has gotten a lick of work done."

Silent, he sat in her red chair and crossed a leg.

She respected his faith. But she didn't understand it. Charlotte believed *in* God; her empirical mind recognized that there had to be a Creator. Yet she struggled to believe God, to trust that He loved her as much as Max and his pastor said He did. That much and more. Truly, Charlotte had such a hard time leaning into the love she literally could see, feel, smell, hear, and even taste, it felt impossible to accept the love that she had to accept by faith. The four-letter word had let her down for so long; she'd grown up on the edges of it. Now that she could hold it, now that it held her, she was afraid that one day, its gossamer threads would break under the weight of her unbelief.

Charlotte sighed and forced herself to meet her boyfriend's eyes that looked black in the shadows of her office, a space that faced east and didn't get as much light that time of day. One wide band glimmered across his forehead and dust motes danced in it. She was surprised when he strode over, leaned over her desk, and lightly pressed his lips to hers. As she enjoyed the sweetness of the hazelnut creamer on his mouth, she waited for him to chide her, to offer a rebuke as gentle as his touch.

But not this time. He swiped a finger down her nose, responded with an "okay," and let her focus on her clients' files in front of her.

For a few minutes anyway.

"Did Annabelle enjoy the biscuits?"

"Y-e-s-s-s, Max." Charlotte slowly rested her pen atop the notes on her desk. As much as she enjoyed his accent, she didn't want to hear him say her sisters' names. "Oliver scarfed down most of them." Her brown eyes locked with his cobalt ones. "I know that's not all you have to say."

"You haven't said much about her, about how she's doing since—"

"Since our discussion at Frankie's?" Charlotte preferred not to acknowledge the possibility of Annabelle's losing the baby. *Surely God wouldn't take this baby too.* "We had a good visit, and she's doing well. Her numbers are good, whatever you call them." She fiddled with the Sharpie. "Anna still can't understand why I visited Mama, why I never said anything about calling her."

"Why didn't you?"

Charlotte reveled in his undivided attention, despite the difficult subject matter. It made it easier to talk. She wondered if this was how Annabelle and Frankie felt with Oliver and Melvin, if her clients felt as safe with her. "Because they would've talked me out of it. I needed to put a face and a voice to make my own memories instead of experiencing theirs." Her chair squeaked as she leaned back in it.

"And did you . . . experience your mama for yourself?"

She shuddered, wishing the beautiful way he pronounced *mama* was the way she felt about Mayhelen Winters. "Yes. I don't know if Anna and Frankie remembered everything one hundred percent. Who does? From my professional and personal background, I know each individual processes experiences and relationships differently. Still, everything they said sure felt like the truth. You know what? Mama's last words were about the store and some man I didn't know from Hope Springs . . . or Spring Hope. Somewhere or other."

His eyebrows drew together. "What about him?"

"It was vaguely familiar, but I can't put my finger on it," she murmured, more to herself than Max. No longer concentrating on him, she studied the play of the afternoon sunlight on the dust and recalled a Sunday school lesson about motes and beams.

"Why don't you talk to your Miss Hattie about it? She might shed some light on what's bothering you."

"Her" Miss Hattie was transitioning to "their" Miss Hattie, as frequently as they'd been talking about their childhoods, particularly Charlotte's.

His voice sounded so far away, but her subconscious recognized his gentle way of poking and prodding to get at what pestered her, whether it was a random idea or a stitch in her side. "Maybe. I might ask her. But not even Miss Hattie can address the fact that Mama didn't say a thing about Frankie or Annabelle when I was with her, though she did cry about Greg. I do believe it was some terrible accident—"

"Or neglect . . . ?"

Dragging her eyes away from the window, Charlotte swiped her eyes, sniffed, and returned to the present. *Where are these tears coming from?* "Or neglect, yes." She nodded slightly. "Which is still awful. Unbelievable. But that day, she didn't have the wherewithal to express remorse or seek forgiveness."

"You mean, she lacked the mental capacity?"

"Max, from what I recall, Mayhelen never had the heart for sorrow or regret, let alone repentance—to borrow one of your words. You church folk would say she had a heart of stone. She had to, to cut and run and not look back for decades."

"But something made her reach out to you . . . or Someone."

She swallowed. "Only He knows, I'll give you that. But far be it from me to live or die that way, Maximilian Demos. Mama taught me this much: I'm going to love hard as long as I have the breath within me."

"Including your sisters? And forgiving your mama? That's going to take more than human will, baby." Max pointed upward.

Chapter Thirty-Six

ANNABELLE GRASPED THE EDGE of her desk and was about to pull herself toward the stacked drawers over on the right. Then she thought better of it. Fearing she might strain herself and endanger the baby, she lightly hopped down, walked the few steps to the other end of her workbench, and squatted. But instead of reaching for the black knob to open the drawer, she cradled her head in her hands. This wasn't going to work.

She was exhausted from rethinking and regretting everything: Did her soldering iron emit dangerous fumes she didn't know about? Should she stretch for the light above her? Had she napped long enough, and had she rolled off her left side when she was asleep? What about all the painting she'd insisted on doing herself before she knew she was pregnant? Had it caused a problem? And picking up Henry—not to mention Nora—something Oliver had warned her about. Too much. Everything presented a risk.

Annabelle knew if she kept this up, she'd have to hang up her pliers and bolt the door to her studio. Dr. Nagele told her that at this point, working was safe. The crisis was past. Besides, it wasn't like she was helping Oliver build the new maple cabinets in the kitchen, what he was doing at that very moment. She wasn't pushing Henry on the swing, though he'd pleaded with her over the weekend and couldn't understand why she begged off. She wasn't running around the yard, digging up stones to use in her jewelry. Annabelle wasn't running anywhere, not even to the bathroom—which meant doing some major quickstepping to get there in time. And speaking of . . .

Bracing her fingertips on the wood floor, she clambered to her feet and reached her arms above her head for a long, juicy stretch. Her hands flew to her mouth. "Oops!" she cried, remembering her fear. As she hotfooted it to the bathroom she sighed, knowing life with an infant was going to be so much harder and rife with questions and unknowns. No wonder Frankie kept her parental helicopter gassed up and ready to fly at all hours of the day and night. And she still couldn't keep the snake from getting to her daughter.

Just like she couldn't protect you from Mama. "Speaking of snakes . . ." Annabelle murmured and paused in the doorway of her studio, her thoughts on everything but her tools and the wire she'd never retrieved from the drawer. Like the serpent in the Garden, Mayhelen was always looking for something more than what she had, something *else.* And she did what she could to make her girls want it too, whatever that elusive thing was. Her serial monogamy planted the seed within them that they weren't enough—individually or corporately—and she fed and watered that idea until it grew too big for her to manage. That was when she destroyed what life she had. What life they had. But Annabelle was determined that the specter of her mother wouldn't steal the life she was building for herself.

She glanced at the slim watch on her wrist. Quickly calculating that her sisters would arrive any minute, she closed the door to her studio and took her time climbing the stairs to her bathroom to get ready. As she finished, Oliver rounded the door, holding Poppy, who'd become more his than Henry's. She smiled at them both, thinking the puppy was almost as cute as the man wearing the khaki shorts and green polo. "Think that's the only baby girl you'll get?"

He shrugged. "If so, there's always next year."

Annabelle threw a hand towel at him. "Keep dreamin'. Don't forget I'm AMA." Then she spun in a circle so he could admire her new maternity dress. "What do you think?"

"I think it's time to go, beautiful," Oliver whispered in her ear, bringing a whiff of a recent shower and warm puppy breath. "They're here."

Frankie spied Annabelle twisting to check the full three-hundred-sixty-degree landscape through all the windows in the car. *That took about forty minutes.*

"Where are we going?" she asked. Her fingers rounded the headrest in front of her, Charlotte's seat. "I thought you said something about furniture shopping? And where's MJ? I figured I'd be squeezed beside his car seat."

"We are, and the baby is home with his daddy and a ton of defrosted breast milk." Frankie had counted on the sisters' typical back-and-forth to keep Annabelle distracted until it was too late to turn back. In fact, she'd even enlisted Charlotte's help.

"You mean, you *want* us to bicker?" she'd asked, incredulous.

Seeing Frankie's grin, she'd pronounced, "Consider it done." And her obedience had paid off. Annabelle was only just suspecting their true destination, a "surprise" sanctioned by Oliver.

They passed one large old house after another. "This is Jasper's historic section. Why are we driving through this neighborhood? I don't remember any places to buy cribs around here."

Frankie glanced in the rearview mirror and saw Annabelle retrieve her phone and type quickly. Then she flipped the device and pushed it between the seats, close enough to Frankie's face that the map app on the display looked distorted.

"All the stores are that way!" Annabelle aimed a thumb behind them, in the direction of the interstate.

"We want furniture that lasts, with a story to tell. This is where you find it." Frankie signaled a right-hand turn where a red rectangular sign at the corner announced in large, blocked white type, *Estate Sale!*, with an arrow pointing straight ahead.

"Estate sale." Annabelle shook her head. "Where I come from, that's called used furniture. You know how I feel about that. History has never been a friend to me. Memories, the past. Old things."

They approached another sign. "I thought we could poke through some stuff for a little bit. Maybe you'll find some jewelry you can use in your pieces." It wasn't exactly a lie.

"I don't see the sense in acquiring someone else's cast-off pain when I have enough of my own to bear. I like working with brand-new material."

Frankie turned left and slowed. She sensed Charlotte repositioning herself in the passenger seat and taking note of her surroundings. Her fingers drummed on the armrest between them.

Annabelle's nose nearly touched the window between the hands she'd pressed to the glass. But she was no child filled with wonder and anticipation; she could very well see they weren't headed to Disney World. "Frankie . . . where are you taking me?"

"Just you? What about the rest of us?" Charlotte grumbled. "I take it I don't count."

Frankie cut an eye at her partner in crime. "You thought Anna was the only one who needed distracting?"

Charlotte's eyes delivered a hard, accusatory punch. "I thought when you said 'estate sale,' you meant someone else's. This was supposed to be a joke on that one in the back seat who doesn't like used furniture. What are you thinking, Frances Mae? Next week we have to see to Mama, but first *this*? Is this a good idea, what with Annabelle's just finishing her two-week . . . er, confinement?"

"*Confinement?* When were you born, the 1800s? It's called bed rest, Charlotte." Annabelle rolled her eyes for the benefit of Frankie, who'd glanced back at her. "When I said we were 'all in,' I didn't mean . . . well, I'm not sure what I meant."

The sisters' discussion at Nora's birthday party was derailed by the snakebite and everything that came after, so Frankie had convened the entire family at the McMillans'. The children played in the fenced backyard while the adults gathered in the wood-paneled den. With Annabelle ensconced in the recliner across from a solemn Miss Hattie, "the mysterious Max," Oliver, and Melvin Sr. were charged with keeping a watchful eye on the children through the newly installed triple window.

"It doesn't matter where you bury her, as long as you do," Miss Hattie had ordered from her corner perch on the sofa, sounding like she expected to be obeyed. "No more diggin' up all the should-haves and could-haves." She agreed a service was unnecessary, more about form and fashion; it didn't take a church full of mourners and a funeral procession to bury the past. In the end, they decided they would leave Mayhelen be and forego the emotional and financial cost of bringing her back to bury her in Jasper since she'd never intended to return.

"That's the best way to honor her. Truly," Annabelle had averred.

"You *would* say that," Charlotte snorted, "but I have to agree with you."

"Cremation is definitely the most cost-effective." Frankie nodded at her husband.

"And *you* would say that!" Both Charlotte and Annabelle had cried as one, clapping their hands.

"Yes, but we're certainly saving ourselves some pain and sufferin' too," Frankie had pronounced.

And that was the end of it, until today's drive.

Charlotte continued her infernal tapping on the armrest.

Annabelle released an audible breath in the back seat, and murmured around her curled fingers, "The irony of this. We missed most of her life and nearly all of her death, but we have to witness her burial to free ourselves. And now, here we are practically resurrecting trouble by going back to the house. Why can't Mama rest in peace like everybody else?"

As in life, Frankie concluded and turned at the familiar junction where the gravel met the asphalt. The crunch of her tires provided the background music as they slowly drove up to their old house. She navigated the minivan around back and parked where Mama's Cutlass used to bake in the sun. Frankie considered leaving the car running but decided against it. Those two might drive off, and without Miss Hattie living across the way, they'd leave her stranded.

Charlotte gazed out her window. "It looks about the same as I remember it. How is that possible?" Her voice was hushed. "From the way y'all have described it, I pictured chalk outlines on the grass and blood dripping down the windows. Some house of horrors."

Again, Annabelle's heavy sigh filled the car. She shot daggers when Frankie dared meet her eyes in the mirror.

"Are you okay? How're you feelin'?" As necessary as she felt the trip was, Frankie refused to take risks with her future nephew or niece's life. Her relationship with her sister was another matter; that could use a little pulling and stretching to get it into shape.

"Fine." Annabelle settled against the seat.

"Well, it's going to get pretty stuffy in here without the air-conditioning." Frankie dropped the keys in her purse and climbed from the car. After slamming her door, she studied the house from her side under the nearly bare oak. She wasn't quite ready to go in. The paint was peeling, shutters were missing, and one of the gutters was hanging off. But she agreed with Charlotte: it was the stately, imposing home she remembered . . . The *chunk* of the passenger door told her Charlotte had emerged from her comfort zone.

"I can't believe you've never been back, considering you only live on the other side of town." Charlotte rounded the hood and neared the tree. Gone was the tire, though the fraying rope dangled from a branch, twisting in the slight breeze.

"I didn't say I've never been back."

Charlotte looked surprised.

"I haven't gone in," Frankie expounded, "but I've driven by. I even turned in but didn't make it far. There wasn't a need. Until now."

Now that we have to make a decision about selling the place, she thought but didn't say. That afternoon in Annabelle's den, Miss Hattie had handed over the keys to the Winters' homesite. "It's *been* time," she told Frankie and brooked no further discussion.

She'd overseen the sale of McNair's decades ago and banked the money for the girls. At first, the savings had sat untouched. None of them seemed to know what to do with it.

"Blood money," Annabelle had called it at the time. "Y'all can have it. I want no part of it."

Miss Hattie had pursed her lips and waved her off. "That's just your pride talkin'. Pure foolishness you'll shed with age, like dead skin." Stubbornly, their caregiver had refused to let any of them touch the savings account until all of them agreed to, just as she'd handled the decision about Mayhelen. "Y'all been revolvin' like separate planets most your life, but no more. You're family, and you're gon' breathe the same air if I can help it."

And she had helped them. Eventually, they'd divided the money, after first setting aside an amount for the woman who'd saved their lives. Annabelle had invested in her jewelry making and travel; the store that supported her childhood enabled her to run away from it. Charlotte funded her advanced degrees. Frankie used it to help purchase her family's home . . . a mere two-and-a-quarter miles across town. Miss Hattie had rented out their old house for them until a few months ago, when the last family had moved out after a small kitchen fire.

She'd called Frankie that same night. "That's enough trouble. It's time to move on."

The van's back door retracted with a soft whir, and Annabelle spun and put her feet on the ground, her growing belly leading the way. She frowned. "What estate sale? There's nothing for sale here!"

Frankie wiggled her eyebrows. "I hear they're giving away peace."

Chapter Thirty-Seven

ANNABELLE STOOD WATCHING the cloud cover build, with a hand shielding her eyes from the slivers of sunlight peeking through. Gazing up at the darkening skies, she prayed for the Lord to give her a new perspective, a different way to see her past and her relationships for what they were. He knew how to redeem the good.

They remained outside a good long while, nobody daring to try the door Miss Hattie had given them keys to. Charlotte trooped around the side of the house to see if their old skates were still under the bucket but returned empty-handed. Frankie peeked under the porch steps, wondering how in the world anybody had ever fit under there, let alone dared to.

Annabelle held out a palm and caught a heavy drop of rain that ran between her fingers. It fell in dribs and drabs, not enough to send them running to the car but enough to frizz her hair and cause her roots to swell. "Who decided this was the best day to come out here?"

Charlotte must have caught Annabelle patting her head as she rounded the corner of the house because her laughter preceded her. "You should get it braided or twisted like mine. Then you won't have to worry about a little rain or this North Carolina humidity."

"Oliver checked the forecast and thought it would be perfect, and that you'd agree. He said something or other about granite." Frankie stared at the leafless branches of the tree. "That old thing could've used more rain in its time."

Annabelle's sigh had lost weight since their arrival. *That Oliver.* She wondered if she'd been looking at her childhood under artificial light. As if in answer, the sky lit up and thunder chased it a few seconds later.

A ding from Charlotte's hip area sent her digging in one of her back pockets. She came up with her phone.

"Can't get away from the office, Doctor?" Annabelle teased.

Charlotte read the screen and tapped out some words before swiping away moisture from the cover and stowing it away again. She hunched over and ducked her head, as if she could make herself a smaller target from the raindrops and possible lightning strikes. "Standing out here doesn't feel like the best idea. Maybe we should seek shelter inside."

"Never thought I'd hear one of us say that." Frankie hugged herself and took the steps first. They sagged in the middle and each wooden tread creaked louder than the one below it as her two younger sisters trooped behind her.

Charlotte clomped up to the porch and stretched out her hand to Annabelle, slowly bringing up the rear. "Are you good?"

Annabelle inclined her head twice but said nothing.

The three paused at the door, and Frankie peeked through the mullioned diamond. Charlotte recalled again one of her few memories of living here, the way the sun shone through the window in the door, creating a patterned dance floor just for her. That was how she always wanted to see herself—twirling in the light—not stumbling through the darkness toward whatever awaited them upstairs.

"I don't think we'll be cuttin' a rug today." Frankie seemed to share the same thought.

Annabelle cocked a thumb over her shoulder at the voluminous, dark clouds trudging toward them. "Not today." Frankie made eye contact with each of them before at last she withdrew the keys and forced one into the lock. She pressed the latch, pushed open the door, and swung it wide.

Charlotte half expected a horde of mice to skitter across their feet and out into the yard, but only a musty smell rolled from the house and assaulted their noses. She flung a braid over her shoulder. "Well, did we come all this way to stand here?"

Frankie cocked an eye at her. "I might have liked the quieter version of you."

"Ha! Too late for that. Are you coming, Annabelle?" She bumped Frankie aside and strode into the house first, stopping in the middle of the parquet floor and spinning to face the open door, watching Annabelle put a foot in, retract it, then step in slowly. All the while, she cupped her belly, and Charlotte wondered if she felt the need to protect her little one.

Frankie brought up the rear. At first, she went to close the door but then let it drift back against the wall. "I think I'll leave it open, usher in a breeze. Sometimes it takes a storm to really clear the air."

"Sounds like someone's been sitting on Miss Hattie's knee."

The slap of Charlotte's footsteps punctuated her words. They echoed against the dusty floor as they all marched as a unit deeper into the house and stopped at the base of the wide staircase angling to the darkened floor above. There, she spun with her arms outstretched, trying to measure the area. "This space used to seem so big. How did we ever have room for you to set up a table for us to eat here?"

Frankie winked. "You're talkin' about the tea parties?"

"Yes! You were the best big sister."

"Who? *Frankie?*" Annabelle's right hand ventured to her hip.

"Who else?" laughed the woman in question.

Feeling left out or worse, the butt of the joke, Charlotte squinted at them. "What? What did I miss?"

"This woman wasn't playing Martha Stewart, hostess with the mostest, out of the goodness of her heart!" Annabelle's belly jiggled, and she covered her smile with her hand. "She wanted to watch her soaps or whatever was on TV—"

"Or just enjoy a moment to myself. I was a teen mom, basically."

The truth tarnished the silvery edges of Charlotte's memory, and her shoulders slumped.

Annabelle used a finger to lift her baby sister's lower lip. "Cheer up, Charlie. The 'why' doesn't change the 'what.' Frankie could've sent us outside, but she didn't. Instead, she chose to serve us lunch and let us play dress-up."

Frankie squeezed Charlotte's hand and didn't let go. "Come on. Let's check out the kitchen."

Frankie and Annabelle tugged Charlotte around the stairs to the left side of the house, and she complained the entire way.

"Why do you want to go in there? I thought the fire took it out." Charlotte pointed to her feet. "I should've worn my combat boots because these flip-flops won't cut it."

Frankie covered her mouth when she laid eyes on the charred wall behind the range. She barely noticed the increased pressure of Charlotte's fingers enfolded by hers.

Annabelle edged around them and moved farther into the room, halting by the table in its center. "I see what you mean," she whispered. "This room is puny! And *ugly*!"

Frankie pressed her lips together. No need to admit the obvious. Strips of red paint hung from the cabinets, revealing the blackened wood. Warped laminate countertops buckled under a white powder. Debris littered the floor. Mayhelen had rarely placed a toe there, and Frankie's sisters acted as spectators, cheerleaders, assistants, and critics while she slapped together sandwiches and created something from nothing for them to eat. She dragged her attention from what remained of her former domain, nearly choking from imagined plumes of smoke. "My kitchen . . . Miss Hattie didn't tell me it was this bad. How did this happen?"

Charlotte rubbed her shoulder. "I don't think the 'how' is important either. Not anymore."

Hearing sincerity, not sarcasm, Frankie leaned into her sister. She managed to return Annabelle's smile. "Miss Hattie was right to give up on this house."

"Still, she never gave up on us, did she?" Annabelle crunched across broken glass. "I think what made it worse was that these cupboards were bare most of the time for no reason—it was because Mayhelen *wouldn't* provide, not because she *couldn't*. But God gave us what we needed when we needed it."

"You sure knew how to make the most out of some Little Debbie cakes." Charlotte giggled.

Annabelle pointed at her. "Don't even try it. If anybody was going to get a full-course meal out of this place, it was you!"

"And you can see where that got me!" Charlotte continued laughing.

"Yes, with a man who's fine as wine." Frankie pretended to fan herself.

"Don't you mean *w-h-i-n-e*?" Annabelle ran from the kitchen to avoid Charlotte's hands.

Panting, Annabelle gripped the newel post and tried to catch her breath. She listened as her sisters' footsteps followed at a more sedate pace.

Frankie reached her first. "I didn't know a pregnant woman could tear out of there so fast! Are you all right?"

"You could join me on my power walk tomorrow morning, with that type of vim and vigor." Charlotte marched in place, raising her knees toward her chest. "Your confinement did you some good."

Annabelle ignored Charlotte's attempt at humor and gazed up into the shadowy flight of stairs. Thunder shook the house, and seconds later, a flash lit the second floor.

Frankie looked in the same direction. "So, are you ready?" Her voice was quiet.

Annabelle brushed off some dust clinging to the hem of her dress before placing her right foot on the first step and bracing her weight on the rail. *Why? Why, Annabanana?* she asked herself. *You understand the how, the why, and the when. The who is long gone.* She bowed her head and stepped down. Shaking her head, Annabelle faced her sisters. "I think I'm good. Y'all can go ahead if you want. I have better hiding places now."

"I'm good too." Charlotte responded quickly.

"Me, three." Frankie looped her arm through Annabelle's and waited as she locked arms with their youngest sibling. "Let's go before the storm breaks."

They headed toward the back door, but then came the sound of tires crunching on gravel, drawing the women's eyes toward the windows on the right of the house. Charlotte dropped Annabelle's arm as Frankie strode to the porch. A familiar weathered F-150 lumbered down the pit-filled drive. "What's going on?" Annabelle didn't wait for Charlotte to answer. The rain battered the roof as she crossed the threshold, her younger sister a half step behind her. They watched the truck park behind the minivan as Frankie closed and locked the door behind them. Then the oldest and the youngest Winters women flanked Annabelle as the skies opened up.

Oliver climbed out of his truck and sprinted to the porch, his hand a poor covering over his head. "Hey, babe."

Annabelle returned her husband's kiss, ignoring his rain-splattered cheeks and shirt. "What are you doing here?"

"There are some people who wanted to meet you, and I thought I should be with you when they arrived." Oliver wrapped an arm around her shoulders.

"That phone call you fussed about?" Charlotte added. "It was your husband, making sure neither of us had talked Frankie out of coming here. We've been kinda working on a project together, and I wasn't sure it was going to happen." She swallowed. "I guess it is."

"O-k-a-a-y." Annabelle squinted at him first and then at one sister after another. "Who are these people?" She could feel Frankie move closer.

Charlotte took a deep breath. She trained her eyes on the ground at the bottom of the porch as if searching for the stones to face a giant. "Frankie, I'd planned to talk to you today while the three of us were together . . . and it makes sense to do it here." Her smile was small and tight as she faced them directly. "God-ordained, you might say."

"Girl, what have you been up to?" Frankie's voice filled the small space.

"I'll make this quick by giving you the abridged version. We can go into greater depth later, but I don't know how much time I have. Mama called me some time ago before she died, and I went to visit her—" she held up hands to restrain Frankie—"Wait. Hear me out. During my *brief* visit, she rattled on about some man and the store."

Frankie whirled on Annabelle with narrowed eyes, tension building in the thick, waterlogged air. "You don't seem surprised by this."

"Believe it or not, Charlotte told me. Only because I must have caught her off guard that day. And to her credit, she was going to tell you at Nora's birthday party, but . . . well, you know a lot has happened since then." Annabelle shrugged. She must have made her point because Frankie's shoulders relaxed.

"Anyway, I thought Mama was talking about one of her husbands, but Max encouraged me to do some research . . ."

Thunder rumbled along with Frankie's outcry. Lightning rent the sky. "*Your* Max? And I gather you know too?" She tilted her chin toward Oliver.

"I overheard the two of them talking about it when everybody was at the house, so I added my two cents." His arm tightened around his wife. "I wasn't sure this would work out, so I didn't want to bring this up until you were . . . ready . . . and we were sure."

"Sure . . . ?" Annabelle's soft question played a duet with Frankie's "About what?"

They all turned as an older model sedan slowly lurched up and over the divots in the drive. It came to rest near the two other cars parked in the back as Charlotte's words again tumbled end over end, as if no one else had spoken.

"And when I dug deeper, it turns out the man Mama was going on and on about had sent letters to the store, looking for someone who used to work there. I think she wanted me to know about it. About him. Annabelle, I think she wanted *you* to know." Charlotte finally came to the end of her confession, out of breath and out of time.

Annabelle felt compelled to clasp Frankie's fingers, marveling at Charlotte standing there, chest heaving, perhaps unused to having the spotlight trained on her this long. It was hard to believe her baby sister had taken this upon herself, without any direction from Frankie. Before she could say anything—before she could figure out *what* to say—a man disembarked from his vehicle, holding a large black umbrella. He scooted around and held it over the woman Annabelle presumed to be his wife, and the two splashed across the concrete pad toward the house. Raindrops splattered off its curved vinyl top and dripped from the ribs as they gazed up at the three women and Oliver once they reached the stoop.

"Please come up," Charlotte beckoned toward them.

Frankie waved slightly at the friendly-looking couple but remained standing in the middle of the entryway to the porch, still holding on to Annabelle. "Hello. How can we help you?"

The man reached into the breast pocket of his blue short-sleeved shirt. "Uh, I'm not sure." He studied the paper in his head. "I'm Milton, and this is my wife, Nancy. We're over by way of Griffith, a little town west of here. You might know it?"

Beside her, Charlotte nodded. Annabelle could tell her sister wanted these strangers to hurry on with their mission.

As if she'd picked up on Charlotte's impatience, Nancy murmured, "Move it along, Milton."

"Well, we understand this is where my father once lived. We're trying to track down anybody who knew him." His voice was barely audible over the pounding of the rain.

Frankie stepped closer to the roughened edge of the wood. "I'm afraid this house has been rented out for several years, and I don't know the people who've lived here, not right offhand. Do come up out of the rain. If you'll write down your names, I can check with Hattie Mason. She has the records, and maybe she can help you."

"They know about all that, Frankie," Charlotte broke in. "Just listen."

Frankie shook her head at Charlotte, apparently confused. "You did some research for them? Is that what you're talkin' about?"

The two clomped up the steps, Milton's hand on his wife's elbow. He shook the umbrella and continued to talk as he worked to wrap it closed. "This would've been a long time ago, not recently. He used to live in Spring Hope with my mother, Beatrice, where I grew up, and then he moved to Jasper. From what I understand, he worked downtown and ended up married to the woman who owned this house here, but not for long. You could say, 'Papa was a rollin' stone . . .'" His huff wasn't quite a chuckle. "Daddy moved on and later died, but folks say not before he had a child. Another child, I mean." Finally succeeding to snap the umbrella, he looked up. "I hope I'm making sense."

Annabelle cried out.

"What is it?" Charlotte reached for Annabelle but didn't touch her, as if she wasn't sure what to do. "Oliver, is she okay? Did we make a mistake?"

He nodded, then shook his head, his eyes on his wife. "I think she sees what we see."

Frankie shushed them all. "Calm down, Charlotte. Oliver . . . Annabelle? Somebody, tell me somethin'. Who are these people?"

Annabelle brushed away all the hands and the questions and moved toward the eyes that sought her out. The gray eyes just like the ones that looked back at her every time she looked in her own mirror. She coughed to clear her throat. "Did your father wear a fedora, by chance? A soft one that matched the color of our—I mean, your eyes?"

Nancy edged closer to her husband, and she looped her arm through his. "Milton . . ."

For a few seconds, the rain pelted the roof of the porch and puddled on the ground below them. Annabelle, standing at a crossroads between hurting and healing, considered what it meant to be whole, redeemed. Not someone's half or step anything, but a sister, a wife, a mother, and yes, a daughter. And to this man, perhaps even an answered prayer.

She stumbled forward, thanks to a nudge in the middle of her back. At first, she looked up, but she saw only a crack where squirrels had gnawed through the wood.

"That was me, silly girl. Not the Lord," Charlotte whispered, her breath warm in Annabelle's ear. "Does He need to send a bolt of lightning for you to ask your brother inside?"

Everybody laughed, including Milton and Nancy. Charlotte took the key from a suddenly speechless Frankie and jiggled the rusty lock. Finally, she worked the door open.

"Please, y'all come in. I have so many questions." Annabelle moved aside. "And between my sisters and me, we have quite a story to tell you."

A Note from the Author

THE SETTING FOR *DYSFUNCTION JUNCTION* is centered in my "universe" which includes the fictional town of Jasper, North Carolina. But truly, Frankie, Annabelle, and Charlotte's story is rooted in the real place in each of us that cries out for truth, unconditional love, and complete acceptance. A place that can only be filled by the Father.

And speaking of my universe, I hope careful readers will enjoy seeing familiar faces and places in each of my novels, particularly this one. Let that serve as a reminder that our world is not such an enormous place. You never know when you might turn a corner and run into your mama's best friend from grade school who married her cousin, some of your daddy's people from round the way, or one of the Agnews who happened to be in the vicinity. At some point or another we'll find ourselves at a similar junction, deciding whether to move forward or retreat, to love or learn, leave or cleave; it's a matter of choosing which road to take. In my mind, we're all part of a family, and I pray, dear reader, you feel you're a beloved part of mine.

Acknowledgments

SURE, there's more than one way to skin a catfish. And there's more than fifty ways to explain how you caught it. Ask any fisherman. Better yet, ask any of my peeps, the ones I grew up with and the ones I'm growing. When we share "what happened," the telling of it is never naked, bare bones. It's dressed to the nines from head to toe, decked out with our own perspectives, backstories, hurts, impressions, biases, and relationships. I always take "me" with me, and my inner Robin sees, experiences, and shares life through slightly blurred lenses. If only an optometrist could sit me in a chair and ask, "Is it one or two? This one or that one?" and correct my vision and version of an event or a person. Then we could get to the truth of the matter. The *heart* of the matter, at the junction of hurt and healing.

But that's who Jesus is and what He does. And so lies the inspiration for *Dysfunction Junction*, in which three women sprout from the same root; yet their relationship to the Son determines who, what, why, when, and how they grow.

Talk about growth! All parts of me have to sit back and wonder how in the world I'm on my fourth novel. A novel that had a title years before there was ever a story about Charlotte, Annabelle, and Frances Mae. But wait—what about birth order? How dare I mention the baby of the family first?! That's because I'm the baby of the family, and sometimes we youngest need a little shout-out. I'm sure two women in particular would say I got plenty of attention, and for all of that and to both of my sisters, I offer a sheepish smile and my gratitude. Somehow, we three survived sharing two parents, one bathroom, and one telephone line and lived to tell myriad versions of the same tales—a few of which flowed quite effortlessly out of the mouths of my characters. They're part of the beginning of the story I'm blessed to live; my oldest sister, Atondra, unwittingly helped me end this one I was called to write.

Of course, there are seven oh-so-precious siblings whose passion, fearlessness, creativity, perseverance, and beauty (not to mention chocolate-chip-pecan cookies!) have changed Eddie's and my life from the ground up. Kate, Faith, Hillary Grace, and Hallie, little Henry McMillan would say you're our sugar and spice and everything nice, and I'd agree. You add sunshine and gray hair to our every day, just like our three "son"-shines—Nicholas, Benjamin, and August—who radiate from a different, yet equally strong and faithful, direction. When it comes to my menfolk, there's not a snip or a snail or a puppy dog tail in the bunch . . . unless I count Oscar, who contributes his own furry shoulder to lean on. But really, it's Eddie I turn to when the nights and the unfilled pages stretch without end. He willingly watches hour upon hour of *Blue Bloods*, *Home Town*, and *Beat Bobby Flay* to stay awake while I type furiously in the armchair beside him. Hubby was my first family, and we've traveled many a road together. Whenever I stand at a confusing or painful crossroads, he takes my hand, tells me a joke, and leads the way. I thank God for His promises in Isaiah 26:7,

> The way is not steep and rough.
> You are a God who does what is right,
> and you smooth out the path ahead of them.

While I'm on this road, I must thank the family who chose to embrace me, not only the ones who have to because I feed and house them. Beth, Jana, Christie, Cathy, Deb, Liz, Joni, and my Community Bible Study class know when to pray, message, and share an encouraging word. They've provided good company when I trekked through the wilderness. When I needed to send up an email flare with the subject line, "Um, can you chat?" Cynthia Ruchti has responded. She's more than my literary agent; she's a beautiful gift wrapped with a snarky red bow who's as passionate about my stories as I am (well, nearly). I can't write *just* or a semi-colon without thinking of her. Without Cynthia and Books and Such, these novels wouldn't have found a home at Tyndale House with my publishing partners, Jan Stob and Karen Watson; my editor, Kathy Olson; and my cover designer, Eva Winters; and the rest of my team—and I use *my* because that's how much I love them. (No baby likes to share!) There's nothing like launching a book by praying with them, knowing that we share a belief and hope that God will direct these words to the eyes and ears that need them, wonderful readers who know how to love on this needy author.

But truly, what would a family be without our Abba Father, who provides over and abundantly, more than we could ask or think? Like Charlotte, Annabelle, and Frances Mae, we all have our own version of events, our own way of ending "See, what happened was . . ." We believers honor the God of all Truth, who is the Way, the Truth, and the Life. In all of our dysfunction, in all of our seeking and searching, we have the hope that we "might grope for

Him and find Him, though He is not far from each one of us; for in Him we live and move and have our being, as also some of your own poets have said, 'For we are also His offspring.' Therefore, since we are the offspring of God, we ought not to think that the Divine Nature is like gold or silver or stone, something shaped by art and man's devising" (Acts 17:27-29). I may not always be up to running with the vision the Lord gives me, or even see it clearly with these ever-thickening glasses of mine. Yet I trust Him to faithfully carry me where He intends me to go—and all that He places in my hands. I pray you find the truth of His Word in my fiction.

Blessings!
Robin

About the Author

Award-winning author **ROBIN W. PEARSON**'s writing sprouts from her Southern roots. While sitting in her grandmothers' kitchens, she learned what happens if you sweep someone's feet, how to make corn bread taste like pound cake, and the all-purpose uses of Vaseline. She also learned about the power of God and how His grace led her grandmothers to care for their large families after their husbands were long gone, a grace that has endured through the generations. Robin's family's faith and superstitions, life lessons, and life's longings inspired her to write about God's love for us and how this love affects our relationships with others. In her Christy Award–winning debut novel, *A Long Time Comin'*, Robin weaves a family drama rich in Southern flavor that a starred review from *Publishers Weekly* called "enjoyable and uncomfortable, but also funny and persistent in the way that only family can be." Her second novel, *'Til I Want No More*, also earned a starred review. According to *Publishers Weekly*, "Pearson's excellent characters and plotting capture the complexity and beauty of family, the difficulty of rectifying mistakes, and the healing that comes from honesty," and her third novel, *Walking in Tall Weeds*, "skillfully captures the complexity of family dynamics and the ways racism's scars persist across generations."

Armed with her degree from Wake Forest University (Go, Deacs!), she has corrected grammar up and down the East Coast in her career as an editor and writer and in her calling as a homeschooling mama of many. Since then she has freelanced with magazines, parenting journals, textbooks, and homeschooling resources and has spoken at conferences and writers' groups such as Breathe and the 2024 Vision Christian Writers Conference in Mount Hermon.

At the heart of it all abides her love of God and her husband, seven children, and dog, Oscar. That's what she writes about on her blog, *Mommy, Concentrated*, where she shares her adventures in faith, family, and freelancing. And it's the source and subject of her fiction—in her novels, in the new characters currently living and breathing on her computer screen, and in the stories waiting to be told about her belief in Jesus Christ and the experiences at her own kitchen sink.

Follow Robin on robinwpearson.com, on Amazon, and @robinwpearson on Instagram, BookBub, Goodreads, and Facebook.

Discussion Questions

1. The story revolves around three adult sisters dealing with issues from their past in very different ways. Which sister could you most easily relate to? Why?

2. Miss Hattie befriends the girls when they are young and eventually becomes integral to their lives. Has someone outside your immediate family invested in your life in a similar way? Have you had the opportunity to be this kind of a mentor or caregiver to others?

3. Charlotte says, "Mama and all her shortcomings changed the trajectory of our lives." She wonders about her mother's power to ruin her and her sisters' lives, and what God's role was in all of it. What answer would you give her?

4. Frankie and Annabelle recall that Charlotte, age six at the time, stopped speaking after what happened to their baby brother, and they began speaking for her—a habit that continued into adulthood. Do you see any patterns in your family's life that may have started in a time of crisis but became habits continuing long after the crisis had passed? Why are patterns like this sometimes hard to change?

5. Frankie confronts Annabelle for choosing to live in a different part of the country for much of her adult life. What issues was she trying to address by leaving, and was she successful? Why did she come back?

6. Annabelle wrestles with the idea that she's more closely related to her nephews and nieces than to Henry. Who are you closest to? Do you think family is biological? Or chosen?

7. Miss Hattie challenges the sisters to make their peace with their mother, even though she might not deserve their forgiveness, and the sisters have strong, differing opinions about doing so. Have you ever had to forgive someone who wouldn't or couldn't apologize? Do you agree forgiveness is an important step to take for our own well-being?

8. Annabelle's husband tells her, "Your childhood left a big hole in your life, but hasn't God filled it by now? Instead of thinking about all you've lost, all the what ifs and what was, think about me. Think about Henry. Baby Mac. Charlotte. Frankie. Miss Hattie." How would you feel about hearing this if you were in Annabelle's position?

9. Charlotte has always kept men at arm's length, but Max is different. How does he wear down her defenses? What helps her to let him in?

10. Oliver feels a stigma about being a divorced Christian, even though he did everything he could to save his first marriage. Why is this such a challenging issue in the church?

11. Near the end of the book, Annabelle prays for the Lord to give her a new perspective, a different way to see her past

and her relationships for what they were. In what ways do we see this begin to happen? What are some areas of your life that you'd like to ask God for a new perspective on?

12. If we could visit with the sisters again a year down the road, what kind of changes do you think we'd see? What might they still be struggling with?